THE AUTHOR

Dorothy Vernon White was born in 1877, the daughter of Horace Smith, police magistrate for Westminster and a minor poet. Later, her family moved to Beckenham, Kent where at the age of twenty-two she began taking Bible classes for poor boys. A lively, independent character, she also ran a week-day club and a cricket team, becoming 'famed as a demon over-arm bowler in an era of lobs and long skirts'. Her short stories appeared in periodicals such as the *Academy* and *Outlook* and in 1907 her first novel, *Miss Mona*, caught the attention of the novelist William Hale White ('Mark Rutherford'). She already admired his writing and, although he was seventy-five and she thirty, their first meeting was the start of an intense relationship leading to marriage in 1911. Dorothy published two more novels, *Frank Burnet* (1909) and *Isabel* (1911), but after Hale White's death in 1913 she virtually ceased to write apart from editing his journals and letters and the remarkable *Groombridge Diary* (1924), her account of their life together. She continued to teach and, in the 1930s, published three books for children. She died at Sherbourne in Dorset in 1967, at the age of ninety.

FRANK BURNET

Dorothy Vernon White

New Afterword by
Irvin Stock

THE HOGARTH PRESS
LONDON

To
My Sister
Marion

Published in 1985 by
The Hogarth Press
40 William IV Street, London WC2N 4DF

First published in Great Britain by John Murray 1909
Hogarth edition offset from the original British edition
Copyright The Literary Estate of Dorothy Vernon White
Afterword copyright © Irvin Stock 1985

British Library Cataloguing in Publication Data
White, Dorothy Vernon
Frank Burnet.
I. Title
823′.912[F]   P′R6045.H1563/
ISBN 0 7012 0564 4

Printed in Great Britain by
Cox & Wyman Ltd
Reading, Berkshire

PART I

FRANK

" Since this was written and needs must be."

FRANK BURNET

CHAPTER I

MARCHINGTON was a family living. There had been
Burnets at Marchington for generations. You could
read the history of the Burnets round the walls of the
church. Frank read it on Sundays from the Vicarage
pew at Morning and Evening Prayer. They were
handsome tablets. Perhaps the largest and most
handsome was that which was fixed (Frank wondered
how) into the chancel-screen just opposite where he
sat. It was the memorial to his grandfather, the
Rev. Seymour Frank Hedley Burnet. Frank's father's
name was Hedley ; his own name, of course, was Frank.
The lettering was plain. Frank knew the words by
heart :

TO THE GLORY OF GOD AND IN MEMORY

OF THE

REV. SEYMOUR FRANK HEDLEY BURNET,

VICAR OF THE PARISH OF MARCHINGTON IN THE COUNTY OF
———, WHO DEPARTED THIS LIFE ON JULY 4, 18—.

"Though I walk through the valley of the shadow of death, I will
fear no evil."

And these words come into the Psalms for the fourth
evening of the month—any month—the month of July
amongst others—so that if you happened to be singing

them you would notice. " Now that," thought Frank, " is an odd coincidence."

He also thought that " the shadow of death " was a remarkable expression. He remembered thinking so when he drove home late one winter's night from a service at another church, where Mr. Burnet sometimes went to preach. It might very likely have reference to the sad way in which his grandfather had died. He had heard the servants talk of it in the kitchen. It had been the summer of the smallpox. The servants said they would as soon " have anything " as have the smallpox. They called it a loathsome disease. Frank pricked up his ears—not that he wanted to know about the smallpox and the loathsome disease ; he would have given a great deal *not* to know, never to know, never, never, never—and then he was much relieved because his father called to him down the passage to come and say his Sunday collect, and he went into the library and said : " Almighty and Everlasting God, mercifully look upon our infirmities, and in all our dangers and necessities stretch forth Thy right hand to help and defend us ; through Jesus Christ our Lord." It was simple enough, and he said it without a mistake, and when he had finished he went out of the room as quickly as possible, because he was suddenly afraid that his father would begin to talk about the smallpox and the loathsome disease.

It was six months afterwards that he was in the kitchen and heard the cook say to the new parlour-maid : " It's the hand of God, and there's no escaping from it."

" I'd rather have anything than smallpox," said the new parlour-maid.

" It's a loathsome disease," said the cook. " Hundreds of people died of it that year. They say there wasn't decent burial for them ; and it's a strange thing it should have fastened on the Rector, for he was a hearty man, as tall as master, every bit. But it was the hand of God, and there's no escape. *He* tried to escape, poor gentleman ! He had packed his boxes, and the cart was at the door when he was took. It was the hand of God."

That was all. Frank heard it, every word. He was by the pantry sink, very tall for his age himself. . . . Well, it was over ; he had heard it, and he knew the worst. The knowledge at last had come to him ; it could not come again. . . . Ah ! but it could stay. He was haunted by the terror. One morning he woke to find red spots upon his arm. . . . It was the morning after his mother had taken him down to the church to see Mrs. Brett's little baby christened. Such a sweet little baby ! and they sang, " In token that thou shalt not fear," and Frank knew the words and tune. He sang lustily ; he heard, he felt, he saw himself singing ; his mother, too, sang as she held the baby. They shouted and sang. But when he sat down to tea, he saw that his nurse had been crying ; she bade him " get on," and she spread him a slice with strawberry jam, and went out of the room. She was whispering with Kate, the cook.

" What were you saying to Kate ?" he asked, when she came back again.

" Never mind, dearie," said nurse.

" Somebody's dead," said Frank—" *died of the small-pox*," he nearly said, but the words somehow stuck in his throat.

" It's poor Mrs. Brett, love," said nurse. " She wanted to stay, poor soul ! but God knew what was best, and He took her. It was the hand of God."

Frank said nothing ; there was nothing to be said. He heard the words and tune of the hymn, and saw the light streaming over the font. Strange that they thought they were happy ! Their joy was false, and the sun had much better never have shined. He finished his meal of bread and jam bite by bite, and afterwards played in the garden. His mother took him to feed the fowls, and he thought no more about poor Mrs. Brett. . . . And then the very next morning

he woke to find red spots on his arm. He bore the
agony all day. At night in his little bed he shivered.
He heard his mother on the stairs, softly, lest she
should disturb him.

" Mother !" he cried.

" What is it ?" In she came, her face, her fair, soft
hair. She swept the floor ; she put her arms about
him. He clung to her convulsively. " You've been
dreaming, sweetheart," was all she said. Her lips
were on his brow.

He recollected suddenly, and started from her in
horror. " Bring a candle, quick !"

She lit one very slowly.

" Quick !" he said. He bared his arm. "What's that ?"

She burst out laughing. " You funny mannikin !"
She rang the bell. She asked for oil, and Frank distinctly heard her saying : " It's those wretched
fowls."

The oil came, and with it came Frank's father. He
had heard the servant running. " I thought the house
was on fire at the very least," he said.

Mrs. Burnet was dipping her slender fingers in the
oil. " My dear Hedley," she replied, " I do not know
which is the greater baby—you or Frank."

Mr. Burnet wandered round the room.

" Mother," said Frank in a whisper, " I want to ask
you something. I want to know if there is any escape
from the hand of God."

" Frankie boy !" She was astonished.

Frank's heart sank within him. There *was* no
escape ; he read it there. He hid his face amongst the
pillows.

" My darling, what is it troubles you ? Escape
from the hand of God ? No, thank God, never ! It
is always over us, God's kind hand."

" Kind ?" he faltered. His head came up ; his
thoughts surged to and fro.

" Yes, kind," said his mother—" kinder than any
hand. . . . Oh, Frank, kinder than mine."

He looked at hers, so slender, dipping in and out.

"Father shall tell you."

"Tell you what?" said Mr. Burnet. He had been rearranging Frank's little store of books in the shelf upon the wall according to their shapes and sizes.

"Frank and I are wondering if God's hand is kind."

Mr. Burnet came over and sat on the bed. He did not speak at once. Frank hung upon his words; he saw an arm steal round his mother's waist. "Kind? Yes, very; absolutely; very."

"Frank is an odd child," said Mrs. Burnet as they went downstairs.

"You are disposed to spoil him," said Mr. Burnet.

Mrs. Burnet said nothing. It would have been foolish to say anything, for that was not what her husband meant.

"I will ring for prayers," said Mr. Burnet, and he rang, and the servants came in, and he read the whole of the second chapter of Genesis.

CHAPTER II

THERE was another tablet in Marchington Church which Frank had often studied. It was to the memory of the Rev. Hedley Seymour Burnet. He was lost off the Cape of Good Hope. This was, perhaps, why Frank was always a little nervous when they went to the sea. Perhaps if Frank had gone more often to the sea he would have been less nervous. Once they spent their summer holidays in Cornwall—that was when Frank was five—and again, when he was twelve, they stayed three weeks on the coast of Norfolk; and since he had been at Winchester he had spent one or two "leave out" days with an uncle at Southampton. There was also, of course, the yearly excursion with the whole of the Marchington Sunday-school. This, however, was all, and it was not sufficient. He just saw enough of the sea to realize that it was very wide, very deep, very changing, cruel, and greedy. So he thought as he paced up and down with his father and mother on the yearly excursion. His mother professed to admire the sea. " Look, Frank," she would say, " what wonderful colours !" She thought he would like to sketch—he painted such pretty pieces at home— but Frank had no mind to sketch. If he were to sketch anything, he said, it would be the old Crown Inn. Buildings were more picturesque ; and he turned his face to the land.

But if he would not sketch he more or less had to bathe : there was no way of getting out of it. Whilst the children paddled along the sands in charge of the superintendent, Mr. Burnet would take Phillis and Frank to the rocks, and they would undress, and then, for perhaps ten minutes, enjoy themselves in the water. Enjoy themselves ? . . . Frank used to say : " What's the good of enjoying yourself for ten minutes if it takes you half an hour to get there and half an hour to get back ?" But his father always said, " Come along !" and Phillis always said, " Do let's "; so they invariably went.

On the whole they had very good fun at the summer Sunday-school treat. There was no end of them, boys and girls, and they always ran a special. It was quite a business getting off. Everyone had to be up by five, and there were sandwiches to cut, and baskets to pack, and the bathing-suits, and the walk in the chill of the morning. At the station they found the scholars. There was a most exhilarating sense of excitement. The boys touched their caps, and the little girls nodded. Mr. Burnet made his way in amongst them, and Frank followed behind ; then Mr. Burnet shook hands with the superintendent, and afterwards Frank did the same, and he felt very jolly, though rather shy. The shyness, however, wore off when the train came in, and he had to assist his father in keeping the children back from the edge of the platform.

It was just as much of a business coming home late at night. They always tried to number the children, to make sure that no one was missing. They made careful arrangements beforehand. Mr. Burnet should stand by the station entrance and count the children as they came in, Frank at the barrier count them again ; but somehow it never worked. The two totals never agreed, though both of them always showed a certain proportion missing—about a dozen or so. The dozen or so were there, of course. If they were boys, they climbed over the railings, and there were plenty of mischievous girls ; anyway, no one was ever lost that Frank heard of. Still, if you take a hundred and odd children out to the sea, you may think yourself pretty lucky if one of them is not drowned. I mean, what happens to *another person* might just as well happen to *you ;* and one year it is a fact a couple of boys who had been staying there at the sea, not a month before the Marchington Treat, ran down to those very rocks, and were brought back dead . . . drowned. . . dreadful. If you looked at the waves, you could see them floating. It was no good to shut your eyes, for they were floating still, and at any minute they might be washed up at your feet. They *had* been washed up and buried, but what difference did that make ? It all cast rather a gloom. Several things had gone wrong about that particular excursion. In the first place Phillis was left at home with a cold, and in the second place the superintendent failed. Consequently Mr. and Mrs. Burnet had to devote their entire attention to the hundred and odd children. Consequently Mr. Burnet told Frank he must bathe alone.

Frank said : " I'm not keen."

" Oh, take a dip," said his father.

" Well, you come too. It's slow bathing alone."

" I'll come presently and look on," said his father.

So Frank got his towel and went. He lingered, and once or twice looked back, but his father was still with the children, tiny black dots on the sand, half a mile off, he supposed. He undressed in a crevice, and then came out. Last year he had undressed in the very same crevice, and Phillis, who, because of some slight affection of the heart, was not permitted to bathe, had waited outside ; and then she had come and watched him and called to him, and he had shaken the water out of his ears, and said : " What ?" He wished Phillis was here again to stand and call, so that he could shout back, " What ?" There was not a soul to shout to ; the children were far away. If anything were to happen, no one would be the wiser. Meanwhile he sat in his scanty bathing-suit upon the ledge of a rock. He thought his father was never coming ; he sat and shivered ; half the morning would be gone. . . .

. . . Mr. Burnet came with a book, and seated himself behind the rock. They were within a stone's throw of one another. What kept the boy so long ? Mr. Burnet peeped to see. What he saw was Frank's thin body up against the sky. His back was turned, his arms were clasped across his breast. Mr. Burnet bit his lip. He had been reading " Pickwick Papers," but the words that ran in his head were words from the Litany : " *To comfort and help the weak-hearted* (the boy was going in) . . . *to raise up them that fall* (he was stopping to rub his thighs) . . . *and finally to beat down Satan* (now for the plunge !) . . . *under our feet* " (he was gone).

Mr. Burnet heaved a sigh ; before he had heaved the sigh a terror was on him. He dropped the " Pickwick Papers," and sprang over the rocks. There was Frank swimming . . . swimming ?—floundering ! He was making for the shore, trying to gain a footing, while the breakers rolled him back. Mr. Burnet's coat was off ; the gulls flew screaming up into the sky. Was there a human scream ? . . . Anyway, Frank was safe.

His father clutched him by the neck of his little bathing-suit, and swam with him out of the surf.

" Oh, oh !" gasped Frank.

" Stand up !" said Mr. Burnet—" stand on your feet."

Frank stood. " I've swallowed such a lot !" he moaned.

" You should have struck out," said his father. " You were right enough."

" Then what did you jump in for ?" said Frank. He was fast recovering.

Unfortunately, at that moment Mrs. Burnet appeared with her sunshade. She had brought Wattie Brett to hunt for crabs.

" Oh, Hedley, have you tumbled in ?" She saw her husband's state.

Mr. Burnet looked annoyed. " The boy gave me a fright," he said. " I'll go to the Crown and get dried." He regretted the whole incident, and did not know who was most to blame. He scrambled up the cliff.

" Father is too absurd," said Frank. " There was no earthly reason why he should jump in. It's enough to make a fellow nervous." He was also annoyed, and he went back to his little crevice to dress.

" Frank is very highly strung," said Mrs. Burnet that night. " He has a nervous temperament. He will gain confidence as he grows older. I think he is a little bit ashamed of this morning's work. Don't remind him of it, Hedley."

" I have no wish to remind him," said Mr. Burnet, " or myself, for that matter."

" You think he has no pluck. Perhaps we are both mistaken. He has not at present a very strong character. Perhaps he will be stronger after his Confirmation."

Of course, there was a chance of that.

CHAPTER III

THERE was yet another tablet in Marchington Church. It was the tablet to Frank's great-great-grandfather, the Rev. Frank Hedley Hedley Burnet. He had climbed the church tower one windy night, and fallen from the top. They had been clearing out a pipe, and left the ladders behind ; and he must have run up the ladders, and then a squall must have come and blown him down, where they found him at the bottom. The lettering on this tablet was not so clear, worn faint, perhaps, with age, and Frank never had time to make it all out, because whenever he looked round his mother always said, "Hush !" and pulled him back again. And his father, who seemed to know whenever Frank's thoughts were wandering, looked over the big Bible, and went on reading : "Son of man, stand upon thy feet." Which was just what the Rev. Frank Hedley Hedley Burnet had failed to do.

Years afterwards Frank quarrelled with Phillis over the tower. Phillis was not Frank's sister. Though she lived at the Vicarage, she was only a distant sort of connection, somehow related to Frank's mother. She had nearer relations, of course, than the Burnets—her uncle and her cousin Daisy, and her aunt, old Miss Elizabeth, who once stayed at the Vicarage—but they were all of them abroad. The quarrel about the tower was this :

They had been together to Marchington Manor. Marchington Manor was always a sore point with Frank. It was a beautiful place : a large house, with three long terraces, and a moat with a reflection, and lawns, and cedars, and paddocks, and a little rambling copse, and at the end of the copse a rustic gate leading out upon the road. Frank loved Marchington Manor, and what vexed him was that Phillis (to whom Marchington Manor would one day, when she was quite grown up, belong) did not care for it a bit. Frank loved the Manor, Phillis the Vicarage.

" We'll swop," said Frank that very afternoon. " Pity you're not a boy, Phil, then you could be the parson. I know there'll be a row sooner or later over that."

" Over what ? "

" The living. How can I be a parson ? My gifts don't lie that way. My gift, of course, is art. It's absurd for me not to be an artist."

" Well, be both."

" Both ! "

" Wouldn't they go together ? "

" Together ! My dear Phil ! Why, to be an artist one must devote oneself entirely to the job. Art must be everything, first and last. One must give one's life, and soul, and strength ; one must not have a thought beyond ; one must strain every nerve. . . ." He stopped, for Phillis had plunged into the hedge after a bit of honeysuckle.

" Go on," she said . . . " *every nerve.* . . . I'm listening."

" Oh, I see . . . honeysuckle ! "

" Never mind the honeysuckle. Go on about art, and life, and soul, and strength."

Frank was walking on. She caught him up, winding the honeysuckle into the ribbon of her hat. " You'll never make a parson," was what she said.

" Why not ? "

" You're not good enough. On the other hand, you might make an artist."

" My dear Phil ! I only know this, that I could easier preach a hundred sermons than paint one single picture."

" Clearly, then, your gift's not art. I thought you said it was. You'd better preach. Oh, I should like to hear you preach ! "

" The chances are you will," said Frank. " The chances are," he said again, " you will. I see no

possible escape at present, unless, of course, father goes
on living until I have had time to *prove* myself an
artist.   But, then, the question is—*the question is, am
I an artist ?*"   He had a stick in his hand, and as he
said " the question is—*the question is,*" he swept off
the heads of the nettles.

They crossed the meadow by the church.   A ladder
leant against the old grey walls.   They had been cleaning the gutters and pipes.   Sometimes the jackdaws
would build in the pipes, and then Frank's father had
trouble.

" *The question is, the question is,*" said Phillis.   Her
hand was on the ladder.

" What are you going to do ?" asked Frank.

" *By straining every nerve,*" she said.   She was
already half-way up ; her skirts were blowing.   From
the parapet she looked down at him and laughed.

" It's nearly tea-time," shouted Frank, consulting
his watch.

" Bother tea !" said Phillis.   " I'm going up the
tower."

" Don't be an idiot !"

" I'll try not."

" Don't be an idiot, I say, and come down !"

" I shall be an idiot if I *do* come down. . . .   *You*
come as well."

" I loathe heights."

" Why don't you say straight out that you're afraid
of them ?"

" I'm not afraid.   I've been up that old tower
before now."

" Have you ?   When ?"

" Last holidays I went up."

" Did you ?"

" Yes."

" What—on the roof ?"

" Yes."

" Up the tower ?"

Frank nodded.   She looked at him curiously.

Frank looked at his watch. " It's half-past four," he said. But she was gone.

. . . " I say, Phil!" He had climbed the first ladder. There she was again, up the second ladder leading to the top. The daws flew out in a commotion. " I say, Phil, come down. It's not a thing for a girl to do."

Phillis went on ; she was singing aloud. The daws croaked round her head.

" It's all swagger," shouted Frank ; " you only make yourself absurd. . . . Phil, it isn't safe, I say." It was perilous. He noticed a bit of the piping was new.

" *You've* done it."

" . . . No."

" You *said* you had."

" I—I meant *this* part—the roof. I never went up there."

" You *said* you *had*." She looked unutterable scorn. Frank clambered down. He waited for her at the bottom, wretched, miserable. From where he stood he could not see her. Someone saw her, though— Wattie Brett, the blacksmith's boy. He was standing by his father's forge with Gracie, the foreman's daughter, and he saw Miss Phillis up against the sky. Miss Phillis on the tower where the jackdaws build ! . . . Hooray ! Hooray ! Miss Phillis ! . . . Hooray ! Hooray ! . . . He knew Miss Phillis well ; she played the organ, trained the choir. Run, Wattie, run ! He ran with all his might. It took him possibly three minutes to reach the meadow ; then came the church-yard wall. He jumped the wall, the graves, mound after mound, and pitched head-foremost in the ditch. . . . She was coming down ; he could not see—he heard her. Then he heard her voice. It was not her Sunday voice ; they were not Sunday words.

" I hate cowards and liars," was what she said.

Dreadful words, thought Wattie, with tingling ears. Cowards and liars ! . . . Then he saw Master Frank, his long legs walking right away. There was a silence ;

Wattie held his breath; then the faintest sound. He summoned courage, stooped, and peered between the hedge. Miss Phillis lay face downwards on the grass, and her whole body shook with sobs. Wattie turned and fled.

CHAPTER IV

BUT really by far the most remarkable thing in Marchington Church was the little rose-window over the east. It had a curious history, and is quite well worth describing. It had been set up by a former Squire—Phillis's great-great-grandfather—in memory of two favourite steeds. Those were the days of the Rev. Frank Hedley Hedley Burnet, he who fell from the tall church tower. Had he not been so ill at the time, no doubt this would never have come to pass. The Squire went up to the Vicarage on purpose to talk the matter over. There had always been a plain rose-window with a plain perpendicular underneath. The Vicar had said that coloured glass would be a great improvement. Nobody in Marchington could afford such extravagance—except the Squire; and the Squire now (that is to say, on the death of his favourite hunters) came forward with a suggestion. He would commission a certain friend of his to make a window in memory of the white mare and the strawberry roan. When he went to consult the Vicar, the Vicar said he was "*far too unwell*" to be consulted at all, so the Squire went away. He wrote a letter to explain his plan. The Vicar subsequently maintained that he had been "*far too unwell*" to comprehend the meaning of that letter, that he had understood the window was to be only in pious memory of two faithful departed creatures, and not a representation of the animals themselves. When he was sufficiently recovered to come back into his church and take a part (here and there) of the daily service, his indignation knew no bounds. But it was very shortly afterwards that he fell off the tower.

There were, of course, disputes about the window. Some people said it was profane, others ridiculous ; some people said it must be taken down altogether, and others that it might be left up if only a sacred flavour could be introduced—if, for instance, the perpendicular window beneath might be filled with holy Apostles ; but as no two people could be got to agree, and nobody could afford the Apostles, and the new Squire lived in Italy, and the new Vicar would express no opinion, the matter was dropped. People now took those horses for granted, and the present Vicar, the Rev. Hedley Burnet, would even occasionally introduce them into his excellent sermons, perhaps as illustrating " the animal creation " or " faithful friendships." Anyway, as Frank thought, there could be nothing profane about two such very unlife-like horses. If the holy Apostles were to be done on that conventional pattern, it would be profane indeed ; but these two stiff-jointed ecclesiastical creatures, as they could never exist *outside* the church, might surely be allowed to come *in*.

He stared at them from the Vicarage pew—why, he did not know ; for they always looked just the same, just as stiff and absurd. It was the only place where you got any colour ; and, besides, you must stare at something. He stared and stared whilst his father preached, and then he would shut his eyes, and then he would open and stare again. It was all more or less boring. Not that his father preached so badly ; he preached really rather well. He wrote his sermons, and then got them off by heart. He could never trust himself to preach extempore, and he always took the manuscript into the pulpit. Also, he always repeated the sermon to Frank's mother on Friday after tea. You might think it would get stale ; but when he came to preach you really never would suspect he was not pouring out an unpremeditated flow. A flow, a

gush : the words ran out ; he never stopped for breath.
From the moment when he stooped to place his Bible
at his feet (which he did, because once, at the grandfather's funeral sermon, he had pushed it over the desk)
—from that moment till the moment when he would
jerk an abrupt and unexpected finish, he was—what ?
He seemed—what ? Inspired ? . . . Frank shut his
eyes. All sorts of odd considerations crowded in your
head about principle and conduct, faith and practice ;
and if you began to think of it, how curious it was to
go on saying the same sort of thing week after week,
year after year, and perhaps without any result !
Where you were probed, the wound soon healed.
Sometimes (to be strictly honest) you were the better,
he supposed. Still, did one always care ? . . . People
attended church for various reasons (a funny institu-
tion !)—his father because he was the parson ; his
mother because his father did, and there was the
Vicarage pew ; Phillis because she thought she ought ;
he because he knew he must ; and then you looked round
at the congregation, and so on, and so on. He would
scan the faces of the choir ; they, at least, were quite
oblivious, the row of girls, the row of boys—the girls
with their hat-elastics, the boys with open mouths . . .
and then he would catch Wattie's eye—Brett's boy,
who sat against the organ—and Frank would turn his
chin over his collar, and gaze up at the conventional
stiff-jointed horses in the rose-window as before.

By the way, they had a rather horrid tale attached
to them. The strawberry roan had been all through a
fearful campaign ; twice its master had been shot, but
the strawberry roan escaped. Escaped ! And escaped
for what ? Reserved, of course, for its fate. It came
home in the troop-ship, and travelled from Portsmouth
to London, from London to Brinkley, from Brinkley
home. No doubt there had always been something
a little queer, if anyone had eyes to see, only nobody
ever has. For instance, they said, when it went to be
shod, the Squire must always go too, and sit in the

saddle. . . . Strange, unaccountable, captious ways.
The groom went to meet it at Marchington Station,
and he was leading it round to show to the Squire, who
sat by the cedar on the lawn, when the poor brute
slipped his foot down a rabbit-hole, stumbled, and
fell. The next day it had to be shot. And that is
not all; for the white mare foaled that night, and died.
Calamity!

CHAPTER V

IT was a very hot summer. The hot days began in
June—cloudless days, glorious days—and then through
hot July. When Frank came home from Winchester,
he found the Midlands all burnt up. It was a serious
matter. Mr. Burnet prayed for rain. That very night
the clouds rolled up, great, sullen, threatening clouds—
rolled up, rolled over, and dispersed. Mr. Burnet read
the prayer again. He looked white and fagged, and,
taxed by his wife, admitted a headache. Frank, too,
lost his appetite. Phillis alone was undisturbed. She
used to lie out in the hammock under the poplars on
the lawn. She went there on Monday afternoon with
" Three Men in a Boat." She read half a dozen pages,
and then dozed. A little wind came up and shook the
poplar-leaves—shook them down into her skirt.
Frank passed that way; he had been sketching in the
meadow just beyond the church; he trudged along the
path with both hands full. He was in flannels, his
collar open at the throat. He said, " Hallo !"
    Phillis did not stir. He was vexed to find her fast
asleep; he wanted somebody to talk to. Sitting down
there in the meadow, odd feelings had crept over him,
and he had packed his tools and come away. It was
horribly sultry. He did not like to wake Phillis; he
stood looking at her for a bit, and picked a little poplar-
leaf out of her lap. Nothing ever upset Phillis. . . .

Then he felt the odd sensation creeping back again, and walked on up the path. . . .

It was pleasanter indoors than out. Mr. Burnet generally began next Sunday's sermon on Monday afternoon. He took great trouble with his sermons; he made several drafts : a draft on Monday, another on Tuesday, an entire revision on Wednesday ; Thursday and Friday he spent in committing the sermon to memory (for he was nervous, and could not preach with notes), and Saturday he rested. He had been making his first draft now. He had chosen for his text, "Ye know not what manner of spirit ye are of." It was a text he very often quoted, but he did not believe he had ever made it the subject of a sermon. He had, of course, a great deal to say ; he had to gather some, all, or any of the thoughts which had run in and out of his head, and lodged there, from the early boyish days when he besought God to deliver him from evil, to the present time when it was working up for rain. . . . It would perhaps be cooler if he shut the window down. The breeze was hot ; moreover, it rattled the venetians. He looked out of the window before closing it. There were clouds, but the experience of the last ten days had told them that clouds might come and go. . . . He returned to his sermon . . . the manner of spirit. . . . Where was his wife ? The house seemed unusually still. Where were the children ? No, he would *not* go and see. He would at any rate finish the sermon first. . . . The point being—the point whence one starts, and where ultimately one arrives—that we *know not*. *We* know not, but *God* knows. Oh, thanks be to God that He should know ! What peace, what hope, what security ! . . . He jotted so much down. Well, it was shaped. He thrust the notes into his desk, and went out of the room.

He called his wife's name once, twice : "Amy ! Amy !"

She came to him from the drawing-room, looking so fresh and cool ; he smiled with pleasure.

"Where are the children?" he said.

"I don't know," said his wife.

"And what have you been doing?"

"Doing my accounts. It is delightful in the drawing-room. You have been sitting in your study. How is your headache? Better?"

"I think we are going to have a storm," said Mr. Burnet.

"It will clear the air; do us all good. . . . That was thunder."

He had heard it too. "I hope the children won't get caught," he said.

"A little rain won't hurt them; besides, here's Frank coming up the garden. How the boy grows! . . . Hedley, I want you to speak to him about his report."

"An excellent opportunity," said Mr. Burnet. It would give them all something to think about while the storm rolled up and away. "I have the report in my desk." They went to the library.

"Frank!" called his mother.

"Hullo!" said Frank. He came to the library-door. He saw his father and mother together—his father so tall, his little mother. He also heard the distant murmur. All sorts of storms were brewing. . . . Well, this would take the edge off that.

"We wanted to have a talk about your report," said Mr. Burnet.

He brought out the scanty document; he cleared his voice, but it was Frank's mother who spoke.

"You have disappointed us this term, Frank," she said. "I do not think you made the effort you promised you would make."

Frank stood there with his palette and canvas. "You mean the Greek," said Frank.

"Not the Greek especially," his mother said.

"Well, what?" said Frank.

"You have seen the report yourself."

"I know. There wasn't much in it. He always

says that sort of thing ; he says it about everyone :
'Want of earnestness and application.' He only has
two phrases ; you either ' want earnestness and application,' or else you ' are thorough and painstaking.'
Both equally objectionable, perhaps, but I think I
prefer the first."

Frank put his palette and brushes down, also his
canvas, face upwards, and turned towards his parents.
It was a pretty bit he had begun.

" Why ?" said his father. " *I* prefer the second.
The first is a ·charge of weakness, the second an
admission of strength."

Frank said nothing.

" Your father is right, Frank," said Mrs. Burnet.
" It would, at any rate, please *us* much more to learn
that you were ' thorough and painstaking ' than that
you ' wanted earnestness and application.' "

" Oh, of course," said Frank, " if you put it that
way."

" It is the way you put it yourself," said his
father.

Frank held his tongue.

" At the same time, young people like bright colours,"
said Mrs. Burnet—she glanced, too, at his picture—
" and prefer the more brilliant virtues—I was going
to say, even the more brilliant vices—to the plainer
qualities. We all want rather to be thought clever
than industrious in childhood. I am sure *I* did."
She looked at her husband, hoping he would on his own
part acquiesce, but he merely said :

" Frank is no longer a child."

" That is just what I think," said Frank. He
advanced to the attack ; his heart went pumping up
and down, for it is so difficult, so impossibly, cruelly
difficult to make one's parents understand. "That
is just what I think. I am no longer a child, and I
wish to goodness people would realize the fact."

" What do you mean, dear boy ?" This was his
mother.

"I don't mean anything particular," grumbled Frank, drawing back a little, "only—only I think I've stuck to things long enough, and it's time I had a change. Besides, I'm wasting precious years. People don't consider that. Just because other fellows go along the old accustomed lines, they suppose there are to be no exceptions. There are exceptions to every rule."

"You are an exception, I imagine," said his father. There came a distant murmur.

"I don't know. I don't set myself up for anything very remarkable or out of the way," said Frank, looking towards the window. "But still, there's a difference in people, that you'll allow. Some people are better suited than others for the ordinary routine of life."

His father interrupted him. "My dear boy," he said, "those are very fortunate people."

"So they are," said Frank coldly.

Mrs. Burnet was vexed ; she thought her husband did not give the boy fair play. "Your father is right," she said again. "Sooner or later we must all face the fact that life—every life—has its ordinary routine. You know it is considered very wrong to have one law for the rich, another for the poor, and personally I think that it is quite wrong, quite mistaken, to suppose that there is a different law for the distinguished and for the commonplace. We are all bound, whatever our station, whatever our gifts, to *do* our best, to *be* our best, and this means for all of us—yes, for all of us, I am sure—*taking trouble*. That is every man's routine ; there is no escape from it, and it is often irksome. Even when you are an artist, dear boy, there will be the daily grind."

"Grinding at art isn't grinding to me."

"You are not an artist yet," said his father.

Frank treated that remark with deserved contempt.

"Your father means," began Mrs. Burnet, "that an amateur——"

" My dear mother," said Frank, " you need not trouble to explain. I've no wish to argue, or to put forward my ideas. I would a thousand times rather keep them to myself, as, in point of fact, of course, I do. . . . Besides, I've often thought over these things. I thought them out ages ago. There is not the slightest reason for you to vex yourselves. . . . You want me to pay more attention to my Greek. Very well, then, I will. I'm sure I've no wish to distress you. That settles the matter."

There came a thunder-clap.

" We had better open the window and door," said Mr. Burnet, rising from his chair. He flung up the window hastily ; Mrs. Burnet opened the door.

The report lying on the table fluttered in the sudden draught. " The lightning will then pass through," said Mr. Burnet, sitting down again. " I do not mind about the Greek. Rather than that you should pay more attention to your Greek, I wish you would pay more attention to what your mother tells you."

" He does," said Mrs. Burnet, and then she went on : " Frank is very good ; he will always listen to reason."

" I object to that phrase ' listen to reason,' " said her husband. " A mere boy has no business to judge what is reasonable or unreasonable. His business is to listen to *what he is told*, reasonable or not."

" I should imagine that to listen to my mother was to listen to reason," said Frank, scoring a point.

" Hush, Frank," said his mother ; " you forget yourself."

The tears came into the boy's eyes, tears of vexation. His mother picked up the canvas. " This is very pretty," she said. " Look, Hedley !"

Mr. Burnet looked, and nodded. Frank's cheeks flamed. He wanted to chuck it out of the window, palette, box, and all.

There was a vivid flash ; it made Frank jump. Mr.

Burnet stood and counted : " One, two, three, four, five." Then came the clap.

" This is the storm," said Mr. Burnet. " We shall have the rain here in a minute. We want it badly."

" Where is Phillis ?" said Mrs. Burnet. " She will get wet."

" In the hammock," said Frank. " I'll call her." He was glad to go ; he ran up the garden path, brushing the tears away.

" What is that ?" said Mr. Burnet.

She listened. " The church bell ! Why, my dear Hedley, it is St. Bartholomew's Day ! I had forgotten Evensong." (That would be Wattie ringing the bell.) " How stupid of me !" said Mrs. Burnet.

Mr. Burnet looked twice at his watch. " I must go at once," he said.

" What is the time ?"

He looked again. " Half-past five," he said.

" I will put on my hat," said his wife. " Yes, please. I should prefer it. It is only ten minutes' walk."

She went out of the room. As she ran down the stairs she met Frank coming in from the garden. Phillis followed more leisurely behind.

" Frank," said his mother, " you will come, too ?"

" Where ?"

" Church. We had forgotten it is St. Bartholomew's Day."

" I don't mind," said Frank ; " but it's going to pour. I advise you not to go. Nobody in his senses would." Zigzag went the lightning through the hall.

" Come, my boy, if you're coming," said his father briskly ; he could not find his umbrella. " Though," he added, " there is no reason why you should come if you don't want to. We shall only get soaked to the skin."

" Rain won't hurt Frank," said his mother. She found her husband's umbrella. " I think he would like to come."

" What's up ?" said Phillis, with a yawn. It was overpowering sleepiness.

" We are going to Evensong. We had forgotten it was a saint's day."

" What saint ?" asked Phillis.

" St. Bartholomew," said Frank.

" Frank is coming," said Mrs. Burnet.

" I'll go, if you'd rather," said Phillis, with another yawn.

Mrs. Burnet said, " No." It was not what she wanted.

They set out, the three together. The rain had ceased almost as soon as it had begun. It was a wonderful sky. The storm came from the west, and westward it was dark and lowering, eastward calm and light ; far away, strange and unearthly, the sun shone on the outspread hills. Down the drive they walked, and out on to the road. It was a straight, long, level road, with sloping fields on either side. This way it led into the village, that way up the narrowing valley, whence the storm approached. It hung like a thick pall, with lightning playing in and out the skirts. Frank looked back once or twice, and each time the pall seemed nearer—seemed by some invisible hand to have been shifted up the valley—invisible, for when he looked it hung there motionless ; and yet, so surely as he turned his back, it stole a march upon him. It was a very evil sight. Moreover, there appeared another strange phenomenon : this pall took shape ; it grew into a cloud, bold, heap on heap against the sky ; and then, more curious still, a little fragment of pure white detached itself and stood apart—stood, and yet moved . . . yes, the white cloud was moving ; there must be wind behind. Wind ? A tempest ! hurricane ! It whisked the white cloud into a flying form, and puffed it up the valley. Frank saw it tearing along the black hill-sides.

" Look !" he said—" look !"

Mr. Burnet did not look, but Mrs. Burnet did. " Very fine, Frank—very fine !"

Fine ?   It was horrible !   Alas ! his mother had no
eyes to see such things ! She thought it was an ordinary
cloud ; she did not see the apparition, the dreadful
judgment in pursuit, nor feel its breath upon her.

" Let's get on," said the boy.   His mother teased
him—he had such long legs ! . . .   He strode on by his
father's side.

" I can't keep up with you," laughed Mrs. Burnet.

Mr. Burnet slackened speed.   " We are almost
there," he said.

Frank turned once more.   Oh, mercy !   It was even
nearer than he thought.   It had leapt upon them,
bound on bound.   Here it was, large and white, like
steam or smoke ; its ragged fringe blew in advance ;
he almost felt it flapping.   Yes, he felt it, the first
shiver.   They were passing between a double row of
aspens ; the aspens trembled, wondered, and then
rocked.   His mother's cloak was caught about.   It
was the prelude to the storm.   " Look out !" cried
Mr. Burnet.   He held his hat ; he ran before the
wind—he ran, they ran, in at the wicket-gate and up
the path.   The wicket slammed behind them, and as
it slammed, lightning, thunder, blast, and rain. . . .
The door stood open, and they were blown inside.

How strange within !   So dark !   Yes, but such
peace !   And Wattie ringing the bell.

Mrs. Burnet shook out her skirt.   " I'm only a little
wet," she whispered.

" Shall I shut the door ?" said Frank.

" Yes," said his father.   He looked round at the
windows.   The windows were all shut.   Either it
should be that, or let a current through.

" Wipe your boots," said Mrs. Burnet.   And Frank
shut the door and wiped his boots.   Together tiptoe
they went up the aisle—the father to the vestry,
stooping through the little arch under the tower wall.
Overhead the bell clanged with a dull, metallic sound.
Then the bell stopped.   The Vicar had come out, and,
robed in white, walked to his seat.   You could hear

his step, his cough, the rustle of his robe as he knelt down to pray. Why, then, was that ? Well, it was odd ; the thunder, like the bell, had stopped. There was peace and quiet. It might be only for a moment—a momentary lull, a breathing-space—but Frank believed the storm was passing. He swallowed something in his throat. He dropped upon his knees down by his mother's side. " *Almighty and Everlasting God. . . .*"

Well, but it was true, every word of the Confession ; and every word that followed, when his father stood and spoke to God alone—every word true, and quite distinct. That was the strange and solemn part, and yet the voice subdued. Not a sound in the church, not a sound but that voice. The storm had ceased. " *Through Jesus Christ our Lord. Amen. . . .*"

In the pause he heard his mother's breathing. Strange silence ! He lifted up his face. How dark ! Darker than ever, so it seemed—too dark, too silent ! No rain, no wind ; the silence utter and complete. . . . Then the voice again. " *Our Father. . . .*"

They got through the Lord's Prayer.

" Mother," whispered Frank. He plucked her sleeve.

" Hush !" She shook her head.

He knelt on by an effort. He tried to listen to the words.

" *O Lord, open Thou our lips.*"

His mother made the response. His heart was leaping so.

" Mother," he whispered again, " I feel sick."

She grasped his arm ; her face was stern.

" *O God, make speed to save us.*"

" *O Lord, make haste to help us.*"

Frank struggled to his feet. She looked at him, then nodded to the door. He found his way, went out ; it was like walking into night. The whole world swam before his eyes. Something was going to happen. He got as far as the railing which ran beside the path ;

he seized it, clung to it, leant his whole weight upon it. This was all he knew. Whether that white light which clothed him was in his fevered brain alone, whether he had gone mad, whether a real wind came and swept him off his feet, whether this torrent beat upon his head . . . " Mother !" . . . He must get back again. He wanted somebody. This was the tower up above. He fought his way. " Mother oh, mother ! . . . Oh !"

*   *   *   *   *

Years afterwards they put another tablet in the church. It faced the tablet to the Rev. Seymour Frank Hedley Burnet. The words on the new tablet ran thus :

TO THE GLORY OF GOD AND IN MEMORY

OF THE

REV. HEDLEY BURNET,

VICAR OF THIS PARISH,

AND OF

AMY HIS WIFE,

WHO WERE STRUCK DEAD BY LIGHTNING ON THE 24TH DAY OF AUGUST IN THE YEAR 18— DURING DIVINE SERVICE IN THIS CHURCH.

" Ye know not what manner of spirit ye are of."

PART II

WATTIE

" Sing, riding's a joy ! For me, I ride."

CHAPTER VI

THERE was written inside Wattie's Prayer-Book, "Walter Brett, from his godmother," and the date. Mrs. Burnet was his godmother, and she had given him this book as a christening present. Wattie had often heard tell of that christening—how Mrs. Burnet had taken him in her arms to the church, and Mr. Burnet had poured water over him out of a little shell. So said Mrs. Moon, who minded him, and she kept the Prayer-Book in its original wrapping of paper, and never let him touch it. Each Christmas Mrs. Burnet brought him a Christmas-box, and also one time, when his father was killed by a kick from a horse, she gave him a suit of clothes—at least, she gave them to Mrs. Moon—and he had them once a week. Also, she came every quarter to bring his Sunday-school card. Mrs. Moon always sent him out to play in the back, so he never knew what Mrs. Burnet had said ; but Mrs. Moon always said the same thing after Mrs. Burnet had gone : " If you're not a good boy, you shall have a thrashing ;" and from time to time, of course, he did.

Mrs. Burnet lived at the Vicarage up the long white road, with Mr. Burnet and Miss Phillis and Master Frank. Sometimes Wattie would have to take a message there for Mrs. Moon, and if it was summer, as he crossed the garden he might see Miss Phillis in the hammock and Master Frank on the lawn ; and Master

Frank would look up from his painting, and Miss
Phillis would open one eye. If it was winter, they would
pass, perhaps, through the hall as he was sitting there
under the lamp, Master Frank with a book and Miss
Phillis with nothing ; and then Mr. Burnet would say :
" Can you find your way back in the dark ?" And
Wattie would wonder what this meant, for the way was
easy enough to find ; and when he got to the shadows
he used to turn round, and the light was still streaming
over the path.

Mr. Burnet often talked of the dark. In church, as
he went down the nave with the boys on one side and
the girls on the other, he would say : " Some little *boys*
are afraid of the dark ;" and they screwed round their
necks to follow him ; and then, as he went up again,
he said : " Some little *girls* are afraid of the dark ;" and
then he would turn on the chancel steps and lift his
finger and say : " Boys and girls must *not* be afraid ;"
and then he would say : " Dear children, stand," and
give out the number of the hymn, and Miss Phillis
would start on the organ.

Mr. Burnet would often tell them not to be frightened
of this or that—of thunder and lightning, or dogs, or
cows, or horses—and then he would point to some
horses there in a window and say they were made by
God. And before they went for the summer excursion Mr. Burnet told them about the sea, and said they
must not be frightened of *that*, because it was in his
hands ; and he told them about that Leviathan, and
about the crabs which they must not hurt, though
given them for food, and about the time they must be
on the platform. Mr. Burnet was never late for the
treat himself. The superintendent arrived first at
six, and Mr. Burnet at a quarter-past, and Mrs. Burnet
at a quarter before seven, with Miss Phillis. Then
came the train at seven. Master Frank kept with
his father ; he walked after his father in cricketing
flannels, and did whatever his father did ; just as
Mr. Burnet shook hands with the superintendent,

so did Master Frank shake hands ; and then when the train steamed in, they both pushed along the edge of the platform and said : " Stand back ! stand back !"

And so it was all through if you happened to notice : Master Frank and his father up and down. If one went to swim, so did the other ; if one went to sail, the other went too ; and when Mr. Burnet said the blessing at tea, Master Frank stood by his side. They both of them counted the boys and girls before they came home : Mr. Burnet counted them out in the yard, and Master Frank at the barrier. Wattie would never be counted himself. And when they got back, Mr. Burnet said : " Well, children, we have had a happy day, and, thank God ! no accidents."

About accidents the less said the better. Wattie had a distinct remembrance of once going with Mrs. Burnet (the time when Miss Phillis wasn't there) along the shining sands, and while Mrs. Burnet lingered to speak to her husband (who had been for a swim in his clothes), getting over the rocks and pitching clean into a pool. He went right down, and didn't come up, and knocked a hole in his head, and though he concealed the hole under his cap, he felt rather guilty when Mr. Burnet said more earnestly than usual, in his clothes which had dried : " Well, children, we have had a happy day, and, thank God ! no accidents."

CHAPTER VII

BESIDES being in Sunday-school, Wattie also sang in the choir. There was this undoubted advantage about singing in the choir : you sat where you could see. Boys and girls sat together, a row of girls and a row of boys, and they could see almost everything they wanted to see, in front and on either side, and behind

was only a wall. Not that things weren't always
pretty much the same, but just because they were the
same, you noticed every difference—the difference
between morning and evening, or summer and winter;
which way the shadows slanted, and whether the sun
burst out on a sudden, or streamed in all the time.
You noticed as well every change in the congregation.
There was the Manor pew—you never could really
be sure who would be sitting there, for the Manor was
let; it never belonged to the people who lived in it.
Various people lived in it. At one time Wattie remembered an old man and his wife, who followed in
very large books; at another time a number of girls
who sat with an elderly servant; then he remembered
the pew being empty, until he was taken aback one
day to find a stiff lady and gentleman sitting together,
and a small child wedged between. These were Colonel
and Mrs. Jones, and they stayed. They stayed to
this very day; and yet, did the Manor belong to
them? No; it belonged to Miss Phillis—Miss Phillis,
who played on the organ, and drew the little
curtain round her, and disappeared, but was always
there when you stood up, the top of her hat just the
same.

On the other side of the nave fair Mrs. Burnet sat
alone. Sometimes she had a friend; more often she
was alone. Once she had a white-haired old lady;
Mrs. Moon called her old Miss Elizabeth, and said that
she was Miss Phillis's aunt. Master Frank, of course,
she had in the holiday season. He came from Winchester. So did Colonel Jones's nephew. It was a
school for young gentlemen.

Every time Master Frank came home he seemed to
grow taller and taller; he was nearly as tall as his
father, who must stoop his head to come out of the
vestry, and took the whole of the nave in six strides.
Master Frank could not stride the nave, for he walked
on the heels of his mother. Mrs. Burnet went first
into the pew, and seated herself at the far end, and

Master Frank went in after her over the hassocks. Sometimes Master Frank would move up close to his mother, sometimes he stopped where he was. Whenever he moved up close he seemed to have something to say. Mrs. Burnet would nod or shake her head ; she kept her eyes to the east. Master Frank kept his eyes there, too, when he had once settled down. He stared at the little rose window before him ; and he stared and stared so hard and so long, as if he were trying to make something out, and then he would frown, and then he would turn his head with a jerk and look round over his collar, first at the girls and then at the boys, and then he would stare back again at the window—all through the lessons, all through the sermon. Sometimes, however, he shut his eyes— during the sermon, perhaps, for a minute, then for more than a minute, then shut them and kept them shut, and then it became a habit. So soon as Mr. Burnet had read his text and put the Bible down at his feet and begun, " My dear friends, brothers and sisters in God," Master Frank's lids would drop. But still Wattie thought he was listening, and directly the sermon was ended he would catch hold of the pew and pull himself up, and then back at once his eyes would go to the window.

Wattie could also see that window. He stared at it, too—in fact, he had frequently come to himself in the Psalms, to find his mouth wide open, not singing at all. He had been wafted away and away, up in the red and the blue and the gold. It was the colour he liked ; the shapes were absurd. Mr. Burnet had said they were made by God; but anyway, it was a thousand pities that a horse should be chopped into senseless bits by the framework of stone. In itself the framework was pretty enough, dividing the circle into six parts—a perfect circle, and equal parts, and all sorts of tracery and device ; but it bothered you when you came to the horses, and you had to be blind to the stone divisions in order to see each beast entire—legs

and body, breast and head, standing complete and
compact, a white mare and a strawberry roan upon a
ground of shaded tints.

Could you imagine (yes, you could) a window of one
sheet of glass—one smooth, round level sheet of glass—
where you might put those horses, and where, bounded
only by a circle like the circle of your eye, they should
be free, and, to their own astonishment, find themselves alive ?   Yes, you could *imagine* it, but that
was all !   Glass so fragile, could it be lifted safely,
fixed securely—could it resist one puff of wind ?
Fragile, fairy glass, with the morning sun behind it,
so far away, set between earth and sky—might he
but stretch one finger out and dip it in the blue !
He would go up if he had wings. . . .   And at this point
a friendly pin would prick him back ; he would shut
his mouth rather suddenly, and burst into hurried
song.

By the way, how had the horses come to be there ?
He had often heard.   Miss Phillis's great-great-grandfather had loved his mare and his strawberry roan ;
they were both magnificent hunters, and jump ?—well,
it wasn't jumping ; it was certain the white mare flew.
And the Squire loved them.   Why, when the strawberry went to be shod, the Squire would always go
too, and sit in the saddle.   Very likely they could not
bear to be parted.   But the Squire let him go out to
the war, and he was so brave that when he came back
they hung round his neck young master's medal.   And
being such wonderful, beautiful, brave and beautiful
horses, it seemed hard they should not be allowed in
a church ; it seemed hard they should die and be forgotten.   Die, of course they must.   The strawberry
caught his foot in a burrow, and had to be shot ; the
white mare died when she foaled.

CHAPTER VIII

IT was a very remarkable thing that Wattie should have seen that particular window fall when it fell with the church in the famous storm. It was perhaps two minutes after Master Frank had walked out, looking so sick and white, and Mr. Burnet beginning the Psalms, and Mrs. Burnet standing still, when the storm came on again. Wattie had thought the storm was over; the thunder had stopped; he had noticed how quiet it was with Master Frank's boots coming down the nave, and the creak of the door, and Mr. and Mrs. Burnet's voices; and then all at once something happened; it sounded like hail on the roof, and the church seemed to rock and to flash in and out . . . he was finding his place for the twenty-fourth day . . . yes, he remembered that . . . and he remembered looking up, and a hissing and singing, and horrible smell, and he remembered shielding his head . . . and then he distinctly saw this one remarkable sight — the east wall swaying to and fro, and the east-end lights falling in. They said he could not possibly have remembered all that he said he remembered. After that he remembered lying in bed with something cold on his forehead.

He was not hurt, only stunned, but they kept him in darkness. He begged to get up. Mrs. Moon, who nursed him, said : "Hush, my dearie !" She said "Hush, my dearie !" to everything, and "Never mind, my pretty lamb !" She also said : "Never mind how it's come about ; you had an accident, that's all—a kick from one of the horses."

Wattie was amazed at her ignorance. "I was in church," he said. "How could I be kicked by a horse ? Whoever heard of a horse in church ?" And then he sat up suddenly, for he remembered the horses in the window, and he said : " They're smashed to smithereens."

" Someone's been talking," said Mrs. Moon.

" Only you," said Wattie ; and he flung back his clothes, for he longed to get out and have somebody else to talk to.

" The first thing you do," said Mrs. Moon, " is to thank the good God on your knees for saving your precious life when He took the Vicar and Mrs. Burnet."

" Took them where ?" asked Wattie. " Are they dead ?" He understood.

" Dead and buried yesterday, and a funeral half a mile long, and a wonder you're not too. It was little short of a miracle."

Wattie said nothing ; he buried his face in the pillow, and pretended to be asleep, but really he was thinking. It was curious and sudden, and Mrs. Moon's explanations only made everything more odd. He was glad when Mrs. Moon left him. She told him not to stir, but he got up and dressed himself, and said, " Our Father," and went out.

He walked rather slowly up the street to the church. When he got there he stood quite still. Very strange and sudden ! He was glad nobody was about ; he never knew he cared so much.

Why, half the church had gone, and a tree was lying on the top ! The east end lying under a tree, one of the biggest of the elms ! . . . What would the sexton say, who kept the grass and rang the bell, and sometimes gave Wattie a penny to ring it ? . . . The west end stood, and the jackdaw's tower, and the wall as far as the porch, but after the porch came a break, and though the wall began again, it very soon came to another stop. Should he turn back ? He bit his lip. No, he would go on.

He had seen ruins before. There were the ruins of Brinkley Castle, but they were different to this. At Brinkley you had a keep covered with ivy, and ramparts smothered with jasmine bloom. Brinkley had died a natural death, and ferns and flowers were springing from it. That could not have happened in a day. Marchington Church had gone in a day. Besides, it had been an accident, quite a mistake—a flash of lightning—and so far from flowers springing there, flowers lay crushed beneath ; grave after grave, laid desolate. He was climbing over the wreckage, and now he stood inside.

Here the havoc was even greater. Strange that what first caught his eye was his own little Prayer-Book jammed under a pew. He wiped the dust off with his sleeve, and smoothed the crumpled pages. This, then, was where he had been standing when Master Frank went out, and he had not been hurt. Instinctively he looked above ; there was the over-arching roof, and then behind—why, if one shut one's eyes to fact one could be easily persuaded that the church stood as it had always stood. There were the last half-dozen seats, there the vestry-door ; the vestry-door was closed, which was left open as a rule, but still it was the door, same lock and awkward handle. And then above, the great bare tower wall—grand wall, strong wall, calm wall, not a stone out of place ; sweet and peaceful, too, for the sun was shining there as it had never shone before ; all the light of the outside world poured in and broke upon it. Whence came the light ? He turned to look, and then he remembered how it was, the trembling, swaying, and collapse. Yes, it had gone, the little window ; one absurd bit of tracery hung there, caught between two tumbled blocks, and beyond that the sky. Gone where ? Well, it must lie upon the ground. Poor little rose ! How should he find it ? He began to shift the rubbish. . . Glass ! . . . Glass ! . . . But was this his pretty window, these dim and dingy scraps ? Why, there was no glory in it, not if he breathed with all his body and rubbed with both his wrists. It wanted light behind, perhaps, and also the parts put together, the colours shown up side by side. In any case he must be careful,

picking over the shivered fragments, and laying them
in his coat on the ground. . . . This was from the
strawberry roan. Oh, the giant ! Oh, the beauty !
What a size his nozzle, and this long strip only a portion
of his never-ending nose ! . . . Somewhere at hand
might be the jaw ; here—in a dozen pieces ! . . . This
would complete the head. . . . When you came to
examine that head as a whole, there was something very
stiff about it. The eye was enough to make you laugh :
it glared a wild glare which was really mild ; it was
either meek or ferocious ; the meekness was in the
round ball, the ferocity in the corner. It was rather
stupid. To tell the truth, the effect was so stupid near
at hand, he was a little ashamed to think it had pleased
him before at a distance. He had always supposed it
was because they were so very far off that he seemed to
know so little about them ; but now they were closer he
seemed to know less. It was the head of the roan. What
roan ? Certainly not the roan which went out to the war,
and came back with the medal slung over his breast.

Here was a slice of the body, preserved by a beam
from the roof. A good bit of colour, too ! . . . He
should like to know how it was done, this business of
painting on glass. He spat and rubbed with his finger.
Was it a regular trade, like shoeing ? Was it as good
to be a painter—not a house-painter, but window-
painter—as to be wheelwright and blacksmith ? Would
he rather paint horses in Marchington Church, or shoe
them in Marchington forge ? It was said of his father
he turned a shoe better than any man in the county.
. . . This was a wisp of the mane ; streak upon streak
he stroked it down. . . . It was real enough, but it
wasn't *real*, and he would choose the *real*. There was
always a job coming in at the forge ; shoeing was
reckoned a regular trade, but this would be more of a
" fad," and there comes an end to all fads. Windows,
unlike horses, suffer no wear and tear. When you have
filled in an east-end light, you won't have to fill it
again ; *your* work is up, except for a storm ! Of

course, there are other churches. In every English town and village Wattie believed you would find a church, but then each church would have its own painter; in every village and town a boy who would give his eyes to scramble up and scratch some fancy on the walls.

This was as much as his coat could contain. He must carry the coat to the space by the vestry, and there, on the clean stone flags, kept clean by the arching roof, he would set out the contents. It was a picture puzzle. He emptied his coat, and came for more. Absorbing occupation, proceeding now how slowly, a fragment here and a fragment there; and then again, with some larger piece, springing out at a touch from under his hand. He lost all knowledge of time. The moments slipped away, the hours struck unheeded; they were striking now; he heard that—*four*. The boys would be out of school. There was the school-bell ringing; then followed a far-off hum. The listless afternoon awoke; a light cart rattled down the street; Wattie stretched himself. . . . Some of the children were coming this way; those were other children's voices. They came, a short-cut under the wall, under the hedge, little companies of them, twos and threes, in at the lychgate, up the path. This was something new to see, the parish church in ruins.

Playmates of Wattie's. " Hullo, Wat !"

CHAPTER IX

THEY all must look; they crowded round. " Stand back, can't you !" each one said. They did not long delay. The little girls left first. Tired of Wattie, they ran to the elm, for the elm had a trunk to scramble over; and then they must skip amongst the rubble, so cleverly, with such bursts of laughter, that the boys must follow too; and then boys and girls all mingled together, and were suddenly somehow gone.

So suddenly gone that Wattie half doubted if they had ever been there at all. He thought he might have imagined it, the chatter of voices and busy steps. With that silence before and this silence after it seemed like a dream, something which for a moment visited part of himself, a part of himself which was not himself and which was, which seemed outside of him, yet within, so that you did not know it was there till it came, nor know it had vanished till it had gone. He believed he could bring it back now if he chose. . . . " *Hullo, Wat !*" *And there they all trooped in the sun.* . . .

He had nearly completed his task. Search as he might, however, a bit here and there still escaped him. He could guess well enough what was missing ; he knew what he wanted to find, but, alas for this sparkling dust ! not the most painstaking boy in the world could piece those atoms together. So it would never be properly mended. None the less reason in rescuing this, laying it decently out, and bidding a sort of farewell.

He was tired now ; his head was aching ; also he felt a little sick. He went and sat down on a grave. That over there was the new-made grave ; you could tell by the flowers ; it was where they were buried, and he should never see them again. Of course, he might not want to see them, but supposing he did want to see them, he couldn't. They were gone. And yet in a way he saw them still. He had only to shut his eyes, and there was the church, and fair Mrs. Burnet coming inside and passing along to the Vicarage pew ; fair Mrs. Burnet kneeling to pray ; dark Mr. Burnet brushing out of the vestry, taking his six steps up the nave ; dark Mr. Burnet climbing the pulpit, putting his Bible on the ground. . . . " *Well, children, we have had a happy day, and, thank God, no accidents.*"

No accidents. *This* was an accident. Perhaps this was what he had meant. But Mr. and Mrs. Burnet were both a good age ; they would be about fifty, and old enough, therefore, to die. Besides, they would go on living—nothing could alter that—from the very beginning to the end (only—"world without end"—there *was* no end) ; for ever and ever they *were, would have been,* and *would still continue to be,* Mr. and Mrs. Burnet. Could either of them be anyone else ? Could anyone else be either of them ? . . . Wattie yawned ; he was hungry, perhaps ; presently he would go home to tea.

Presently. It was nice to be here, lying flat on your back, looking up in the sky, where the birds were perpetually flitting. . . . Somebody coming ! That was not nice ! Hush !—yes, a footstep—the far side of the church. It might be the sexton bringing a broom, and then what chance for his precious window ? He could not have told the sexton, and the sexton would never see for himself, and Wattie would have to sit there and look at him brushing it into a heap. . . . Hush again ! Whoever it was, the footsteps were trailing nearer. Such an odd sound ! It might be the sexton beginning to sweep, or was it some creature cropping ? . . . Why, look ! it was only a horse, and after him came another. Whose horses ? He did not know ; he had not seen them before, and he knew every horse in the place. . . . A pure white mare and a strawberry roan. . . . He held his breath. It was funny— "funny" was hardly the word—it was wicked, for they had walked right into the church. They must have come out of Buttercup Meadow, and this was the fault of the boys and girls—the last boy who went through and left the gate open. What were they after, picking their way ? The clear space by the vestry-door. A very odd feeling came over Wattie, but it went as soon as it came. He had eyes and wits, and what were the *facts ?* The facts were simple enough : a strawberry roan and a pure white mare, like those in the painted window, had strayed out of Buttercup Meadow, and wandered into the church. It was not so curious after all. There must be hundreds of whites and roans, and not one of those hundreds but would stray, supposing you left the gate open ; and supposing the walls of a church were down, what should prevent them going inside ? . . . They were walking through shadow into the light, and when they came into the light they stopped. They flung up their heads, and turned to the sun, and there was the clean tower-wall behind them. So they stood for a moment, and then moved on, and carefully, one step at a time, trod underfoot the Squire's window.

CHAPTER X

THE year of the big storm was a year of great changes for Wattie. It was the year when he grew from a child to a boy. He had turned ten that August, and insisted on leaving school. He found a good opportunity, for half of Marchington schools had been wrecked, and half the children had lost their places ; hence, when Wattie absented himself with one or two other adventurous spirits, nobody troubled to bring them back. It was more than human nature could endure to sit cooped up between white-washed walls when the outside world was all agog. The storm had made Marchington famous. Men and women actually came from London to have a look at the place— " special correspondents," so everyone said ; and they stayed at The Bell, and strolled round the village, and asked questions, and wrote down the answers on pieces of paper, and made rapid sketches of lasting misfortunes.

There was a great deal of talk. The boys hung about all day and picked up the news, and no one had time so much as to cuff their inquisitive ears. Wattie, too, had a job at the forge ; and as the forge was one of those buildings which suffered most in the storm, and as it stood over the road from The Bell, the " special correspondents " were constantly in and out. " Special artists " came also, and sketched. At one time there were no fewer than five gentlemen and six ladies at work on characteristic studies, one side of the forge or the other. The foreman did not like the ladies and gentlemen " coming about "; he said the forge might do for a picture, but it wouldn't do for his work ; and he began to put things straight, tearing the wooden rafters down and chucking them into a heap by the road. He was very sharp with the ladies, the foreman was ; and when one of them spoke to Wattie, he called to him to get something to do.

The six ladies and five gentlemen were all very good to Wattie when the foreman wasn't looking. One gentleman gave him a piece of indiarubber for standing as part of the foreground ; and a lady gave him a half-empty tube of cobalt blue ; and another gave him some drawing-pins ; and he missed their company when they were gone. Afterwards, in the illustrated London papers, he saw what they had been doing. He did not think the pictures were like anything in Marchington, but he made them all out by the names : " Marchington Church as it was . . . as it is," " Marchington Forge," " Marchington Vicarage," " Marchington Vicar's Grave." Wattie looked them through one after the other, and then he came to " The Boy who was ringing the Bell," and there he was with his apron on, though it wasn't *his* business to ring the bell, and he had taken his apron *off*.

He also read about the distress—that it was very great ; that Marchington was in a desperate way, and many people homeless ; that so many pounds' worth of damage was done ; and all about the church. The church took a column. It began with Edward the Confessor, and went on to Henry VIII., and then to the Squires of Marchington Manor, and finally offered its heartiest sympathy to the present Squire (a young lady not yet out of her teens), who, owing to the extravagances of her fathers, would, it was feared, not find herself in a position to restore—at least, for the present —the sacred edifice.

All this was in the paper, and Wattie read it out to the foreman and mate over their breakfast, because he came last from school. The foreman had another paper, which contained scraps of intelligence under various headings. One of the headings was, " *Horses in Church*," and began :

" *Whoever heard of horses in church ?*" The foreman dropped all his " h's."

" I have," said Wattie, but he spoke to himself.

And the foreman read on about the rose-window, and Wattie did not listen at all ; only he heard the last sentence : " *And that Marchington Church will ever hold horses again is highly improbable.*"

" No, it isn't," said Wattie under his breath.

" *In the meantime,*" proceeded the foreman, " *there will be no service in Marchington Church for many a long day to come.*"

The foreman and mate both sighed—not that it could matter to them, as the foreman went to the Methodist Chapel, and the mate only went for a walk. It seemed, however, a dreadful thing to be without church or schools. But the schools were to be rebuilt ; there were workmen already about the place, and workmen were up at the church. What were they going to do for the church ? A cruel pity ! The church was to be shut up, closed down—Wattie hardly knew what. The rubbish was cleared, and the grave-yard swept, and the broken pews, and the chancel-screen, and the organ, and pulpit, and eagle—oh, and a number of other things—were carried away in vans and carts, and stored in Marchington Manor. Some day, when Miss Phillis was old enough to manage her own affairs, they said she would put them all back again, and build up the broken walls. They said she had set her heart upon it, and Wattie gathered that it would be for a kind of memorial to Mr. and Mrs. Burnet, and perhaps Master Frank would preach there. If only someone could put it in hand ! But Miss Phillis had gone to the South of France, and (so it seemed) for

the next three years must only do what she was told.
In three years Wattie believed that he could have built
up the church himself, taking a turn at it every night
after his work was done. He dreamt of it sometimes
in bed rising stone upon stone, and sometimes it grew
to a wonderful height, and then he would lead Miss
Phillis in, and the air would strike quite cold ; and
then he would wake, and pull up the blankets, and
dream about nothing at all. Only Wattie thought it
was rather a pity you must always be paid for the work
you did.

It was also a pity Miss Phillis was poor. That was
why Marchington Manor was let, and why Colonel and
Mrs. Jones lived there ; not that they *lived* there
after all, for they were mostly away. They went away
after the storm, and did not come back for fifteen
months ; they did not, of course, belong to the place.
But they paid Miss Phillis a lot of money ; they had
been paying her year after year. It was a puzzle to
Wattie why she should want so much, and what she
should spend it on ; and it was only now for the first
time, when all these questions were being discussed,
that he learnt what became of the money. Why, she
never got it at all ; it went to somebody else ; *it was
owed*. Poor Miss Phillis in debt ! It was sad she
should be so poor and in debt, which you ought to keep
out of. Wattie could not help thinking sometimes,
when he sat down to supper at home, how Miss Phillis
was far away, giving *her* home up to people who did
not want it, and for a sum of money which she wasn't
allowed to keep. And yet, for all this, though she
wasn't allowed to keep her own money or live in her
own nice house, they allowed her to keep the three
little cottages which tumbled down in the storm.
They let her keep those, and build them up. " That's
only right and proper "—so the foreman said.

And the foreman said they had opened a fund—a
Lord Mayor's Fund for " the distress "—and the mate
said that money was pouring in, and they both put

their heads out and looked up the street. Wattie put his out too, but he did not see any money, only a little gilt badge in the gutter, and he stuck it in the front of his cap.

CHAPTER XI

THERE was nothing so very remarkable about the high stone wall which ran (as it always had run) along that bit of the Brinkley road ; and had there been any facilities for gaining the top, Wattie would never have wanted to get there. As it was, in his Sunday clothes he stopped. He was on his way home from Sunday-school—the usual way, the usual wall—but the impulse was irresistible. Was it the usual wall ? It seemed to have suddenly grown so high, and also (now you came to examine) allowed no possible sort of a foothold. A jutting branch of a tree, however, lent a support to his back, whilst he clawed with fingers and toes. He fell a dozen times at least, but eventually he discovered the trick, and found himself arrived. He had cut his hands and torn his trousers, but he wiped the sweat off his face and looked down. What had he come for ?—that was the question—never mind how he had come. What he had come for was something so wonderful, so unexpected, that he almost fell backwards into the road (only, being there, he wanted to stay there), and he could have shouted for joy (only better far hold his breath), for this so wonderful, so unexpected, and with so broad and glossy a back, was nothing less than a horse. Who would have guessed it ? Nobody. Any number of people had gone up and down this very afternoon—single people, who walked without talking ; pairs of people, who talked as they walked—and not one would have guessed that under that wall a horse might be twitching his ears.

This in itself was sufficient, but, stranger still to relate, it flashed upon Wattie all of a sudden that here

was the strawberry roan. Not very strange, however.
The fact he had once seen the strawberry roan only
made it more likely to see it again. It had strayed out
of Buttercup Meadow ; why should it not have strayed
here ? He supposed this was part of the Manor estate.
Those were the tiles of Manor Farm. Perhaps the
roan belonged to the Farm ; perhaps it belonged to
Colonel Jones ; perhaps it belonged . . . What was
he doing twitching his ears ? Was he listening ? No,
not exactly ; Wattie thought sleeping—not sleeping,
but dozing, perhaps. He had found it too hot in the
burning field, and so had come into the shade, under
the trees, close to the wall, closer and closer, quite
close. . . . Ah ! . . .

Wattie worked himself round (a delicate business !) ;
the horse did not stir. There were flies crawling over
his back. What a back ! . . . He did it. . . . He
slid off the wall, and sat plump. What would happen
he hardly knew ; he had just time to seize two handfuls
of mane before he was flung up and down, and whisked
through the air at a pace which shook all the breath
from his body. He supposed he was riding ; that was
his first intelligent thought, and it came to him as they
swept the first corner. On that thought followed
another—namely, that he should never be able to
sweep the second. But the second was coming. He
took a fresh grip. . . . He could, and he would ! . . .
Afterwards, when he got up, he told himself that he
should have swept the second as well as the first if it
had not been for the offending bough of a thorn, which
smote him across the face ; and presently, when the
field stopped going round, he saw he was somewhere
about the middle, and also that the horse had gone
back, and was twitching his ears again by the wall.

Wattie twitched his ears also. Perhaps, on the
whole, it was time to be moving. He would be late
for tea. But at this point came interference in the
shape of a man (with a stick), who arrived, not over
the wall, but through a gate from the Farm, and

approached (with the stick) in a threatening manner.
And this was just when Wattie had made up his mind
not to trespass again, not to ride strange horses, not
to be late for tea.

"Come out of it !" yelled the man (swearing awful,
thought Wattie). "Just you let me catch you !"

Never ! And as the man made a grab, he ran under
his legs and, emerging, made out a straight course for the
Farm.   Over the meadow and through the yard—a
vision of pigs, a flutter of fowls—but there he was
on the road. The man with the stick was far behind.
He would just have finished his Sunday dinner, and
there was a chance he might reach the gate by the
time that Wattie reached home.

"Wattie, you're late," said Mrs. Moon ; "and, bless
the boy, where have you been ?" She saw the state
of his trousers.

Where had he been ?   He hardly knew ;—the top of
the wall, the strawberry's back, the grass, and somebody's legs—he had been in so many places. He
stirred his tea and said nothing.

CHAPTER XII

ONE day Wattie was loitering down by the forge, when
the groom from the Manor arrived with the strawberry
roan.   The first thing he remarked was that the roan
had got bigger. He supposed, when he saw it before,
it must have been quite a young horse ; now the head,
as it turned upon Wattie, seemed as if it would swallow
him up. It pretty well filled the forge.

"You get outside," said the mate, and Wattie
walked all round the horse and got out. He now had
another view. The girth was enormous, so was the
thigh ; the legs were gigantic, and strove on the ground.
It was more like a picture ; but whether this might
be due to the sun slanting in through the open door,

or to the shape, the bold and magnificent curves, Wattie was puzzled to know. To his joy he perceived that the mate had gone, and he ventured inside again.

The groom was very good-natured. He stood and talked for a bit. He asked if Wattie was fond of horses, and Wattie said, " Not so wonderful fond," and he said it was a powerful beast, and he called Wattie " Young Hopeful," and the strawberry roan he called " Necessity."

" You let him be," said the groom, when Wattie went to pat his neck. " He's got a nasty way with him."

Wattie withdrew, but presently, when the groom wasn't looking, he went and patted Necessity. Necessity kicked out; he kicked out straight and sharp—too straight and sharp for Wattie.

" I told you so," said the groom, and he propped Wattie against the wall; and the foreman was very angry, for he had to have his eye sewn up.

Wattie did not see Necessity after that for a long, long time, and then it was outside the saddler's shop, and he ran up to him. He did not really believe that Necessity had a nasty way, and he came quite near, and caught hold of his nose. He was holding Necessity's nose, when he saw the groom standing there in the door.

" If you want a job," said the groom—for Wattie was turned fourteen—" if you want a job, you can take him down to the forge."

" Give us a leg," said Wattie. He saw the groom meant what he said.

The groom only laughed. " Oh, that's it, Hopeful, is it ?" And he shoved Wattie up on top.

The saddler came out at that minute.

" You're never going to let *him* ride !"

" If you call it riding," said the groom.

" You'd better mind what you're doing, my lad," said the saddler.

" Or you'll hear of it," said the groom. But the groom was laughing all the time.

Wattie felt very queer, for he had never sat in a saddle before ; but he said, " So long !" to the groom, and began walking Necessity down the street. The saddle was most uncomfortable. It was shiny and new, and while Necessity's back was broad enough, this horse-hair and leather arrangement made it considerably broader. If only he could get near the stirrups ! But he would not try with the groom looking on. He was scarcely sorry to turn out of sight along the Brinkley Road.

Here he would trot. He was not quite sure who began it, Necessity or himself, but as Necessity trotted, he would trot too. He wanted a little stick ; he should like to make Necessity go. Necessity *went*, of course, but more on his own account. It was not an easy sensation, but that was the fault of the saddle. He had really felt far more at home that day galloping round the field. He began to have some misgivings. They were fast approaching the hill which led down to the forge. If Necessity got away down that hill, there was no telling what might happen. Wattie could never pull up at the forge, and the mate would come out, and when should he hear the last of it ? It was down the hill he started slipping. Necessity rolled from side to side ; he heaved his haunches left and right, a jerk one way and a jerk another. The brute was trying to get him off—would do it, too ! One glance at the forge. . . . Suppose a head should be poking out. . . . No head. Very well. He seized the mane ; he threw himself shamelessly forward on Necessity's neck. Necessity seemed to wobble. Slower and slower and slower each deliberate bump. It was the end of the hill. Wattie believed even now, if only he could regain his balance . . . he clawed with both arms ; his fingers met, and he clasped them round Necessity's throat. He had gone so far there was no getting back. His left boot was scraping the saddle. Necessity gathered his purpose. Wattie was looking into that eye ; his cheek was pressing Necessity's cheek ; their warmth and breath were mingled. They mutually understood. Here was the forge, and Necessity drew himself cautiously in as Wattie slid over, hung for a second, and dropped on his feet.

The foreman came out with the mate. " Hullo !" said the foreman. " What's this ?"

" Side-slip," said Wattie, and (meaning the groom) " He's coming behind."

" So I should hope," said the mate.

" Well," said the foreman, " it doesn't matter what happens to you so long as the horse is all right."

The mate, on the other hand, said : " It doesn't matter what happens to the horse so long as you're all right."

And Wattie said to the foreman, " I reckon it does," and to the mate, " I reckon it doesn't."

And the groom turned up at that moment and said : " Young Hopeful again !"

They called him Hopeful after that, and although the foreman and mate were always agreeing that Wattie was never meant for a blacksmith, but more for a kind of clerk, yet they sent him out with the horses now, and trusted him once with a couple to Marchington Manor. So Wattie was always up and down, and he cut himself a little stick one Sunday out of the hedge ; but when the foreman saw it on Monday, he took it away. " You'll have no little stick," the foreman said.

CHAPTER XIII

ONE night Wattie dreamt a dream. He dreamt he was in a great wide valley. The grass was fresh, and sweet and growing, and it was full of dew. The sun had not yet risen, but there was a look of twilight, and the air was very cold. He was standing there alone,

how or why he could not tell, and he wondered what
he waited for.

Then, on a sudden, up the valley he saw a sight to
make him dance, to make the blood leap in his veins.
There came a small white horse. Was ever anything
so dainty? She was trotting down towards him out
of the green folds of the valley. Very fast she came,
and white and pure, just as the sun got up. Faster
and faster—oh, what little feet! Should he dare stop
her? If he dared stop the greatest lady in the land!
Yet someone called to him distinctly, "*Stop her!
Stop!*" Was she only a runaway? Had she broken
loose? Where was the bit and bridle, then? No,
Wattie knew that she was free — free and wild and
beautiful—and never tamed by man before. "*Stop
her! Stop her!*" cried the voice—no voice at all; he
did not even turn to see. "*Stop her! Stop her!*"
He must summon courage, then, for she was close
upon him. He moved a step, and stood out in the
drenching grass full in the way she came; and as she
came, thud, thud, he struck her with his doubled
fist. It was a cruel thing to do; but, oh! she stopped
herself, swung round, and ran back straight into his
arms. He found her whole head buried there. Sweet
and warm sensation! Was anything so soft, and clean,
and gentle! He did not look at her; he held and felt
her beauty. It was enough . . . and he woke smiling,
but his pillow wet with tears.

Now he saw that white mare at the forge that very
morning. Why should he be surprised? for he knew
that she was real. He had known it in his dream,
and that if only he could look at her (but he must
hide his face), he would see she was just the same
white mare that had walked with the strawberry roan
into church.

He was positive now. There she stood in the sun,
and the groom and the foreman and mate stood
round her. It was a different groom, and Wattie
wondered. He wondered where they came from. He

hung about to hear. He did not hear much, but he heard her name. It was Choice. The groom said it was Choice, and also he said, " She's a beauty !"

So she was. Wattie ventured to look at her now, and she seemed to know what he was thinking, for she turned her head away. Meanwhile the mate was busy, first with one hoof, then the other. He did not notice the mate, but when the foreman went to shoe her, Wattie drew near.

" Four black feet in sixteen minutes." That was what the foreman said, and he looked at the clock as he said it. It was sixteen minutes to ten.

. . . You saw things somehow in a flash—important things, at least—a flash, and all was over. Nobody else had seen — nobody else, for Wattie had so often noticed that when things grouped themselves, nobody else was looking. Nobody saw just then when they stood out in the sun ; nobody saw just now when they were standing in the shade. " *Four black feet in sixteen minutes*," that was what the foreman said. It was vivid, like a flash, and like a flash it came and went. If he could only hold it, just for a little while— hold it and then examine, and afterwards set down truthfully what he had seen, and not only that, but (it sounded absurd !) put himself there as he felt him- self just at that moment and in that spot ; *then*— why, then other people would see what he saw, feel what he felt, and they would be able to turn to each other and say : " Isn't it so ? And isn't it jolly !"

· Could he say that to the foreman, and be grinned at for his pains ? Grinned at ? Have his ribs punched, put in the ashbin, ducked in the drinking-trough, more like. The foreman allowed no nonsense, and Wattie must never air an unasked opinion. Not that the foreman despised opinions ; only they must not be unasked, nor must they be too much your own. More- over, they must be intelligible, and Wattie feared that the foreman would never be able to comprehend those strange and sudden seizures when horses and men sprang into life, and stood out for a moment (which seemed an age) in bold relief against the colourless and shapeless background of *what generally went on*. Admiration with the foreman was instinctive ; he felt his way unconsciously to the good points of a horse, and would chuckle, never knowing that he chuckled, let alone knowing the reason why. And if by chance he felt an admiration which did not rise instinctively, but burst upon him from without, would he confess as much ? To admit it to another would hardly be consistent with his dignity ; nor to admit it to himself, with common-sense.

It was not common-sensible. Did Wattie say it was ? Such queer sensations are not felt with the common-sense at all—the five common senses. You were not hearing, smelling, seeing ; you did not taste nor touch ; it was this other part of you which, waking, held you for a minute whilst the world went on. It did not happen often. Day after day he would see horses in and out unmoved, or sunshine on the old stone floor ; then all at once, another day, he would stumble upon something ; things would grow big and group before him, and stamp themselves upon his mind. . . . Wait ! Did he stumble on it ? Did things grow big and group for him only here and there ? Were they not always everywhere, but *he* made so compact and neat within his human frame as to be quite unable to stretch a point beyond—could just hear, taste, see, smell, and touch—until, hey presto ! the neat compact frame fell to pieces, the wheels stopped going round, a sixth sense fought for freedom, and he knew *this* and *now*. . . . Then, presto ! pass. Here he was home, compact and neat, and ticking like a clock. . . . It was towards the clock he looked, starting from his reverie, and as he looked the clock struck ten.

" Four black feet in sixteen minutes." And they led the mare away.

CHAPTER XIV

WHEN Wattie got home that night he could not help
thinking of Choice. In the first place, he should very
much like to know where she came from. Supposing
she was the mare that had strayed out of Buttercup
Meadow—and he firmly believed that she was—then it
was obvious she must belong to Colonel Jones. Necessity certainly did ; it was Jones's groom who had
brought Necessity down to the forge, and Wattie was
wellnigh positive that on one of the rare occasions
this spring when he had seen Colonel Jones in the
village he had been riding the strawberry roan. And
if one of the horses in Buttercup Meadow had proved
to belong to Colonel Jones, so, no doubt, would the
other.

But there was the groom to account for. Wattie
had his suspicions ; the whole thing struck him as odd ;
he should not say a word about it, only, all things
considered, it looked like a change at Marchington
Manor. Nor did he forget the fact that the last time
he went that way they were putting new iron railings.
Meanwhile he felt a change in himself ; there was so
much stir in the world—new grooms down at the forge,
new railings up at the Manor—that he must be stirring
also ; he must be done with the old. There were things
to discover and to do ; the groom and the railings
declared it. As he got up from tea he felt taller, and
all but forgot his grace. He would like to find the
field, for instance, the meadow he had dreamt about.
He should never find it in Marchington—of that he
was sure—but he believed he should find it somewhere,
maybe miles beyond Brinkley, and even the chance of
it pointed to this, that he must take longer walks now
on his Sunday afternoons.

Besides, he should like (shy thought !), supposing he
did not discover the meadow, to put down on paper all

he remembered—how Choice had turned at that tiny
blow, and run back into his arms. He would like to
fix it somewhere, the warm, soft head and panting
breast, so that others might know and he never forget.
When should he do it ? Why not next Saturday ? . . .
All of a sudden time spun round. He began to reckon
his Sundays and Saturdays—how many he might
expect in his life if he lived to be about sixty.

He worked it out as he went to bed ; but before he got
into bed he opened a cupboard. This cupboard contained his treasures. Here was the rubber the gentleman gave him, and the drawing-pins from the lady.
Both rubber and pins had proved very useful ; he
always rubbed out the best part of what he put in, and
the pins had again and again fastened his sheets of
white paper, which he got from the shop, to a smooth
bit of board which the foreman had found him. He
had also a few sticks of charcoal and a small stump of
chalk, and to replace the empty cobalt he had almost a
dozen other tubes, some of them flat and some of them
full, and a brush, and at least two-thirds of a sketch-
book which the dustman had saved him out of the cart.

And yet he had never really painted—that is to say,
not planned to paint, to paint any one particular
thing, Saturday after Saturday for all the rest of his
life. He was planning now, as he punched his pillow,
and it would be his own fault next Saturday if he failed
to do justice to Choice.

He did fail. Regarding what he had done on
Saturday, by Saturday's candle-light, he had his strong
misgivings. He had no misgivings on Sunday, and he
tore Choice in two. He must now wait another whole
week till Saturday came again. Meanwhile it was
Sunday morning, and he meant to walk twice as far
as he ever had walked, and get a friend to go with him.
This was to look for the meadow. He did not find the
meadow, but he walked twice as far as he ever had
walked, with a friend, and they missed their Sunday
dinner, and got home for church.

Monday they were busy—Monday, Tuesday, Wednesday ; so the days whirled round, running out of a morning, running in of a night, half asleep in the kitchen, fast asleep in bed. Thursday not so busy— leisure, that is, to remember they had broken the back of the week. Friday busy again ; but Friday night he could tell himself " *To-morrow's Saturday*."

It started raining at noon on Saturday just as the men knocked off, and finished some time in the dead of Saturday night ; but on Sunday morning, when Wattie looked at Choice, he thought her not so bad. He wrapped her in tissue-paper, and put her away in the cupboard, and the day being fine (for Sunday is usually fine if you'll notice), he went again with his friend for a walk, only they did not walk so far, and returned in time for dinner.

PART III

FRANK

"What hand and brain went ever paired ?
What heart alike conceived and dared ?"

CHAPTER XV

FRANK had another year at Winchester. He went back that very autumn term after the sad summer holiday. He hated going. He did not believe Phillis cared a bit. She was to go abroad with a cousin, and study music and French ; but then it was easier far for Phillis to detach herself—for example, see this : she did not *belong to* the Vicarage, though she had lived there all her life ; she did not *belong to* the family. . . . Family ? What family now ? . . . The best thing for Frank to do was to drive the whole matter out of his head, forget he had ever *belonged* himself to place or people at all. Only the hard part was that wherever he turned his thoughts, they came back to the dreadful days which had passed. If he opened a novel, he would flash from a page written there to a page of his own lived life, find himself talking again to his father or mother. . . . *I would far rather keep my thoughts to myself, as in point of fact, of course, I do.* . . and then, with a start—dead ! killed ! a tragedy ! terrible storm in the Midlands ; loss of life !—horrors brought home to his door. So it was if he opened a newspaper—avoided the horrors (*that* he would)—read of some exhibition of pictures, his fancy coursed in and out as he read . . . painting, art, his own canvasses, the piece in the field by the church, odd feelings, Phillis's skirt and the poplar-leaf, the gravel path. . . . *" Frank !" called his mother .* . . . *" Hullo !"* . . . Then the mind recoiled, beat

63

(and covered) a hasty retreat, calmed itself, set
out an opposite way, as surely as ever came back
again !

And returning to Winchester would not cure that.
He was positive. Mind you, he knew, for he had ex-
perienced this sort of thing many times in his life before.
The fact was he had no power to shake himself free—
self-detachment, that was the proper word ! . . . such
as Phillis had, who (curious creature) actually argued
about her " black," and wanted it made in a certain
fashion. " Black !" he would like to be dressed in the
gayest colours, so that no one should ever know what
had happened. And here came in letters by every post
. . . " My dearest Frank " . . . " My darling boy " . . .
" This terrible trouble " . . . " The hand of God." That
had always struck him about the ostrich hiding its
head in the sands. " Silly creature !" says everyone ;
" *things are there*." Ah, but to shut one's eyes successfully, systematically, automatically *as things appear !*
He had to face the men in college.

He had often in old days imagined what his own
death and funeral would be like. Dying quite young.
He had written some verses from which the outside
world would be able to see how future events had been
forestalled. To himself he had pictured the news going
round the school, the hush in Chamber Court, and in
chapel some reference . . . nonsense ! absurd ! he would
come back ashamed, and then very secretly, down
in his heart, he would think with hot blushes :
" What could they say of *me* in chapel ?—idle,
selfish, timid, vain, jackass, idiot. . . ." And all
this while he was turning the leaves of his lexicon,
and had not the smallest idea for what word he
sought !

And here was death in reality—not his own, but his
parents' death. Both ! Both dead, both together !
The train which whirled him from Waterloo, past
Surbiton, past Weybridge, seemed to be thumping
the words to a tune. . . . *Both dead, both together ; both*

dead, both together. . . . He thought the lady sitting
opposite must have heard, for she looked at him and
nodded, as much as to say : " Yes, I know, it is *you.*"
And he felt himself leap when she suddenly spoke, but
only about a restaurant-car, and then he was glad
she had spoken, for it opened a conversation, and she
was a lady—that Frank saw—and spoke of everyday
things ; and good for him that she did, for a wretched
feeling of nervousness, the horror from nowhere and
everlasting, jumped on him unexpectedly, and he
knew (by experience also) that his one hope was to
" talk it off."

It would have been better if only he might have
turned up with the rest of college, but the rest of college
went back last week. This was a fad of his guardian.
He had kept Frank at home—*his* home, South Kensington, ugly and dull (the museum to visit, that's about
all)—because . . . because . . . oh, why not let him
forget ? Forget ? Why, every night at dinner (how
he swallowed his food he never knew ; he once dashed
upstairs and was sick)—every night almost his guardian
would say, " Your dear father, my boy," or " My poor
boy, your mother. . . ." And, curious as it may seem,
the only thing Frank felt, the only definite feeling, quite
apart, of course, from the vague indescribable wretchedness, was a sudden desire for Phillis, uncontrollable,
yet, needless to say, controlled ; curious, because
there was nothing so very special in Phillis : she
was not remarkably brilliant, and certainly not
" artistic."

Anyway, he would far rather have turned up in
college with the rest of the college men. It would have
created less *fuss,* and if he was to endure life at all just
now—just now ?—*from now till the end*—it would only be
by conforming to habit, by going on precisely as he had
always gone on before. And that he should do at
once, so soon as he had got away from his guardian, so
soon as he had satisfied people's curiosity ; for one
thing was clear, wherever he went now amongst old

friends he must inevitably be greeted—looked at, stared
at, spoken to, what you will—once *for the first time*
since his calamity. Well, so far as "men" were
concerned, the trial would soon be over. It was
half-past six, and at seven o'clock he should be back in
college. He reckoned what everyone would be doing.
He planned to slink up and take out his books with a
show of having a lot of work to get through. Moreover, he had a slight cold and sore throat, and he might
make this something to grumble at. Grumbling covers
so much ; if only you can succeed in grumbling, no one
suspects you really ail.

As for these plans, he might just as well have spared
himself the trouble, for when he *did* arrive, he found
the whole place in an uproar. There was a fire—one
of Commoner's in a regular blaze. Such a pack in
Southgate Street ! It was no joke, either, as he saw,
when he had fought his way through the crowd, for
there they were chucking things out of the windows, and
Frank heard more than one person declare they would
never be able to " get it under." What a mercy it was
a fire !—not a flood, not a storm. There was no
danger ; it was not terrible—it was beautiful, and you
could watch it in comfort. Had there been any wind,
the flames might have leapt to one side, licked hold of
adjoining buildings, but (such a calm September !)
the flames shot straight up to heaven, roared impotent
in the sky. Besides, you knew all the time there were
engines " putting it out "—so far as *you* were concerned, too soon ! Unlike the sea, unlike the storm,
fire is an element over which (at least, in the city of
Winchester) you have a certain amount—a *sufficient*
amount (that's the point)—of control. . . . The heat
of the flames was intense : he was roasted and scorched ;
that he liked, and he liked the flicker over his face.
He almost envied the firemen, giants themselves,
looming in and out, with gigantic shadows dancing
around them. So much fascinated was he by the
whole of this picturesque scene (and the lurid light on

some commonplace garden-bushes, laurels, he thought, was extraordinary) that he did not remark the fact that the rest of the crowd had retreated, until one of those very firemen sprang up at him with spidery legs and said : " Now then, young gentleman, stand back ! We don't want the house a-top of you." And Frank, aghast at being spoken to—found out of place— with dignity moved away, and afterwards looking back, did not believe for one moment the house would fall in at all—wished it would, of course !

And that night everyone talked of the fire.

CHAPTER XVI

It was during Frank's last year at Winchester that he became proficient in swimming. Perhaps it might be because the weather was hot. He won quite a name for " purling "—diving. Why he should suddenly take to diving he had not the remotest idea. It happened like this: He was feeling unusually jolly—and had felt so, by the way, ever since term had begun ; he had spent his Easter holidays in Switzerland, and had felt very jolly there—in fact, he could not have said exactly when it was he began to feel jolly—but, anyway, he was feeling so that sweltering summer's afternoon when they came from the practising-nets, and somebody said, " Let's go down to Gunner's Hole."

He had never tried diving before. It is true he had tumbled head-first—call it upside down—into the sea once or twice, but so far as the river was concerned, he very rarely went there, and if anyone suggested a dive, he could generally fake some excuse and go off without being noticed. But this afternoon—such an afternoon !—the water was blue and transparent, and rippled rather than sucked at the edge, and the sun slanted in through the trees, and ran in a great broad

beam to the end, where the divers stood—this afternoon Frank found himself mounting the steps, felt a
burst of joy, put his hands up, feet together, poised—
consciously, like some Greek statue, God's creature,
beautiful, happy youth—then tossed himself up,
rushed down. . . . Oh ! oh ! oh ! . . . here he was !
Beat the water away . . . (recollected . . . all right !)
. . . away from his face. Here he was ! He was *here*,
and stroke after stroke, steadier, steadier, made for
the opposite bank. Sitting there in the shadow, he
suddenly knew that one of the men had seen it all.
He got up, went round, climbed the steps ; he felt
sure that someone was going to say : " Very good,
very good ! That's your first ;" put his feet together,
his hands above, leapt up, flew down, cut the water,
emerged, shook himself free, then swam with ease,
with grace, *with repose*. Extraordinary ! . . . And
the same man had watched him again. Ah ! and what
did he care ? *That* wasn't his first, anyway. And
if he dived once more and once more (four perfect
dives in all), he could say, " When I dive," . . .
" When I dive, as a rule," . . . " Sometimes when I
dive." . . .

He did not get to sleep all at once that night. He
lay awake on purpose, to enjoy a certain sense of
exhilaration. To such a sense he was not altogether
unaccustomed. It came by fits and starts. So he
could dive ! Perhaps he could do many other things
which he had not attempted before, or in which hitherto
he had failed. Perhaps there was such a thing as
growing up—growing from boy to man ; perhaps with
growth came confidence ; perhaps—wait a bit ; had
he hit on a truth ? Perhaps with growth came confidence. A discovery ! Ah ! you might laugh, you
might call it simple—was it so simple, after all ? Mere
copy-book philosophy ? Don't be too sure. It had
come to him in the form of genuine revelation. It was
as if he had opened a new door in his heart, reached a
room deeper down, and found nobody, nothing, but

a secret—a pervading secret, full of eyes, which folded
him round, and the secret this—you are growing up,
and with growth comes confidence. . . . In this room
he fell asleep.

CHAPTER XVII

THERE was one thing which Frank had always hated—
the interminable discussions at night. When he was
in Second Chamber, there were four of the older men
who argued and argued. Frank used to roll up his
head in the sheet, but still he could hear them, now
loud, now low, and although he might shut out half
what they said, he caught the other half, and it was
wearisome in the extreme. He supposed you would
call it a philosophical kind of talk—about Religion and
Science, and Art, and Humanity—and the same words
and phrases recurred and recurred. How he envied
the men who could lie like lifeless logs through it
all! He was thankful when he was moved into
Sixth Chamber the following term (this, of course, was
some time ago), for Prefect of Hall slept there, and as
he was always writing prize poems, he never allowed
the slightest disturbance. Men had to get into bed as
fast as they could. When Prefect of Hall got into
his bed nobody knew. Frank used to start up sometimes out of a dream and find the light still there, and
the head still bending over the books, and the pen
still scratching away. Subsequently Frank went back
to Second Chamber. The four men who plagued his
first years had gone.

In fact, the whole situation had changed. Frank
was now in sixth book, and a prefect, and they talked
or not, as they liked. There was himself and three
other fellows, and the young ones all in bed. Rather
a distinguished set. There had never been quite such
a set before, and when one by one they left, things
altered, and there never was quite such a set again.

One was in Lords; another was working up for a science "schol"; the third on two occasions had been in print in the *Westminster;* and the fourth—well, the fourth was Burnet, and at present Burnet. . . . But wait a bit; Burnet would one day do something, distinguish himself. He used to look at the other three and think, "*Yes.*" He felt that it was more than possible, more than probable : it was inevitable. He felt he was marked out for a career. If not, to what purpose this almost volcanic disturbance within—this strangled, suffocated feeling, this painful desire for self-expression ? Somehow or other it must come out—by " it," of course, he meant genius, talent, call it whatever you like ; he had no wish to boast ; he was dealing now with facts — somehow or other, by this way or that. Secretly he was convinced that the way would be Art. It would not be Greek ! That was his present quarrel. Where was the sense in painfully picking the meanings of some remote age, when you could gather in easy handfuls just the same meanings nearer at hand ? How about Shelley ? If education meant, as he imagined it meant (thanks to that classical training !) the bringing out of one's mind, was it not best brought out under the most natural circumstances ? Does one carry away the infant from its native land in order that it may grow up (all stunted and misshapen) in another climate and under totally foreign conditions ? . . . This was what Frank thought, and perhaps when he got to *totally foreign conditions* he would jump into bed ; or suppose he was doing his lines, he would—well, go on doing them.

Frank did not by any means always say what he thought about things. He kept his thoughts to himself. He partly knew why he did this. It was because what sounded well enough spoken in silence (one swallows so much !) would sound flimsy spoken aloud ; somebody else might choke, and you would start choking, too. On the other hand, which seems like a contradiction, some of one's thoughts, the deepest down—the thoughts which one does not consciously, elaborately think—the thoughts which *per se are there*—exist so much nearer the truth than opinions we utter ; and Frank was for ever catching himself in the midst of some argument for or against, making the whole while mental notches, subversive of what he had even now said, the chief notch being this : " Ah ! but is it so really in practice ?"

For wonderful theories were propounded between eleven and twelve at night ; every department of life was examined, pulled to pieces, and sometimes Frank thought, as he dropped off to sleep, left scattered about ; but this was an afterthought, when everyone else was snoring. Still, it was, on the whole, a wonderful four. All points of view were represented—Science, and Poetry, and Cricket, and Art. Science was cold, Poetry was warm, Cricket was funny, and as for Art— that is to say, Burnet—well, Burnet, he could be funny, too, or cold, or warm, just as you please ; but down at the bottom, though talking as fast as anybody, he believed he had nothing in common with the rest, that he was *far behind them* (this was a secret ! not a word !), inasmuch as they dealt (did they not ?) with principles and theories, large ideas, while he had never got beyond the details and the facts. For example, when, one night of many, Science dissected Religion, pulled it to bits, and the Poet began to toy with the pieces, and " Lords " set them splitting with laughter, till Burnet said, " Look out ! look out !" and a small boy sat up in bed ; Frank, as he turned to the small boy and told him to lie down, found himself, as it were, face to face with *a thing which had really happened*, and he heard himself asking his mother whether the hand of God was kind, he heard the question passed on to his father, the solemn hush, the weighty answer, " Kind ? Yes, very ; absolutely ; very," beating like beats of a heart or ticks of a clock. Nothing to the point, of course ; but the scene recalled as plain as possible ; and it was as if

he had been talking only with his tongue, while
his heart was feeding far below. Or again, for example, in the midst of some argument about Social
laws, Prejudice, Convention, Freedom, and the like,
Frank would hear Phillis saying : " Go on about Art,
and Life, and Soul, and Strength ;" and he would
wince—actually wince, there in Second Chamber—
just as he winced on the dusty road when he swept
off the heads of the nettles. So, you see, he must
always go back to something which had really happened, and therefore might really happen again—
trivial details, childish facts. Alas ! he was no philo-
sopher (this is a secret !). He was (not a word !) a
commonplace being.

Yet he would pretend to be something else. He
would *make* himself something else. He thumped his
pillow, and told it so. Why not he as much as
another ? And perhaps he really was, and only diffi-
dence held him back—perhaps he really was, but he
had just decided that he wasn't. Never mind, tingling
and quivering, fit to sob, he would *pretend*. He could
paint—that he knew—and he would persuade the
world, himself too, that what he painted was what
he thought and hoped and believed, though it wasn't—
it wasn't. For his thoughts were of the most ele-
mentary kind, and his beliefs the beliefs of his baby-
hood, and his hopes the hopes of a child. And the very
day after that night when they had talked with flushed
faces of the Prejudice of Principle and the Piecrust
Pretexts of Life, he had suddenly recollected Phillis's
nineteenth birthday, and turned in at Wells's, the
bookseller's, and bought a nice little copy of Omar
Khayyám, and sent it to her (the address all exact)
in Paris, where she was quickly recovering from a
slight attack of German measles.

PART IV

WATTIE

" As the world rushed by on either side."

CHAPTER XVIII

ONE afternoon Wattie heard horses coming along the road. They drew up at the forge, and somebody called. He ran, for it was Miss Phillis—he ran, leather apron and all.

" Why, it's Wattie !" said Miss Phillis.

" Yes, miss, it's me." He looked at the young gentleman—Master Frank, of course.

" How are you, Wattie ?" said Miss Phillis. " How's Mrs. Moon ? How's everyone ? . . . It's a stone in Necessity's shoe."

Wattie cheered up and went for a pick. He came out, no longer ashamed of his apron. The foreman came also, and watched. It was done in a minute.

" How old's that nipper ?" said Master Frank.

" Fourteen," was the foreman's reply ; and Wattie ran back with the pick. The pick he took to a very dark corner, and stayed with it for a time. When he peeped out, they were still standing there. Miss Phillis was riding Necessity, Master Frank was on Choice. . . . Well, he had had his suspicions. Would it turn out in the end that Joneses had left the Manor, and that Choice and Necessity did not belong to the Colonel at all, but really belonged to Miss Phillis ? *Would* it turn out ? Why, it had turned out ! Here was Miss Phillis for proof, so smiling and jolly, enjoying her own. Her own, that was sure. How they were laughing! The mate had come up across from The Bell, wiping his hand. "How are *you*?" "How are *you*?" ... And the horses—the foreman first slapped Necessity, and then went over to Choice. The mate followed the foreman; they were perpetually changing places, and Miss Phillis kept looking this way and that. When she looked this way, you heard what she said.

"Plenty of fun ... fond of them both? ... Think so, indeed! ... Choice and Necessity. ... Colonel Jones ... *that* is Choice. ... Necessity? ... I'm getting used to him now. ... Famous old breed ... my great—no, my *great-great*-grandfather. ... Jump? You should see! ... Plenty of fun."

Plenty of fun! He wanted to shout, he wanted to laugh and sob and cry; and call the foreman a fat-head, and the mate a pudding-face; and he wanted to call himself an idiot, and hide away for ever and ever. And yet he was brazen bold enough to crane his neck for a better view. Oh, he was glad they were home again, Master Frank and Miss Phillis—dark Master Frank and fair Miss Phillis—Master Frank under that very large straw.

"Good-bye ... good-bye ... good-bye!"

Master Frank was in reverie. He sat up with a start.

"Good-bye, Wattie, good-bye!" That was Miss Phillis.

He found himself at the door; he had joined the group in the sun.

"Isn't it jolly weather?" This was Miss Phillis again.

"You've brought it with you." That was the foreman.

"It's been that shocking!" That was the mate.

"You haven't admired us yet." This was the foreman again.

They all stared up at the new red brick.

" Beautiful !" said Miss Phillis. She always liked things jolly.

Master Frank did not look so content. The foreman asked his opinion.

" What's your opinion, sir ?"

" I liked the old place best," said Master Frank.

" Of course !" said Miss Phillis. " You're an artist, and prefer things tumbling down."

" If that's what the gentleman wants," said the mate, " he should have seen us after the storm." They still used to talk of the storm.

" I dare say," said Master Frank. He seemed to want to be off, and he gave a sign to Miss Phillis, but Miss Phillis was in a dream.

" Staying up at the Vicarage ?" said the foreman to Master Frank.

" No," said Master Frank.

" Plenty of changes since your time."

" No doubt," said Master Frank.

" Come, sir, we looked for you back as Vicar, we did, to tell you the truth."

" Me !" said Master Frank, laughing under his straw. " Preaching is not in my line."

" And your father such a preacher, too. Always heard him at harvest. Beautiful sermons, wasn't they, now ? Beautiful sermons, Miss Phillis ?"

Miss Phillis nodded, half in, half out, of her dream.

" And the Vicarage house and all ! . . . Oh, we like the new gentleman well enough, but there's been a Burnet for generations. Marchington don't seem the same since your father died, Master Frank."

" Possibly not," said Master Frank.

" Shocking thing !" said the foreman, and heaved a sigh.

" I believe," said Master Frank, " it is one of the very worst storms on record. Come along, Phil," he said to Miss Phillis.

" You're not looking much," said the foreman, as Master Frank gathered his reins.

" It's the heat," said Master Frank.

" There's no earthly reason," said Miss Phillis, " why we need stand in the sun. . . . Good-bye !" And they rode away.

Wattie wondered a good deal all that afternoon about Miss Phillis and Master Frank, and about Choice and Necessity. He wondered if in any way Choice could belong to Master Frank ; he was pretty sure not— judging, that is, from appearances : everything seemed to belong to Miss Phillis. Why did she give them such odd names ? Why did she call one Necessity ? Perhaps because she had to. And why did she call the white mare Choice ? Very likely because she chose. He wondered why Miss Phillis had come. Had she been saving up her money ? Had she paid back what she owed ? Would she now live at the Manor for good ? And what was Master Frank doing ? There were dozens of questions he wanted to ask, but never should think of asking. He should learn in time, however, for the foreman and mate would be certain to talk.

They talked the very next morning.

" And what's *he* doing ?" said the mate. (This would be Master Frank.)

The foreman made no response ; he finished a little job, and then he gave Wattie fourpence and told him to fetch the beer.

It used to take Wattie precisely two minutes to fetch the beer every morning. He had just to dash across to The Bell ; the girl at The Bell, looking out of the window, would have both the pewters ready ; and then he had only to go back rather more cautiously than he came. But he knew you could miss a good deal in two minutes, and he knew he had missed it now.

" I reckon the poor young chap looks miserable." The mate said that as he finished his beer. " Where's he stopping ?"

" Up at the Manor."

" *That* won't be let again in a hurry."

Wattie pricked up his ears. He was busily sorting nails, and he grew more busy and absorbed.

" *That* won't be let again in a hurry." The mate repeated what he had said. It wasn't exactly a question, and yet it needed some sort of reply. You might think that the foreman would give no reply ; but you'd see, if you waited, he would. Presently, quite by chance, he said :

" She'll be here this winter, I know, for a fact."

" Will she ?" That was the mate.

" *Will* she ?" said Wattie, and then he was covered with shame.

But, fortunately, no harm was done. They looked at him with a stupid stare ; only the foreman seemed to realize that Wattie was somehow at fault, and sent him back with the pewters.

CHAPTER XIX

THE forge could not possibly have been built in a more advantageous position. Every carriage that passed from Marchington Station to Marchington Manor was bound to come rattling down the hill and pass between The Bell and the forge ; and carriages were always passing two or three times a day.

That Monday Master Frank went off. He drove— at least, was driven—to catch the 10.14. The new groom held the reins, and Master Frank sat by his side, leaning a little forward as they approached the hill. There was only one yellow bag. Tuesday brought strangers—a tall and elderly gentleman and a very sweet young lady. They drove in the dogcart, too, with the groom at the back. They were gone like the wind, but Wattie could see the young lady look first at The Bell and then at the forge, as she clung to her hat with one hand, and said what she wanted to say with the other.

Then their luggage turned up, three or four pieces ; and, sure enough, they were in church on Sunday— the little new iron building—and everyone stared as they went to their seats—Miss Phillis, then the young lady, Miss Daisy, then Miss Phillis's white-haired relation, and last of all the elderly gentleman. This was Miss Daisy's papa. He had come with Miss Daisy to stay for a month, so one of the girls from the Manor told Mrs. Moon ; but the girl was wrong, for they went the following week. And they took Miss Phillis with them, while they left Miss Phillis's aunt behind. She *was* her aunt, so Wattie discovered ; he learnt it from the gardener, and that her name was Miss Elizabeth ; " the old lady," they seemed to call her, " though *she's* no lady," the gardener said. It appeared she had dismissed him on account of some early " fallings." Her temper was something shocking, and the gardener had been obliged to say that if she was not perfectly satisfied she had better get somebody else ; and she *had* got somebody else, Wattie found out at the end of the story.

Wattie did not think that old Miss Elizabeth's temper could be so very shocking, for he frequently saw her with Miss Phillis, and they seemed to be excellent friends, always jolly and laughing. He would like to have closely examined her features. Once he was passing the post-office just when the carriage stopped, and Miss Phillis jumped out and ran with the letters. . . . Well, after all, there might be some truth in the gardener's statement ; she certainly looked severe ; she had very dark eyes and deep furrows, and her lips were firmly compressed. . . . Her lips moved now, and she spoke to Wattie.

" I beg your pardon, mum," said Wattie.

" *Boy, touch your cap*, was what I *said*."

And Wattie touched his cap, and then ran round the corner.

She was always there, was old Miss Elizabeth ; she made the Manor her home, and as a general rule, when Miss Phillis went off (as she went this time with Miss Daisy's papa), Miss Elizabeth stayed behind. Wattie heard her telling the clergyman how she hated " gadding about " ; it was " all very well for young people." Miss Elizabeth must be old, quite old, quite fifty or sixty, Wattie thought. They said she was a spinster, which meant she had never been married, and she had to be treated with great respect. Wattie, in fact, felt rather awed until that afternoon when he found her out in the fields, more than a mile from the Manor, fanning herself in the sun. Had he known she was there he would never have gone ; he came on her un-expectedly. He thought she was fanning herself because she was hot, but she cried : " Come, boy, at once ! Can't you see I've twisted my ankle ?"

He managed to help her home, though she was such a terrible weight, leaning upon his shoulder. He had to stop more than once to get out his pocket-handker-chief ; but she had to get out her handkerchief too, and when he said, " It makes you sweat," she said, " I quite agree with you." This was all she said, except " *Oh dear ! oh dear !*" and at the hall-door where he left her, " *You are a sensible and obliging boy.*"

So much for old Miss Elizabeth ; she stayed on and on. Others came and went. Miss Daisy for ever was coming ; such a sweet young lady ! She always looked first at The Bell, then at the forge, coming down the hill ; first at the forge, then at The Bell, going back again. Once she brought to the Manor a small Aberdeen, and it somehow strayed into the forge. Wattie took it that night after work, and he met Miss Phillis and Miss Daisy going in at the iron gates. They both cried out at once, " Alexander ! Alexander !" and Miss Daisy snatched the puppy, and smothered it with kisses. Wattie could not help laughing, and he laughed still more when Miss Daisy blushed, and said,

" Oh, wait a minute, please," and opened her purse, and there was nothing inside.

Miss Daisy's papa did not visit so often. He was supposed to have business in town. The foreman told the mate he had been Miss Phillis's guardian, and he it was who had tied up her money so tight, and only let her repair so few of her cottages after the storm ; he, too, so the foreman said (and his wife did the servants' washing), who had put his foot down about the church. He allowed five hundred pounds for a temporary iron building, but he would not permit any restoration. Of course, Miss Phillis could do as she chose now she had come of age, and everyone knew a scheme was afoot, and Wattie had actually met a gentleman measuring with a tape. Still, when Miss Daisy's papa came down and sat in the temporary iron building, bolt upright by Miss Phillis's side, Wattie could not help thinking that even although Miss Phillis was turned one-and-twenty, she was not allowed to have her own way.

There was also a noisy fellow called Major—came whizzing and hooting down the hill, past The Bell, and stuck at the forge.

" Serve him right," said the foreman, and the mate said the same sort of thing. But presently Major poked his head in, and said : " Where the deuce is everyone got to ?" And the foreman and mate went out and stood in the road for thirty-five minutes. Major sometimes would stop after that and exchange a few words. He once spoke to Wattie the day of the Derby race. He wanted to know which of two horses Wattie was backing (" Which of the two are you backing, my boy ?"), but as Wattie had never so much as seen (let alone ridden) either one of the horses in question, he naturally was not backing at all.

Then there was young Mr. Fred. He was supposed to come after Miss Daisy. That was what Mrs. Moon said, and so said the foreman, and so, in fact, said everyone, and everyone also said that they hoped she would never have him. Nobody cared for Mr. Fred, and everyone loved Miss Daisy. Mr. Fred often looked in at the forge, and he called Wattie " Handsome William," and frequently tipped him half a crown ; but if ever Miss Phillis came by with a question, and Mr. Fred happened to be about, Mr. Fred slunk outside. It was easy to see they didn't get on, and once when Wattie was turning a shoe (if you could call it a shoe), and Miss Phillis stood watching, and presently said, " Ah, I should like to do that," Wattie felt positive what she wanted was Mr. Fred's head, and the hammer and anvil.

Master Frank rarely came—once in the summer, once in the autumn, and once again after Christmas.

CHAPTER XX

In September began the cubbing season, a busy time and very delightful. The ladies and gentlemen rode out quite early, and Wattie would sometimes hear them go past, supposing the meet was Brinkley way, when he was warm in bed. Sometimes, however, he would be up. Either he or the mate must get to the forge by half-past six o'clock, and often when Wattie's turn came (especially in the cubbing season after the idle summer days) he would be there soon after five, just to see, if he might, a bit of the fun, and feel the foggy weather.

One morning he heard Master Frank.

" Here, somebody ! Where are you ?"

Wattie plunged through the mist.

" Is anyone here ?" Yes, it was Master Frank ; he came leading Choice, and he seemed put about. " Is anyone here ?"

" No, sir," said Wattie.

" What a confounded nuisance !"

Deadlock.

" What's the matter ?" Miss Phillis drew up. (A very dark bay.)

" Why, there's nobody here," said Master Frank. " Just my luck !" he said.

" Won't Wattie do ?"

Master Frank stared at Wattie. Wattie did not like being stared at by Master Frank, so he went and picked up Choice's foot—the foot without the shoe.

" Yes, that's the foot," said Master Frank.

Wattie put it down.

" Well, can you do it ?"

" Me !" said Wattie. " Me and my mate together might." For shoeing's a trade, like anything else.

" There, Phil, I told you so." Master Frank was quite annoyed.

Wattie picked up the foot again. The shoe had only just dropped, that was certain ; there were the nail-holes clean. . . . " Wait a bit !" He ran ; he came running back ; he had found the shoe with the mist shining on it.

" Good !" said Miss Phillis.

" Bad !" said Wattie. " That wasn't any of *our* work, miss."

Miss Phillis laughed ; she told him : " No ; Choice was last shod in London town."

" Oh, London town !" said Wattie. He took hold of the bridle. Of course, he could fit the same shoe on. Master Frank seemed to doubt.

" How long will it take you ?" he said.

" Sixteen minutes," said Wattie. (The foreman was four times as sharp as himself.) He led Choice tenderly into the forge ; he looked at the clock ; it wanted the quarter.

Whilst he was tying her up he could not help hearing some snatches of conversation. There was nothing he should not have heard.

" Hullo, Major !" (Master Frank ! . . . A third party had come up.) " I'm afraid I'm delaying you all."

"Not a bit," said Major. (Yes, it was Major. . . . *" Which of the two are you backing, my boy ?"*)

"Do go on," said Master Frank.

"That's what we thought of doing," said Major.

"I'll walk home," said Master Frank. "It's no good messing about. It'll take that nipper an hour, and only be half on then. I'll walk home," said Master Frank.

"Better than that," said Major ; "*you* can ride Fred's horse."

"What's up with Fred ?"

"Sick and shivery, that's all."

"It was stupid of Fred to come "—this was Miss Phillis. "Everyone told him not. Yes, Frank, it gives us a good excuse for sending Fred home."

"What brute is he on ?" asked Master Frank. There seemed some hesitation.

"Necessity," said Miss Phillis. "You know Necessity."

"I don't," said Master Frank. "Never ridden him in my life."

"My dear Frank ! Well, *I've* ridden him, and he's a——"

What ? . . . Wattie was hammering ; heard no more. Between the strokes of his hammer he was aware that others had ridden up ; there was a buzz of conversation, and every few seconds somebody sneezed A few minutes later, a lull. . . . They had gone.

Young Mr. Fred groped into the forge.

"Take her up to the Manor," he said ; "there's no hurry, and say she's not wanted." He lingered as if he had something else he wished to communicate, holding his hands to the fire, then sneezed, and said, "Beastly raw morning !" and went out again.

There might be no hurry for young Mr. Fred, but Wattie had reasons for hurry. In the first place he must make his boast good, sixteen minutes for one black foot, and in the second place—but that would come after. . . . Master Frank ought to be more civil

when Miss Phillis gave up to him so ; she let him have
Choice, then Necessity, and got not so much as a look
or a word. Nay, Master Frank actually grumbled
because she had never before mounted him on
Necessity ! Just as if Miss Phillis could always be
giving in ; could always be setting aside her own fun ;
ride any sort of a new bay mare in order to let Master
Frank and the other sickly young gentleman have
what they wanted themselves. Miss Daisy would not
have served her so, nor Miss Phillis so have served
Master Frank. . . . Six o'clock striking ; the last nail
home ; a moment, and there she stood. *One black foot
in sixteen minutes.* A sweet little foot to be sure !

Now for the second place. . . . He knew where they
met—at Brinkley Hole. He had no scruples of conscience. Were there not several ways to the Manor,
and one of them by the Hole ? That was the way he
was going. The mate would be up by half-past six,
puzzled, of course, to know what had happened. He
should know later on when Wattie returned—so much,
at least, as Wattie would tell him. He led Choice out.
Shame and confusion ! Folly and nonsense ! If he
wasn't fit to ride Choice, " let him be hung," as the
mate always said. Or rather, this, a more practical
thought as he got his seat : if he was not fit to ride
Choice, Choice would probably kick him off.

Well, he had grown some inches taller since he was
last in the saddle. It was a couple of years since that
day when he asked Jones's groom to give him a leg.
He remembered about the stirrups. Now, with a very
trifling adjustment, he could find them and hold them,
too. This in itself was a great advantage ; and his
limbs were more of a shape ; he had less disposition to
wobble ; he felt the grip of his knees, the flat of his
thighs ; he could sit upright like a gentleman. . . .
Perhaps it was as well there was nobody to admire.
If anyone had admired him, he might have heard
more about it. A boy with a milk-can emerged round
one corner, rubbing his eyes, but he did not see Wattie,

and Wattie rode on. . . . If he were groom at the Manor, he should keep bridles better than that ! He might have been groom if he wanted. The coachman had often said he could get Wattie into the stables, but his father had been a blacksmith, and his grandfather too, and there was always a Brett in the trade. And yet it must be jolly enough to go out in the morning, and saddle Choice, and rub every scrap of steel up bright. . . . He began to consider. It was like this : he must be at the meet, and yet not at the meet ; he must be with the hounds, and yet not with the hounds ; he must see without being seen. . . . Was that baying ? Hullo ! Was that baying ? Something whispered to him, " Beware !" A little green track was on his right, and he drew in his reins and listened. He felt the sun striking through on his shoulders ; he had got upon higher ground. . . . Baying again ! . . . Choice ! Choice ! He had to kick her with both his heels. He was less than a mile from Brinkley Hole, and at any moment the burst might come. . . . He fancied now he could hear Master Frank, " *Never ridden him in my life* "; and Miss Phillis, a little bit nettled, " *Well, I've ridden him, and he's a——* "

What ? " Something like *you*, I expect," said Wattie ; and he stroked one of Choice's silken ears. The horn ! The horn ! So far away ! Again, the horn, so near ! . . . Far and near, faint and clear— was it a horn—a human horn ? Was it an angel above the mist ? Was it a trumpet in the skies ? . . . The horn ! the horn ! the human horn ! Men, not angels, about. Oh, hurrah for the cubbing season ! The horrid Wattie smelt blood. He stood upright in his stirrups, which belonged to somebody else. . . .

" Stand still, can't you !" For Choice had plunged, and Wattie sat down without meaning to. " If you want to go cubbing," said Wattie, talking into those silken ears—" if you want to go cubbing, you must learn to behave."

She whinnied once, and he smacked her nose. He listened attentively. The horn ! the horn ! . . . He smacked her again. She stood ; he listened ; the fog poured into his open mouth. . . . How very still ! how very strange ! What an odd fancy came over him ! . . . This bramble, for instance—he would not touch it—but was the dew hanging there never to drop ? And the hedge and the cart-ruts—were they caught too, bound by a spell, while the rest rushed on ? . . . And how did this slip here, this little cub, twisting one way and looking another ? Nothing had moved, and yet here it was, fixed like the bramble. . . . Oh, wake up ! Look again ! *There* is the hedge and bramble, and the cub has straightened itself out of sight. And oh, it was really the cub, and there's such a tumult, and here they come on him—the hounds !— thudding past him, one by one, altogether . . . giddy moment . . . they were gone.

CHAPTER XXI

So was Wattie :—after the hounds, with the field upon him ; yelling and tearing and rending, they were in hot pursuit. Soon he would be in the thick of it ; and if Choice would not run mad—as, indeed, she bid fair to do—he might go with the hunt up the lane, take his chance at the other end, and then push on to the rising ground, and follow at discretion. So long as he kept under shelter, with the steep bank above, he would do very well, supposing that Choice's behaviour was good, and supposing that he could hold her. She was pulling now as the hunt came up. A flash of pink through the hedge, a dip in the ground, a scuffle and shuffle, up the slope, and away ! . . . Then Major, riding alone. It was Major, without a doubt. Besides, he could hear him speaking.

" The fellow's a fool ! The fellow's a fool !" And

then he called unmistakably, " Burnet, is that you ?"
Wattie drew back and said, " No."

He drew back on a line with Miss Phillis. Miss
Phillis was not speaking at all—too much in earnest
for that. Perhaps she had started away from the rest,
and meant to show her paces. Choice knew Miss
Phillis, and pulled. Wattie had checked her because
of Major ; now he urged her on. Miss Phillis had
broken into a canter ; so should Choice. There was no
fear of detection ; Miss Phillis was all for the matter in
hand ; not a word, not a breath escaped her ; she was
making straight up the field, with eyes for nothing else
but the distant hedge and the brow of the hill, and ears
for the hounds and the horn alone. When he got to
the end of the lane—very well, he would stop ; for the
present—oh, joy ! . . . Hullo ! what's this ? Scatter
and splutter, Master Frank ! No doubt about that
when he spoke.

" I say, Phil ! Phil, I say !"

" What ? I can't stop." (Oh, Miss Phillis !)

" Phil, I say, this precious beast . . . he's all very
well. . . . Bah ! get up, confound you ! . . . This
beast——"

" Come along. I can't hear. Come along"—
laughing and shouting against the wind.

Another dip in the ground. . . . They rode level.

" What were you saying, Frank ?" (Miss Phillis is
out of breath. Good ! she may be more patient.)

" I was only about to remark . . . Good Lord !
. . . By Jove, Phil, he's a bit of a brute . . . a nasty
ill-tempered——"

What ?

(Then Miss Phillis, expostulating.) " Of course,
Frank, if you make up your mind " . . . (*What ?
what ? what ?*) " Creature's back " . . . (*What ?
what ? what ? He lost that too.*) " Nasty ill-tempered
brute ! Then you must expect . . ."

Expect what ? Well, Wattie had dropped behind ;
besides, he had come to the end of the lane. . . .

Talking of brutes, here was Choice like a hundred she-devils let loose ! Only he had got her in hand ; he pulled her here, and he pulled her there—yes, he would pull her just into the place where he had meant her to go ; then they would wait, deep in the ditch, whilst the rest of the hunt went by. They were passing now, helter-skelter, two and three at a time. He counted them—first a couple of gentlemen ; . . . *that* was Miss Daisy's papa, of course ; . . . two more gentlemen, three more ladies . . . *that* was Miss Daisy ; . . . two other young gentlemen . . . then a long pause. . . . That was all.

Now was his time. He forced Choice out of the ditch, he tugged at her, left and right, got her nose forward, and worried her up the bank. They pushed through into the field together. Oh, it was gorgeous here in the sun, with the open country whirling round you, so that you must look down at your feet. And looking down, what turf for a gallop ! He must follow them where they had gone. Looking up, where *had* they gone ? Some have gone this way, some gone that. Who is it leading the Manor party ? Major ? Then you lead them astray. (*The fellow's a fool—the fellow's a fool !*) There you go bobbing ; and if you looked, you would see up the hedge a splash of scarlet with a few dark specks behind. And if you lead, Miss Phillis follows ! Miss Phillis ought to know better, but perhaps she knows *even better than that ;* perhaps she is following Major because she knows it must end in a jump. This would be like Miss Phillis. . . . Well, he would follow too. One glance back to make certain ; not a creature in sight ; only the world falling from you, field after field sloping down and away. . . . He is off ! It might mean fines, imprisonment, flogging—what did he care ? For the moment he was supreme, and Choice was under him, spurning the ground. Oh, those black little feet ! They were swifter now—swifter and stronger than when she first trotted into his dreams. Was this the meadow ? Not up here !

No, nor anywhere ! Only a secret way by which Choice ran out of heaven. *This* was not heaven ; let her bear that in mind ; here were no secret ways ; she had got plain earth before her ; turn this way or that, the earth would not turn, and what she met she would meet. This being so, she would meet a hedge over the brow of the hill. She could not see it, but it would be there. What fun ! Then they meant to take it ? Well, whether they meant it or not, they *must ;* they must either go over, or else go back, or else break off at right angles and go for a certain gate. Who would sneak out of his course a couple of hundred yards for a gate ? Not Major, for instance, riding alone—(*the fellow's a fool—the fellow's a fool !*)—nor Miss Daisy, riding with her papa and one of the two young gentlemen ; nor the other young gentleman with Miss Phillis, who was also with Master Frank. . . . And yet they were changing places. Miss Phillis had left Master Frank, and was now abreast of Miss Daisy's papa. The two young gentlemen dropped behind ; Miss Daisy was going ahead ; Miss Phillis caught up Miss Daisy ; Miss Daisy's papa caught up Master Frank. . . . Ah, but the two young ladies—they are gaining the brow of the hill ; they are rising up into the sky. See, head and shoulders, up they come ! They are laughing and nodding ; is it the hedge ? There ! they are off ! They drop out of sight. . . . One, two, three, the rest come up ; each for a second is there, and goes over. Each ? Has he time to count ? He is one of the hunt himself ; he is galloping up the slope—can catch the top of a sycamore-tree on the downward slope beyond. . . . There's Miss Daisy's papa again !—and the gentlemen ! There is Miss Daisy ! There's Miss Phillis in front ! Hooray, hooray, Miss Phillis ! . . . Miss Daisy is after her, though, and both of them after Major, and all of them after the hedge. . . . Yes, it runs straight across. . . . Miss Daisy's papa is pointing and waving—led into a trap. Not that he fears for himself, but he fears for the two young ladies. Nor

is he very far wrong if he condemns this jump on the
view as one of the worst in the neighbourhood. Only
it is too late ; he is shouting against the wind ; besides,
if they heard, would they stop ? . . . Miss Phillis is
up with Major. Is it Major she wants ? She has
passed him by ; Miss Daisy has passed him also.
(*Which of the two are you backing, my boy ?*) . . .
Which is it now—Miss Phillis, Miss Daisy ? The
horses are straining to see what's before them. They
are level . . . not so . . . Miss Phillis is first. Now
for it ! She gathers ! Ease her, and over ! Fly, fly,
like a bird ! The hedge never quivered. Then Miss
Daisy, so close—it was only a glimpse. Then Major—
an ugly performance. Who cared for the rest ? The
birds, they had flown. Oh, who would not be a bird
like one of those sweet young ladies ?

A bird or a boy—it is all the same ! No time now
to consider, no time now to repent. Has Choice ever
jumped in her life before ? Such a hedge ? She must
jump it now ; they could never stop, he knew, and she
knew—he with his wits, she with her instinct. He felt
her mad beneath him ; he felt his own control. . . .
He settled himself, then touched her up—touched her
up with a heel. . . . What ! she would shirk ? For
shame ! . . . What ! she would twist her neck ? He
slapped it, one side, then the other ; then he slapped it
again—the other, the one. . . . A wriggle, a toss, a
snort ! She had got him ; she leapt with him into the
air. . . . Was he thrown ?—thrown high, chucked
up, flung back ; but he held the reins, and he held his
body, every limb loose and compact. . . . Then down.
Where ? Why, here ! Somehow home, lodged in the
saddle, a victor, a king—a king on this the most
splendid of queens, beautiful creature, beautiful queen.

Beautiful, splendid ! Alas ! not his. Could he deny
it any longer ? There were the others careering away—
wild sport for an autumn morning. They had crossed
the next field. Good-bye, good-bye ! The fun was
up ; he must turn about. . . . Good-bye, good-bye,

good-bye ! They had slipped out of reach, and were gone. . . . And he was left quite alone, quite alone, with Choice. Good Choice ! He wanted to tell her what he thought, only he did not know how. He certainly would not jump her again ; he would walk her quietly up the field, two hundred yards to the gate.

When he came in sight of the gate, he was passing under the sycamore-tree, and under the sycamore-tree he stopped. He stopped because he saw somebody— somebody tall and slim and proper—open that gate from behind the hedge, lead his horse through, then shut the gate, mount, and go after the others.

CHAPTER XXII

ONE day at the forge there was a bit of a scene. Mr. Marshall, the groom from the Manor, brought Necessity in to be shod. Now, long ago, when Necessity first came in, it was not Mr. Marshall who brought him ; it was the groom who called Wattie " Young Hope-ful " ; but the odd thing is that Mr. Marshall said to Wattie just what the other groom had said : " You let him be. He's got a nasty way with him." And this he said because Wattie went up to Necessity, as a matter of course, and dealt him a jolly smack.

" You'd better come out of it," said the groom ; and this he said because Wattie, having smacked Necessity once, smacked him twice, and then stood leaning his weight upon him. " Boys know everything," said the groom.

" We've had him in scores of times," said Wattie, and he smacked Necessity once again, and began to pick the hairs off his coat.

" Now then, Young Ornamental !" This was the foreman coming, and Wattie got out of the way. He thought he would show Mr. Marshall his utter indiffer-ence, so he went to the back of the forge, and busied himself with the bellows ; but after a while he forgot, and left the bellows and watched.

Horses were strange creatures. The foreman often said that no two horses were just alike, and that their habits and ways and tempers were mostly those of a Christian person. He was saying it now in his high-pitched voice. " Irritable " was the word he used. Irritable, indeed ! Every time the foreman stooped to grasp Necessity's leg, Necessity's leg flew out. Wattie thought he would cop it soon, cop it properly. The foreman seemed to think so too, for he drew back at last, and gave it up, wiping his streaming brow. Then came the mate's turn next. He spat on his hands (how Wattie laughed !), then he got down, then up, then walked a little to left and right (if the mate was to cop it properly Wattie should die of laughing !) ; then a fearful plunge. . . . It wasn't very successful, and everyone roared.

The mate rolled over, and felt his bones.

" You never got kicked !" roared the foreman. " You never !"

" Kicked !" yelled the mate.

" No, you never ! . . . You ask Mr. Marshall there."

Mr. Marshall wouldn't say yes or no ; that was the first thing you noticed. Mr. Marshall had an amiable face, which did not look kind. What he said now was : " It's just as I told you. There's no doing any-thing with him."

This appeared to be true. Wattie had ventured out.

" Don't you go near him," said the mate. This was just like the mate.

" All right, I won't," said Wattie. The mate was beautifully sold.

" If you do," said the foreman, " I'll give you a hiding as you'll never forget." The foreman, however, meant what he said.

" He's been like it this fortnight past," Mr. Marshall explained, with his amiable face ; he looked at them all one after the other, as if he liked them all equally well.

" It seems as if he's upset. Nobody can't do nothing with him only the young missus."

" She's a rare one with horses," said the foreman ; and Wattie walked right away ; and presently Mr. Marshall went out, taking Necessity with him, and Necessity had not been shod.

What would be done ? Wattie wondered. He hung about to hear ; but although the foreman kept telling the story to everyone who passed by, he only told the part where the mate fell down and thought he was kicked, and never broached any suggestion for getting those shoes on Necessity's feet. An idea did just flash into Wattie's mind. He dismissed it at once as foolish, but all the same he looked down the road whenever he ran across to the Bell. And then, to show that even the maddest of dreams may come true, on returning one day from an errand he found Necessity at the forge, with Miss Phillis perched in the saddle.

Thinking it over afterwards, it seemed strange that he should have felt instinctively something was wrong ; yet she laughed as he sidled in.

" Good-afternoon," she said.

" Oh, good-afternoon, miss," said Wattie ; he began to get something to do.

" Can Walter shoe a horse ?" He heard her ask that question. He knew what the foreman would say. He would shout to the back of the forge (as he did) : " Young Wat ! Hear that ? Can shoe a horse ?"

This was the signal for him to come out, at least a step or two. He mustn't say anything, only grin.

" I expect he can," said Miss Phillis. This was a vague remark. Miss Phillis would hardly know whether he could or couldn't.

" I won't say," proceeded the foreman, taking a nail from his mouth—" I won't say but what young Wattie's a handy boy ; but shoeing, miss, is a trade same as anything else. There's a powerful deal for a boy like young Wattie to learn. . . ." And that was how he went on.

In the end they all helped more or less. It seemed odd to be going about just as usual, and yet not as usual, for you had to be more particular, and you talked in a different way ; at least, the foreman talked ; he talked all the time, and the mate on and off, and forgot himself once, and was told of it afterwards. And, oddly enough, it was just at this moment when Wattie looked up to see if she heard that the thought flashed into his head again that something was somehow wrong with Miss Phillis. But then it flashed out, for she was telling how her great-great-grandfather used always to bring *his* strawberry roan to the forge, and must needs sit in the saddle if he wanted to make *his* strawberry stand just as *her* strawberry now was standing, perfectly quiet, perfectly good. . . . "There were Bretts in Marchington, *then*," she said.

Bretts in Marchington then and now.

"Wat, lad, you shall finish." This was the foreman speaking like that.

Wattie did not much fancy the job, but he wiped his hands on his apron, and got down and wedged Necessity's foot between his trembling knees, and reminded himself how only a few days ago he had given Necessity two or three smacks. Meanwhile Miss Phillis was talking. Wattie neither knew then, nor could he remember afterwards, what Miss Phillis was talking about. He remembered saying "Yes" and "No." He had, besides, his job to do. . . . Then he began to feel easier ; he began to hear what Miss Phillis was saying, and it was only this and that, and he began to see that the mate had gone, and the foreman betaken himself to the bellows. The foreman was lost in the roar.

"It's a very odd thing," said Miss Phillis, "that Necessity always behaves with *me*."

"Does he, miss ?" said Wattie ; it was the first time he really spoke.

"Yes, it is," said Miss Phillis.

Wattie said nothing, for Miss Phillis would often pay no heed, and go along just as she pleased.

"I'd ride Necessity," said Miss Phillis, "from here to London, and take every hedge and ditch on the way."

"Would you, miss ?   What for ?"

"What for ?   Nothing, but to show that it could be done."

"Oh, it could be done," said Wattie.

"Have *you* ever jumped a hedge ?" said Miss Phillis.

"Yes, miss," said Wattie ; "once."

"A stiff one ?"

"Not wonderful stiff."

"What were you on ?"

"A horse."

"What horse ?   I mean, I should like to see you put Necessity to a really big jump."

"Yes, miss," said Wattie respectfully.

"After your boast."

What was his boast ?

"I wonder what you'd say," said Miss Phillis, "if a thing happened to you which once happened to me." (He had guessed as much !   She stirred in the saddle ; now it was coming.)   "You give me an honest opinion."   She was leaning forward, stroking Necessity's ear.   Wattie clumsily dropped a nail.

"There's your nail," said Miss Phillis. . . .   "It's only a story, but it's true.   It may have been years ago, and it may have been here or miles away, in some tiny corner of England you never so much as dreamt of. . . ."

"Yes, miss," said Wattie.

"We were out riding, a lot of us, ladies and gentlemen, and we set ourselves to a certain jump.   It may "—a bright idea occurred to Miss Phillis—" it may have been a jumping race, or it may not."

"It may have been a jumping race," said Wattie, " or it may not."

"Anyway we jumped, and we all got over.   It was a pretty stiff jump."

"How stiff ?" asked Wattie.

" Well, you know that field on the Brinkley road, near the short-cut through the woods."

" Yes, miss."

" Well, that isn't the field. But you know if you go on you come to a lane with a field on your right."

" Yes, miss."

" Well, it isn't that ; but you know beyond there's a long slope up, and a dip, and a hedge with a sycamore ; you can't help seeing the sycamore, because there's only one. . . . Well, that's the hedge—I mean, it was quite as high. *My* hedge was quite as high as *that* hedge, and that's the highest hedge hereabouts."

Wattie nodded.

Miss Phillis also nodded. " We all got over," she said, and stopped.

Wattie wished she *would* stop.

" *Except one*," she went on. " He didn't jump ; he hung behind, and came through a gate."

Wattie was trying to laugh, and the funny thing was there was nothing sad in this story.

" He came through a gate," said Miss Phillis again.

" Well, miss," said Wattie, wiping his cheek, " you're not *obliged* to jump."

" No-o," said Miss Phillis. " Mind you," she added very quick—" mind you, I think you *are*. . . . Anyhow, that's not the point of my story. What happened was this. We were talking of how we jumped that hedge ; it was a pretty stiff hedge, and the one who did not jump the hedge, he—he——"

" Talked about how he came through the gate," suggested Wattie.

" Ah, if he *had*, who would have minded ? No ; he talked——"

" I see," said Wattie ; " you needn't go on. He talked about how he jumped over the hedge. Well, miss, do you know, I don't blame him."

" I hate cowards and liars," said Miss Phillis.

" Do you, miss ?"

" Don't *you ?*"

" They don't trouble me much," said Wattie. " Is
that all the story, miss ?"

" Not quite."

" I thought it couldn't be."

" Well, I *knew* he hadn't gone over—I knew it,
never mind why."

" I don't mind why," said Wattie.

" Never mind why, but I *knew* it, and so I *said* I
did."

" Yes, miss, of course."

" And he began to excuse himself. I hate excuses
at any time, and it only made worse of it. He was
riding—well, he was riding *this* dear old thing. . . .
You know, we had our horses in town, so you needn't
suppose it happened *here*."

Miss Phillis, who hated liars !

" He was riding Necessity, and he doesn't like
Necessity ; that vexed me from the first. He prefers
Choice. Choice is always a favourite."

" Beautiful manners," said Wattie.

" I have not a word to say against Choice, though,
personally, I would as soon jump Necessity any day."

" *Would* you ?" said Wattie. It was not for him to
say anything, though he had ridden them both. He
longed to tell Miss Phillis how Choice had flown, but
it would have been impolitic, also, he thought, imperti-
nent ; and meantime Miss Phillis proceeded.

" It was just an excuse. I don't believe for one
moment that if he had been on Choice he would ever
have gone for that hedge. The excuse annoyed me ;
I cannot tell you how much it annoyed me, and I said
——" She paused again.

Wattie had finished his job, but still kept down and
plied the hammer.

" I said," went on Miss Phillis—" I said what—well,
what I said to you just now—that I hated liars and
cowards ; and afterwards they told me that I'd spoken
much too strongly."

" Is that all ?"

" Yes ; only, there's the question.   You give me an honest opinion.   *Did* I speak too strongly ?"

Wattie shook his head.   He was standing upright now.

" Of course, of course, I know, I *know* the mistake was in the beginning.   *He should have jumped the hedge.*   I know *that*."

Wattie shook his head again.   He pictured it all, with Master Frank.   He went to lead Necessity.

" What I can't see, miss," he said, " is why, when you jump, you talk about it."

Miss Phillis did not reply ; she hadn't really the time to, because the foreman came out ; and as the foreman came out, Wattie went in and turned up his collar as if it was cold.

CHAPTER XXIII

WATTIE could never make up his mind which of the two he really loved best, Necessity or Choice.   A good deal depended upon the ground you put them on. There was a certain tint of paper which suited the roan exactly.   He had got it from Mrs. Moon.   It had come from the draper's, and was rather creased, but at once, when he saw Mrs. Moon untying her parcel, he thought how well the strawberry colour would look on that particular tint.   Mrs. Moon let him have the paper, and the string too, if he liked, and she also let him have half of the kitchen table, and " anything in reason."   So Wattie sat for two whole hours, until the light had gone, painting Necessity, which seemed in reason, as he thought.

Necessity soon wore out ; the string had cut the paper here and there, and one of these cuts ran right across the body ; moreover, though he damped the paper, he could not quite get rid of the wrinkles.   Only it had been very pleasant matching the roan against that tint.

It was just as pleasant three weeks later matching Choice on a sheet of brown. He bought that at the Marchington Stores—one brown sheet for a penny. It was very large ; it measured (by his little rule) thirty-two inches from top to bottom, and thirty-six inches across. He was going to cut it in quarters, and then it would serve for four, when he put down his little rule and his knife, and said to Mrs. Moon :

" May I clear the tea-things off ?"

" Bless the boy !" said Mrs. Moon, " you'll want the whole room next."

" I only thought I'd clear the tea-things off," said Wattie ; and he began putting them away. Then he spread out his sheet of paper, and it suddenly passed through his mind that possibly Mrs. Moon was right, and he should want the whole room next.

Wattie could not have reckoned up the number of times he had sketched out Choice and Necessity. He had sketched them in pencil, in charcoal, in chalks, and in paints. You would never have thought—at least, so *he* thought, stirring his tea of an evening— you would never have thought it possible to sketch them out in so many shapes and sorts and sizes. You would have thought—at least, so *he* thought—that a time must come when you had put down all you could ; but that did not prove to be the case.

Take Choice, for example. There was his dream. He had tried that again and again ; he had tried her trotting up the valley, with the green hills folding behind ; then as she came on him ; then with her wild look passing him by ; then as she turned at that tiny blow—yes, he had tried her turning, pulled up short in her run ; then as he felt her head in his arms.

He had also tried her as down at the forge. That was so utterly different. You would hardly have guessed that she was the same. *He* had thought her the same until that flash. . . . *Four black feet in sixteen minutes.* . . . Fifteen minutes ticked along like fifteen other minutes, fifteen sixty-seconds ; but the sixteenth

minute, or the sixtieth second of that minute, dropped
out of all the other minutes, dropped out of all the
other seconds, and was left there behind. . . .   Horse,
forge, and men for ever. . . .   The foreman here, the
mate there, Choice set in the middle. . . .   Was that
all ?   Or was this all—just two dark forms against one
white ?   No, there was something else.   There was all
Choice felt, and all he felt, and all the foreman felt,
and the mate.   For the foreman, he came stooping,
and the mate went leaning back, and Choice, she hid
her face from Wattie, and Wattie hardly dared to look.
She was so free and beautiful.

And then that afternoon when they came to the
forge, and Master Frank sat *so* in the saddle, thinking
under his shady hat, and Miss Phillis sat *so*, looking up.
. . .   " *It's the heat*," said Master Frank. . . .   " *There's
no earthly reason*," said Miss Phillis, " *why we need
stand in the sun*."   That was the flash ; there was the
sixtieth second—the heat, the sun, Master Frank, and
Miss Phillis and Choice.   " *There's no earthly reason*,"
said Miss Phillis, and laughed.   And you could draw a
long sweeping line from the top of Miss Phillis's head to
her waist and her skirt ; then over the haunch, down the
leg and the hock, to the ground.   That was the sweeping
line which he traced again and again.   He only traced
the line, however, and afterwards he rubbed it out, and
he painted Choice as she was before—that is to say,
without the saddle ; and though you might think it
ugly—Choice with her back towards you—it was really
not ugly at all ; for the glimpse of the head was charming, and wonderful, too, the body compact, the length
and breadth running up through the thin sheet of
paper as if cut out in a block.

Or take, if you like, Necessity.   He had tried him
again and again—not as he saw him first, looking down
on his strawberry coat, nor racing him round that
field, but as he saw him triumphantly twitching his
ears close under the wall.   Then the day when Necessity
came to the forge, and Wattie was told to get outside,

and he walked all round and got out, and saw every
limb so clean he could not possibly fail to follow—the
gigantic legs that strove on the ground, the haunch and
girth, two magnificent curves—and the puzzle if this
was colour or shape. . . .   And then as he trailed
through the hedge, disconsolate, led.   It was easy to
see what was wrong with him now.   If Master Frank
blamed Necessity, would not Necessity blame Master
Frank ?   Would he ever forgive him ?   Would he ever
allow mortal man to come near him again ?   He must
have caused trouble that day.   He had caused a deal of
trouble all round.   Mr. Marshall could do nothing
with him, in spite of his amiable face.   The foreman
could not so much as get near him.   The mate shied
off from the first.   Wattie had kept on a line with
the foreman.   " He's been like it this fortnight past."
Now, if any of them had known what Wattie had
known, what had happened a fortnight ago, there
would have been less surprise.   Little wonder, indeed,
if his mistress must come !   " A rare one with horses !"
the foreman said. . . .   That brought him down to
the forge again.   And now it was as it was with Choice.
Just the same sweeping line, the same laughter, the
same looking up, the same interchange of voices. *" Can
Walter shoe a horse ?"   " Young Wat, hear that ?   Can
shoe a horse ?"*   And Necessity, standing so still the
while, letting them come, first one, then the other,
cleaning and fitting and filing—most still of all when
with trembling knees they both of them heard Miss
Phillis say, " *You give me an honest opinion.*"

CHAPTER XXIV

IN those days everyone talked of " the new church."
It was wrong, Wattie thought, to call it " new."   The
site was old, at any rate, and much of the old would still
remain.   The tower, for instance, and the vestry, part

of the south wall, and part of the north ; and, besides
all this, there were many of the original fittings to be
in due course replaced—a number of pews, the reading-
desk, the block on which the pulpit stood, the brasses
and memorial tablets . . . well, no need to go through
the list ; the church would *not* be entirely new ; there
were " old associations," so the Vicar said.

He said it in his sermon ; that was the first they heard
about it. Only fancy ! Miss Phillis had kept it a
secret from everyone but the Vicar. And the Vicar
began by saying that he had something to communicate which would be of paramount importance to all
the inhabitants of Marchington, and they wondered
what it was. And then he read a verse out of the
Psalms, and said a great deal about King David, and
you listened because you felt something was coming.
It did come. *The parish church was to be restored.* . . .
What followed was hard to gather ; only at last, bit
by bit, Wattie discovered that the Vicar was speaking
about Miss Phillis, though careful not to mention her
name, and the church seemed crowded and hot.
Everyone talked of it on the way home. As a rule,
when they trooped out of church, the people would
stop and nod to their friends who had not been in, but
this morning nobody nodded or stopped. It was small
good stopping to ask, " What do *you* think ?" of a man
who had had no opportunities for thinking at all.
Afterwards, when the first excitement wore off, and
when those who had been in church had grasped the
facts of the case for themselves, they were proud enough
then to spread the news through every house in the
village.

The mate asked Wattie questions on Monday. The
foreman sat by and heard the answers. The foreman
did not show any particular interest in the scheme,
until a certain gentleman, who came down the road
and inquired of him the way to the Manor, turned out
to be the architect. You could see this gentleman to
and fro pretty often now. Wattie saw him one day

with Miss Phillis walking along the Brinkley road.
Miss Phillis had a great scroll of paper, which she was
studying as she walked, and the gentleman had his
hands behind him and an umbrella under his arm.
Miss Phillis was so intent that she never looked up,
and just as Wattie was passing she said : " There seems
to me no earthly reason . . ."

It was very likely that scroll of paper Miss Phillis
studied so hard which was put up in the iron church
for the congregation to look at. Everyone looked at
it going out. Wattie, as you might say, only got half
a look, for in all the press and confusion he found himself caught with some of the gentry, and freed himself as
fast as he could. So he turned in another day. There
were really three plans : a plan of the church as it had
been—an exterior view ; then two of the church with
proposed restorations—one from outside, and one from
within. It was interesting to note how the new would
work in with the old, how the tower and west would
combine with the east, and that bit of the south which
stood intact would be absorbed in the whole.

Beneath the plans was another paper, a kind of list
of subscriptions. Miss Phillis was giving the Fabric.
It would cost her several thousands—so, at least, they
said. Anyway, as the foreman put it, " the architect
knew what was what " (this gentleman who inquired
his way), and it leaked out in the *Brinkley Observer*
that no expense would be spared. The Fabric, then,
from Miss Phillis ; the pulpit from Master Frank ; the
organ from old Miss Elizabeth ; the east-end window
from Miss Daisy's papa ; the altar-cloths from Miss
Daisy ; and many more things besides. Also there
was a sixpenny fund opened to provide pews, kneelers,
and hymn-books, and you were asked to send your
sixpence to the Vicar ; there was a penny collection in
Sunday-school for the children ; and also for boys like
Wattie, who would neither, of course, send to the
Vicar nor pay a penny in Sunday-school, there was a
box at the door.

At first a good many people used to walk up of an evening, and see how the work was getting on. It seemed a desperate slow affair. This was the mate's opinion. He said he reckoned a job like that should be done in no time, and got out of the way, and that if you had the money to start, you ought to be able to see it through. He also reckoned that the more hands you employed the more work would get done, and that as it was Marchington Church, they ought to be Marchington hands; and he spoke very ill of Miss Phillis when she turned a Marchington man away.

The mate said it wasn't her business.

" It's a great deal more hers than yours," said Wattie. He could not have spoken like this to the foreman. " It's her own money she's spending."

" It's her own money, that I'll allow," said the mate. " What I say is, it's for her to see to the money, but let somebody else see to the work."

Wattie did not go on arguing with the mate. *He* knew why Miss Phillis saw to the work—because she would have things properly done. Why should Marchington men be employed if other men were better ? And as to that one particular man, Wattie knew why she sent *him* away, and anyone else might know, and did know; and although it was said that his work was good, Wattie knew that it wasn't, and anyone else might know it too if they only cared to examine.

Miss Phillis examined. She must always see everything. That was one reason why she would not employ more than a certain number of men ; she would not have one side of the church rising up whilst she was engaged with the other. Once there was quite a to-do. Miss Phillis had been away for a week, and had come home on Saturday morning, and on Saturday evening after tea she brought a party up to the church. The men had knocked off, of course, but Mr. Pigeon was there, the clerk of the works. It seemed that Miss Phillis had sent for him, for he was riding round on his bicycle when Wattie met him in the road, and he asked

Wattie to lend him a hand in getting the place a bit straight. They were sweeping away the rubbish when they saw the Manor party crossing the Buttercup Meadow, and Wattie was still collecting the untidy pieces of paper when Miss Phillis appeared on the scene.

Wattie did not hear what Mr. Pigeon was saying; he went on talk, talk, talk; but he heard Miss Phillis presently : "*I don't understand, Mr. Pigeon.*" And then Mr. Pigeon began again, and Miss Phillis began interrupting him, and there was quite a conflict of voices. And all the time Wattie was there, because Mr. Pigeon had said, as Miss Phillis came in, " Half a minute, my lad," and given him two bits of moulding to hold.

Meanwhile the rest of the party strolled in and out of the church ; there was Master Frank, and Miss Daisy, and Miss Daisy's papa.

" I consider it gross impertinence, Mr. Pigeon "— Miss Phillis was very angry—" and I shall have every bit of it taken down. No, not a word, if you please ! " Miss Phillis was very angry indeed.

" What's the row, Phil ?" Up came Master Frank. (They must have seen Wattie standing there, so it could not have mattered his hearing.) " What's the row, Phil ?" said Master Frank.

" I am more annoyed than I can say."

" Has old Pigeon been doing you ?" (Mr. Pigeon had gone to the vestry.)

" I don't believe there is such a thing in the world as a thoroughly honest workman. . . . Is there ?"

" No, miss," said Wattie, because she happened to address the remark to him.

" There's not a thoroughly honest anything," said Miss Daisy, looking at Wattie. She was looking at Wattie, but she was not thinking of Wattie ; she was dreaming and dreaming away.

" What are you looking at Wattie for ? He's honest enough." That was what Miss Phillis said ; she only chose to say it.

Wattie said, " Sometimes," and laughed.

" You expect a deal too much, Phil." This was Master Frank. " We're a lot of fraudulent knaves."

" Who are ?" said Miss Phillis, and she went up the aisle to where the chancel once had been.

Mr. Pigeon came out of the vestry presently, and he got Wattie to help him shift some heavy tarpaulins, and then, as Miss Phillis came down the aisle, Mr. Pigeon left Wattie with the tarpaulins, and went back to the vestry again.

Miss Phillis was full of her thoughts. " Oh, Frank," she said, and she suddenly stopped ; but Master Frank was not there. He came, however. " Oh, Frank, I never told you how much I liked your design for the pulpit. You have chosen all the best bits—Elijah before Ahab, and John the Baptist beyond Jordan ; only don't you think instead of Christ on the Mount, you might have Him cleansing the Temple, driving the people out with cords ?"

" Hum," said Master Frank, and began smoothing his hair.

" What are you two discussing now ?" asked Miss Daisy's papa ; he had come up from behind.

" Only the pulpit," said Master Frank. " Tell us about the rose-window."

" Yes, and there's Daisy's altar-cloth."

" Daisy's altar-cloth is already in hand ; about my window there's nothing to tell ; only Phillis is bitterly disappointed to think that the horses should not be put back."

" My dear Phil, how could they ?" Master Frank turned away with a laugh.

" I didn't mean the original. Goodness knows what has happened to that. It was smashed, I suppose, to smithereens. But I *should* like those horses again. You know, uncle, the white mare was Choice's great-great-great-great-grandmother. They ought to be re-membered. We used to love them so as children, didn't we ?" She appealed to Master Frank.

"I didn't" said Master Frank. "They were hope-lessly out of drawing."

"He says everything's out of drawing."

"Besides, Phil, the subject—pardon me—is not ecclesiastical."

"I don't know," said Miss Phillis. "The Bible has horses ; why shouldn't the Church ? Anyway, so far as the rose is concerned, I prefer Uncle Jasper's idea of the angels. Only suppose—suppose there had been a window there in the west . . . in fact, I *do* think," said Miss Phillis ; now this was what Miss Phillis said, and she said it quite recklessly : " I *do* think someone might paint them upon the wall."

"I dare say somebody might," said Master Frank, " for a couple of hundred pounds."

PART V

FRANK

"Then we began to ride. My soul
Smoothed itself out, a long-cramped scroll."

CHAPTER XXV

FRANK did not once visit Marchington between his seventeenth and his twenty-first year. He always managed to avoid it. His guardian urged him on several occasions—when the new iron church was put up ; when the living was sold ; before he went to study in Paris ; also when he returned. Each time Frank had a good excuse. On one occasion he found out that the visit would clash with an important cricket week in the south, an invitation he must not refuse ; on another occasion his work interfered ; on another occasion he had a narrow escape : was to travel down next day with his guardian when a merciful cold caught hold of him, and, riding home to his lodgings on the top of an omnibus in soaking rain, and then neglecting to change, he succeeded in passing a feverish night, and sent a wire from bed to say : " So sorry. Laid up. Can't go." And his guardian went alone.

Well, why not ? There was no need for him to go too. What did he know about the living, except that he would much rather have the two hundred pounds a year, and study Art. Thank Heaven, on this point at least his guardian was reasonable ; he used no pressure about the church. For that matter, nobody pressed him, neither his guardian, nor his aunt at Surbiton, nor his great-uncle in Cumberland, nor his old second-cousins at Tunbridge Wells. When he told Phillis that he had given up all thoughts of becoming a clergyman,

Phillis said emphatically, " I'm very glad," and added,
" I never knew you had any."

So far good. At the same time, certain idiotic
persons seemed bent on ruining him, if possible, at the
outset of his career. He thought of them with grim
humour. There was his Surbiton aunt, who professed
surprise and disappointment that he did not go to the
University. Why had not Frank won a scholarship ?
If he could gain one *into* Winchester, why not gain one
coming *out* ? Why not ? Why, simply because he
had never entertained the smallest notion of going to
New College ; simply because he had never entertained
the slightest idea of wasting the best years of his life
in studying stuff which could be of no possible use to
him in the future. Then there was a cousin of the
cousins at Tunbridge Wells who offered a lucrative post
in Japan, and was bitterly offended because Frank did
not cry out for joy at the prospect of writing letters
all day in an office for a salary which he did not
require.

" Still, it was very nice of your cousins' cousin,"
said Phillis. Phillis said this, but then she was not
paying any attention to what she was saying, and went
on feeding the dog.

Then his great-uncle urged the Civil Service, the
Indian police, the Law, and the Education Department,
and Frank must listen to him, forsooth, because he
would one day leave him a beggarly two thousand
pounds. But he got his guardian to listen to sense.
He spent ten days in Kensington, and had it out with
him, and his guardian was gracious enough to concede
that there could be no harm in " a trial." " You may,
my boy," he said, " take a year at the Academy
schools without compromising yourself as to whether
or no you make art your profession."

" I intend to make it nothing else," said Frank,
and closed the discussion. " I've no intention of
playing the fool ;" but this he said to himself upstairs.

And that is how it came to pass that Frank should be in lodgings, and ride on the tops of omnibuses, and eat his supper in wet clothes, and wire to his guardian ; and that is how it was, after a year in London, he went to Paris, and after nearly a year in Paris he came home; and how he tried to get a big subject-picture into the Academy, and failed; and how, on his twenty-first birthday, he received an affectionate letter from Phillis congratulating him, and sending him a knitted waistcoat, which she said had taken her eighteen months to work, adding that both she and her Aunt Elizabeth would be glad if he could come and spend a few days at Marchington Manor now that he was in England once more. She would like to have waited until they were straight (they had only moved in last week), but she was afraid he might be going abroad again soon.

Well, sooner or later he must go ; and now he was a man—twenty-one—he felt more confidence. Besides, he was a little out of conceit with his art. Besides, he should like to see Phillis. He had not seen Phillis for over two years. She also was twenty-one ; she was twenty-one last August, he was twenty-one this June. She had always been a jolly companion, especially in old days. He *did* think, when he met her in town on and off a couple of years ago, that she had grown the least bit stiff ; she had also talked a good deal about clothes, but that might have been on account of Daisy, who was getting her coming-out frock. And, after all, Phillis was always like that : she would talk about one thing or another, and go on until she was tired—long after *you* were, of course. Yes, he would like to see her again. He must thank her for this magnificent waistcoat—Miss Phillis, too, of Marching-ton Manor ! He stood with the waistcoat over his arm. A delightfully funny red silk thread was woven in and out. He really was dreaming, dreams not to be told ; but the upshot, anyway, was to throw the waistcoat down on the bed and counsel oneself to dis-

cretion. For he certainly should not allow Phillis,
let alone himself, to be rushed into any sort of mutual
*mis*understanding by a lot of giddy-pated relations.
He knew well enough what they would say—" Aunt
Elizabeth," and all, " How delightful!" " Brought
up together!" " Quite a matter of course!" He should
be very careful, waistcoat, how he behaved.

Queer to turn up at that station again! The same
long platform, the door where the ticket-collector stood.
The ticket-collector was new. That was rather a
mercy. No one accosted him, " Master Frank!"
Outside in the yard a smart young groom in a cart
touched his hat. " Good-afternoon, sir."

" Good-afternoon," said Frank. The porter shoved
in his bag. . . . There was the same old approach
to the station, where the children swarmed for the
Sunday-school treats. . . . The bag was in? Very
well. Up he jumped. Would the groom guess that
" B." on that bag stood for Burnet, and that he was
the old Vicar's son? Frank sat forward and talked—
talked all about the hay harvest. Here were the Manor
gates. . . . Newly painted, by Jove! . . . So-ho! Miss
Phillis; she means to have everything here in apple-pie
order. . . . Park very neat; grass edges trimmed;
baker's boy dismounts from his bicycle, lets them
through to the drive; " Thanks," says Frank, and the
groom whips on. Rhododendrons out, azaleas over;
lawn with the cedars; glimpse of the house; rhododendrons again; house once more; a sweep between
hedges; all lost; then out. Horror! Confusion!
Here we are, swirling round before the front-door.
Confusion, because it all seemed so strange—one thing
to slink round the house with Phillis as trespasser,
another thing to enter it solitary as a guest.

And here *was* Phillis. Oh, how fine!

" Here you are! How jolly! How nice of you to
come!"

" Nice of you to ask me," said Frank, pleased that
anything so neat should drop so readily from his mouth.

Meantime she was reintroducing him to her Aunt Elizabeth, whom he had only seen once ages ago when he was a boy.

"Tea is ready. . . . You look well. . . . Isn't it funny to be here ?"

"It's awfully funny to have the *right* to be here," said Frank, following out his train of thought. And then he saw Aunt Elizabeth looking at him as if she thought his remark was odd, and he wondered if it was, and what it meant, and added, " Awfully good of you to ask me," which was practically what he had said before.

" Funny world !" said Frank to himself when he went to dress for dinner—" funny world ! . . . She's quite grown up, but not much changed ; exactly the same sort of face. . . . A bit stand-off. . . . Very likely has had some ideas put into her. . . . I wonder who that conceited-looking chap may be who stuck his head in at the window and said " Oh !" and went out. Abominably rude manners. I hope Phil isn't going to be smart, and mix herself up with a lot of tenth-rate mushroom millionaires. If so, *I'm* off. She won't get *me*. . . . Ripping place with the shadows over the lawn ! Who put the honeysuckle there ? She got it, I know, from the road just outside the wicket. . . . Aunt Elizabeth seems a bit of a dragon— runs this show, I suppose. I'm glad I never told Phillis about my subject-picture. By Jove ! what a place ! What a sunset ! What weather !"

At dinner Frank took stock of the party. Phillis sat at the head of the table. She was in white. Her hair was done a new way. He believed it was even not quite the same as it had been at afternoon tea ; if so, she had learnt to be vain. He hoped to goodness all this grandeur and flattery and nonsense would not be the ruin of her. As a girl, you could not have seen a jollier, more unaffected creature. He should be careful how he behaved. Meantime she was talking to the ridiculous and ill-mannered individual who had put his head in and said "Oh," and gone out. She called him "Fred." He might be one of those distant connections of which he had heard on her father's side. Uncle Jasper he had met before. He used to come and see them as children; he was Phillis's uncle and guardian. The decidedly pretty girl was his daughter, rather young and shy, and to her Frank would be especially kind. Aunt Elizabeth was his sister; she had only come home from Canada, where she had lived for twenty years, in order to . . . But at this point Phillis leant forward and said: "Frank, does the waistcoat fit?"

When he went to bed that night Frank had a good deal to think about. He had feared it was going to be dreadfully slow, but then by degrees the company livened. They got chaffing Phillis about the waistcoat (that was when the fun began). She was reputed no needlewoman, and she called upon Frank for justification; did he remember how she used to hem dusters— a halfpenny for every side? . . . "By Jove!" had said Fred, "twopence a duster. Has a duster four sides?" . . . And nobody paid any heed to Fred, but they all were set laughing by memories; for what Phillis forgot, Frank remembered, and Uncle Jasper said, "Ha! ha!" And afterwards, in the drawing-room, Frank quite changed his mind about Phillis, for she seemed to be perfectly friendly; and so was Daisy, too—anxious to be on very good terms. That was his first thought on waking—very good terms. "After all," he said to himself, as he blinked through the blinds, as he blinked round the room, as he lay in his bed—"after all, I don't see why Phil *should* be spoilt. I don't see why she should not be just as fond of her old friends as ever." And he got up and dressed himself, and went out; and the sun was streaming over the lawn, and there all at once came Phillis.

"*You're* up early too," said Frank.

Phillis said, "Good-morning." Perhaps she was

always up at that hour. "Breakfast at nine," said Phillis. "I hope the dog didn't disturb you. Something frightened him in the night."

"This little rat," said Frank; and he pulled the Aberdeen's ears.

"Alexander," she said. "He belongs to Daisy." She carried the Aberdeen in her arms.

"No; I slept like a top. I say, Phil, how jolly it is— this place, I mean, and the being back—I mean the seeing you again! You've not altered a scrap, only grown up. Do you know, last night I thought at first you were going to be stiff, but after a bit it wore off."

Phillis laughed; she was walking towards the house.

"Do you know," she said, "why *my* stiffness wore off? Because *you* began to talk."

Frank blushed; oh, he wished he hadn't. "A pretty compliment," he said.

"Oh no," said Phillis; "you don't understand. I meant *your* stiffness."

To Frank the conversation at breakfast seemed unusually dull. He wished he had not come down so soon. He found himself in the way. Aunt Elizabeth greeted him briskly—"Good-morning." She had letters. Phillis paid heed to Alexander.

In came Uncle Jasper, blustering. He appeared not to notice Frank. "My dear," he said to Phillis, "if your station-master sent off that case by the 10.18, it should have reached Euston the same afternoon. Well, Mr. Burnet, how are you? A glorious morning we've provided."

Frank felt disposed to say he was much indebted, but Uncle Jasper went on about Euston, and Aunt Elizabeth went on with her letters, and Phillis went on with the Aberdeen pup. Frank thought he would just as soon be in lodgings near the Academy Schools, and bolting a dish of ham and eggs, as wander round that loaded table uncertain what to do.

"Please everybody help themselves," said Phillis,

and, Fred at that moment coming into the room with a general bow, turned to the sideboard, and, lifting the lids of all the dishes, partook of some fish, and sat down.

" What can I get you ?" said Frank to Aunt Elizabeth. He spoke with inward palpitation, but with outward, oh, such a studied manner !

" Get me ?　Oh, thank you.　Get me something. Anything will do."

Frank put some fish on a plate and brought it back to the table.　" Where does your Aunt Elizabeth sit ?" he inquired of Phillis.

" Oh, put it down, Frank, anywhere."

" *Where does your Aunt Elizabeth sit ?*" repeated Uncle Jasper.　" Well, *I'm* going to sit here.　Fred, old man, make room for me. . . .　*Where does your Aunt Elizabeth sit ?* . . .　Hey ! what a glorious morning !"

" What's all that about me ? . . .　Fish ?　No, thank you.　Oh, Mr. Burnet, is that you ?　How good of you !　But pray don't trouble. . . .　What are all your plans for to-day ?"

" We plan to enjoy ourselves," said Phillis.　" Yes, Frank, that fish for *me*."

" Oh, anything *I* can do ?"　This was Fred, with his mouth full.　How glad Frank was that she did not speak !

In came Daisy.　" Am I last ? . . .　Oh, you angel, Alexander ! . . .　But am I really last ?"

" Never mind ; you'll have Major Bob to bring up the rear to-morrow."　This was her father.　" Glorious morning, isn't it, Daisy ?"

" I meant to get up early," said Daisy, " and go for a long, long walk."

" A long, long, long walk," said Phillis.

" A long, long, long, long walk," said Fred, and seemed to expect a laugh.　" Can't understand," he went on, " how anyone can go for a walk before breakfast.　If it wasn't for breakfast, I doubt if I'd ever get out of bed."

" You would in this house," said Phillis severely.

" I want you to mow the lawn to-day. Daisy, we'll
finish weeding our border. This afternoon you shall
drive, as you wished, to Brinkley. Meanwhile, Frank,
if you like, you shall ride with me, and see what changes
have taken place since the old Vicarage days."

It was all very well arranged, and all very jolly too.
For the girls did weed the border, and Frank went
weeding as well, and so long as Fred kept out of the
way they got on very happily, and Aunt Elizabeth,
passing, said : " You three industrious people !"

CHAPTER XXVI

AND that afternoon they rode together, Phillis and
Frank. Fred saw them go, stood on the step in the
sun, said, " Oh, I say, I wasn't invited," giving needless
point, thought Frank, darkly under a huge panama, to
a very self-evident, obvious truth.

" You haven't said anything yet about Choice,"
began Phillis, as they walked down the drive.

" I haven't had time to say anything about anything," said Frank, with a laugh ; he was settling into
the saddle.   " Is Choice this nice little lady ?"

Phillis nodded. . . .   " Well, you haven't said anything yet."

" I've said she's nice "—with another laugh.   " I'll
say she's very nice—perhaps—in a minute ; we'll see
how she behaves."

" She always behaves. She has beautiful manners."

" Yours is a powerful beast," said Frank.   " I
suppose you'd call him a roan."

Phillis looked sideways down at him with evident
satisfaction. " His name is Necessity. He's a dear."

Frank watched her, then set off laughing again.

" Why do you laugh all the time ?" said Phillis.

Now, could he possibly tell her why ? He was laughing
for precisely four reasons. One, because of her sideway
look of evident satisfaction ; two, because of the fuss

people (women especially) make with a horse ; three, because the horse in question reminded him of another horse which used to be in the parish church ; four, because he would really rather carry himself than be carried, except, indeed, by locomotives running on properly organized lines.

" If I were an artist——" said Phillis suddenly. " By the way, how does *your* painting get on ?"

" Oh, that gets on all right. . . . Well, if you were an artist, *what ?*"

" If I were an artist, I should paint animals, not men."

" *Would* you ?" said Frank. This was just one of Phillis's speeches.

" The utter impossibility of the premiss," said Frank in high good-humour, " destroys the value of the conclusion."

" What do you mean ?" said Phillis.

" I mean," said Frank at random, " that you must let me be your master. I've a sketch-book in my bag, and a small box of colours, and I'll take you out tomorrow morning, and show you that—that—well, that if you began to paint, you would not stop at dogs and horses, but soar on to the wonders of nature— sunset, star-rise, moonshine."

" Soar on to moonshine," said Phillis. This, again, was like Phillis ; she so rarely understood ; at the same time, she caught hold of words here and there—the beginning, perhaps, and the end—and brought them together conclusively, with, of course, an absurd effect —which wasn't *your* fault ! But they were now in the park, and Phillis had turned her powerful beast aside on the turf, and was urging him into a gallop. Frank followed. Galloping after her kept his attention. When they passed through the iron gates out on the road Frank found himself short of breath.

" One thing I want you to do," said Phillis.

" Anything, anything," Frank gasped out. " Entirely at your service."

" Oh, well," said Phillis, " it wasn't that sort of thing. I want you to come with me to the grave."

" The grave ? . . . Oh yes . . ." said Frank. " Haven't you been there yet ?"

" No ; I waited for you."

" I see. . . . All right. . . . Besides, you must have been busy, Phil. You've got the place awfully jolly. You make a splendid housekeeper." This he really meant. As he had meant it, he repeated it. " You make a splendid housekeeper."

Perhaps he spoke too enthusiastically, for Phillis seemed amused.

" I say, Phil, you'll forgive me, but isn't that chap they call Fred a bit of a stick ?"

" A stick ? My dear Frank, he isn't a stick ; he's a *straw*."

" And why do you have a straw in your house ?"

Phillis only replied with a laugh. The laugh was a little vexatious ; but, then, had Phillis ever in all her life been known to take a hint ? She evidently attached no sort of importance to Frank's remark.

" I hope," he said, " you won't get into the way of picking up with second-rate people."

" Frank, you goose ! I don't pick him up ; he *belongs*. He's somebody Uncle Jasper has to be kind to. Frank ! Frank ! don't lecture *me !* Frank, you were always a prig."

This was in fun, of course. How well she looked in the saddle—more graceful than of old ! and that hat with the ribbon became her.

" I was considering your hat," said Frank, as their eyes met.

She felt it, and said : " Which one ? Oh !"

Frank pushed *his* back from his forehead, then pulled it over again. Besides, they were approaching the church.

He helped her to dismount. " We can tie them up to the gate," said Phillis. " Choice won't stir a foot. . . . There, don't they look pretty ? . . . Yes, you

wonder what we are doing. . . . Don't they wonder,
Frank ? . . . Oh, we'll come back again. . . . Frank,
say something ; do say they look sweet."

Frank said " Yes." He was thinking ; then he
woke up with a start, and said : " Yes, rather ! . . .
Ripping !"

So this was what they had done with the church—
patched it up, and boarded it in. Very likely they
hoped to preserve what was left, and make it the centre
of restoration. He was glad of the patching and
boarding. Somehow it veiled the whole. Also it hid
the detail. He avoided looking, and did not know
when he was passing the door. . . .

The grave. . . . The headstone. . . . Yes, he remembered. His guardian had asked his opinion—this shape
or that ?—and the words ? He had managed to steady
himself and mutter, " Anything anyone likes." And his
guardian had said that certain words had been found
in the desk, the text for the following Sunday's sermon.
" Those'll do," said Frank. . . . There they were :
" *Ye know not what manner of spirit ye are of.*" Frank
saw the meaning in a flash. He had thought the words
were merely scriptural. Merely scriptural ! what is
that ? Well, Biblical, you know—words you had got
to believe, and into which you must put some sort of a
meaning. But they weren't ; they were common-
sense. The meaning was in them already. *Nobody
knows our manner of spirit*—not his nor his father's ;—
his mother's ? Phillis's ? Oh, look at Phillis stooping
there—her plain, her beautiful face—and pulling a
weed from the edging of moss. . . . " Oh, Phillis !"
he said. He caught hold of her arm. He lifted her
up. " Oh, Phillis !" He gripped her still. " I don't
know how it is, but I could *live* with you, I could ;
and I don't think I could live without you."

The next moment he was aghast at what he had
done. He had said something absurd (about living
with her !), lost control of himself (could not live
without her !). And here he was actually sobbing. He

made an effort ; somehow—somewhere—seized upon
his inward being, crushed it back, and slammed
a door. " I say, I'm sorry. . . . Still, it's a fact.
. . . Never mind . . . I was moved. . . . Let's go
away."

" Wait," said Phillis. " Wait !" What was she
going to do ? He dreaded some kind of scene.
" Wait !" Her cheeks were crimson. " You think
you've been foolish, Frank. *I* don't. . . . I didn't
feel like crying at all, but I could cry now. I could !
I could !" She burst into tears.

How he blamed himself, called himself names
secretly and aloud. He hardly knew what he was
saying. " Phil ! Don't ! . . . Don't ! . . . What a
fool I am ! Hush, that's enough. . . . It's all my fault.
Fool ! jackass ! idiot ! . . . Come and look after the
horses !" Was he a coward to leave her ? Coward
as well as fool ? How could he stand and look on
at her, weeping without support ?. . . She joined him
almost immediately.

" I so rarely cry," she excused herself. " When I do,
I'm hopeless. I can't stop."

" Forget it all," said Frank. " Here are these two
wise creatures puzzled to know what the trouble's
about."

She went and kissed each nose. Then she turned
to Frank in a solemn way. " It's a curious thing,"
she said, " but for sympathy there's nothing under the
sun like a horse."

Frank helped her into the saddle. " Talk of the
sun," he said ; "it's piping hot, I know."

And he half believed that afternoon it was the sun
which turned him sick. For they called at the forge
going back, and stood and stood and stood, whilst a
nipper of fourteen or thereabouts, with a leathern apron
and grubby paws, picked a stone from Necessity's
shoe, a job that took half a minute ; but the foreman
and mate must needs jaw, and jaw, and jaw, and jaw—
old times, of course, and the rest of it—until at last

Frank said, "Come along," and the foreman remarked
that he didn't look well. He said it was heat. He
believed that it was, and Phillis said : "There's no
earthly reason why we need stand in the sun."

CHAPTER XXVII

FRANK spent the rest of that summer in town.   Save
for ten days at Rye in August, he never left his rooms
and studio for three whole months.   It was not a
particularly interesting time—not particularly satis-
factory, nor, for that matter, unsatisfactory. He got
through a certain amount of work, and yet, on the
other hand, he did not get through any surprising
quantity.   One day it seemed to him that he had a
good deal to show, and the next day that he had nothing.
His friends found him in varying moods. In strict
confidence, that was rather a knock-down blow he
got last spring over his big subject-picture. It had
been his ambition to exhibit in the Academy before
his twenty-first birthday. That was now impossible.
In other words, his picture was—well—returned. He
made light of the disappointment. He told his friends
—he wished now heartily that he never had mentioned
the picture to one of them, and he had mentioned it
to pretty well all, at least, so it seemed, now that
they came condoling—he told his friends that he
should probably "get in somewhere, possibly Birmingham."   That is, he said this to his serious
friends ; but to his flippant friends he only mocked,
like everyone mocked, each one trying to out-mock the
other.

"And yet," said Frank, when he was left alone with
his picture, "that is not what they *think* of themselves."   It might, of course, be what they thought of
each other. Life was horribly unreal. "Was I such
a rare fool ?" he asked himself, " to think I could paint

Luther flinging his inkpot at the Devil ?" (this was his subject, by the way), " and was I such a rare fool to hope it might hang in this year's Academy ? Am I the rarest fool in London ?. . . I *am* the rarest fool in London !" Hullo, then ! He was face to face with *that* fact, was he ? Very well, and he took his knife and hacked the canvas out of its frame. And when one of his serious friends said to him thoughtfully one day, " Oh, Burnet, how about your picture ? Did you get in anywhere ?" he said, " I didn't send. It wouldn't do." But when two of his flippant friends asked him, " How about Birmingham ?" he said, " They won't have it." And his flippant friends said, " Won't they ? I say, what a shame !"

In his heart of hearts he would sometimes contrast himself with his artist friends, flippant and serious. He would try to place himself just where, in respect of others, he really stood—a most uncomfortable position to take up, since anything is better than one's proper place, which must inevitably seem too low. Still, if he contrasted himself with a fellow like Jim Raikes, he could find comfort. Raikes was of his own term. They started together, and very often they would be engaged upon the same piece of work. It was not that Raikes was stupid, far from it—very, very, far : his natural gifts were great. In a student's competition he had followed a close " second " upon Frank. No, he was not to be sneered at ! But did he put his art before everything ? Did he live for it, talk of it, dream of it ? The idea of Raikes living for Art was laughable. Sooner would he live for a good dinner, and in point of fact, he was known to be particular as to where he dined. His talk, too, ran almost exclusively on sport. Frank was at first pleased to meet a fellow-cricketer, and, on comparing notes, to learn that they had played against one another in their preparatory school elevens. But when he found that Raikes only stopped cricket " shop " to begin football, and racquets, and hockey, and fives, he began to be horribly bored, and also told himself in very plain terms that Raikes would never " do any good." He was very much surprised when Raikes came out " second" in the competition. It only showed what he *might* do. But it would be just a flash in the pan ; and he disagreed entirely with some of the men who said that Raikes was bound to succeed by virtue of his concentration of forces. " Concentration of forces" seemed a curious phrase to use of a fellow who expended his energies in so many different directions. . . . Still, by the way, it *was* energy. Perhaps that was what they meant—concentrated energy at all points ; and Frank eyed Raikes a little curiously.

One is not, however, likely to attain an end which has never been an aim—or, by the way, did it sometimes happen, that a fellow set out not with any intention of arriving anywhere in particular, and then suddenly arrived somewhere, very particular indeed ? With mushroom millionaires—men who had extraordinary strokes of luck—this might be true. Surely it could not be true with men who alone can effect progress by the mastery of all the tedious technicalities of an art. Such men, if they are to mount the rungs, must surely have an aim somewhere at the top of the ladder. Raikes had no such aim. Avowedly, of course, he hadn't, nor in his own conscience, Frank believed. Now yonder little slip of a creature— Jackson was his name—he, if you liked, might climb the ladder. It was generally agreed he would. *There* was concentration of a different kind. Frank envied him his power of patient labour. Yes, *he* worked. No need to question his sincerity. Art came first with him. It was proved without a doubt, not because he talked about it (for he very rarely talked), and not because he dreamt about it (Frank guessed he never dreamed), but because he worked. Day by day he got through something, surmounted something, completed something, and at the end of the term there was always something to show. And you were obliged to admit it was the combined result of genius and infinite pains. He *did* admit it. He admitted it that day of another competition, when Jackson came out first, Raikes third, and Burnet far behind. Frank's picture had been done in a hurry—at least, he acknowledged it now, now that the day was over and he was trundling home, though at the time, when he was engaged in painting the picture (a rather good sunset effect), he had thought it was not so much hurry as inspiration. Jackson's picture had been done in no hurry. The more you looked into it, the more you saw that it was a very finished performance. He did not admit this without a twinge, not of jealousy, but of wounded pride. He had, as a matter of fact, put himself in the way of a rebuff—that is to say, he had displayed some little vanity before a fellow who happened to be possessed of the amiable quality of being able to give the snub direct. Who could have thought it unwise to approach the meek Mr. Jackson, who proved not so meek after all ? Frank had approached him with his picture—his rather good sunset effect—and Mr. Jackson had merely not looked at it ; had set it aside with dignity, and a mild remark about the weather. Frank had turned crimson with shame and vexation. He would never show Jackson a picture again. And yet, of course, Jackson was right—perfectly right—as this afternoon's business had proved, Frank being nowhere in that show. But how does a queer little creature like Jackson become possessed of his amiable quality, and learn to give the snub direct ? His father was a bankrupt pawnbroker—by all accounts not a very pleasant individual—had survived some sort of public disgrace, and had divorced his wife. Jackson—the son—must have had a pretty miserable time of it. He had a wretched, starved appearance (perhaps he did not get enough to eat), and, of course, he had never been to a public school. Now,

if Jackson had been at Winchester, and if his father
had been a parson and his mother a virtuous woman,
Jackson might not have had this amiable quality of
giving the snub direct.

CHAPTER XXVIII

WHEN Frank's aunt, who lived at Surbiton, asked him
whether he was glad he had "embraced an artistic
career" (which she very often did), he always said :
"Oh yes ! What do you mean ?　Yes, rather !"

One of his girl cousins said : " It takes you to such
delightful places !"

Frank said : " Oh yes !　Well, what places ?"

" Why, you've just been at Rye !"

" Yes, but it rained all the time," said Frank.

" You were in Paris ten months," said his other girl
cousin.

" Well, *you've* been in Scotland," said Frank.

" Only six weeks," said his cousin, " and it was
Wales."

" Wales and Scotland, all the same, and Paris, too.
I mean it's all the same world, and the same sun, and
the same moon, and stars, and the same people.　We're
all on the same planet."

" Oh, bother the planet !　Suppose you were a city
clerk."

" If I were a city clerk (though I don't see what
that's got to do with it)," said Frank, " I should be
just as disagreeable as I am now."

" Oh no, you wouldn't, for you'd be less spoilt."

The cousin who said, " Oh, bother the planet !"
was really rather a jolly girl, though she talked dreadfully at random, and almost entirely about tennis.
She played tennis every afternoon of the week at a
club, and on Sundays, when the club was closed, she
played in her friends' gardens.　She begged Frank

again and again to accompany her. Frank did not care much about tennis—the only game he cared for much was cricket—and he generally made it his excuse that Sunday was his only available time, and he did not approve of tennis on Sunday.

" But there is all the rest of the day to go to church in," his cousin objected.

" I know," said Frank ; " but I want the *whole* day to go to church in."

" Oh, I like that ! How many times do you go, I wonder ?"

" Twice."

" Do you ?" An odd look came over his cousin's face. She looked puzzled, distressed, and uncomfortable.

" Besides," went on Frank to comfort her, " I never do anything on a Sunday which I may be called upon to do any other day of the week, except eating."

His cousin laughed ; the distressed look vanished ; she said : " How mad you are !" Then she said : " *I* always go to evensong. We bicycle round to different churches, and it's lovely. Now you can't object to that. Will you come next Sunday ? Heaps of men come."

" I haven't got a bicycle."

" But you can hire."

" My dear, don't tease your cousin," said her mother. " Frank very likely has his own ways of spending his Sunday."

" I'll hire," said Frank.

" There, he *is* coming," said his cousin. " I know you never mean what you say."

But it rained, after all, and they did not go.

The cousin who said he was spoilt, or that he would be less spoilt were he a city clerk, was a different kind of girl—more clever, but not so jolly. She used to vex Frank by her small disparagements of Phillis. She called her " rather a nice little person," and wanted to know what she " did with herself all day."

"Nothing." That was Frank's answer, savage and short. What should Phillis "*do* with herself,"as you call it ? Carry herself about ? Work herself up and down ? Turn nature into mechanism ? Reality into a shadow ? Personality into a thing ? Change from a living girl to an existing type ? *She* was a type—his cousin he meant—and a Citizen, and a future Mother of other Citizens, and a Daughter of the State. It would be unfair to say she was jealous of Phillis, though it was certainly awkward that he, their blood-relation, should be some sort of blood-relation to Phillis, and they no relation at all. Still, it would be unfair to say she was jealous, and it would be unfair to say she was conceited. (Frank knocked off one by one the things which it would be unfair to say.) And it would be unfair to say she was stupid, because she was clever, distinctly so, very well educated, too. She had been to school and college, as, indeed, had all her friends. Frank once made some remarks about women's colleges, but they were rather weak, decidedly weak, and he withdrew them, and when his cousin said, "You see, unfortunately you are not a University man yourself," he was obliged to admit that was so, and, tacitly, that he had spoken with ignorant prejudice and the most ridiculous personal bias and spite. . . . Horrid ! . . . True, however. She was good-looking—in fairness he must say that—pretty eyes, pretty hair ; but she did not seem to intend to use them in any way—for anyone's honest pleasure, that is. So far as that goes, her ideas about marriage were all statistical. Still, he should never laugh at her. She was consistent, he believed, and probably he was less consistent and a great deal more absurd. And really she *did* work hard, fagged herself out, tired those eyes and dulled that hair, as Frank, with the artist's look, discerned. Oh, inexhaustible energy ! She never directly told Frank that she thought him feeble, but she implied it many times. She was always trying to rouse him, argue him into some sort of mental or bodily activity. She did inform him once that he was horribly ignorant of everything going on in the world about him.

"If, instead of painting Luther and the Devil, you would paint some of the miseries of twentieth-century existence," she said, " you would be better employed, and might get your picture accepted into the bargain."

There was some truth in this, of course—in the latter part, that is. But when Frank urged in defence that " all centuries were alike," and that " he didn't think the twentieth century, taken all round, was better or worse than any other," and that " good and evil were inherent principles," his cousin said : " We can listen to that any day from the pulpit." And his aunt, who came in at that moment and heard (he supposed) the last remark, said good-naturedly : " I always *did* think Frank ought to have been a clergyman." And his cousin sniffed, and went out of the room.

" Yes, Frank," his aunt continued, " I cannot understand why some of you young men do not take holy orders—good, steady, clever, religious young men. Why don't you, now ?"

" I can't tell why the other good, steady, clever, religious young men don't," said Frank with a laugh— he liked his aunt the best of the lot—" but I can tell you why *I* don't. It's because I've got no gift that way. If I've any gift . . ." He was going to say, " If I've any gift at all, it's art," but he left that out as unimportant.

" What do you mean by ' gift ' ?" said his aunt. " And what does a clergyman want with gifts ?"

" Oh, well—preaching. My sermons would be so dull."

" I don't see why they should be duller than other people's. Besides, you would have been ordained. I suppose that makes a difference."

" I hope so," said Frank, " or it's a poor lookout."

" Nobody seems to set any store by these things nowadays. My girls never go to church, except when they can ride and make a round. *I* always went. I'm sure I don't know how I should ever have got on without it, for your uncle was so much away on circuit, and there was nobody to ask. Nowadays young people seem so much more capable of deciding things for themselves. I suppose it's better education. Still, neither of the girls can speak modern languages as I could, and they can neither of them keep accounts."

" I'm sure they will have to live a long time to know half as much as you," was what Frank *thought*, but what he *said* was : " I didn't get on with French a bit, though I was in Paris all those months."

" It's in your family," said his aunt.

" What ? The incapacity to acquire French ?"

" My dear boy, I said nothing about French !" (nor had she, but then Frank had). " I meant the Church. Look at your father, and grandfather, and great-grandfather. And you are the image of your father. Such a help he was to me, too ! Such a comfort in my troubles, and I'm sure I've had enough ! I never knew your father make a mistake except in his own affairs, and your uncle always said that he was one of the wisest of men."

Frank said something which was meant to sound like " Yes." It was horribly hot, and he wiped his forehead.

" And you're like him, Frank, as like can be."

" I'm tall," said Frank.

" It wasn't the height I meant," said his aunt ; " it was the similarity in *character*."

Frank said the same sort of " Yes " again.

Though he liked his aunt—sometimes he almost loved her—Frank wished she had rather more sense. He did not know whether it was the fault of the girls, who perhaps put ideas into her head, but she would suggest all sorts of indiscreet plans for the amusement of what she called " young people." " Young people " in this connection was an offensive phrase, for it meant a lot of men and girls who were not young at all—at least, quite old enough to look after themselves and know " just how far you can go." As if anyone knows how far he can go, or where he is going, or where he has got to ! Frank should most certainly be on his guard. When Dolly, his younger cousin, was starting out on her bicycle with a medical student to whom, for the time, she seemed rather attached, her mother would say, " Where are you young people off to ?" But when they were coming back from a theatre, and his aunt said two hansoms would do, " and you can go with Dolly, and Helena " (that was the other one) " will look after me," he resolutely beckoned a four-wheeler, and it extricated itself and came, and they all packed in, and even if Dolly did not like it, it was a great deal better that she should.

Besides, she (that is to say, his aunt) arranged such river-picnic parties. You went and got yourself mixed up with the queerest set of people, and you could never be sure that you would not find yourself paired off with somebody, and placed in a really awkward position. He went to one in June and another in July, avoided one in August, but was practically forced into attending the last, which was fixed for the end of September. He did his best to enjoy it, but he loathed it. His elder cousin—Helena, that is—was very stiff that day. She seemed to have started out with the notion that he either had done or intended to do something dreadfully wrong. When he offered to carry a basket up from the boat, she said, " Oh, I don't think we need trouble *you*," and not five minutes later attacked him before the whole crowd with, " Now then, make yourself useful." She went off after lunch, however, with a certain Mrs. Somebody who was a guardian, and discussed the poor. Of Dolly he saw very little ; she had a bosom friend with her, and they kept themselves strictly apart. There came occasional shrieks of laughter, and once or twice they passed, nodding their heads in talk. They were in that mood when man is no necessity.

Frank found himself consequently thrown with his

aunt, and with two girls his aunt had lately " taken
up." He had met them at a dance before, one in
white and one in pink, sisters, and he had danced
with both. He tried to dance with both twice, but he
missed the pink one till his card was full, and then, just
like his luck, passed her a dozen times standing in re-
proachful attitudes, and had to disappoint her—himself, he should have said. He judged the pink girl had
forgiven him ; she also was in white to-day. At first
he thought them rather pleasant ; then he began to
get annoyed, not with them so much as with his aunt
and the other fellows who had come, some of his aunt's
" young people." Nice " boys " these ; stayed fooling
down by the boats whilst Frank and his aunt laid out
the lunch with the help of the two white girls, then
strolled up—" Oh, I say, can't we help ?" when everything was ready. Nothing then for them to do but
jest over the dishes. And the odd thing was that
Frank felt sure while they jested over the dishes they
were jesting over *him*, and that somehow he was supposed to be a young bird easily caught. What confirmed this opinion was the conduct of the two white
girls, for, having been particularly warm and friendly—
a little inclined to flirt, Frank thought—*before* lunch
and in setting out the table (that is to say, they said
many things they obviously did not mean, and this,
he supposed, would constitute flirting), *after* lunch, all
at once they grew haughty, first chilled him with their
indifference, then froze him up with their pride, and
then, just as he was recovering from that violent
change of temperature, plunged him into another
before tea, ran up in fits of ill-controlled laughter to
tell him some story against the men, and finally, rowing
back with him, paid not the smallest heed to anything
he ventured to say, but seemed to derive a great deal
of amusement from the conversation which they kept
up with Dolly, now grown sociable with three men in
the other boat. And whether the man who was rowing
with Frank was annoyed that he wasn't with Dolly,

or put out about something else, he smoked in grim silence all the way home. Frank rather thought it was Dolly, for when they reached the landing-stage, he waited behind to join the others, and there they flittered and fluttered about, Dolly, her friend, and the two white sisters, whilst Helena and the guardian set off rapidly in the direction of home, and Frank found himself left with his aunt and the cushions.

" It's no use waiting for those young people," said his aunt, and they toiled up the bank together. " It was *so* good of you to come," she said, as he stood on the doorstep with his burden. His aunt had a worried look ; perhaps she was tired. . . . " Oh, not at all. . . . Yes, it has been a delightful day."

" If she's had a beastly head on like I've had the whole of this blessed afternoon," thought Frank, " I should think it *has* been delightful."

And when he got back to his lodgings, there was a letter from Marchington, a letter from Phillis—bold, big hand :

" DEAR FRANK,

" Could you come to us for a few days this week, next week, or any week after ? Uncle Jasper and Daisy are with us now. We've had a lovely summer, and it doesn't seem over yet ; so do come, if you're not too busy.

" Your affectionate
" PHILLIS.

" Aunt Elizabeth sends her love."

He read the note through twice, and the last few words he stared at, and when he went to sleep that night he conned them over again. " *We've had a lovely summer, and it doesn't seem over yet . . . do come. . . . Your affectionate Phillis. . . . Aunt Elizabeth sends her love. . . .*" Yes, even that grim old lady ! And the best of it was, it was genuine ; not a word was spoken in Marchington Manor that wasn't true to the uttermost syllable.

CHAPTER XXIX

PHILLIS, at any rate, spoke the truth—that is the point which matters—Aunt Elizabeth also as a rule, possibly also Daisy.   As to the rest, you could not say that they spoke what was false ; it was neither false nor true, not to be weighed in any scales but a featherweight balance. It was rubbish—an odd, surface kind of talk.   Though it was different in many degrees to the talk of the men in college (for, remember, those were distinguished men with, after all, *something* to say—Science, the Poet, and Lords), yet Frank was reminded again and again of those old sensations he used to have when all the time that he argued he was asking himself, " But is it really so in practice ?"—the sensation now expressed in a different form : " What is the worth of all this rubbish ?"

Take such an instance as this, for example : Daisy lost her dog.   Daisy was genuinely sorry, genuinely distressed.   What does everyone say and do ?   Phillis is equally sorry—more sorry, perhaps, because she is fond not only of Daisy's dog, but of Daisy ; hers is a double distress.   Daisy and Phillis tell everybody.   It is just after breakfast.   Fred comes over the lawn with a putter and golf-ball.   " Alexander's lost !" says Daisy.

" No, I say, he isn't !"   Whack goes the ball.

" Not seen since seven this morning."

" No, by Jove ! but he'll turn up."   After the ball goes Fred.

At the far end of the garden near the copse who but Major Bob.

" Alexander's lost," says Phillis.

" He's not !"

" He *is*," said Phillis, and passed on.   She might, perhaps, have noticed a provoking similarity between Major Bob's and Fred's remarks.

Phillis's uncle next arrived.

" Alexander's lost," says Phillis.

" Not really !"

Says Daisy : " Not seen since seven this morning."

Her father peered into the bushes.   " We must have a good look round."

But when it came to Aunt Elizabeth—" Alexander lost ?" she said.   " Go and find him."

Nobody found him in the end.   He was brought back.   Phillis and Daisy had given up search.   Exhausted by their morning's profitless labour, they sat all the afternoon under shady hats in the glare of the hot September sun.   Meanwhile Frank sweltered on, mile after mile, scoured the country, heard of him here, heard of him there.   Not a terrier, no.   A black Aberdeen ?   Yes, of course—came home disgusted, vexed, and sorry, to find Alexander in Daisy's arms.

" Down at the forge," said Phillis.

" Boy brought him," said Daisy.

" I knew he'd turn up," said Major Bob.

" I guess he *would !*" said Fred.

" Hot, eh ?" said Bob.

" You look it !" said Fred.

Frank only pulled Alexander's ears and called him a " young rotter," but up in his room he laughed a short laugh.   And the laugh was justified.   Who had looked for the dog ?   Frank.   Who had found it ?   Some boy.   Who talked about it ?   Everybody.   Just as if there were nothing else to say but, " *I* hunted here," and, " *You* hunted there," and, " Fancy his not coming back for his dinner !"   And then an occasional burst from Major and cackle from Fred, the joke, of course, being that Frank should have scoured the country, and the little brute down at the forge all the time.

" And by the way, Phillis," said Frank, as if the joke were now at an end, " that fellow might have brought it round before the afternoon."

" Oh, that's Wattie all over !" said Phillis.   " He never puts himself about."

Take another example. Aunt Elizabeth one day hurt her foot. She was in bed for a fortnight. Here was the same irritating uniformity of opinion. No one seemed to believe it was true. First Bob said : " No, not really !" then Fred said : " No, I say !" Even Daisy said : " She *hasn't !*" It was Frank himself who told them, in the drawing-room, gathered for tea. He had helped to carry her up the stairs, so he knew ; and he also knew more or less how it happened, and who it was that brought her home ; at least, from the description, most probably it was the Vicar's son. . . . " Vicar's son ? What was he like ?" says Daisy. " I'll tell you if it's the Vicar's son." " A very nice boy," replies Frank ; " that is your aunt's description. 'A handsome Apollo'—those were her words." " Who was Apollo ?" Fred wanted to know. " In this case," says Frank, " a boy, youth, lad. 'A sweet, clean creature,' that's what she says." " It can't be the Vicar's son," says Fred. Silly observation ! He repeats it to Phillis as she comes in : " Is your present Vicar's son a sweet, clean creature Apollo ?" . . . " Daisy, make the tea." . . . " Yes, but we want to know—that is to say, did he bring your Aunt Elizabeth home ?" " Who ?" " The Vicar's son. Frank said he did."

" Nonsense ! It was the blacksmith's boy. . . ."

You may be sure *that* joke sufficed.

Or, again, for a final example, when they went cubbing one morning, and everything seemed wrong from the first. There was a fuss as to who should ride what. Overnight Fred had bargained for Choice. Frank held his tongue. When appealed to, he said he cared not a rap either way. He himself now believed that Fred, who was ill—sneezing and shivering—that Fred had made up his mind to ride with the rest of the party to-morrow in order that Frank might be spited, and cheated, and fooled, for Frank had allowed in company that he preferred " a horse he understood."

" But you *must* ride a horse once for the first time," had said Phillis. " Yes, I know," had said Frank ;

and he had proceeded in perhaps what seemed a round-about way to explain just when it was, and why it was, and how it was he mistrusted or trusted a horse, ending up where he had begun—that as he had ridden Choice before, he would rather ride Choice again, unless, indeed, Phillis, should wish, etc. Consequently, he had ridden Choice habitually—never ridden any other —until that night when (surely in malice) Fred, with two violent sneezes, protested *he* wanted to try the mare.

"The argument will best be settled," said Phillis to Fred when they all bade good-night—"the argument will best be settled by your keeping your room to-morrow. Will you have some lozenges ?"

"Anyway," Frank decided, a little warm as he went upstairs, "Fred shall not ride Choice to-morrow." There was no good in yielding—positive harm, in fact.

Fred did not ride Choice, but he rode for all that. He sent word first thing to the stables, and appeared a little after the rest, sneezing good-morning to every-one. Frank did not wait ; he went on—he went on with Daisy, then with Phillis. Fred and the Major were left in the fog. Then the business began. Choice lost a shoe near the forge, but what was the good of the forge with nobody there, only a boy? Phillis meant well, but bothered ; tried to be cheerful ; en-couraged the boy. Up came the rest. Frank puts as good a face as he can on the matter ; apologizes for the delay. . . . Odd how people accept apologies ! "Do go on," said Frank.

"That's what we thought of doing," said Bob.

. . . And Fred ? Why on earth did he come at all, if he meant to turn sick and go home, and, as a signal act of unselfishness, bequeath his brute to Frank ? . . . He had never ridden Necessity. There was no way out of it, though. It seemed like some plot against him. He hated himself for the very thought, and yet even Phillis laughed, and said : "Come along ! I can't hear ! Come along ! . . ." It was a thousand

pities he had not kept cool ; it was a thousand pities
he had allowed himself to be worked up into a fever.
His agitation troubled the horse, and when it came to
the matter of jumping a hedge, they were neither fit
to be put to the proof. . . It was all very well to say
that he ought to have jumped that hedge. The most
ridiculous rubbish was talked. They all began about
that jump sitting at breakfast — precious jump !
Well, never mind, they were pleased with themselves,
and Frank would have listened cheerfully, only they
fell on him all at once : How had *he* jumped ? Why
didn't *he* speak ? . . . Why *should* he speak ? he
wanted to know. " My good people, if I had jumped
the moon, would it be absolutely essential to let
the whole world hear of it ? . . ."

" We are not talking about the moon Frank," Phillis
had swiftly said (how words burn into your brain !).
" We are talking about that hedge."

" Well, there's nothing so special about that hedge.
I dare say it's not the first time I've jumped it."

" Oh, then you *did* jump it," Phillis had said. " I
almost began to think. . . ."

Wait ! Was he honest ? . . . Ah, wait ! Let him
set facts in order. He was trying to pass as an instance
of rubbish a series of very vital facts. Fact one, he
feared Necessity ; fact two, he feared that hedge ;
fact three, he had not jumped that hedge ; fact four,
he made out that he had ; fact five, when asked point-
blank by Phillis, he must confess he hadn't ; fact six,
he excused himself because he was not on Choice ;
fact seven, she called him coward and liar. . . . She
called him coward and liar ! Oh, never mind about
rubbish now ; he had passed on to other considerations.
Was all the rubbish talked in the world worth a
moment's debate, worth excusing, condemning, worth
anything by the side of these facts—seven *facts* in one
morning, seven startling facts, unquestionable facts,
proved to the hilt, between getting up and eating your
breakfast ? She called him a coward and liar ! So

it appears he is. Well, well, well—a discovery.
Discovery indeed ! Had he not known it all his life ? ...
There was only one point to consider : should she
have called him a coward and liar in front of other
people ? "I hate cowards and liars !" She said it
with angry, flaming cheeks and hard tears in her eyes.

"Oh, Phillis !" This was Daisy.

"Phillis, my dear !" This was Uncle Jasper.

"Humph !" This was Aunt Elizabeth.

"Steady, my lady." This was Bob.

Frank could have screamed aloud. He really believed now that pains must have somehow run through
him—*physical* pains, a chill, perhaps, from the misty
morning, some of Fred's sneezing sickness. It was
only by a supreme effort that he controlled himself
and sat there.

> "Oh, Woman ! in our hours of ease,
> Uncertain, coy, and hard to please."

Fred, who stood by the fire, back to the company,
quoted the verse.

"Very apt ! Very apt !" said Bob. "I wasn't
aware you knew any poetry, Fred, my boy," he
added.

"It's on this calendar," said Fred, turning round,
and there was the calendar on the wall.

> "When pain and anguish wring the brow,
> A ministering angel thou !

Frank, old man, you've upset the ladies." For
Phillis and Daisy had disappeared. Frank, like the
ladies, went out of the room.

He had afterwards done the only thing to give him
any peace of mind. He had seized his first chance,
ordered Necessity, ridden him out one afternoon,
retraced all the up and down gallop, found himself
in the sloping field, bobbing along, bobbing alone ;
made for the hedge, squashed every scruple—let the
horse do it if he could ! . . . Thought himself dead,

felt himself living ; turned by a single sycamore, cut
out another way home again ; sat down to lunch, and
solemnly weighed and considered whether Phillis were
justified or not ; whether one should or should not
express these decided opinions ; whether lies were lies
and terrors terrors, to be meek a vice or a virtue ;
whether one ought to bluster and brag, to give back
as good as you got, and see to it that when you were
hurt somebody else suffered too.

And yet the very next day he began his design for
the pulpit which Phillis had asked him to do.

CHAPTER XXX

THIS design he completed afterwards when he got
back to town. It took him a long time to finish. It
was to stand in Marchington Church, which was slowly
being restored. The idea was a sort of glorification
of preaching. Though he had often talked nonsense,
as everyone talks, about preaching, he had always
been secretly convinced that preaching (anyway, at
its best) was really a wonderful art, or, rather, it was
not an *art* at all. It was no medium, no expression
of a Thing behind ; it was the Thing itself. It was Life
pouring out through a natural channel—no paint, no
pen, no instrument to force it this way or the other,
and dam it up with a hundred and one technicalities.
The power to paint a picture was something belonging
to you ; the power to preach was nothing belonging, it
was you. It was you with all your beliefs, hopes,
doubts, sorrows, sins, temptations, deliverances, and
so on and so on. You, untrimmed, untrained, unsized,
unsorted : you, big with yourself ; and pray, what else
is there to be big with ? " *You* must be born," said
Christ.

But, argues the Poet, the Painter and the Musician,
and everyone else with a gift to hand, our Art is an

outpouring as well. Not an outpouring, Frank contended, but a setting forth on the stream. One thing to set out in a boat, well equipped if you like, but only a boat to hold body and soul, only a boat to take count of the winds of Wealth and Fame, and the calms of Indolence and Exhaustion ; and another thing to leap naked, body and soul, in the flood—you and the flood, that was all ; just Life, or as near to the intimate living of Life as it seems possible to go.

And yet, of course, if anyone were to come and say, " Then why the dickens don't you preach, and stop this messing about with Art ?" Frank would be annoyed. He would not, in fact, have anyone know these opinions of his about Preaching and Art. Why should he be called upon to leap naked into the flood when other people picked their way daintily in well-equipped craft ? to live this intimate Life, absorbed by it, lost in it, when other people looked on, neither absorbed nor lost ? . . . The Rev. Hedley Burnet, preaching to a score of people twice on a Sunday (and always the same score, mind !), may be nearer to the living Life than Frank Burnet, Esq., his son, exhibitor, then R.A. Only if nobody thinks so but *you*, where is the comfort ? And just because you happen to have a more correct sight than other people, are you obliged to let everyone know and suffer accordingly— be true (as you must) to your professions, leap in the flood and be lost to fame ? . . . " Besides," thought Frank — and here, perhaps, was the real hitch—" I couldn't preach ; I've nothing to say." . . . Nothing to paint, too ? Ah, perhaps ! But who would be sharp enough to discover ?

And meantime he finished his pulpit design. He really believed the treatment was fair. Elijah represented the separation of good and evil, *attitude positive ;* John Baptist the examination, *attitude uncompromising ;* Christ the disposition, *attitude supreme.* . . . When he brought his drawing to Marchington, Phillis made an odd suggestion. Whether it was she did not care for the figure of Christ, or whether it was she had lost her temper with Pigeon, the clerk of the works (for being a knave, which some men can't help), anyway, she said she would have preferred the Cleansing of the Temple. If he had not been so sure that wit was not Phillis's strongest point, and, moreover, that jokes on sacred matters would be to her most distasteful, he should have thought the suggestion had something to do with the fraudulent Pigeon, who was standing there with the boy. He did not say much in reply, only " Hum !" or " Oh !" or possibly " Ah !" because it was no good explaining to Phillis the merits of his Christ on the Mount, and he hated snubbing anybody.

PART VI

WATTIE

"Hush! if you saw some western cloud. . . ."

CHAPTER XXXI

WATTIE had not seen Mr. Frank for some time, when he turned up again one day. He was grown quite the man. Wattie had been sent to the station to fetch some bundles of iron from Brinkley, and the same train which brought the iron brought Mr. Frank ; and just as Wattie came poking about the goods-van, Mr. Frank came poking too.

" I want that carried up to The Bell," said Mr. Frank ; and he hit a smart yellow bag a whack with his stick.

" Yes, sir," said the porter, and shoved him aside, and Mr. Frank's legs went down the platform.

He was wearing a grey flannel suit. Wattie believed that same flannel suit passed him upon the road after dark, walking rapidly, twirling the stick. He was pretty well sure, for it disappeared into The Bell, and only a very few seconds after a light was set burning in one of the windows, and it went on burning a long, long time.

It was certainly Mr. Frank who came out of The Bell soon after ten the next morning reading the news. Wattie, inside the forge, was not so terribly busy but that he could watch Mr. Frank going up and down, flapping his paper and smoking his pipe —up and down, up and down, in his Norfolk coat and without any hat ; and then he returned to The Bell.

He was emerging again just as Wattie went hop,

skip, and a jump for the beer. He had changed the
Norfolk coat for the grey flannel suit, and the newspaper for his walking-stick, and his dark face was
under a big panama. Wattie stood back to let him
come out ; and he came out and strode down the road
in the direction of Marchington Manor.

Mr. Frank did not lunch at The Bell that day—at
least, that was Wattie's opinion ; for when he went
with the pewters at one o'clock the place was deserted.
He was not in the smallest degree surprised to see Mr.
Frank and Miss Phillis in the village that afternoon.
They were walking, and Miss Phillis was leaving
magazines. Wattie was stuck at the saddler's, where
they kept him for half an hour. Under ordinary
circumstances this would have been annoying, but, as
it was, he sat down in the shop and looked out through
the open door. Miss Phillis carried a basket, and
Mr. Frank carried his walking-stick. They were ever
and ever so far away, the other side of the green, and
they kept stopping, first here, then there. Miss Phillis
went to the doors and knocked, and Mr. Frank stood
on the path outside, and stared up and down, and
twirled his stick, and pushed his hat back off his forehead.

Next day they came to the forge together. Wattie
could hear their voices—Mr. Frank's voice, at least.
He caught the word " *pictures* " . . . " accepted " . . .
" rejected " . . . " Lucky for me !" . . . " Hullo !
there's nobody here."

" Yes, there is," said Miss Phillis ; and Wattie came
out.

" Is *this* the chap ?" said Mr. Frank. " I'd clean
forgotten."

Miss Phillis said, " Good-morning, Wattie," and,
" You remember Mr. Frank."

" Good-morning, miss," said Wattie. He saluted
Mr. Frank—Mr. Frank now quite the man.

" By Jove !" said Mr. Frank, " you were the young-
ster who took a stone—I know perfectly well."

How Mr. Frank did stare !

" Good !" he said to Miss Phillis.

What in the world was good ?

" Have you ever sat as a model ?" But this he asked of Wattie.

" No, sir," said Wattie, biting his lip. Mr. Frank was always like this ; he was enough to set anyone off. There was Miss Phillis couldn't help laughing.

" *Of course* he hasn't," Miss Phillis said ; " he has something else to do."

" Well, I'll give him a shilling an hour to sit."

" He'll want more than a shilling," said Miss Phillis, " to get him to sit."

Wattie had not the remotest intention of sitting, but it wasn't for him to speak. He was puzzled to know what they meant. Mr. Frank would say sooner or later.

" Look here," said Mr. Frank ; " I'm there at The Bell, do you see ?" He pointed through the door, and Wattie looked out with interest.

" Very well," said Mr. Frank. " You come across some time, and I'll put you into a picture."

" When ?" asked Wattie.

" I'm working most mornings," said Mr. Frank.

" So am I," said Wattie ; " and afternoons."

Miss Phillis was laughing again, and then she suddenly stopped. " Mr. Frank paints beautiful pictures," she said. " Wattie would like to see your pictures, Frank," she suddenly said. " He tries to paint a little himself. I have just persuaded him to let me see one of his works of art ; it is up at the Manor ; you shall see it."

Wattie hoped not.

" Are you fond of painting ?" said Mr. Frank ; his face lit up as he spoke.

" Not so wonderful fond," said Wattie.

He had better far have said " Yes " and done with it, for Miss Phillis rounded upon him.

" How can you say such a thing ? All the time last year when your arm was bad you painted a lot. I came and saw you."

" What was up with your arm ?" Mr. Frank inquired.

" I knocked it against a horse," said Wattie. He was sure Mr. Frank didn't want to know ; he only wanted to go on staring.

" Yours is a ticklish job," said Mr. Frank, not thinking of what he was saying ; and he turned to Miss Phillis. " Good !" he said for the second time. (Wattie began to have a suspicion.) " Good !" he said. " Excellent ! I think I see my way again to the Royal Academy. Will the chap do it ? That's the question."

" Wattie would willingly help you, I'm sure."

" What *is* it, miss, exactly you want me to do ?" Wattie thought he might just as well ask.

This time it was Mr. Frank who laughed. Miss Phillis was going to explain, but Mr. Frank began first.

" It's like this," he said. " I'm an artist ; that's my job. Just as you are a blacksmith by trade, so I'm an artist, do you see ?"

" Wattie's a *very good* blacksmith by trade," Miss Phillis here put in.

" And I'm a very good artist," said Mr. Frank in an odd, quick way—" at least, I intend to be. Don't interrupt me, Phillis. Well, what was I saying ? . . . Painting's my job ; and this year, mark you—this very year, this very remarkable, memorable year—I've got a picture in *Burlington House*, the *Royal Academy*, you know ; and next year I want to get another, and I doubt if I can, unless you help."

" Which means," said Miss Phillis—" which means . . . yes, Frank, you've talked enough . . . which means, in simple English, that he wants to paint your portrait."

" Oh !" said Wattie ; and then, like a fool, he blushed

up to the roots of his hair ; and he must have looked
very silly, or else said something rude, for Miss Phillis
and Mr. Frank went out, Mr. Frank brushing the sleeve
of his coat.

CHAPTER XXXII

WATTIE hoped he should hear no more of sitting for
Mr. Frank, but the very next day, as he was passing
The Bell, Mr. Frank hailed him from one of the ground-
floor windows.   He was hanging out, smoking a cigarette.   He now proceeded to throw up the window a trifle
higher and jump on to the flower-bed.   Then he came
over the road in his Norfolk coat and shiny slippers.

" How about that portrait ?" said the Royal
Academy.

" What portrait ?" said Wattie.

" Well, aren't you going to sit for me ?"

" Am I ?" said Wattie.   " I didn't know."

Mr Frank brushed his cigarette-ash against the heel
of one shiny slipper.   " What time do you knock off ?"
he said, and stood upright on his feet.

" Six o'clock," said Wattie.

" Famous," said Mr. Frank.   " Six to eight . . . light
evenings. . . .   Call in here at six.   You've only to
ask for me."

" How about my tea ?"

" Confound your tea !" said Mr. Frank.   " Can't
you do without your tea ?"

" No, sir, I can't."

" Bless my soul ! how many times do you suppose
I've gone without *my* tea ?"

Wattie did not hazard a guess.   It was also not to
the point.

" If you stick at a tea," said the Royal Academy,
" you'll never get on in the world."

" I don't want to get on in the world," said Wattie—
" not if it costs me my tea."

" The British workman !" said Mr. Frank, throwing his cigarette into the ditch. " Come what may, he must have his tea."

" Yes, sir, he must," said Wattie.

" *Brett !*" roared the foreman ; and Wattie ran.

Wattie spoke to the foreman—presently. He said : " I want to get done at half-past five."

The foreman said nothing then, but that afternoon, at half-past five, he looked up and nodded, and Wattie went home.

He went home and cleaned himself. For this operation he had the assistance of Mrs. Moon's kettle, which was hissing (most luckily) on the hob. He used plenty of soap and a pumice-stone ; he then plastered his hair to make it lie down ; after this he effected a change of clothes, a white shirt instead of a striped one, and his Sunday suit out of the cupboard. He also put on a high linen collar, and a bright red-and-black spotted tie, which the girl at The Bell had given him. Then, going into the yard, to match the tie, he picked a rose which was almost magenta. Finally he went down the street, and met Mr. Frank with an innocent face.

" What on earth——" began Mr. Frank. (He liked Mr. Frank's expression.) " What on earth—I mean, come in ! I'm glad you've turned up. Punctual, I see, to the minute."

" Ten minutes late," said Wattie.

" Ten minutes late, are you, by Jove ! . . . Up-stairs—the room on your left."

Wattie was made to go first, whether he liked it or not ; Mr. Frank got his revenge ; and now in Mr. Frank's private apartment he turned uncomfortably shy. He stood without moving, and watched Mr. Frank.

Mr. Frank was quite at his ease. He was rummaging in a corner, and cheerfully whistled a tune. Presently he looked up. " Come and stand over here," he said.

Wattie went. Every bone in his body he stiffened.

Mr. Frank sighed. " Well, get along. Sit in that

chair. Turn your face to the window, and hold your tongue."

He began to arrange his canvas. " You needn't sit so desperately still," Mr. Frank went on in a minute ; " I'm not ready yet to begin." There appeared to be a good deal of necessary preparation, but when Mr. Frank said, " Confound !" Wattie knew that he had begun.

" Look up a bit," said Mr. Frank. " Don't stare so ! What are you fixing your eyes upon ?"

" May I speak ?" said Wattie.

" Yes, of course."

" Then I don't know."

" Don't know what ?"

" What I'm fixing my eyes upon."

" Good heavens ! Well, suppose you look out of the window, right out and forget yourself. Look at the roof over there . . . jolly red tiles, for instance."

" It's the forge," said Wattie. " I'd rather not."

" Well, that tree, then—groups of trees—limes— whatever they are. Look at them, think of them. . . . You're *not* thinking of them. I can see you're not."

" I don't know what to think of them."

" Think how jolly and sweet they smell, and how the bees buzz in the blossom, and how ripping if one could only lounge about in the shade of them all the days of one's life. . . . Ah, now ! Wait a minute."

They waited several minutes, if you could call it waiting, going on like that. Then Mr. Frank burst out once more.

" You're fixed again ! Wake up ! You're not thinking of what I told you."

" I've finished thinking of that."

" Think of something else. Think of anything. . . . Stay ! Think of what you were thinking of yesterday when I saw you down at the forge. What was it ?"

" Work, I reckon," said Wattie.

" Think of it now."

" I'd rather not."

" What is the pleasantest thing in the world ?"

" A kicking horse," said Wattie.

" Think of a kicking horse, then."

" With somebody else on top."

" You can think of *me* on the top, if you like,"
Mr. Frank said, splashing away. " The idea," he went
on (how did he know ?)—" the idea seems to yield
you some amusement." He walked to the mantelpiece for a light. " Suppose," he said, puffing,
" you hold your tongue, and let *me* have a turn. . . .
Yes, very good ; keep so till I give you leave to
move."

The silence seemed very long.   Really the next thing
that happened was that Mr. Frank strolled to the
window and threw out the end of his cigarette.   When
he came back he stood opposite Wattie.

" It's incredible," he said, and ran his white fingers
through his dark hair. " Where's it all gone to ?" he
groaned.

Wattie looked sympathetic.

" Are you a young man given to moods ?"

" Given to what ?" asked Wattie.

" Moods.   I mean, are you up one minute, and down
the next ?"

" I'm pretty well up and down all day," said Wattie
blandly.

Mr. Frank burst out laughing.   " Thank your stars,"
he said. " And yet," he went on, as he finished
laughing, " the mystery remains.   What angel was it
visited you yesterday afternoon ? . . ."

Mr. Frank was bending over his palette. . . . " By
which I mean," Mr. Frank went on, " why did you
look like a piece of pure poetry *then*,, and *now—now* . . .
What have you been doing with yourself since yesterday afternoon ?"

" Work," said Wattie.

" *Work !*   That's it ; kills the soul !   Where did you
put my matches ?"

" May I move ?"

" Move ? Yes, confound you ! You're moving perpetually."

" Then they're *there*."

" Thanks," said Mr. Frank. " *Work !*" he said. " Work, work, work !" He seemed to be going to say something else. " What's the good of it all ? What's the outcome, the net result ? What do we do it for, I wonder ?"

" Wages," said Wattie.

" Ah yes, by Jove ! yes," said Mr. Frank, seizing on an idea. " Yes, by Jove ! *you've* got to live ; *you've* got to *live*."

Wattie was puzzled. " *Die*, you mean."

" No, I don't," said Mr. Frank. " Death is a comparatively easy job. It's all done for you, and you assume no responsibility. Life's the trouble—when, how, where, and why to live. And yet one can't help living with the daily bread dropping into one's mouth. Now, *you can* help living. Stop work, and you find yourself dying, and to find yourself dying is, after all, worse than to find yourself living. I've never found myself dying yet, therefore I've never got thoroughly keen about living. *I* don't have to keep myself alive, *you* have ; and you must get awfully keen at times—I mean when it's cold and the fire's gone out, or you're hungry and there's nothing for supper. Jolly !" said Mr. Frank, and he meant it.

" It might be," said Wattie. " I really don't know."

Mr. Frank laughed again. " Very well, then," he said, " you really don't know. I thought you did, but you don't ; there once more is the beauty of it. Still, it's a fact, you've *got to live*, to earn your *living wage*."

" Worse luck I have," said Wattie.

" You may thank your stars," said Mr. Frank. " Thank your stars there's not two hundred a year coming in at the quarters whether you like it or not— much too little and a little too much. Do you suppose for one moment you'd continue to work if you'd got two hundred a year ?"

" Work !" said Wattie. " Stand and look on !"

" Exactly. And you wonder what the dickens *I'm* busy about." He was lighting his cigarette. " It's a queer thing, but as soon as there's no need to take up work, a man finds he can't put it down."

CHAPTER XXXIII

" Look here," said Mr. Frank—it was the following evening—" look here, about that collar . . ."

" It was clean enough when I started."

" Clean enough now," said Mr. Frank. " I wish you'd take it off."

Wattie wrenched at the nape of his neck.

" Much obliged," said Mr. Frank. " You keep that collar for Sunday. . . . Turn your face to the light again. Yes, you can take the stud out and leave the shirt open, so. We could really dispense with the coat . . . waistcoat, too, if you won't find it chilly." (Wattie was wiping his brows.) " Must be particular," said Mr. Frank. " I suppose you think it's a fuss about nothing. You don't understand my job ?"

" What *is* your job ?" asked Wattie.

Mr. Frank picked up his brushes. " I've told you once. I'm an artist."

" Oh," said Wattie.

" A painter by trade. Ever heard of the Royal Academy ?"

" *Heard* of it—yes," said Wattie.

" The place," said Mr. Frank, " where artists hang their pictures—at least, some artists—all who can."

" And the rest, I suppose, hang themselves."

" That's it. Well, look here ; *you* go to Burlington House, and in the left-hand corner of the second room, near the door as you enter——"

" Wait a bit, sir ," said Wattie. " *The second room, near the door, and the left-hand corner ;*" and Wattie looked round at the door and down in the left-hand corner.

" Up on the wall," said Mr. Frank. (Wattie ran his eyes up to the ceiling.) " No, about *here*," said Mr. Frank, and he pointed with two long brushes. " That's what they call ' the line.' To be hung on the ' line ' is a coveted honour ; they put the best of the pictures there."

" And that's where they put yours, is it ?" said Wattie.

" I had the good fortune," began Mr. Frank, and then he went off for the matches. . . . " The picture in question," he said, as he stood scraping the box and finally struck a light on his shoe—" the picture in question—not that it's worth a visit to London—it's about the size of that print . . . and the subject isn't original . . ." He blew the first cloud of smoke in the air.

" What *is* the subject ?" asked Wattie, for he really wanted to know.

" It is called," said Mr. Frank, puffing away and leaning against the mantelpiece—" it is called——" Then he stopped. He blew such rings in the air. " Life's very odd ; life's very strange "—he blew more rings—" no, it's not called *that* . . . Still, life *is* odd, you'll allow. Anyway, if you allow it or not—and you probably don't—yet it *is*. It's a house with a number of doors, and they open and shut you never know when—you never know when or how or why ; and a certain door may stand ajar, and yet before ever you cross the threshold it may be slammed back in your face."

If Mr. Frank went on like this, he might say some-thing that Wattie had not any business to hear. Luckily, Mr. Frank did not go on ; he worked away and away. Wattie got somehow thinking, thinking of this and thinking of that, and gave a big jump when Mr. Frank spoke :

" *Love casts out Fear* is what it is called."

" Oh," said Wattie. " How ?"

" How what ?" said Mr. Frank.

" How did it cast out Fear ?"

" Perfectly simple," said Mr. Frank.

" What was the Fear, then ?" asked Wattie.

Mr. Frank smiled a good-natured smile. " It's an allegory," he said, " and an allegory is—never mind what. It isn't a flower that grows in Marchington, nor in Brinkley, I dare say."

" More of a city plant, perhaps."

" Yes, London's full of them. That's what drives a fellow here—no allegories, but just a lot of nice quiet people, living nice quiet lives in nice quiet places, their loves and fears delightfully natural, no complications, no ' Shall I or shan't I ?' ' Can I or can't I ?' . . . You wonder what I am talking about ? Well, be thankful that you *do* wonder ; be thankful that such allegories mean nothing at all to you."

" Then I imagine," said Wattie, " that I needn't go to *the left-hand corner, second room, near the door ?*"

" Certainly not," said Mr. Frank. " Keep out of it altogether. Avoid it like poison—poison—poison ! . . . And, look here, supposing you hold your tongue. I'm doing your mouth, do you see ? . . . Thank you . . . just so . . . you're not feeling cold ? . . . By the way——" as he lit up again, holding out a neat little case.

" Have you done with my mouth ?" asked Wattie.

" Confound you ! Yes. . . . Don't smoke ? Well, don't begin. How old are you ?"

" Seventeen."

" Are you, by Jove ! . . . Seventeen ! . . . To think of it ! Why, at seventeen I was at school, and here are you earning your living. Don't take to the brush. Two bits of advice : don't take to smoke and don't take to the brush. . . . But I hear you're fond of painting."

" Not wonderful fond."

" Fond or not, I've promised to look at one of your pictures."

" Oh," said Wattie, " promised."

" What is more, I've got it somewhere—no, not here, upstairs, done up in a sheet of brown paper."

This was Miss Phillis's doing. " Oh, that's nothing. I'll take it back."

" Don't be alarmed. I'm a tolerably good-natured critic. Well, what is it ?—a mountain scene, or a river scene, or a battle scene, or a——?"

Wattie could have cried. It was almost a breach of honour on Miss Phillis's part. But meantime Mr. Frank went on : " You'll find, if you wish to do any good at this job, you must stick to Nature—copy Nature, copy something near at hand, something you can really see ; none of those mountains and rivers and battles. Copy your forge ; it's charming." (Wattie laughed.) " Really, it's charming."

" It may be just to walk into once in a way of an afternoon."

Mr. Frank laughed now. " But what am I telling you ? That's all wrong. On no account must you take to the brush—not though I should say the nicest things about the contents of that paper parcel. It's ruinous, like smoke. One is as bad as the other. You spend on smoking what you *don't* earn in painting. See ? . . . You make, I guess, twelve shillings a week."

" Sixteen," said Wattie mildly.

" Sixteen !" cried Mr. Frank—" sixteen shillings a week ! And I've known fellows at *my* job earn *not sixteen shillings a year*."

" I reckon they didn't last long."

" Oh, they lasted. One of them, by the way, made his fortune, only he made it in mines. Oh, they lived all right. They lived on Hope. Come, you are the chap who can't miss a tea. How would you like to live on Hope ? And yet it's what a number of men are doing—men *you* would think a long sight better off than yourself. . . . Take my advice, you live on your tea."

" I shall, sir ; breakfast and dinner, too."

" That's it. Hope's not satisfying. It—it——"
Wattie waited.

" It—it——"

" Blows you out," said Wattie.

" The very word," said Mr. Frank.

" Why don't they take on a more paying job ?"

" Why don't they ? Why don't we ? Because we
can't. The thing is forced upon us."

" I don't see that," said Wattie. " Everyone's got
a choice."

" There *is* such a thing as necessity."

" I know there is," said Wattie, managing not to
laugh. " Only there's no earthly reason——" But
that was what Miss Phillis had said.

" No earthly reason *what ?* No earthly reason why
one should be an artist, I suppose that is what you
were going to remark. Have you ever heard of
ambition ? What is the height of yours, I wonder ?"

" My what ?"

" Ambition. Is there anything you want very
much ? Is there anything you'd give all you've
got to possess ?"

" I shouldn't think there is," said Wattie. " I
reckon I'd have it first on approval."

" Ah, if only one could ! It's a queer thing, too,"
said Mr. Frank, " I stand where you are standing—
seventeen—looking forward to a future which has now
become a past. Very different looking forward to
looking back again."

" Very different, I should think."

" Eight years hence—it *is* eight years—you may yourself be looking back to all you planned at seventeen."

" I don't plan much," said Wattie.

" Still, I presume that you hope ?"

" I don't think I hope much either."

Mr. Frank burst out laughing, then suddenly
sobered. He went to the window, and stood looking
out. Wattie looked too—such rosy clouds and the
room getting darker and darker.

" I remember," said Mr. Frank—he seemed to be speaking to himself, but it could not be wrong to listen—" I remember certain days, gorgeous days, *other* days, when one trotted up and down the world without a fore- or afterthought, and just enjoyed the present ; when the clouds did *not* roll up at sunset, when morning broke fair, and noon was gay, and evening tranquil. I remember it—I remember *them*—yes, *them* ; I could put my fingers on them, though, when I was—what shall I say ?—*left alone* for a few precious minutes, utterly, utterly happy."

" Why not ?"

" Why not ? What do you mean ? . . . Why not ? Ah, *why* not ? If I could catch hold of your good ' why not ?' . . . Very well, you may stretch. It is getting late. Do you want a look ?"

" I don't mind," said Wattie, and he made his way round to the front of the easel.

" You approve ?" Mr. Frank had come back again.

" It's all right," said Wattie. " I suppose it's me."

" Confound your impertinence—yes ! Isn't it handsome enough ?"

" Oh, handsome enough," said Wattie. He could hardly tell Mr. Frank that the portrait was more like himself.

Mr. Frank only laughed. " You're coming to-morrow ?"

" To-morrow's Saturday."

" You can come all the earlier, then."

" I can't come at all."

" Why not ?"

" Well, sir, a chap wants his Saturdays."

" Teas and Saturdays ! . . . Wait till Monday— Monday, the same time. And, look here, I wish you'd come straight from work." Wattie was fixing his collar behind. " It's like this, you know," said Mr. Frank: " anyone can put on clean linen—there's nothing in that ; the clean soul is what I'm after. You bring

your soul with you just as it is.   Remember as well my
advice : don't smoke, don't take to the brush, and
don't have any ambitions.   I've two."

" Two," said Wattie—" two."

CHAPTER XXXIV

THERE were special reasons why Wattie should
not be willing to yield his Saturday afternoon.   On
Saturday afternoon he was sure of a quiet time up at
the church.   The men who were working there knocked
off at twelve, and by one o'clock not a soul was left
on the premises, and Wattie could slink in if he chose
and develop the accumulated fancies of the past week,
and in imagination see them set down on the bare
space over the vestry door.   And on this particular
afternoon a special reason drew him.   He had been
hard at work for many days on a study which he firmly
believed would provide the scheme for the big wall
picture.

The background was a dullish red, of the tone and
hue of the wall of the church.   Upon this background
were fitted in Choice and Necessity.   Choice, as you
looked at the canvas, stood on the left ; she stood
with her back towards you, and yet partly turned, so
that the off-side was hidden from view ; the body fore-
shortened, the legs close together, the haunch and
girth overlapping, and the neck sweeping out and
round, asking an earthly reason why they should stand
in the sun.   Necessity also presented the back, more
full, for you got nothing else till you came on the right
to his shoulder, the neck, and the head, which was
low and sniffing your way, with one ear wanting an
honest opinion.

Now, to be quite exact : take a straight line across
the bottom—that would support the hind feet—a line
a trifle above—that would support the fore ; a line

from Choice's haunch would come just over Necessity's ear ; a line from Necessity's haunch would rest on the nape of Choice's neck ; a line from Choice's ear would cut through her nape and Necessity's haunch ; and then you saw something was wrong : you expected this last line to be broken, your eye to be carried up to a point, whereas you remarked a depression, a flatness— something, perhaps, had been blotted out, something, perhaps, was never put in, and this you began to suspect because both of the creatures looked as if they had carried a burden ever so slender, as if there had been a check ever so slight on the head.

This was the picture he had sent to Miss Phillis. He had taken it up himself, carefully packed and neatly tied. He had been pleased (almost proud) to take it, and now he began to wish he had kept that picture at home. There was another reason for wishing this, besides that Mr. Frank had got hold of it, for he had done rather a dreadful thing, and panic succeeded to pride. It was not so much his impudence in painting Choice and Necessity, but he had foolishly, frowardly painted *her* also. Invisible, yes ! No stroke of the brush had he ventured, but he had foolishly, frowardly dreamt her, and dreamt her into the picture— dreamt her and dreamt her till *she was there*. He knew she was there, as did Choice and Necessity, and as (to his horror) Miss Phillis might know.

And yet Miss Phillis might *not* know. She did not know much about pictures. When she looked at a picture she never could tell what to say. She could not tell if it was good or bad, nor whether she liked it or not. Mrs. Moon was a better judge of a picture, for she sometimes would say to Wattie : " It seems to be coming right at you," when that was how it was meant to be coming; or, " It seems to be going right away." Miss Phillis was more of a practical turn. And if Miss Phillis should *not* know, then he might venture to make a request. But this was a secret. Wait a bit ! Should anyone else be told but

Miss Phillis ? Miss Phillis would have to be told, for
she must give her permission. He could not do this
thing unless she had first said " Yes." Otherwise he
would much have preferred his secret to be a surprise,
to take her in one day unawares, and stand there
saying nothing, whilst she said—— What would Miss
Phillis say to see his horses upon the wall ?

Meantime there was no harm in planning, and on
Saturday afternoons of late he had been up to the
church, first with one fancy, then another, never quite
knowing which of his fancies would be most likely to
endure. And even on this particular Saturday, when
he felt so certain in his own mind that the picture Miss
Phillis had got at the Manor, which was his latest,
would prove his best, a doubt did cross that certainty
whether there might not follow another still better
than the best.

Nobody knew of these weekly visits. How should
anyone know ? The building was now enclosed with
a huge palisade, and the door leading in was securely
locked, and how could you enter without a key ?
Nobody—not Mrs. Moon for one—would ever suppose
it possible. And yet it was more than possible—easy !

There were always planks left lying about. Lean
one plank against the hoarding, raise the lower end
off the ground (usually on a pile of bricks), crawl up,
sit on the hoarding, then throw your whole weight no
this end of the plank, lift it, tilt it, shift it, balance,
seesaw-fashion on the top. . . .   Now throw your
weight on the other end, shove, and prop, and steady,
until you have worked the first end through mid-air,
and lodged it upon the transept wall. . . .   Then
cross. . . .   You have gained the roof ; you can walk
all over it if you like ; but you make your way, first,
at any rate, to the tower end, where the restoration
is hardly yet begun, chuck back the men's tarpaulin,
peer down, catch on, let yourself go, and swing with
your legs astride one of the rafters.

Such a muddle within ! Here he was up amongst

the beams — old oak beams, splendid beams, thick with dust, however. There in the chancel he saw the new beams—bright new beams, beautiful beams, also the new clean stone. *Here* the masonry crumbled away. He pulled it to bits in his fingers. But you loved the old, of course—up there, too, with your fingers on it—loved it because it was old, because it had lived such ages ago, and had had no beginning, and was made by invisible hands. And yet you loved the new—fell in love at first sight, greeted it not like a time-honoured friend, but a fresh and winning acquaintance. And how light it was by comparison ! You looked from shadow to sunshine, then from sunshine to shadow . . . and when you had focused your eyes you saw the dull red of the tower wall. . . .

A couple of hundred pounds ! It was just like Mr. Frank to talk of a couple of hundred pounds. Now, why should anyone want a couple of hundred pounds for painting a couple of horses over the vestry door ? Wouldn't you rather expect to pay a couple of hundred for getting the job ? Still, one must earn a living. If you reckoned the cost of brushes, paints, etc., and then if you reckoned up the time, you could make out a bill. Not that *he* should make out a bill, for he was not a painter, but a blacksmith, and they would be spare hours. . . . Spare hours ! There were none too many. In summer you knocked off at six, and (roughly) then could work till eight. In winter, save on Saturdays, you could not work at all ;—colour was impossible ; and so you would complete your job in something like two years !

Well, was there any hurry ? The church itself would not be ready for another eighteen months, and the finishing touches to the picture . . . Finishing touches to a picture which had never been begun ! Senseless, too, to think about even so much as a beginning, since how should it begin at all ? . . . Miss Phillis makes a vague suggestion (" *Suppose there had been a window ?*"). Master Frank knocks it on the

head (" *A couple of hundred pounds!*"). Nobody
really cares about it—not even Miss Phillis, who made
the suggestion ; for if Miss Phillis had cared, why, the
thing would be done by now.   Besides, if Miss Phillis
had been serious (it was a happy thought of hers),
and if she had made up her mind for good that she
meant to have that picture painted to cover the tower
wall, was it likely that she would have ever allowed
. . . or, rather, to put it another way, was it not *more
likely* that she should commission young Mr. Frank
(the two hundred pounds a joke, of course) to take
the matter in hand ?   Master Frank had trained for
an artist, and would have the necessary gear. . . .
Still, it was quite ridiculous the way some people
deferred and delayed.   Wattie should not be one whit
surprised if, two years hence, when the church was
restored, Miss Phillis and Master Frank should walk
up the aisle together, and Miss Phillis should say :
" I *do* think someone might paint them," and Mr.
Frank laugh and reply, " I dare say someone might
for a couple of hundred pounds."
    Hush !
    Someone was coming. *Hush, if you saw* . . . Never
mind, he was safe.   Voices—familiar voices !   His
heart stood still, then galloped away. . . .   Only
familiar voices !   They came in under the awning
hung over the big south door.   They stopped on the
threshold, silent.   Then Miss Phillis, she stirred and
whispered, and pointed towards the east.   Mr. Frank's
head was bowed, giving his full attention.   Then Miss
Phillis moved away.   She wandered up the aisle
slowly, noting things as she went. . . .   Where was
Mr. Frank ?   Suppose he should be gone !   If Mr.
Frank had gone, Wattie could never stay here alone.
Ah ! Mr. Frank was there, by the door ; a movement
betrayed him.   He had been reading one of the notices
put up by Mr. Pigeon, the clerk of the works.   He was
reading it still—reading, and reading, and reading—
he must have been reading it through and through . . .

suddenly turned his head. Miss Phillis was coming
back. Swiftly, suddenly, all at once, Mr. Frank stood
at her side. And then . . . He uncovered his
eyes. They had gone. He covered his eyes again.
He could never, never tell anyone—no, not even himself. No one must know ; he must not know. What
had he seen ? Nothing ! What had he heard ? Not
a syllable uttered ! What did he know ? Everything.
He knew it all in a flash—in that flash when everything
seemed to happen ; when everything that ever had
happened and ever could happen had happened at
once ; when Mr. Frank pressed suddenly forward, and
Miss Phillis drew suddenly back—suddenly, certainly
back.

They had gone. He thought he could hear them,
crossing the grass, crunching the gravel, then recrossing
the grass again this way. Would the awning move ?
Was that Mr. Frank's step outside the door ?

. . . Nobody came ; it was all his fancy ; and yet that
was Mr. Frank's step . . . no, no ! . . but the awning
moved. Why, that was the wind ! . . . He had better
get down now whilst he could.

CHAPTER XXXV

FACE to face with Miss Phillis !

She stood by the palisade door with the padlock
and key.

" I left it open," she said abruptly.

" Somebody did," said Wattie.

" And *you*, it appears, walked in."

She had been crying. He took the key.

" What were you doing ? Why are you here ?
Have you been into the church ?" Miss Phillis fired
her questions.

" Yes, I've been in," said Wattie. " I wanted to
ask you something, miss."

" Well, you weren't likely to find me there."

" I didn't expect to find you. I came to see if it was really worth while bothering you about what I wanted."

" Bothering me ? You don't bother me. What's this about what you wanted ?"

" I'd tell you, miss, now, if you'd time to listen."

" Plenty of time ! I *want* to listen. Talk, and talk, and talk. I'm much too tired to talk. Let us go in and sit down."

They entered the church together. It was just like the dream which he used to dream, and the church was as dark and cool. Their voices dropped.

" It's a favour. I want you to say yes."

" Yes," said Miss Phillis . . . and then, in the pause that followed, Miss Phillis laughed. " You have not told me yet what you want."

And Wattie came back to himself, and said : " No, I forgot. Well, what I want is to paint some horses in this church." Thereupon he broke out in a sweat.

" Horses in this church ! Why, you are always painting horses !"

" Not always, miss ; on Saturdays."

" Saturdays ? Oh yes !" Miss Phillis was all in a dream of her own. " Paints are very dear to buy." That was the next thing Miss Phillis said, and it showed her practical turn. When she looked at the colours, it was more to the cost. Besides, Miss Phillis was always hard up, and so was Miss Daisy, who opened her purse and found nothing in it.

" Not so wonderful dear," said Wattie.

" But, oh, Wattie, I must tell you," said Miss Phillis ; " talking of painting, I've lent your picture. You've no objection, I hope ?"

" Oh no, miss !" It was too late to object.

" It will come back," said Miss Phillis. " Go on about your horses in church."

This was the way Miss Phillis thrust just anything upon you.

Wattie pulled himself together. " I want," he said, " to paint those horses which were in my picture on this tower wall." He pointed, and Miss Phillis looked. What was she going to say ? Not one of the hundred things she thought.

" That is a good idea."

Wattie marvelled. " You say yes ?"

" Oh, I've said it !"

" *But* . . ."

" But *what ?*"

" *I* don't know what."

The thoughts crossed in her mind zigzag. She caught at one.

" I'm full of troubles. Haven't you heard the sad, sad news ?"

" Which sad, sad news ?"

" I mean about the restoration."

" The restoration . . . oh !"

" We can't go on with it just now—not this year; probably not next year; possibly not the year after that."

Wattie could scarcely ask why. Perhaps she would choose to tell him.

" It's simply this : I've lost some money. No, you needn't look about for it. It isn't here; it's down a mine."

Again he could not put the question. She put it for him. " Won't it come back ? No doubt it will— at any rate, the greater part. Meantime, however, I must wait. I'm *told* I must, and I *know* I must, and it seems a *thousand thousand* pities."

How like Miss Phillis ! She had been *told*, she *knew*, and it was a *thousand thousand* pities. He might at least say one thing. He said it : " I am sorry." It sounded foolish, cold, and brutal.

" Thank you," said Miss Phillis. " Everyone is very kind in saying they are sorry."

"Well, I'm not so wonderful sorry," Wattie went on at once. "I mean, no end of people start a job and have to put it by for a bit. I don't call it *sad*, and I don't see any particular reason for everyone putting themselves about."

Miss Phillis was paying no attention ; her thoughts zigzagged again.

"It's an odd thing, too," she said : "I once had an idea of the kind myself, and I spoke to an artist. I wanted to know if those old horses which used to stand over the east-end window—you would hardly remember —if those old horses could be painted up there."

"Didn't he think they could ?"

She was dreaming ; she woke with a start. "Oh, he thought they could, but he said . . . You know, Wattie—you won't think me rude ?—but your picture is not really like the rose-window, if that's what you meant. Really it isn't. I'd say it was if it was."

"Perhaps it isn't," said Wattie. (Funny, funny Miss Phillis !)

"You've made your horses back towards you, and in the window they were facing," said Miss Phillis, "and they held their heads up too, not down."

"Did they ?" said Wattie. He steadied himself. . . . Choice and Necessity seemed to be turning, seemed to be tossing back their manes. . . . "*Did* they ?" He suffered some kind of a shock. Fancy was riotous in his brain.

"Yes, they *did*, and you *might* remember, though you were only small at the time. You were ten years old, and you're seventeen now, and eighteen soon, on the sixth of August." Miss Phillis's practical brain was clear.

Wattie nodded. "Tell me," he said, "what the artist said. You said the artist said something."

"Well, I told you he said that it *could* be done, only that it would cost a good lot."

"You never told me that. How much ?"

"A couple of hundred pounds."

" A couple of hundred pounds !"

" Yes, and he was an artist—a good artist—and he ought to know."

" Ought to," said Wattie.

" And," said Miss Phillis, " I simply cannot afford it."

" Of course not. But then, you've not got to afford it. *I* don't want a couple of hundred pounds. An artist might ; I'm not an artist."

Miss Phillis caught at his meaning at once, though slow to catch at a picture. " I see—I begin to see. You are one of those people who only want payment in thanks."

" I don't want much thanks," said Wattie. " I do it to please myself." He looked at the tower wall.

" There's the cost of materials," said Miss Phillis. She also looked up at the wall.

" That's nothing. I shall have as much money as time. The amount of time I can spend in a week will just about match the amount of materials."

Miss Phillis may or may not have followed. " You don't think you'll spoil the look of the church ?"

" We could always wipe it out."

" Should you mind if I asked you to wipe it out ?"

" I should wipe it out before you asked me."

Zigzag went her thoughts again. . . . " I wanted to tell you something, Wattie. Do you know I was making plans for you ?"

" Plans ?" said Wattie.

" Well, it has always seemed to me that you had hidden away somewhere inside of you a secret——"

" Sin ?" said Wattie.

" Talent," Miss Phillis said.

Wattie bit his lip. " What sort of a talent ?" he asked.

" Well, a very obvious talent, I should have said, for painting. I don't know much about pictures," Miss Phillis went on—oh no, Miss Phillis, you don't— " but I have heard artists talk—real good artists—so

that I may be said to know *something*, even if I cannot
be said to know *much*."

" Something, of course," said Wattie.

" And the little I know teaches me this : that you
have a very real gift—not a great one, I don't say that."

" Not a great one—no," said Wattie.

" Still, a gift, I dare say, quite worth cultivation.
Would you *like* to get on ?" said Miss Phillis.   She was
looking him in the face.

" Get on where, miss ?"

" Well—get *on*."

" Yes, miss, but *where ?*   I must know where I'm
to get to before I can say whether I'd like to get there
or not."

" Well, that's true, in a way. . . .   Should you care
to be an artist, then—a *real* artist, I mean—like Mr.
Frank ?"

" Not altogether," said Wattie.

Again zigzag her thoughts were crossing.   " Taking
it all round, Wattie, perhaps you are happier."

" Much," Wattie submitted.   Besides, he probably
was ; for the immediate present, of course he was.
And the future ? . . . well, the future . . .

" *Our* lives change such a lot. . . .   *You* aren't leaving
Marchington."   (What ! was she ?   He must not ask.)

" *I* am.   The Manor is let.   I suppose you know."
(He did not know.)   " I must cut down all my
expenses.   What does it mean ?   Well, for *me* it
means leaving everything and everybody. . . .   Oh, if
I were you, how I should hate and hate the strangers !
I don't believe I *could* serve them.   I don't believe
when they came to the forge I could ever let them
inside."

" At our job," began Wattie vaguely ; he had not
the remotest idea what he was going to say, and then
he remembered how the foreman would sometimes say
that " no two horses were just alike," so he thought he
would say that now.   He did.   He said : " No two
horses are just alike."

" Yours aren't, are they ?" said Miss Phillis, trying to understand. " One is roan and the other is white." (He almost shouted the words aloud : " One is Necessity ; one is Choice." It was surely impossible she had not seen !) " I don't know which I like the best. . . . Wattie, Wattie, listen, listen ! You are the funniest boy in the world, wanting to talk and talk and talk, and painting those horses turning their backs and hanging their heads on the ground."

" I may make them pick up their heads," said Wattie. " I dare say they won't look a bit like those "—he swallowed a lump—" when they are done."

Miss Phillis, of course, misunderstood him. " Oh, but I think those are beautiful creatures. I only said they weren't copied exactly. I'm sorry if I have hurt your feelings, but your feelings should not be—what shall I say ?"

" So easily hurt," said Wattie. " Only, miss, if you think I care for that particular picture, you're out of it utterly."

" Wasn't it finished ?"

" No, it wasn't ; and if it was it wouldn't have done. It's the wrong idea."

" I know nothing about the idea "—(No, Miss Phillis, you don't, and that is a mercy, for if you did, you would see more than you ought to see)—" I know nothing about the idea, but I thought it was beautifully finished, quite wonderful for a boy . . . and all the time, Wattie, I've wanted to ask if you would let me have it—buy it. . . ."

" I thought your money was down a mine. No, miss ; of course, if I sell, I shall sell in a shop and get a proper market value."

" What would you get ?"

" Two or three guineas, I dare say."

" Oh, Wattie, could you ? Is it worth it ? I'm afraid I've been praising you up too much. It isn't likely a boy such as you, living in Marchington besides, should have any special sort of a talent."

" Well, I don't care," said Wattie. " I don't want to sell, but that's what I'd get. It's only fit to be sold. I'm sick of it—straight."

" Never mind. I've hurt you. I'm bound to hurt somebody. I say all the wrong things."

" There's only one thing I want you to say."

" What's that ?"

" You know;" he nodded up at the wall. " It's *yes.*"

" Oh yes," said Miss Phillis, " I'll say yes."

PART VII

FRANK

" My mistress bent that brow of hers."

CHAPTER XXXVI

IT was strange after all those buffeting years to fall on happier times. There *are* men, thought Frank to himself that day when he learnt that his picture was hung—there *are* men who have to wait until middle life to achieve their first success. Yet he had waited long enough ; he was nearly five-and-twenty, and he had had five years of disappointment. He did not know many fellows who could boast that, and the iron had all but entered into his soul.

Not quite, however, and he enjoyed life that spring and early summer as he had never enjoyed life before. He felt as he had felt those last two terms at Winchester when everything went well, and he forgot his regrets for the past and his fears for the future. Ah, little did he guess then what was before him ! Never mind, he had come through.

He had an absurd notion this year that he grew an inch and a quarter—positively *grew*. People do sometimes grow after their teens. Anyway, he seemed more conscious of his strength and height and breadth, and would pull himself up and expand as he walked through the streets. And how the days whirled round !

What famous jolly things happened one after the other ! His great-uncle in Cumberland died—well, that was not quite what he meant to say, only he got the two thousand pounds, and it turned out to be three.

On the strength of three thousand pounds he took his aunt and his cousins to the theatre. Both the girls were now engaged. Helena was to marry a rather stiff fellow, the editor of a Liberal newspaper ; Dolly was to marry, *not*, you mark, the medical student— nobody thought she would—but a friend of her father's, twice her own age, and she looked supremely happy, a little sobered, too.

"We shall hear of *you* getting married soon," said his aunt in the theatre. She was in very good spirits, firmly believed that she had brought about the two girls' matches, when she had all the time planned something quite different for both. Frank, of course, laughed amiably, stood at once on his guard. Ah, if his aunt only knew ! . . . He wanted them all to have coffee, ices, Dolly a box of chocolates. And below them and beside them, in stalls and balconies and pits, the people buzzed and laughed and nodded, and only here and there by seeking did you discover a serious look. There was no need for people to be miserable ; plenty of happiness in the world—it only wanted seizing on. " *He either fears his fate too much, or his deserts are small* "—favourite lines just now. The three thousand pounds were his, anyway ; they had come without any seizing ; then the picture accepted and hung, and a heap of jolly congratulations —everyone seemed most awfully pleased ; after that a Press notice, short and sweet : " Amongst others we remarked Mr. Burnet's *Love casts out Fear* ;" then three weeks on the Norfolk Broads—three weeks (only think of it !) of unclouded skies and magnificent sunsets ; the return to town and Dolly's smart wedding ; then—well then, why then, he gathered his forces, packed his new bag, and took the train to Marchington.

Fine weather again ! Hot, dusty, golden, late June weather, buttercups, and gorse ! He did not come by invitation. No ; he put up at The Bell. He should go to the Manor to-morrow. He had written a note to Phillis to tell her of his arrival, and to promise a visit in the morning. Some measurements for the pulpit, which was now in the sculptor's hands, provided an excuse for his sudden appearance. Afterwards he regretted the note, since it made it impossible for him to call that afternoon, and he found the time hang heavy. Also he found himself fidgety, unable to settle to anything, and eventually, after his evening meal, started out and walked for miles and miles across country westward into the light, then turned and walked miles and miles back again eastward into the dark. Even then he sat smoking in his room facing a couple of candles until the first hour of morning struck. There was so much to think about. The tide which had ebbed so long was now in flood, and he was about to seize an opportunity. Phillis was his from the first, but he had never yet had right to claim her; he had always been too young. It was only when you got to a certain age that you discovered how hopelessly young you had been all the years before. And yet at Winchester, afterwards in Paris, afterwards in London, he had thought himself so wise, sometimes so aged; he seemed to have drained the cup of bitterness, which surely is the last cup a man is asked to drain. How stupid now it all appeared! . . . What was the wisdom? A little Shelley! And perhaps he had yet to learn wherein the real worth of Shelley consisted! What was the bitterness? Some trumpery disappointment, a rebuff from the Royal Academy, a sneer from a fellow-student, a somewhat irritating but innocuous lecture from his guardian, a cold in his head, a shivering fit. Bah! He had outgrown *that* stuff! He was past the time of illusions, illusionary fears and joys; he understood just what life had to offer, and the spirit in which you must take the gift. His hand was perfectly steady now as he filled another pipe, and told himself that he might or might not succeed in his suit. A cynic, of course, would say he was calm because he was virtually sure, because his instinct and reason told him that there was no " might

not " in the case. They had always been fond of one
another.

He would not go to the Manor until twelve
o'clock. Phillis was probably busy. It was a jolly
day, and he sauntered up and down in the sun reading the morning news. At eleven he went in and
changed. It was whilst he was changing that he
tossed off a glass of cold water, and discovered that he
was nervous. It came of all this waiting about and
sauntering in the sun and flapping the morning paper.
He believed that if this cowardice had attacked him
yesterday at Marchington Station, he should have
taken the next train back. Well, it would do him
no good to stand there comparing last night with this
morning, telling himself it would always be so, your
confidence easily shaken, your grounded philosophy
undermined, your ballasted logic blown about. The
walk to the Manor would restore him. He had
pictured this scene too often of late : just such a hot
summer's day, and he would find Phillis in the garden,
and she would not guess what was in his mind—would
not guess what was going to happen until it had
happened, for Phillis was the most unsuspicious,
straightforward creature in the world. There would
be no sort of " proposal." He would just take her,
at the right moment, the nick of time—take her, and
she should be his. They would be married that
autumn. He saw no reason for delay, and he particularly liked the music which Dolly had had at her
wedding. He thought in the autumn you could
not do better than go for a month to Italy. He
should love the ripening vineyards, and he should
sketch, and Phillis should sit by his side. He would
make her happy—oh, ye gods ! If a man so brutal
could be found as to give that girl cause to be anything
else but radiantly happy ! Afterwards they would
come back to town. Half the year they would spend
in London in a nice little house near the Chelsea
Embankment, provided out of that three thousand

pounds and his own little bit and all the pictures he meant to be painting, the other half at Marchington. Oh, and he *would* work hard for her ! Not that she had any need, but because it would be such pure pleasure to make her offerings fairly earned, to give her some of the sweat of his brow.

Why, then, with life so pat did his heart sink as he came to the gates, as he turned in and stalked up the park, as he found himself on the gravelled drive, as he faced the great front-door ? The sun was obscured, too, at that minute, and there crept a little chilly breeze.

They told him Miss Phillis was out, but Miss Elizabeth in, and, " Oh yes, sir, the ladies expect you ! This way, sir, if you please."

He was in the drawing-room. He had not found Phillis in the garden ; so far his dream did not come true. The place was uncommonly quiet. It suddenly entered his head that the man was wrong : he was *not* expected, and he wished he had never come. If he was left here much longer, he should ring the bell and tell the man he should call another day. . . . Call another day for what ? What was he calling for ? Why, of course, it was to—— The object dwindled, shrivelled, and collapsed. . . . It was no good proposing to Phillis unless he was quite, quite sure that he wanted to marry her. . . . And here was Miss Elizabeth.

He was flustered, for she had come in at a critical point. The ground had just slipped from under his feet, and yet he must stand up on that ground—that carpet, anyway—and say, " How do you do ?"

" I'm very well, thank you, Mr. Burnet. Pray sit down."

He sat down gladly. His knees had begun to tremble.

" My niece is out. She will be out for lunch, but at home this afternoon. She hopes you will stay and lunch with me."

" I'll come in the afternoon," said Frank, half out of his chair.

" Oh, very well."

" I mean—I beg your pardon—I'll stop and lunch with you." He did not usually make such a fool of himself. " I wanted to see Phillis. It's some time since I heard anything of you all. I really came down about the measurements of my pulpit."

" Perhaps you would rather lunch with your pulpit," said Miss Elizabeth.

Frank laughed and blushed. He did the one on purpose, and the other he could not help. When should he give up that horrid habit ? As to laughing, it was the best thing to do. Besides, the old lady meant no harm, and, like all people who love their own wit, she must sometimes sacrifice nice feeling.

" I'm horribly muddled this morning," said Frank. " I didn't get to sleep till I don't know what time last night."

" How's that ?"

" Oh, I don't know. Busy and overworked, I suppose."

" Indeed ! And what have *you* been overworking yourself about ? I thought you were the young man without a profession."

" Without a profession !" laughed Frank. " I'm afraid it's rather an arduous one. Painting's a trade, you'll allow."

" Oh, that's what you call your profession ! You don't mean to say it keeps you busy."

" Doesn't it ! We don't have regular hours, of course, and a good deal of our time is necessarily spent in going about——"

" I believe it is," said Miss Elizabeth.

" You have to keep the mind open and fresh," said Frank, " and one must meet others of the trade. As much is done by talk as by anything else."

" I quite agree."

"But it's not all talk," said Frank. (She made him nervous.) "Witness my picture hung this year."

"What's your picture?"

"In the Academy. You've been, I suppose."

"Never! Burlington House in winter for me."

"I'm afraid we can't compete *there*," said Frank, "though old masters were young masters once, you know." He must be pleasant, yet hold his own.

"Yes; but you don't suppose they would ever have had the face to show the work that some of you young men show nowadays."

"Stop!" said Frank. "That is rather unfair. You condemn us unseen. You should come and have a look at the pictures, you and Phillis. Why not?"

"Oh, Phillis can go! Her head can stand it. She hardly knows one end of a picture from the other."

"I shall persuade Phillis. It's rather a great occasion."

"Why such a great occasion?"

"Well, I've never had one in before." She was doing this on purpose.

"Never had one in before! And I thought it was your profession."

"Well, yes, so it is; but one does not always succeed at once in a profession. There are briefless barristers, you know." He did not mean to give in.

"My dear Mr. Burnet, I *know* it"—funny emphatic old lady. "I am keeping one of them alive at this very moment—keeping him from starvation—and, if you can credit it, he has engaged himself to be married on two hundred a year. I beg his pardon, I believe he can bring it up to three."

"I suppose he thought things were so bad they couldn't possibly be worse," said Frank. If the old lady was grim, he would be grimmer.

" He need not have been in such a hurry," she went on.

Perhaps, thought Frank, he was best judge of his own affairs.

" And, pray, what else do you do besides hanging a picture ? That can't take all your time."

" Paint others," said Frank.

" And what happens to all these pictures? that's what I want to know. Who buys them ?"

" The charitably inclined," said Frank. He would pay her back in her own small coin.

" Then I hope there are plenty of that inclination, or it's a very poor lookout. *Everybody* must turn artist nowadays—everybody ! I've three nephews and four nieces studying Art at the present moment. Thank goodness Phillis can't draw a straight line."

" Excuse me, I believe it is the only line Phillis *can* draw. But perhaps your nephews and nieces do not intend to make Art their profession?"

" Well, they're young yet. They may come to their senses in time."

Frank laughed good-naturedly. He really felt slightly annoyed. " You seem to have a bad opinion of our calling."

" Oh, dear me, no ! Not when it *is* a calling."

" When *is* it a calling ?" He laughed still more ; felt rather more annoyed.

" When it's an unmistakable calling."

" When is it an unmistakable calling ?" This time he got red as well as annoyed.

" When a man has a great natural gift."

" Oh, well," said Frank ; " and who's to know who's got that ?"

Just then the gong sounded for lunch. Frank was relieved. If the conversation had gone on much longer, he would have been obliged to adopt a different tone. He considered one or two of Miss Elizabeth's remarks in very bad taste. That one especially about the briefless barrister. It was meant, of course, for

a side-thrust ; and if there was a thing Frank loathed
and despised from the bottom of his heart it was a
side-thrust—loathed and despised it, but always forgave
it (for there is something in the weakness of these side-
attacks—no, call them *thrusts*, they are not *attacks*—
which disarms you, checks your full blow back) ;
whence, the gong sounding, he opened the door and
followed Miss Elizabeth into the dining-room, where
they talked (as he hoped) agreeably over their lunch.
But when Phillis came in, fresh and strong, as she did,
like the morning sun, and said, " Oh, Frank, this
is jolly to see you again !" Frank thought, what a
shame ! What a shame these ugly, worldly considerations ! What a shame to suppose that Phillis, provided she cared for him at all, would care for him less
because he had only two hundred a year ! If they
were made for one another, were braver, gayer, tenderer,
better, in one another's company ; if they were moved
to tears and laughter ; if *he* felt confidence and *she* felt
joy (and he looked at her over the table), then must
they say " No " to all of this because Phillis's father
had left five thousand a year behind him, and
Frank's a couple of hundred—begging your pardon,
he could bring it to three. If neither of them had a
penny, very well, money considerations must then
come in. The idea of Phillis in poverty was not
exactly terrible ; it was more laughable. You looked
across at her happy face, and could not conceive it
pinched or careful.

Frank wondered whether it was Miss Elizabeth's
side-thrust which had made him so uncertain as he
walked and talked with Phillis after lunch. On the
other hand, it might have had nothing to do with Miss
Elizabeth, but rather with Phillis herself. Perhaps
she was in too boisterous good spirits ; perhaps she
was preoccupied in her own affairs, bent on leaving
magazines—in at one gate, out at another—or perhaps
she was in a captious humour, for, having eagerly
persuaded him to go to the forge to engage a certain

boy as a model, arrived at the forge, she seemed to make jest of the matter ; and, if that was to be the case, why go at all ?

Perhaps the time was not ripe.   That was the only conclusion he could come to after tossing on his bed, after cursing the crowing cocks in The Bell Inn yard outside, after watching the dawn creep through the window, steal round the walls, then push its way out in the room.   He hardly knew his own mind, and if that were really so, was he in fit condition to help Phillis make up hers ?   By this morning's grey light he could not have persuaded Phillis to anything. Still, he should see as the day wore on.   Meantime he hung from the coffee-room window smoking a cigarette. One consolation he had, and he told it again and again to himself—his picture, his first real success, and that notice : " Amongst others we remarked Mr. Burnet's *Love casts out Fear.*"   This was something to the good.   Whatever happened, he could say to himself, " There's *that.*"   Whatever happened !   What did he mean ?   Why did he always suggest his own doubts ? The doubts settled down upon him.   He was now at his zenith, should never climb higher, never again succeed ; henceforth one after another the objects of his ambition were doomed to escape him. . . .   He saw the boy across the road, and flung up the window, jumped the border, and was out talking before he knew why.

It was all more or less by way of amusement, something to do, something to carry him on for a time, as it were mechanically, to help him to shape the next definite move.   Whether it shaped a move or not he could hardly tell at the end of one sitting ; but he found himself engaged on a rather remarkable piece of work—a pure bit of human nature—and decided that he would spare no pains to see it in next year's Academy.   It wasn't only that young Cock-a-hoop was handsome, but that he stood for so much.   He stood for everything healthy in body and soul.   Lucky beggar, if only he knew ! No credit to him, of course. If Frank had been brought up on bread and cheese, with the whole of his life planned out for him—so much work, so much play, so much sleep (and sleep it would be !)—he could also have sat for his portrait with a face serene as an archangel's, sublime as a seraph's. And he could have kicked his seraph heels and talked nonsense out of his archangel mouth, and worn a red and black spotted tie, and a pink magenta cabbage rose, and " reckoned " this and " reckoned " that, and cried out for his tea. And yet that boy was not entirely a bread-and-cheese hero. He had more than a dash of poetry in him. Phillis said that he painted. " You should look at his paintings," Phillis had said. . . . That was the worst of being an artist : wherever you went, people asked you to look at their paintings. There was always somebody in the family circle who sketched, or drew, or etched, or copied, and because you were an artist (and had consequently learnt the only important fact which an artist pays the schools to teach him—namely, that you must " go through the mill ")—because you were an artist, it was supposed that you would have something to say about each sketch, copy, or etching put in front of your nose, the family standing round meantime to hear your "trained opinion." . . . Still, of course, if Phillis wished it ! . . . And he had carried off a brown paper parcel— it was there on the table in his room—and some time he would open the parcel at leisure and see what the fellow could do. Only he always made the mistake of over-praising everything. Meanwhile he painted the archangel, and gave him good advice.

CHAPTER XXXVII

LIFE is odd—very odd. You set out one day with the
intention of doing *this* thing, and you come back having
done *that*, and perhaps convinced in your own mind
(as convinced as this morning you were to the contrary) that what you did in the end was right. He
had been so certain about his intentions when he
turned up at Marchington Station. He had come
to a crisis, a turning-point ; he had travelled the
thorny path of youth, had survived a good deal of
disappointment, trouble, tragedy—never mind what—
and here he was on the other side, successfully arrived.
He should hesitate no longer, but enjoy the privileges
of his new estate. He was a man now, and he might
make a home. If anyone had told him that this
intention was not the unalterable, inevitable conclusion to a long chain of events, he would have—well,
smiled patiently. And yet he had not been in Marchington twenty-four hours before his whole purpose
was shaken, and he found the long chain of events
twisted and tied in a hundred knots, and the unalterable, inevitable conclusion lost in the coil. He found
himself wondering whether the time had come, whether
he was as old as he thought, whether he had not a
great deal still to learn so far as his art was concerned,
whether fame were so easily established, and he so
near his goal. And then the question—*what* goal ?—
cropping up. Most annoying, when surely at five-
and-twenty one ought to have found one's direction
at last ! . . . And then, behold ! on Friday night he
dines at the Manor, and never has felt more confident.

" Have you measured your pulpit yet ?" said
Phillis.

They had gone out into the garden, and now walked
up and down on the terrace. Aunt Elizabeth sat
indoors.

" No," said Frank.   He was going to excuse himself,
and then he suddenly thought, " Why should I pretend
any longer ?   Why shouldn't she know it isn't the
pulpit ?"   So he said : " The pulpit can wait."

It was strange that a chance observation like that
should open the way to so much.   There was something in Phillis's manner when she said : " Yes, it *can*
wait," to set Frank's nerves in a tingle. " Frank, I've
tiresome news."

" What's up ?"   He armoured himself.   He had
scented the enemy.   He put on the cool and casual
air.

" Oh, it's nothing to trouble about."

" I'm untroubled," said Frank.   " You don't mind
my cigarette ?   Well, what's your news ?"

" Lost money again.   Aren't we unlucky ?   It
seems as if we are never to live here in happiness long.
It isn't the money I care about."

" Not a hang, Phil, I know.   I must say, I'm most
awfully sorry . . . but go on.   Wait a bit, while I strike
this match. . . .   You're not cold ?   Shall I fetch you
a shawl ?"

" No—oh no, thank you !   Well, about the money.
What I mean is I shouldn't care if I had only a pound
a week, and could live here as a tenant : live in the
lodge or at the farm, or be one of the gardeners' wives—
I mean, wife of one of the gardeners—because I
should still be at home and enjoy it all."

" And see other people in possession ?—sit in your
garden, eat at your table, walk on your terrace, ride
your horses——"

" Never ! . . .   Choice and Necessity go to Daisy.
She has promised to take them.   I'm selling the bay,
and the pair lets with the house."

" Lets   with   the   house ?   Are   you   letting ?"

" I've let ; at least, the deed is almost done.   Uncle
Jasper is coming next week to settle the business.
Don't tell anyone.   Nobody knows at present but
Aunt Elizabeth, uncle, Daisy, and you."

Frank walked on. " I'm glad you told me," he said briefly.　He smoked at his cigarette.　" Of course, it is all very sudden."

" I only learnt two months ago that things were bad."

" What things exactly ?　You're so vague."

" I'm not vague ; I'm ignorant.　Uncle Jasper has explained it all, but I never understand money, and he will talk about it late at night when I want to go to bed, or early in the morning when I want to go out.　It has something to do with mines, and the securities were supposed to be safe, but they weren't, and yet in a year or two the money may all come back."

" Well, but that doesn't sound very dreadful.　*Must* you leave ?"　Frank said that ; what he thought was : " This sweet woman shall not suffer.　If I were Leighton or Alma Tadema, and could get one thousand guineas for every picture I painted ! . . .　I *will* be Leighton and Alma Tadema. . . ."

But Phillis went on : " Uncle Jasper says I *could* stay, only the conditions are so distasteful I told him I'd rather not.　Give up my horses ?　No !　Shut up half the house ?　No !　I hate shut rooms.　I shall have all the rooms open as long as I live.　Cut down expenses ?　Oh yes, I know : charities first of all, then servants, then friends—a minim measure for everything.　No, no !　I can't endure it !　Could you ?"

" Rather not !　I loathe all measures.　Where are you going, by the way ?"

" Abroad.　I can retrench much quicker there, and I might be back in a couple of years.　I shall get back as soon as I can.　It is horrid to think of strangers coming.　No one will like them.　They won't *belong* . . . Oh, but the pulpit !　I forgot.　We began about the pulpit.　The church for the present *must* be at a standstill.　Everyone says, ' Why don't you make an appeal to the county ?'　An appeal to somebody else

to finish the work I've begun ! Do you think it sounds
nice ?"

" No, not at all."

" And then they complain that I spend too much
money and time and trouble, and that the whole
could be done with half the labour and at half the
cost, and nobody know the difference."

" Nine out of ten wouldn't, perhaps, but I always
consider the tenth."

" And, anyway, *I* should know."

" Of course. Well, Phillis, look here, I repeat I'm
awfully sorry ; but, bar leaving this place for a couple
of years, I don't see there's much to trouble about.
The church can wait, and fine it shall be when it's
finished ; and we shall walk there with clean con-
sciences, and the Master Builder shall approve. As to
the horses, I think we might find some plan for . . . well,
well, well, we shall see."

Did she guess what that *well well, well* might
mean ? . . . He checked himself. It wanted a fierce
bit and bridle, for he was hot to tell her the truth, to
take her now in his arms and hold so much goodness
and wisdom and love, and bind them for ever to himself.
But wait ! . . . We shall see ! . . . Too hot, too hot !
Yes, suddenly mad, overpowered, not fit to make any
rational proposal, such as, " *Phillis, it would be better
for you,*" or, " *It would be better for me,*" or, " *It would
be better for us both . . .*"

" I'm glad I didn't," he said to himself that night,
as he swung down the dark avenue of trees, out on the
road, back to the village, back to The Bell. " I'm
glad we went into the drawing-room just at that
point. There never was a sweeter, stronger, saner
woman, and I love her ! . . . Ah, we shall see about
that ! . . . But my first duty is to lay the matter
before her. I don't want the thing to be done in a
moment of passion."

It should be done to-morrow. They had agreed to
go together to the church. Frank, if he liked, could

measure his pulpit, and, anyway, there was a good
deal to see. "Oh, we've got on !" said Phillis, and
talked very busily by his side. Did he listen ? He
may have listened ; he seemed to hear it all ; but there
was so much to settle, and his mind was making
vigorous plans. . . . They would be quietly married.
September ? — October ? — winter in Florence . . .
come north to the Lakes for the spring . . . summer in
Switzerland . . . autumn, back to the Lakes . . . south, in
the winter, to Florence again. . . . He was conning it
as he came up the path, over the crunching gravel.
He was glad Phillis talked so much. He should have
found it hard to talk, having the one thing only to
say. . . . Still talking in church—subdued whisper,
of course ; very eager now to explain : "What made
me so *savage* . . . What I can't *stand* . . . and there's
no earthly reason why I *should* . . . What I wanted
to have and *mean* to have . . . What they said I *must*,
only I *wouldn't* . . ." And then : "Look here . . . and
look there. . . . Don't you like this ? . . . Do you
like that ?" . . . He stood, hat in hand, and gave his
attention, stared up at the roof, the shadowy rafters,
round at the walls. "Yes . . . yes . . . yes."

She had gone up the aisle. How swiftly she moved !
He turned all at once, and was reading something . . .
old Pigeon's latest instructions ! . . . Should he speak ?
Should he speak ? . . . What did old Pigeon say ? . . .
"*Fresh hands apply to the foreman.*" . . . He found
himself in the aisle. She was coming back.

"Phillis"—he tried to control his voice—"Phillis,
I wonder if the time has come to speak to you about
something."

What had happened ? She had stopped him. How
had she stopped him ? By a look ? Yes, a strange,
penetrating look, and by a word, "No," very decided—
"no." . . . Did she mean no ? Did she know what
she meant ? Did she know what *he* meant ? He
tried to catch at that straw, but the tide rushed up
and caught it away ; for she gave him another look, per-

fectly steady, perfectly plain, and said the word once
more : " No."

He must have followed her out. They were there
on the gravel. Ten minutes ago they were coming
up, and now they were going down, just the same, side
by side . . . only it was a nightmare, and presently
he would awake. . . . And yet he was holding the
wicket for her. This was true enough ; and here was
the road. Besides, he was conscious, terribly conscious, with a cut-and-dried consciousness. "The
whole of my life, every thought and purpose, has come
to an end. There is no more faith. How can there
be ? Everything I believed to be true is now proved
to be false. Everything goes ; God goes. I can cling,
of course, to accustomed beliefs. . . . I shall go to
church on Sunday. . . . What has that got to do with
it ? Just as much as anything else. . . . Can't you
see that every stone you set carefully in its place has
proved to be rotten ? You can either heap them
together again, or else build again . . . that's good ! . . .
with quite new stones. . . . What stones ? Will the
new stones be any better ?"

He believed she was speaking. Some excuse. She
wanted to go this way. . . . Good-bye. He supposed
he went back to The Bell alone.

CHAPTER XXXVIII

A NOTE came to him that night. " Who brought it ?"
asked Frank.

The girl said it was Mr. Marshall, and then explained
that Mr. Marshall was the groom at the Manor.

" Has he gone ?"

The girl said, Oh yes, he had gone, and then put
her head back to say he had gone to the station.

Frank tore open the envelope. How often he had
stood with an unopened envelope in his hand ! once

half an hour, and then, after all, it proved good news.
Half a moment now was sufficient. He knew the
worst already. . . . Not that he hoped—not that he
hoped . . .

    " DEAR FRANK,
        " I was very abrupt, but you took me un-
awares. Besides, I had no hesitation. I knew my
answer at once, and no amount of thought could have
made it different. It is cruel to look into friendships,
to begin to inquire why, when one loves so much, one
does not love a little more ; but I believe there is
some radical reason which would make it a thousand
pities for us to be married when we might be such true
friends. It is a great mistake for two people to get
married if they are not quite sure that they are absolutely necessary to one another ; and I cannot be sure
that I am absolutely necessary to you ; in fact, I am
sure I am not. If, in the heat of the moment, you
protest that I *am*, this will be because you do not
understand what I mean by ' absolutely necessary.' "

Understand ! He read her words again and again.
He would force some intelligible construction upon
them. Did she really doubt the genuineness of his
need ? Not necessary ! Not necessary, of course, if
one can afford to do without the joy of full possession,
to do without the sunshine in the world ! . . . He
thrust the letter in his pocket. He should go at once.
It was dark outside ; no moon, no stars—rain ?
Would it rain ? The road dimly wound before him.
As he turned into the Park he was lost, but he caught
the lights of the Manor. . . . "*Shut up half the house !
No ! I hate shut rooms ! I shall have all the rooms
open as long as I live.*" So she shall ! So she shall ! . . .
Bang went the long white gate. Here he was in the
garden, hot in spite of the cool night air. He rang the
bell.
    " Is—is—Miss Elizabeth in ?"

" Yes, sir. Will you come in, sir ?   Or can I deliver a message, sir ?"

It was an unusual hour to call.

" I'll see her," said Frank. He stood inside. He was shown into the drawing-room. Nobody there. They might not have finished dinner. It was nine o'clock. In came Miss Elizabeth.

He caught her hand.   " Where's Phillis ?"

" I thought you asked for me ?"

" Yes, but I wanted Phillis."

" I am sorry to disappoint you.   Phillis has gone."

"'Where ?"

" To the station to catch the train."

" To London ?"   He would follow.

" No, Scotland ; to my brother." He could not follow there. "Sit down," said Miss Elizabeth. " Have you dined ?"

" Yes, yes !" So he had after a fashion. " There is a mistake," he said.   " I must see her, and see her at once.   What time did you say that train went ?"

" I did not say any time.   Nine-thirty at Brinkley."

" I'll catch it.   There's no sense in stopping here."

" I said nine-thirty ; it's nine now."

" Who is with her ?"

" Her maid ?"

" There has been a misunderstanding.   I would give all the world for one moment's explanation."

" There is plenty of time for explanation."

" Plenty of time ! What do you mean ? It must be now or never. A misunderstanding gets worse and worse the longer you leave it.   I want this cleared up at once. . . . At once," he repeated, as Miss Elizabeth made no comment.   " If I had got here an hour sooner ! If I had only got here an hour sooner !" He stared at the clock—not that staring would bring back the hour, but because he must somehow rouse Miss Elizabeth to some sense of the gravity of the situation.   " A word would set the matter straight."

Miss Elizabeth spoke. " You can write, you know."

" Oh yes, of course, I can write. I shall write. I expect I shall write. I shall think what I shall do. She has utterly misunderstood something I said to her. Her going away so suddenly proves it. Yes, it *does* . . . why, so it does !" He saw it in a flash—in a dozen flashes. She had loved him all the time, but being in doubt as to the reality of his feelings, she had refused, hesitated, made herself a loophole in the shy, quick way a woman will, then turned and fled. . . . " Aunt Elizabeth," he sobbed, and he went on his knees before her, " you are Phillis's aunt—aunt to the sweetest creature that ever breathed. . . ." He was kissing her hand.

" What have you got to say to *me ?* Nothing, it seems, but to call me somebody else's aunt. Get up. . . . Come. . . . You are a very young man. I am a very old woman. Your case is not hopeless."

" Not hopeless ? What do you mean ?. . . Isn't it hopeless ?" He caught at that. He found himself seated at her side. " Isn't it hopeless ?" he asked again. Then he leant eagerly forward. " That is what I thought," he said. " That is what I dared to think ; and you, dearest lady, have come to give me confidence."

" Dropped from the clouds for your convenience ! I haven't come at all. I was here."

She spoilt herself by this sarcastic way. Never mind, she meant to be amiable, and perhaps she meant to help.

" Of course, you know what has happened," said Frank, a little stiffly.

" Oh yes, I do."

" She—she told you ?"

" No. Phillis, at present, has told me nothing. No doubt she will tell me something some day."

" How did you know, then ?"

" Well, to tell you the truth, I guessed."

" Guessed ? Oh, well, yes ; it was a likely thing to happen."

" That you should fall in love with her ?"

" Yes ; that she—that we—that I—yes, that I should fall in love with her."

He waited for Miss Elizabeth. It was her turn to speak. She did not speak, however, so he said : " And I have reasonable hopes—quite reasonable hopes," and stopped.

" I am glad to hear it," said Miss Elizabeth. " For my own part, I like to see people happy." Was she sarcastic again ? No, she meant what she said, and she continued : " I agree that your hopes are reasonable, though they may not be realized all at once. Phillis is fond of you, I know. . . ."

" She has told me so. Virtually she tells me so." The letter was burning in his pocket.

" And, at any rate," said Miss Elizabeth—she seemed to ignore the interruption—" even if she is not fond of you, there is one point in your favour."

" What ? What ?"

" She is fond of nobody else."

" Ah !"—a long-drawn " Ah !"—" that is just what I thought. And Phillis is so straight."

" There are one or two," went on Miss Elizabeth, " who would, I know, have liked to approach her ; but they never got farther than approaching *me*. She has never permitted any addresses."

" She's a queen !" burst out Frank. He would let the world know.

" There are queens and queens," said Miss Elizabeth.

Frank laughed at Miss Elizabeth's pleasantry. His thoughts had flown back to the letter.

" I can't for the life of me think what she means."

" Phillis usually means what she says."

" I was afraid at first she meant it," said Frank— he felt himself turn crimson—" but then I got her note, and saw at once a misunderstanding. She seems to have an idea in her head that she cannot give me what I want. This is absurd. Surely it is for *me* to give ; for *her* to demand. If *she* is satisfied,

what more is required ? I shall be satisfied well
enough. Satisfied! What does she mean ?" He
waited for an answer.

" I don't know," said Miss Elizabeth.

" To quote her own words, she does not feel that
she is 'absolutely necessary' to me." He waited
again. Miss Elizabeth said nothing, but it was evident
she was listening, so he went on. " It is all a huge
mistake. Who is the best judge of what I need ?"
Once more he waited. " Well, I suppose I ought to
be." He had much better state, not question, his
case.

" Perhaps she is afraid that at a supreme crisis she
would not be of use."

" Of use ? Supreme crisis ? . . . Yes. . . . I don't
quite understand. I mean, of course, if anything big
turned up to be tackled, I suppose I should naturally
tackle it myself. I've no notion of making my wife
(be it Phillis, be it whom you will) a drudge—a beast
of burden."

" No. I think you would be a very considerate
husband. However, that is not quite what I meant."

" Isn't it ?" said Frank. He paused so that she
might have an opportunity of explaining ; but as she
did not take it, and probably did not mean anything
very particular, he went on : " I know, perfectly well,"
he was still thinking about the drudge, " that it isn't
money Phillis wants. Besides, she is a little less well
off than she was, and I'm a little better off, so we can
both cry quits. No, it must be some ridiculous notion
of not being good enough—I mean, clever enough.
Just as if I wanted a clever wife, a wife who understood my pictures. Why, there are hundreds of those
to be got any day in London. I would far, far rather
have Phillis look at my pictures upside-down. She
has done such a thing, you know."

" I can believe it. Personally, I do not think that
an inability to appreciate your pictures would stamp
Phillis as not ' good enough.' "

" That is just what I was saying."

" And I am sure," continued Miss Elizabeth, " that
Phillis would say so too !"

" Well, I hope she would have sufficient sense,"
said Frank. " But, then, what can she mean ?"

" Perhaps she was not thinking of pictures. A
picture is not a supreme crisis."

" I don't know," said Frank ; " it might be. Anyway, I have already come on one or two supreme
crises in my life when Phillis would have been of
inestimable use. I should again, and again, and again
have been the better for her advice."

" I am sure you think so."

" Well ? I suppose Phillis thinks so too ?"

" Apparently she is doubtful ; and you know it
would be a sad disappointment for Phillis to find at
a crisis that you wanted help which she could not
give."

" You have a poor opinion of Phillis."

" Oh no ; on the contrary, a high opinion of her."

" You suggest that she is incapable of giving a man
any help."

" I was not speaking of *a* man ; I was speaking
of *the* man—*you*. There are plenty of men Phillis
might help, and glad they would be of her assistance—
glad, and proud, and satisfied."

" Oh !" said Frank. He was making that out.
" The fault is in *me*, is it ? I want a peculiar kind of
help, do I ? . . . God knows I do !" He suddenly
covered his face.

" Fault ?" said Miss Elizabeth. " I do not quite
see that it is to be regarded as a fault."

Down went his hands again. " It *is* to be regarded
as a fault. *I* should regard it as a fault—a grievous
fault, if I were incapable of being glad, and proud,
and satisfied with whatever assistance Phillis might
offer, and whenever she chose to offer it."

" Whatever and whenever ! That is my point.
It would be sad, I repeat, for Phillis to offer any kind

of assistance but just that which you wanted, and to offer it at any time except just when it was required. *There* is our ' absolutely necessary.' You see, we open up the question whether you have a nature which, in the first place, is empty without Phillis, and, in the second place, can be filled with her exactly."

" Empty without Phillis ! Why, is it likely, if my life were full, that I should be crying out to fill it ? . . . And I'm crying enough," said Frank bitterly. " I'm afraid I'm keeping you. I'm sorry. I'll go. Besides, it appears to be a difficult task—a task beyond me— to convince you that I have any serious feelings of respect or affection for your niece."

" Oh dear no !" said Miss Elizabeth. " You prove yourself quite serious, and I am sure you will be married in the end."

" In the end ! Thank you. It is very easy to say that."

" I understood you to say you had reasonable hopes yourself."

" I said that there had been a misunderstanding, and so there has, and I marvel less at it after this evening's conversation. It seems to me that mis-understandings are none too rare."

" They are very common. . . . But ' reasonable hopes ' you said."

" I may have said so. I don't know. Yes, I did say so—yes, I did."

" And there, at any rate, Mr. Burnet, we agree. I entertain reasonable hopes myself. A calm survey of the matrimonial affairs of my friends and relations through the course of a long life has persuaded me that most men and women find their mates for better or worse, and that it is only one in fifty, perhaps, who is the object or the subject of a blunder."

Frank stood up. He was staring into the shaded lamp.

" Meantime," said Miss Elizabeth, " there are all manner of prizes to be brought to your lady's feet."

" Oh, Phillis cares nothing for prizes !" said Frank very shortly.   When he said that he nearly sobbed. He just saved himself in time.

" I am sure she does—I am sure she must.   Some sort of prizes, anyway.   She will want to be proud of you, of course."

" Of *me*, perhaps.   Prizes won't help me."   He suddenly thought that they wouldn't.   He suddenly thought of himself.   He felt a horrible sinking.   What had buoyed him up ?   A puff of air ?   And now had he fallen to solid earth ?   He must say something ; he must talk.

" So far as prizes are concerned, any work I've ever done—and I *have* worked, though I haven't always succeeded—not by any means ; in fact, very rarely. . . . Still, I got a picture—I mean, I never supposed I was good enough for her—at least——   Yes, I did, and in a sense I *am*, for you can't do much better than love loyally ; I swear I think you can't."

" Come, that's true."

" I'll say good-night," said Frank.   He could not control himself much longer.   " I've kept you an age, and it's all to no purpose.   Thanks very much. . . . No, don't ring. . . .   I can let myself out."   He kissed her hand.   There was no sense in that.   He was not fond of her, but, then, she had struck him.   He went through the hall and opened the door, and shut it quietly after him.   For a moment he stood on the steps.   It had stopped raining, but there were no stars.

PART VIII

WATTIE

"Only a memory of the same."

CHAPTER XXXIX

THERE were children up at the Manor—a little boy and a girl. They arrived one day in a governess cart, and stopped outside the forge. The nurse was driving. She probably said, " Sit still. The man will come "; and Wattie came as fast as he could. But meantime the boy flung open the door, missed the step, and pitched headlong into the road. There was a fine to-do. The pony plunged forward, the nurse pulled the reins, only the little girl sat quite still. Wattie picked up the young gentleman, who burst into tears in his arms. " He's a naughty boy," said the nurse, and took him away from Wattie. She propped him up with one cushion ; the little young lady gave him another ; and he buried his face and finished his sobbing. He was sobbing as they drove away, but he lifted one eye to look at Wattie. The little young lady was looking across the road at The Bell.

That governess cart was always about. It jingled past the forge regularly once a day. In the afternoon they went for a walk. Wattie met them in Marchington village.

" Hullo !" said the little young gentleman. He seemed about eight years old. " Hullo !" The nurse had hold of his hand, and as she walked on, he had to walk too. It was the little young lady who looked behind.

After that they came to the forge, bringing their

ponies to be shod.   They ran in together, then stopped,
partly because the mate was there.   The boy very
soon made friends with the mate, and was wielding
one of the heavy hammers.   He wielded it very nearly
on to the little young lady's head.   It caught the tip
of her shoulder.   He yelled to her to look out, and she
looked out, and stood in another place.

" Hi there !   Who'll shoe my horse ?"

" Don't shout," said the nurse.

" I shall shout if nobody comes.   Hi! somebody,
come !   Who'll shoe my horse ?"

At this minute appeared the foreman.   He seized
young master, lifted him up, and set him on one of
the ponies.

" It's hers !   It's hers !   Take me off !" he screamed,
and he scrambled down for himself.   He had lost the
little young lady.   " Where are you ?   What are you
doing ?   Oh, there you are ! . . .   He's only blowing
the bellows."   He came and watched too.   Then he
got tired and grabbed her skirt, and pulled her towards
the door.   " Don't you hurt my pony's foot," he said
to the mate in passing (the mate said just anything
in reply), and then he saw a flock of geese, and ran
out and cheered them along the road.

Wattie took the ponies back.   The children were
racing up the drive as Wattie turned in at the gates.
(They had been painting the iron railings.)

" Hullo !   It's you. . . .   I hope they're properly
shod.   Get out of the way.   I want to look."   He
was squatting down with his tiny crop, and rapping
at one of the little white feet.   " We go cubbing
to-morrow," he said, and as it was no good rapping,
he got up and dusted his breeches.   " We've never
been cubbing before. . . .   Dinner !" he cried, as
somebody beckoned, and he cut away over the grass.
" Come !" he screamed.   But she did not come.   She
was stooping to pick up first one, then the other, of her
own little pony's feet.

It was just a week later that Wattie heard the wheels

of the governess cart. They were rattling down the hill, going home in the grand October sunset.

" Stop ! Stop !"

And the nurse pulled suddenly up. " Whatever's the matter ?"

The young gentleman waved with both his arms. " I want to show him my leg. Hi! come and look at my leg ! . . . Please move " (he was getting it out). " There's my stocking. Isn't it fat ? It's lint underneath. Bother my garter ! . . . Now then, look !"

" Nobody wants to see your leg. Cover it up," said the nurse.

" *He* wants to see. . . . I got that cubbing. I went at a hedge ; it was ever so high—quite as high as . . . as high as . . . how high ? Oh, she wouldn't know ! *She* wasn't allowed to jump it. You weren't allowed, were you ? Only the men, and *that's* what happened. But it's what you've got to expect ;" and he patted his leg.

" Till you learn to keep your seat," said Wattie.

" It's a good thing they wouldn't let *her* try." He pulled up his stocking. " Nurse, can't you make this lint lie down ? . . . It wouldn't have been very nice if *she* had got cut about."

" The little young lady, perhaps, knows how to take a hedge."

" Oh no, she doesn't—not a hedge like that. She only jumps quite little hedges. Ask her how little is the biggest hedge she's ever jumped. But she wouldn't know. . . . Look out for yourselves ! It's coming back on the cushion. Good-bye ! Good-bye !" And they rattled away.

On Sunday the children came to church, young master with a stick. " An accident in the hunting-field," Wattie heard him whisper, hobbling in, " and I'm not to kneel down."

He sat between his father and mother, and the little young lady sat beyond. Their heads appeared over the back of the pew. They recognized Wattie as they

came out—"*The man is in church*"—and then they
followed him up the street.

"We didn't know you came to church. We've
never seen you there before. We aren't obliged to
stay for the sermon. We stayed to-day because we
had each got sixpence to put in the bag. It's for the
pews in Marchington Church. That isn't the real
church where we went. There's an old church. We
know. *She* wanted to get inside, but she couldn't,
because it was locked."

"It isn't always locked," said Wattie.

"When isn't it locked ? We've been three times,
and it's always locked."

"The time to go," said Wattie, "is on Saturday
afternoon."

"No, it's not, for it was Saturday afternoon that
we went."

"Ah !" said Wattie. "Did you tap at the door ?"

"I banged for all I was worth."

"Yes, but you must not bang. Now, suppose on a
Saturday afternoon someone came and tapped very
gently, I've a sort of idea the door would open."

"Would it ?"

"Tap very gently, mind !"

"*She* shall tap—her tiniest tap, like this. . . . Do
you hear ?" He ran to her across Wattie, and then
ran back. "But it isn't true. I don't believe—
I don't believe it ! I don't believe. Come along ;
they're calling. Don't run, because of my leg. Good-
bye ! Good-bye ! Good-bye."

CHAPTER XL

IN a village like Marchington, where everyone knew everyone's business, it was strange that it should escape observation when Wattie began to go up to the church. Now that the building was stopped, very few people went that way; and if it had come to anyone's ears that Wattie was seen to go up the path and try the lock of the little north door, all Marchington would have heard about it, and inquired what he was doing there. But Wattie could always slip in and out, and no one be any the wiser. No one in Wattie's case put two and two together. Mrs. Moon, who cleared the table week after week for Wattie, would never associate Wattie with painting. As to where he might spend his spare hours, he was grown up now, and must see to himself. Nor were the foreman and mate any better at sorting and summing their facts. The foreman would ask Wattie in to tea of a Sunday. They sat round the table, old and young, and talked for more than an hour. And yet, as he came, so Wattie went. They knew not a pin's point more than he told them. The mate knew nothing, of course.

And now he was going to tell the children. There was the soft rat-tat on the door.

" . . . Lock it behind you, or nurse may come. Did you hear our knock ? You must have been listening. I didn't know *you* would open the door. You said *it would open*, and I thought . . . Oh, what a mess ! Why, you're painting ! Who gave *you* leave to paint in church ? I say, he's painting in church. . . . Where's she gone ? Oh, there you are ! Come here and see. He's painting in church."

Wattie went back and took up his brushes ; the children came pressing near.

" What on earth are you doing ? What on earth is he doing ? I don't believe you know what you're doing.

Do you know what you're doing ? . . . That's a horse.
Whose horse is that, if you please ?"

" Are you sure it belongs to somebody ?"

" It must belong to somebody. Every horse in
the whole of England belongs to somebody. I would
give a hundred thousand pounds to know to whom
this horse belongs. . . . He's going to pretend he's
too busy to tell us. But he could tell us at once if
he liked. I've got a paint-box at home. Who taught
you how to paint ?"

" I don't know," said Wattie. " I learnt."

" Somebody must have taught you. You know,
but you don't mean to tell. He's not going to tell
us anything. Ask him a lot of questions, and see ! . . .
Well, if nobody taught you to paint, you can't know
how, and you may as well stop. If nobody taught
him to paint, then he doesn't know how. . . . You
haven't noticed one thing : I'm walking without a
stick."

" When are you hunting again ?"

" Perhaps next week ; but I'm not to jump."

" Not to get thrown, you mean."

" I could have jumped if I'd been on Fun. *She* rode
Fun, and she got over."

" Why, I thought you said . . ." began Wattie.

" Ah yes, I said she wasn't allowed, but she jumped
when she thought we weren't looking. Only Major
saw her, and then it came out. It didn't come out
for ever so long. She wouldn't tell, because, if she
told, they might not let her go cubbing again."

" Did they ?"

" Oh yes. She may jump if she likes, but I mustn't,
because of my tumble. I wish I had been on Fun that
day. . . . Who gave you leave to paint on the
wall ?"

" Somebody told me I might."

" Somebody told you you mightn't, and that's why
you lock the door. We know all about you now. Is
it a secret ? Have I guessed ?"

Wattie nodded his head.

"A secret! a secret! Tell us more. Tell us," he cried, "or I'll run away with your paint-box, or I'll stamp on your palette, or I'll break up your brushes!"

"It's a long story," said Wattie.

How the little young lady clapped her hands! She dropped at his side, the boy at the other.

"This is a very old church," began Wattie, cleaning the paint off his fingers.

"How old? Older than you?"

"Years and years older than me."

"It's not all the same age—like you."

"That's very true. It is being restored."

"We know that," said young master. "That's what our sixpence was for. Was it so old that it tumbled down?"

"Certainly not. I believe it would still be standing if it hadn't been for the storm."

"What storm? Tell us what storm at once, or I'll smash your box, and stamp on your palette and . . ."

"A storm many summers ago. We had had some piping hot weather; then it got sultry and close. The streams were all drying up; then came the storm, and the streams were filled."

"*Ah, but the church?*"

"Well, the church was destroyed—no, partly destroyed—by lightning."

"Lightning? Was anyone killed?"

"Only two persons."

"Were they in church?"

"Yes."

"What were they doing?"

"Saying the Psalms."

"How do you know?"

"I was in church, too."

"Why weren't you killed?"

"I was right at the back."

"Ah, but supposing the lightning had struck at the back?"

" It didn't."

" Ah, but supposing it had ? Once in a very bad storm we got into nurse's bed. I hate thunder !"

" I have more to tell you about the church."

" After the storm ? Go on."

" There was a window . . . well, look round . . . not Christ with the twelve Apostles, but the angel-window above. . . . When I was a boy and looked up at that window, what do you think I used to see ?" They stared with open mouth. " Two horses stained on the glass."

" Not *really !* You would never see horses in church."

" It does not sound likely, does it ? And I doubt if you could have found such another church in the whole of England with just such another window, and just such a curious story attached."

" What was the story attached ?"

" The horses belonged to a fine old man who lived where you are staying now."

" What do you mean ? We are not staying any-where. We've not stayed anywhere all this year, and we shan't until we go to London for a week at Christmas."

" I meant the Manor. He lived there. It belonged to him. It had belonged to him and his fathers, and then it belonged to his sons."

" And now it belongs to us. Go on about the horses."

" One of them was a strawberry roan, and the other a pure white mare."

The little young lady nodded her head.

" The roan was sent out to the war. He went with a cavalry regiment, and the Squire's son rode him ; and day after day they rode into battle—day after day, day after day."

" I know ; don't tell me. One day he was killed."

" No, he wasn't."

The little young lady drew in her breath.

" He returned safe and sound."

" But what happened *then ?*"

" They welcomed him home, and they pinned round his neck the cross which his master had won at the war."

The little young lady sought his face.

" But what happened *then ?*"

" Nothing. That's all. He died. But the Squire, he said he should like to remember the good old roan ; so he ordered a window to be set up to remind himself and his people."

" You said there were two, and one was white."

" About the white very little is known beyond the fact that she lived and died, and was mother to one little foal. But the Squire was fond of her, so it seems, for he gave her a place by the roan, and there they were standing side by side."

" Why don't they stand there now, instead of those silly angels ?"

" The angels are not at all silly. They are painted and drawn a great deal better than ever the horses were. Still, we were sorry when they went. They went in the storm."

" How did they go ?"

" They fell in with a crash."

" And the glass was broken. . . . And what became of the bits ?"

" I tried to put them together."

" What, in the lightning and storm ?"

" No ; it was three days later—a very fine afternoon. I went to look at the church, and I thought I might just as well hunt for the picture."

" It can't have been broken very small if you managed to put it together."

" It *was* broken very small, and I didn't manage to put it together, but I very nearly did."

" How long did it take ?"

" Two or three hours, perhaps. I pieced it out here just where you're sitting."

" Only fancy !   He pieced it out here, just where
we're sitting. . . .   *Then* what did you do ?"

" I went and sat down on the grass.   There were
big gaps in the walls, and you could walk in and out.
I went and sat down on a grave."

" To think ?"

" Not to think so much as to look about me.   And
whilst I was there I suddenly felt some creature was
coming."

" I don't believe it's true.   You're going to make
out an ogre came and ate you up, and yet you're
here."

" I'm here, yes ; and it wasn't an ogre.   It was a
horse, a young horse, a strawberry roan ; and there
were two great rents in the walls—one in the north wall
and one in the south —and where I was sitting I could
look through to the Manor fields and the Manor
chimneys ; and then I lost the fields and the chimneys
because the strawberry roan stepped in."

" Into the church ?"

" Into the church, and after him came a pure white
mare.   They filled the gap, they filled the church, and
they came along over the rubbish and rubble, and then
they stopped."

" Where ?"

" Just here.   They were in shadow.   I didn't know
it until they came into the sun, and then they were
picked out like these on the wall in bold lines like I am
painting."

" Are those bold lines ?"

" I think they are.   The strawberry stood a little in
front—here was the mare ; and they both turned round
to look at the sun."   (How it shone on their breasts
and beautiful bodies !)

" Why ?"

" I don't know why, nor perhaps did they.   They
were just enjoying themselves."

" Wasn't anyone there to look after them ?"

" Nobody.   They had strayed away.   I don't believe

they had ever been bridled." (Living, moving, deliberate creatures !)

"They ought to have been."

"So they were afterwards, I'll be bound ; but then
they were free to go as they pleased, and they chose
out the sunniest places." (It was a glorious, glorious
time !)

"I thought that was where you pieced your window."

"Yes, it was ; and they trod upon it." (So they
did, with deliberate feet !)

"What a shame ! And it was spoilt. . . . Oh,
look ! a tear fell out of her eye. . . . Those weren't
real horses, were they ?"

"I saw them."

"I don't believe *I* should have seen them."

"Oh yes, you would."

. . . How could he explain ? There are strange,
unaccountable things in life. Some people see them,
and some people don't. . . .

"Of course, if you want to see anything, you must
happen to *be* there and happen to *look*."

"I wish I had happened to be there ; *I* should have
looked. I would give one hundred thousand pounds
to see them come walking in. I would give one
hundred thousand pounds to find this church with the
walls knocked down. You never saw them after
that ?"

"Yes."

"Where ?"

"At the forge."

"They came to be shod ? Then they *were* real, and
somebody must have had them. Who had ? Somebody must."

"Somebody must, as you say."

PART IX

FRANK

" Fail I alone, in words and deeds?
Why, all men strive and who succeeds ?"

CHAPTER XLI

It was one cold day in winter when Frank was changing
lodgings that he came on an unfinished portrait. It
took him a minute to recollect. Even then the name
escaped him. It was the lively youth, anyway, who
hung about The Bell. No, he didn't; that was a libel:
he really worked at the forge. Frank stared at him
for a bit, then blew on his frozen fingers. " I wonder
if that boy is as philosophical in this biting frost as
he was eighteen months ago on a summer's evening."
And then the past rolled back. How had that canvas
come there? Who could trace its history? Why,
he had several times changed lodgings within the last
half-year—bundled his goods together in one place,
and pitched them out again in another. He had lived
in hopeless confusion. Not that he liked confusion:
he hated it. He would have liked every drawer,
every cupboard, opened and scoured, every portfolio
overhauled, and in earnest some day he should see it
was done; but not now, not now. He must wait till he
was healed. Time would heal, time would heal. When
he came back to London the summer before last he
was ill, really ill. He never knew how he managed
the journey. He travelled by night, and arrived in
the morning. He had gone straight to bed. Perhaps
it might have been better to have kept on the move,
called on his friends, only he turned so horribly sick;
frightened the landlady; *she* sent for the doctor, and

there he was laid by the heels for six solid summer weeks. When he got up, he went abroad. He attended to no business. He reached home again about Christmas-time—better—yes, better, but somehow shaken—that is to say, he had lost the power of facing things. He shrank now more than ever. He had all sorts of escapes and by-ways, where he instinctively fled if any unpleasantness came along— unpleasantness of a sort, that is. For example, his friends wished him to send pictures to two winter exhibitions, but he dared not risk the shock of refusal, though this was not a reason he could exactly give. Also, in that desk—that desk which the men were moving now, struggling under their burden—in that desk were Phillis's letters, unsorted, undestroyed. Something he ought to have done with them. If he opened the desk, which he rarely did, he kept his eyes from that left-hand corner, where they lay all upset, tossed about. He had put them back so in a hurry the night before he went down there, and had never touched them since. And now, supposing he were to die in a muddle, who would know what to do ?

What memories this canvas revived — this portrait of young what's-his-name! " I'll have you out," said Frank, and stuck the boy's head on an easel. Here was a funny thing ! He must be better ; a few months back he should have turned that portrait with a shudder to the wall. " We'll have you in next Academy," said Frank. " I said we should, only I meant last Academy, and last Academy I was not in a fit condition to put the crowning touch upon your head."

And at that moment Dolly came in, without her husband, and said : " Oh, I thought you moved in years ago."

" Then you haven't been near me for years ; that's proved," said Frank. " What brings you now ?"

" Nothing but pure affection. Mayn't I come to see a friend ? Oh, what a dear ! The boy, I mean ; only he isn't finished."

" That is what just struck me."

" Who is he ?"

" A blacksmith."

" Where does he live ?"

" Not here ; far away in the country."

" Oh ! . . . How's Phillis ?"

" All right. I mean, I don't know. She's in Italy."

" I say, Frank . . . it isn't true . . ."

" What isn't true ? Don't sit down on my paints."

" . . . That she refused you ?"

" Who said so ?"

" Oh, everybody !"

" Everybody ? My dear Dolly, I don't know everybody, nor does everybody know me."

" I mean, heaps of people. Well, mother for one. And I suppose you've been fool enough to take her at her word ?"

" . . . Dolly !"

" Yes ?"

" You're happily married ?"

" Rather ! Look, he's given me this pendant only this morning ; and he always lets me do what I like so long as I don't interfere with him. We said *that* from the first—not to fuss one another, but go our own ways."

" I see."

" And it works very well—at least, so I think. Jealousy seems such a stupid thing."

" It does."

" But we were talking of you and Phillis, not about Warner and me."

" I know. All I meant was that you must manage your own (apparently very simple) affairs, and leave me, etc."

" You're not offended ?"

" Not in the least."

" You should never take what a woman says. I said ' No ' to Warner twice. I knew he would ask me again. Phillis can't help being fond of you ; nobody could—the dearest boy in London."

" Hum !" said Frank ; " that settles it."

" Mother always says so ; and talking of mother, by the way, I wish you would go in some time and see her. She's so much alone, and she gets quite mopey."

" Isn't she well, then ?"

" She's not ill exactly ; just allows herself to get miserable. We took her for a ride last Saturday. We went sixty miles in little more than a couple of hours. Warner said it ought to make her sleep."

" Doesn't she sleep, then ?"

" She fidgets so. She worries, and there's nothing to worry about."

" No," said Frank.

" And it seems so stupid."

" Yes. How is Helena ?"

" Going strong, and the baby. He has thrown up the paper, you know—no, I don't mean the baby. He disapproved of the management. He is going to write books instead. He has written one, which has gone into two editions. Something to do with religion. You wouldn't like it ; you're orthodox—at least, you used to be. Well, I'm most awfully sorry, Frank ; you deserved better luck than that, though I shouldn't be surprised if it all came round in the end."

" Oh, it will come round," said Frank. " Go round, I mean—the world will."

" Oh, the world won't stop, I hope," said Dolly, " though I sometimes shouldn't mind if it did. But don't you expect too much of life—of love, that is. The great thing is not to worry. Husbands and wives worry too much. They try to be too fond and affectionate. Now, if you hadn't cared a snap about Phillis, she'd have married you."

" Poor Phillis !"

" Why ' poor ' ? Of course, I'm supposing that she hadn't cared a snap about *you*."

" We should have made a loving couple."

" You're much too sentimental. I might have known you would be. Well, keep your sentiment, dear boy ; it suits you, and I rather like it, but it's bound to bring you misery. You sit here in this studio of yours, painting all these wonderful pictures, and what do you know of life ?"

" Nothing," said Frank. " And where are all the wonderful pictures ?"

" That one, for example."

" We've seen that one before. The rest appear to be missing."

" All the better. I suppose they're sold. Anyway, I've seen hundreds of your wonderful pictures."

" Dozens, not hundreds, Dolly, and not very wonderful."

" But as to your knowlegde of life, it's—it's——"

" It's ignorance, isn't it ?"

" And you live in a fool's paradise."

" Oh, oh ! do I ? Perhaps you mean I *try* to, though."

" Try to, then. And, dear me, why shouldn't you ? Why shouldn't some of us be happy ?"

Poor Dolly ! That was a slip ! But she did not perceive it, and Frank never stirred. Or perhaps some shadow of inconsistency may have crossed her mind, for she broke off abruptly, and said : " Anyway, Frank, I wish you would look in on mother."

He did. It was more than a year since he had called at the house. No river picnics now ! He remembered how he had stood on the steps with the boat cushions under his arms. The girls had been very successful. If you thought of Dolly as she *was*, with her bosom friend and her three young men, and Helena with her Poor Law, and then thought of them both married—Helena with a baby, Dolly without—

you could not help smiling. . . . And here was his aunt alone in the drawing-room.

It was quite true that his aunt was in rather low spirits, but she cheered up before he left. On the whole, it struck him that she had more to say of real interest than in the days gone by. Perhaps this was because there were fewer interruptions ; in fact, there were no interruptions, except for the lamp and the tea-things ; and he sat and sat, and they talked and talked, and they actually got on to Wordsworth and Browning, and when the maid came in with the taper, his aunt had just quoted the line " Moving about in worlds not realized," and had to wait till the blinds were down before she could go on to explain that she did not know what the words meant, but thought them very beautiful, and she supposed it sounded ridiculous, but she believed she *felt* the meaning without *understanding* it.

" It isn't ridiculous at all," said Frank ; and he tried to show her that this was the very essence of poetry —the heart ever before the head, the spirit half out of the body—and that her very apology proved her a poet. Whereupon, of course, she took fright and beat a hasty retreat to the safe shores of common-sense, the plains of platitudes, and declared that she never could learn any poetry by heart, and that Dolly was so quick at it, and Helena had written very pretty verses.

There was this to be said for the unmarried woman (so Frank thought) : she was a unity ; she had not divided herself into pieces and shared herself round in a family. You lived again in your children—yes ; but in other words your children lived, *you* died. Might not some means be found for preserving the life of parents ? His aunt had died before her time. It was Helena's, Dolly's, turn to live. Now what a thousand pities ! He had always dimly perceived that his aunt had something to say, even in the picnic days when he helped her with the cushions—something to say between her talk, stray thoughts let out unawares as she chattered. She chattered less now than of old. There was no need to chatter—no one to whom, by-the-by, she might chatter. Now that the girls were married she found herself much alone. Those picnic days were for the girls, and, of course, it stands to reason that it cannot be much fun to arrange a lunch, and set it out, and see it eaten, and carry back what's over, including the cushions. Still, she had got the girls married; the absurd part being that the girls had got themselves married after all, and would have done so without any river picnics. Would they? Don't be too sure. They must sharpen their faculties somehow, somewhere, and even if three men in a boat were to suffer, they would not suffer much. Oh, Phillis, Phillis! you are different. Phillis, listen—listen all the way over from Italy; you and I, Phillis, walk in another world. . . . He opened the door of his lodging, and slipped inside in the dark. . . . And yet, what would Phillis make of Dolly's and Helena's mother? Pity her, perhaps; say, in the very kindest tones: "But, Frank, you must allow, she's rather dull."

CHAPTER XLII

PERHAPS he liked things dull. Perhaps it was not dull to sit and talk about things which really mattered, to talk the truth for once in a way. Perhaps it was not dull to be given a pile of his father's sermons in manuscript to read. Other people might think it dull.

"It is not your father's handwriting. I copied them myself."

"I thought I recognized your *t's*," said Frank, and he ran his eye down the first page. Should he re d? Should he put it from him? "Are they any good? I mean, have you ever read them? I would always

rather hear a sermon extempore." He laid them
on the table.

His aunt took them up again. "Your father's
sermons were never preached extempore," she
said.

"Oh, I know!" said Frank. "I was thinking of
that fellow I go to hear now on a Sunday, only I can't
remember his name."

She still held them in her hand.

"Every one of these I copied. Here and there are
scraps your father wrote. . . . This, for instance : his
last sermon. He never preached it, though."

She was holding it towards him. He must take it
or refuse.

"It's very neat," he said, and gave it back again.

"You keep it, Frank. Indeed, I should like you to.
Dear me, how one stores up things ! Who will read
these when I'm gone ? The letters would not interest
you. I used to consult your father sometimes, especially about investments—he never liked more than
three per cent.—and I asked his advice as to where
I should send the girls to school, and he said, ' Let them
stay at home'; and I think it has answered, for they have
neither of them given me any trouble, and both married
well."

So she talked on, and he folded the paper in half
with deliberation, making the edges meet exactly,
and then he put it back on the table.

"And, Frank, to change the subject " (he was relieved), "I was so much upset to hear " (what was
coming now ? . . Phillis ?)—" to hear what I heard the
other day. Dolly told me. But I hope that will
come all right in the end."

She *did* mean Phillis, then.

"I should never have satisfied Phillis," he said.
"She's a proud, exacting creature." And oh, how
tender ! . . . Yes, by the way, those were curious
adjectives, and his aunt expressed some surprise.

"Proud and exacting ! Then, Frank, it is a good

escape. You with a tyrant for your wife! That will never do. Come, you wait a year or so, and you shall find yourself happier than you ever hoped to be—happier than you ever deserved to be (I believe we are all of us that), with some gentle, unaffected, modest girl. I've just such a girl in my mind."

" No match-making, if you please. That would be hard on me and on the unaffected girl."

" I'm sure it wouldn't! She's the daughter of a very successful barrister, and—— But you're laughing at me ; and I'm glad you're laughing, for you are much too grave, and it is a sad sight to see a man break his heart over a woman ; and the women men break their hearts over are usually not worth it."

Frank made a plunge. He crossed his legs and said : " It is a solemn fact, aunt : I wasn't good enough for her. At one time I thought I was, but now I see I wasn't."

" Good enough in what way, please ?"

He paid no particular heed to her question. He plunged forward again. He was shaping the matter in his head. " I've always somehow shown up badly before Phillis. I *will* say that I think she has seen the worst of me."

" Shown up badly ! Seen the worst ! . . . What sort of a character do you give yourself ? . . . I should like her to see you here, with a dull old aunt, wiling away a winter's evening."

" By enlarging on my own affairs ! I don't think I should rise in her estimation. Oh, it's all right ; Phillis and I are very good friends. We understand one another perfectly, but——"

" But what ? You are very good friends, and understand one another : how much else do you require ? Young people expect a good deal, it seems."

" Phillis can command a good deal."

" She may command too much and get nothing," said his aunt. " *My* girls are happy enough."

Frank crossed his legs the other way.

" She might at least expect to have somebody she admired," he said.

" And why not admire you ?"

" Well, I don't know. I think on that score I can enter into her feelings. I admire *her* enormously—always have admired her since I was a boy."

" And yet you call her proud and exacting."

" Yes ; those were not the words to use : they would give a false impression ; to me they give a true one. Anyway, I repeat, I admire her enormously—honest, fearless, starry creature. What is there in me to compare with that ?... Oh, well, never mind. Besides, what is there I can offer ?"

" A very loyal heart."

" Oh yes, I know. My dear aunt, there are scores of loyal hearts about when it comes to a woman like Phillis. The majority of men are not such louts as to be insensible to all that truth and goodness. . . . But I've made such a hash of things."

" I don't see that," said his aunt. She spoke rebelliously. Of course she would, seeing that she did not, could not, mean what she said.

" I used to think I could paint."

" And so you can. Why, there was your picture in the Academy."

" My picture ! Yes, my one and only picture. One picture doesn't make a painter any more than one swallow a summer."

" But you will paint more. Last year you had been ill. You did not send anything up."

" No ; and I sometimes think I never shall again. I've not even the pluck to court refusal. It's an awful thing to make a start and then get stuck. You look a bigger fool than if you'd never made a start at all. Besides, you've just so much of the road to return upon before you start again in a new direction, though I should never do *that*. One can't at my time of life. Besides, Art is the only thing I'm the slightest good at."

" I wish you had been a preacher, Frank."

" Preaching isn't an art. . . . Well, it *is*, but it doesn't *seem* to be."

" I don't see why that matters."

" No more do I. . . . What rubbish it all is ! I believe, I still think, I can paint ; that I have in this poor head of mine (which aches horribly) some divine conceptions. I suppose conceit dies hard."

" I wish you did not get these headaches." This was what his aunt said. The headache at least was a thing of the present ; the preaching and painting, and the divine conceptions, could wait for another day.

As he was leaving the house that night, his aunt ran after him into the hall.

" You've forgotten this."

This was the folded scrap of paper, carefully folded edge to edge. He said : " Oh, all right, thanks !" put it in his pocket ; took it out when he went to bed. He found himself reading it ; carried on and on. If you once begin that sort of thing, you must see it through to the finish. *Ye know not what manner of spirit ye are of. . . . Self-examination.* (That was the first note jotted down.) *Most people examine themselves.* (Some of us too much. Introspective age. If he ever had a son, and that son examined himself, he should. . . . Never mind . . . go on.) *Confidence of youth.* ('Tisn't confidence at all ; it's blindness— stark, staring blindness. At Winchester he was a fool.) *Doubts of young manhood.* (Rather call them *certainties*, or else he was old for his age ! He had no longer the slightest *doubt* about his own futility.) *Disappointments of middle life.* (Then is life worth living ? Stupid old question ! *Wicked* old question ! That's not *our* business. Besides, life *is* crowded with joys. We forget the joys ; we remember the sorrows. Oh, vile, vile, vile ! Wrong, wrong, wrong ! He had dropped on his knees by his own bedside, not to pray— you can't call that praying—only better to kneel and sob than to stand and blaspheme. . . . And the paper

still in his hands.) *Review of the past : awful abyss ;
blank waste ; nothingness. Oh, wretched man that I am !*
(Then came the letter B. That meant Part II. Yes,
above there was letter A, worn very faint indeed.)
*Christ's compassionate look ; the Samaritan village ;
the men in that village.* (Yes, very good—not the
village, but the *men ;* and not the "men," but *this*
man, *that* man.) *The failures in that village.* (Just
so ! But don't drive a point too hard.)   *Ye know
not their manner of spirit—nay, more, ye know not your
own. Tender rebuke.* (So he thought ! Just the word !)
Hardly rebuke at all. (Ah, better still ! His father
thought so, too, did he ?) *Comfort, rather.* You *do
not know ;* God *knows. Comprehensive understanding.
Blessed security. Thou understandest my thoughts long
before.* (A very apt quotation.)

　. . . Was that all ?   Turn over the sheet. . . .   Nothing
on the other side.   Turn it back again. . . .   Just the
same.

　Still kneeling ?   Get up ! get up !   Had he a right
to dwell upon the past (his own futility), or look into
the future (Is life worth living ?)?   Had he a right
to anything but the immediate present ?   A day's
work, a day's wage, a day's sunshine, a day's storm.
He would like to be at the day's work now.   Pity
these thoughts come at night, so that your first plain
duty is sleep.   This is always the way.   He would
not toss ; he would lie quite still, quite resolute ;
resolutely crush down every vexatious imagination ;
shut his eyes and refuse to see the blank waste and
awful abyss ; idle terms at Winchester ; profitless days
at home ; empty years in London ; and on and on,
stretching on, ever so, idle, profitless, empty. . . .
Down, down ! . . .   Let him remember something
good.   How could he ?   How could he steady his
mind, with that yawning gulf in front of him ?   It
was enough to hold himself back, to keep a firm foothold, to gasp for help, to find he was still on the land,
to find he could summon up strength to say : " It is

not reasonable. Go on with your life. Finish it up. It can't be as bad as you suppose." Strange comfort suddenly ! And why comfort ? and why now ? But he slept—slept sound and secure—and yet, as he thought next morning, he had dreaded a wretched night. He woke fresh, too ! Felt better than he had felt all that week, and wanted to get to his work.

CHAPTER XLIII

As a matter of fact, he saw no reason for changing his plan of daily life—up at 7.30, breakfast at 8, studio 9 to 1, lunch, open-air exercise, tea at home or abroad, reading, dinner at home or abroad, reading again if at home, bed at 11. This had been his routine for many months past, with accidental modifications. Of course, you might be in your studio from 9 to 1, and yet come away ashamed of yourself. You might yawn and wander about, and shift your position a dozen times, and smoke—no ; he had given that up ; had not smoked at his work for six whole weeks, and painted worse in consequence—and you might read the *Times*, and write a note, and clean your palette—in a hundred ways you may keep yourself skirting the one business which should be on hand, and employing yourself with a hundred others.

Now to-day—to-day was different. If one always worked as one worked to-day ! . . . He should make something, he hoped, of this Marchington boy. It was a face to delight him. Such health and innocence ! And yet there was something behind that innocence. The fellow was no fool. Once or twice a bit too sharp, as Frank remembered with a blush. He would now be almost two years older—would be about nineteen ; the " boy " in him departed, the man appearing or just appeared. And this altogether knocked on the head any notion of going to Marchington and looking

his model up.   Better by far to finish the portrait from
memory (not such a difficult thing to do) than to find
himself face to face with a gawky, half-fledged youth,
who cruelly gave the lie to every stroke which had
gone before, grown either vulgar or coarse, with something worse than a cabbage-rose to spoil his natural
boyish beauty.   The cabbage-rose, by the way, he
half believed was a piece of nonsense—had half believed
it at the time.   So that if he went to Marchington . . .
Hullo ! one o'clock. . . .   A very successful morning.

Again over lunch.   *If he went to Marchington.* . . .
He had more than half a mind to go.   He should avoid
the Manor : he had no wish to see strangers in and out
of the gates ; also he should avoid The Bell ; also the
forge, which was opposite.   He should cut all those
middle years out of his life, and return to the years ago.
He wanted to see the Vicarage.   He should not call,
but get round the fields at the back ; afterwards go
to the church and the grave.   He should choose a day
haphazard.   Supposing to-morrow was fine, he should
take the early train ; he should pack sandwiches in his
pocket ; he should be a boy once more, with a boy's
deep-rooted antagonism to all maturer folk, and an
instinct to carry him under the hedges out of sight of
the conspiring world.

To-morrow *was* fine.   He packed his pockets, and
caught the train, and rushed through the country north.
It was the month of January, but would you think it ?
The sun was hot on the brown ploughed fields, there
were flights of larks like flights of swallows, and the
road from the station-yard was powdered as in the
month of June.   There are winter days that are more
than summer.   He ate his lunch in the meadow below
the church, where as a boy he had found a capital bit
to sketch.   He found the same sketch again ; not a
stick or a stone was altered.   There was the half-open
gate, the peep through to the Vicarage garden, the
glimpse of the poplars on the lawn, and here in the
foreground he could have sworn the very same broken-

down cart as of old.   He had got into trouble with the
perspective.   It was the meadow where he sometimes
felt odd.   He did not feel odd just now.   He was all
in a glow with his walk, and could sit quite cheerfully
in the hedge munching his sandwiches.   Then he must
push his way nearer, nearer . . . as near as he dared.
A bachelor lived there now, probably shut up with his
sermon in the study overlooking the drive.   The hammock had gone from between the poplars, but the grass
underneath was still worn in a patch, and the path
still wound to the garden-door.   Well, so it would. . . .
If he craned his neck he could see his bedroom window
facing the rising sun.

Ah, should he like it all over again ?   Was it not
happiness, on the whole ?   And such glorious plans for
the future, laying your head on your pillow at night
with schemes for remote or immediate glory, and a
general sense for the present of comfort and all things
provided as a matter of course !   Should he like it all
over again—the arguments with Phillis, the walks to
and from the church with his mother, the saying of
Collects on Sundays ?   Why, yes, he would—even to
being scared to death by nameless fears, which he
now understood.   Sandwiches have been known to
produce them, and he had all but swallowed the last
intact !

He would take a turn through the fields to the
church.   How he loved the perfect stillness, the earth
bound up in iron bonds !   Sleep, deep sleep, contented,
powerless to resist, and yet above the blue sky mildly
blessing you ! . . .   So in the churchyard sleep, deep
sleep . . . real sleep.   No quiver of decay, no stir of
resurrection, but an unutterable forgetting, a pause, a
long arrest—quite distinct from *death*, which is *something*, which is *passing*, which is *moving*, which is
changing, which is *life again without cessation*. . . .
Oh, to lie here in the winter is better than the
spring !

That gentle mother ! . . .   One never comprehends

one's parents until one is grown up. . . .   If he had
them back again they would meet on equal—at any
rate, more equal—terms.   He should be a man—a man
beside his father, a son beside his mother.   He had
loved her, sometimes could have broken down over
her, wept over her, clung to her—a part of her he was ;
but he should not dispute so much.   Dispute ?   Who
disputes with his parents after a certain age ?   He was
not so big a fool as to interrupt his mother now at
every other word, and put the concluding stop to all
his father said. . . .   And yet he would not have them
back.   The dead are very safe.   Besides, he should be
jealous over his mother.   He did not want to see what
he was bound to see—that he was only the child after
all—*their* offspring, born of *them*, and they all in all
to one another. . . .   And they had died together.
Often he had thought it might have been as well had
he died, too, and wondered what the pain was like, and
what it would be to pass—three souls, father, mother,
son—on to the other side of life, floating in close company, possibly hand in hand, to the region of the
spirits, of the angels—who knows what ?   It may be
God Himself, or perhaps the Jesus of the Gospels ?
. . . So he would think in flashes, when other people
were talking, when he was talking himself—at Winchester in Second Chamber, at Surbiton with his aunt,
rumbling back on the top of a bus from the Academy
Schools.   Did he think so now ?   No ; now he was
more accustomed to life, no longer confused life with
a " career," something into which you got comfortably
shaken and settled by, let us say, your twenty-first
birthday.   It was something more intricate than that
—a web to take all your time in weaving.   Not that
you wove it.   It got itself wove, whilst *you* continued to live—as, indeed, you are bound to live—
without question, and if not here, why, somewhere
beyond.

But only once since that grave was dug had he
come and stood beside it, and that was with Phillis.

How long ago ? Four, five, nearly six years ! . . .
An odd thing had happened. He had been overmastered, completely overmastered for the moment,
by a sort of hysterical longing. He had even, as people
would say, made a distinct proposal of marriage—well,
not very distinct. Anyhow, with the curious wisdom
of a girl she had put it aside, had treated it as if it
never had been ; consequently, had saved him hours,
days, months of shame and remorse. You do not
exactly want to weep on a woman's neck and say,
" Will you take me ?" and then be taken. She had
broken down, too ; that was some comfort. Sympathy,
he supposed—no suffering of her own—and she quickly
cheered (he remembered that), and they dropped a
shoe, and called at the forge, and how she chattered
and nodded and laughed ! Blessed, unconscious
creature ! . . . Ah, she refused him eventually,
because he was not good enough. It had taken him
some little time to arrive at *that !* and then not by
sudden inspiration, but a slow process of reasoning.
He was unworthy at so many points. He had learnt
them one by one. He was bold, attempting too much ;
timid, achieving too little ; rash to do something ;
slow to do anything ; steady in untried virtue—oh yes,
but subject to awful collapses. No hero he, and Phillis
should have a hero ; Phillis would glory in ribbons and
stars. He had thought of that long ago—of joining
the army, and serving abroad, and coming back with
an empty sleeve, and of Phillis's pride and compassion.
But no ; he had pushed that away—a bogus hero !
Should he be any the less himself—the more brave—
because some doctor had shorn off his arm willy-nilly ?

And yet *he* should never find a woman to be what
Phillis might have been ; for it is highly probable—
nay, certain—that you are perfectly loved and understood only by one person. *That one* we'll hope we
find ! But when for some folly on our part, some
feebleness which hinders us from representing ourselves as we really are, so that we are not recognized—

oh, what a pity ! None of that feebleness in *her!*
She was recognizable from the beginning ; he had
known her from the first. A woman properly com-
posed, a woman of such equal parts ! . . . And to
see that ladder against the wall reminded him of how,
as a girl, with aggravating common-sense (*he* had
called it bravado), she climbed on to the roof, and
then went higher, and he, with just as aggravating
common silliness, told her some foolish yarn—that is
to say, a direct lie—to the effect that he had been up
there before.

There being no particular danger in ascending a
safely-lodged ladder, he would climb up now himself.
On the occasion of Phillis's common-sense or bravado
he had got as far as the gutter. He remembered he
noticed a new bit of piping fitted in with the old. Now
the piping was new altogether. This was Pigeon's
work. And had Phillis, he wondered with a smile,
come up herself to be satisfied over each of the joints
from the head to the ground ?

Here was a second ladder. You could mount it
with just as little fear, seeing you had the roof beneath
you. His great-great-grandfather was mad, and had
scrambled up in a tearing gale. *He* was perfectly
sober, and perfectly sane, and the air was hardly a
breath. This, then, was where she had stood. Well,
there was a parapet. Moreover, he had learnt to look
down ; he had also learnt to know what he was doing,
comprehend his own actions, and say, " I have
climbed the tower *to look at the view."*

What a pretty village ! He had never seen it spread
before him—the Vicarage, the drive, the garden, a bit
of the lane running down to the church, a cluster of
tiny cottages, the white patch of the station-yard
with a glimpse of the railway-line beyond it, Jones's
farm and the top of his wall, a snatch of the Brinkley
road as it wound up the swelling hills towards Brinkley
over the brow, the same road stretching the other
way past The Bell and the forge (swallowed up in the

dip) to the Manor gates, which you partly guessed, and on, if you only could follow it, but you followed instead the Manor drive, and stopped at the lawn and the great front-door, and watched as if, from that sleeping house, somebody should awake.

Yet he was vexed when round the bend came a man with a couple of trotting ponies—mice at this distance—and out on the steps ran a couple of children —miniature children you would say. And with their awakening the world awoke. He saw the rooks float out of the elms ; here they came cawing and wheeling towards him ; and under his feet the noisy jackdaws giddily mingled and swirled. The sky was full of commotion. He could not stand it. Down, down, down ; he had been up long enough. That's the last rung ; here's the gutter ! What a fuss and to-do ! Leisurely, leisurely, to the ground.

CHAPTER XLIV

ALL those early January mornings Frank worked hard at the portrait. He was tolerably well content. He invited his aunt to come to his studio. Did she want anyone else to meet her ? No, she preferred to come alone, or, if not that, in a crowd ; for it is so embarrassing to look at a picture in company : nobody knows whose turn to speak, each overhears the other, you all start talking and suddenly stop—a racket with dreadful pauses.

" There can be no crowd, anyway," said Frank, " and therefore you shall come alone."

When she came, despite the fact that only Frank was there to greet her, she was flurried and nervous, also flushed.

" Where's the picture ?" she asked. " I'm sure I shan't know what to say. . . . Oh, is this it ? How charming ! But don't expect me to *say* anything,

Frank—not to *say* anything—though I can see at once it is beautiful."

" Now," said Frank, " you sit down here—you look rather tired, by the way—and make a thorough examination, and don't say a word."

" Well, if *I* don't talk, *you* must ; we can't have silence," said his aunt. " You tell me about the portrait, Frank—what I ought to think. He's a delightful boy, I'm sure."

" You think that, do you ? I believe you're right. Have you a headache ?"

" Nothing to speak of. I've not been very well."

" Cold ?"

" I suppose so. I lay awake shivering all last night."

" Oh, I'm so sorry ! Why did you come ?"

" Because I felt better."

" And now you feel worse ?"

" No ; at any rate, not as poorly as I felt last night and on Monday afternoon. But tell me something about the painting—tones and values, you know. . . . I love that bit of open collar. What a clean skin ! That boy washed."

" Do you think so ? I dare say. But he kept his clean skin carefully covered. I could hardly persuade him to take out that stud."

" And, oh dear, the stud appears ! That's just a boy ! The stud all ready for use, but discarded. Well, I like that ! But the picture, Frank ; you don't explain. I want to know what to think about it. I look at that boy, and he *tells* me something."

" Do you think so ? Yes, by Jove, he could talk. He told me a lot, I remember. . . . I believe you're in for a horrid cold."

" Never mind that. The eyes are wistful."

" That's all wrong. There was nothing wistful about the beggar. He told me he had no hope."

" Oh, the poor dear ! But, then, he was young, and the young are terribly hopeless. It's only when you are quite grown up you expect life to treat you properly."

What gleams of philosophy do appear in apparently commonplace middle-aged women! That was just about the point *he'd* arrived at.

" But you mistake my meaning," he said, waiving the gleam of philosophy. " I meant he *desired* no hope. He seemed to think he had all he wanted."

" Did he? Had he? I could hug him! But we forget the picture. I know what it is. You think a stupid old woman like your aunt has no appreciation, and so you spare your breath and pains. I am sure I should know what to think if you told me. Now what is that boy so eager to say? Do you see his lips are opening, Frank?"

" Are they? Yes, so they are—just parted. Oh, he'd no end to talk about."

" And nice sweet breath comes out of his mouth. He never smoked, I'm positive."

" No, he never smoked. By the way, I told him not."

" Example is better than precept. You, I suppose, smoked all the time."

" I dare say; very probably; I forget. But, then, this chap was young. He hadn't already gone to the bad. . . . Look here, I don't believe you ought to be out."

" Oh, never mind me! Besides, I kept in the best part of three days, and it's very warm for January—only the 8th of January."

" Horribly muggy and close. Well, have some tea, and you'll feel better. . . . You're a capital critic."

" A critic! My dear Frank, what have *I* to say? It is for *you* to instruct. . . . What do *I* know about technique? . . . There, that throws more light upon it." (He had lit a couple of candles.) " How his face comes to greet you! The rest disappears. It's the innocency I admire—the fresh, candid, welcoming

look ! . . . It's the innocency I admire—the fresh——
Oh dear ! . . . Wait a bit. . . . How very odd ! . . ."
She had been standing ; she groped for her chair.

" Aunt, you're not well."

She covered her face with her hand.

" You don't think you're really bad—sickening for
something ?"

She removed her hand and laughed, but her laugh
broke off short with half a groan. Frank came quite
close, then as quickly drew back.

" Aunt," he said, " I don't want to alarm you, but
you've got something like a rash on one side of your
face ; or perhaps it is only where you rested your
cheek." He came nearer again to look.

" Oh, rubbish, my dear !" said his aunt. But she
got up and went to the mantelpiece, over which, of
course, hung a mirror. " Bring a candle," she said.
He brought them both.

" It's a fact," he said, and set down the candles.
" It's a regular rash—little red pimples."

" Humph !" said his aunt. " Those weren't there
when I started out."

" Nor when you came in an hour ago. It's something you've picked up here." He laughed, rather
feebly, perhaps.

" I think I'd better go home, Frank."

" I think you had, and get to bed." He picked up
her umbrella and opened the door. " Wait a bit !
Wait a bit ! I'll call a cab." He ran in hot haste.
He whistled and whistled. . . . Confound the cabs ! . . .
His aunt had followed him down the stairs. " Keep
away from the draught," said Frank. " By the way,
who's at home to look after you ?"

" I was going to ask if you wouldn't mind . . ."

" Mind what ? Here's the cab !"

" I've no one to send to the doctor. Both my
maids . . ."

" I'll go for the doctor. You get in. What about
your maids ? . . . I'll tell him to come round

at once. . . . Hullo, though! who'll take care of you?"

"Oh, the maids will be home by ten. It was a wedding. Good-night! Bed is the place for me."

"Just a minute!" said Frank. He flew back into the passage, and felt in the dark for his hat. It tumbled to the ground, but he caught it up and ran down the steps, and jumped in beside his aunt.

"My dear boy, why should you trouble? Frank, *do* go back." But they had started. She leant against the cushions, shutting her eyes. Frank looked round at her once, had an awful fear she had fainted, was dead; but no, she was breathing heavily. As they passed the flaring lights of a shop he saw the marks on her face again. He had guessed at once, though he dared not say. The word had come into his mind, though unspoken—smallpox. It was a nightmare drive, but one by one they turned the corners. Suddenly his aunt sat up. "Frank, it might be infectious! Are you afraid?"

"Oh, I don't care. I never catch diseases."

She tried to see herself in the glass. "It might be chicken-pox. I hope it isn't anything worse. I didn't know I'd been near any illness. This is bad weather for infectious complaints."

"We want cold to kill the germs," said Frank.

"I was with somebody yesterday who had been with somebody else who was nursing a case . . . Here we are!"

"A case of what?" said Frank.

"That was only influenza; and I don't think influenza ever brings out spots."

"I'll pay," said Frank. "You go inside." He followed her into the house. "I've sent the man to the doctor's. I think I'll wait here till he comes."

Of course, his aunt protested—he knew she would—but she was too ill to prevail against him, and he helped her up the stairs. At the top of the stairs he felt her whole weight on his arm. He struggled to the bed-room. The door stood ajar, and he carried her in and laid her on the bed. It was dark, but he had in his pocket the minute silver matchbox won years ago at one of the Surbiton card-parties. He lit the gas, and came back to the bed. His aunt had opened her eyes.

"I'm very ill, Frank," she whispered. "You'd better go."

"Can you get off your clothes?" he said. He began to unfasten her brooch, her collar, the hooks on her shoulder, and down her side. Then he took off her boots; then lifted her up. "If you've got a hot-water bottle . . ." he said.

She looked round the room. . . . "In the kitchen."

"I'm going to fill it," said Frank. "Try to get into bed before I come back."

What an age it took him to find the bottle! and then the kettle had to be filled, and was ever water so sullen? When he got back his aunt was in bed. She did not open her eyes. He bent over her. She was still breathing—that was one mercy—but he feared that at any moment the breathing might stop. He slipped in the bottle. This was all he could do, except, per-haps, for lighting the fire, and he put a match to the grate.

On the mantelpiece there were photographs of the girls: Helena with her baby, Helena without her baby, the baby without Helena; Dolly in a large metal frame all alone at one extreme edge, her husband in a similar frame all alone at the other. Dolly came fairly often to see him—funny Dolly, with her know-ledge of life. Her husband had a stupid but kindly face; and yet you could call people stupid from habit. He looked out of that frame at Frank with a couple of rather intelligent eyes. Frank lowered the gas. Nothing now to do but to wait for the doctor. He stole to the bookcase on the wall. A Bible, a Thomas à Kempis, a pamphlet on "Nursing," a "Guide to

the Lakes," a green edition of Tennyson, one or two
paper-covered novels in French, and a couple of old
Monthly Packets. The pamphlet on "Nursing" was
wedged in between the Bible and Thomas à Kempis,
and one of the novels divided the first and second
volumes of Tennyson's "Complete Works" (which
also proved to be incomplete), and there seemed no
harm in restoring order. Then he took out the
Thomas à Kempis, and read. He had read it
all before. Never mind; he ran his eye down the
pages.

In came the doctor; Frank knew him well.

"Hullo, Burnet! I didn't expect to see *you*."

Frank rapidly explained, then stood on the hearth,
while the doctor made his examination. He jumped
when the doctor touched his arm.

"Sans doute," he said. "We've several cases."

"What?"

"Smallpox. How long is it since you were vaccinated?"

"It was my second term at Winchester. That's
thirteen years ago this spring. There was a smallpox scare."

"Well, I'll come round to-morrow and see to you.
Very likely you'll escape, but we'll take the necessary
precautions. You say the servants are out at a
wedding; well, when they come back from the wedding, you slip home. What's your address? Still
the same?"

"The same street, but I've moved to Number 14."

"Number 14. Very good. I shall send a nurse
round here in less than an hour."

CHAPTER XLV

OH, the weary weeks of sickness ! Three long weeks in
bed ; two long weeks half in, half out ; and a still longer
week out—out of bed, that is, but confined to his
room. His room ? A private room in a public hospital. They carried him there when too ill to remon-
strate ; and yet he had tried to say that he would far,
far rather die where he was. Now that he was up again
he felt from time to time that he would far, far rather
he *had* died, whether he died in his lodgings or in this
little white-tiled room. The white-tiled room was
beautifully clean ; this at first had been some comfort,
by " at first " meaning the first days when he began
to care or notice ; but latterly those tiles provoked
him : he had an odd desire, a passion, a mania, to
cover them with pictures. Sometimes he dreamt of
offensive pictures, and this was horrible. The sim-
plicity of the furniture, too, which at first had certainly
pleased him, became now a constant source of annoy-
ance. Time after time his head would turn from the
chair by the wall to the three-legged table, then on to
the washhand-stand, then back to the chair, and round
once more—a mechanical hypnotic movement which
he only checked by shutting his eyes. Or when he
roamed with his thoughts far away, out through the
window, out of the room, and suddenly, by a sharp
turn, came in to find himself starting again at the chair,
he would groan aloud in wearied disgust, " I've seen
you before," and bury his face.

Of course, no one could come to see him. Friends
and relations sent presents and sympathy—those, at
least, who knew of his illness, as they heard of it one
by one. Raikes sent a barrel of oysters ; he was the
first to know ; he knew because he often walked into
Frank's studio, and happened to walk in that very
day when they drove Frank off in the ambulance. One

of the two remaining elderly cousins at Tunbridge Wells sent a cardboard shoe-box packed with roses; his old guardian a pamphlet on Church and State; grapes came from various sources (Dolly sent a magnificent bunch); letters innumerable came too. Dolly wrote frequently; was very sorry Frank was ill; wished she could come and see him; wasn't afraid of smallpox; shouldn't care to be marked, but, as to being ill, wanted some such sort of amusement; town was horribly dull—would be more lively when Frank came back, etc. It was a pity Dolly wrote so often, wrote so much, and sought so far for her woes and joys. Perhaps it was just as well Frank could not answer her letters, or he should have told her so—told her, too, that smallpox was horrid (loathsome disease!), that to be ill was—to be ill, and there's no making anything else of that! And then Frank would think of Dolly's mother (there was always a postscript about her mother—" Mother is heaps better," " oceans better," " pretty nearly well "), and of that night when he helped her to bed, and the metal frames on the mantelpiece, and Dolly's husband's intelligent eyes, and " sentimentality " and " caring a snap," and " the great thing not to worry."

Of course, there were periodical visits from the doctor, who began at first with professional jokes, and afterwards, learning that Frank was a Wykehamist, used to stand by the bedside asking advice about public schools for his eldest son. There were also the nurses. He had two. A third came in for a fortnight, but was then removed. He was glad when the third was removed, because she would not give him enough to drink; and when the doctor told him he might have more, she gave him less, from which he concluded that there was some little hitch between this nurse and the doctor, or else that the nurse considered his request (an innocent one, he had thought it!) a breach of honour, and took a dislike to him accordingly. Anyway, he could not regret her departure, but so weak he was in body, or irresolute in will, that he let the new nurse go in and out five times before he made a similar request, or, rather, ventured to say, " I'm very thirsty."

" That's soon cured," said the nurse, and brought him drink at once. She prepared a special drink for him, and set it by his bed. She also moved the chair one day, at Frank's desire, to the other side of the table. " I get so horribly bored at the order of things," he explained. Not that she seemed much to comprehend this piece of explanation; she fancied it was because of his " artistic sense," as she called it. His sense—oh, his sense was at a low ebb.

" You *are* an artist, aren't you ?" the nurse inquired; for he had made no rejoinder to her remark.

" Well, that is what puzzles me," said Frank. " I lie here questioning whether I am."

" Oh, you'll feel differently when you are up."

" I dare say," said Frank. " I have a very bad habit of ' feeling differently,' as you call it."

" A very bad habit of feeling differently ? I'm sure I don't know what that means. I am going now. Is there anything I can do for you, Mr. Burnet, before I go ?"

" Nothing, thank you," said Frank.

This was what they were always saying : " Is there anything I can do for you, Mr. Burnet ?" They did too much for him. He was never allowed to do anything for himself ; and, whatever you may say, it is unnatural for a man to lie full length or recline in an easy-chair and be waited on by a woman—by a woman, too (making worse of it, though you may not agree, but in point of fact it does)—a woman who might very well be your own sister ; and the idea of sending Phillis for one thing and another—a pencil, a sheet of paper, a sponge and towel, a clean pocket-handkerchief ! . . .

By the way, what did Phillis know about him ? He was thinking of this one day when the letters were delivered, and there was one with the foreign post-mark and Phillis's large hand. She was " very sorry ";

hoped he was " better "; hoped he would " soon be
well "; had heard of him through Daisy, who had heard
from Bob, who had heard from somebody at Marchington. She herself was very well, only rather tired of
pictures ; there were too many Early Italian masters.
It was only a short letter ; it took, perhaps, one minute
to read from end to end, another minute to read again,
but many minutes to ponder. What was the post-
mark ? Florence. She was at Florence. He should
not go *there* to recruit. In a fortnight's time the doctor
wanted him to be up and away to a warmer, sunnier
country ; and he had thought of Florence. He would
go to the South of France instead. Then he took up
the letter and examined it more particularly. A year
ago he would have been fool enough to have read
wonderful things between those lines. There was sufficient space indeed ! He amused himself by hunting
out the trifling mistakes. Perhaps if one read any letter
penned by any most careful person five, six, seven,
eight times, one would find something amiss—some dot
or a comma. Phillis had made three pretty big mistakes. She had dated the letter Monday, February 10,
and Monday had been the 11th—he knew because of
the Psalms on Sunday ; also she had spelt " discriminate " " discrim*e*nate "—" I can never discrimenate
between the pictures "; also she had omitted " it " in
the sentence, " Daisy heard about from Bob." This
set him thinking of Bob and his rather raucous laugh,
and of Fred, who sneezed, and of Uncle Jasper, and of
many trivial circumstances such as haunt the memory
long after the dates of the Kings of England have
vanished away. That time when he careered half over
the Midlands in search of the Aberdeen pup, what a
noble fellow he thought himself, something approaching a gentleman, compared with Bob the lout, and the
idiot Fred ! In reality, he had been a bit of a fool—
not, indeed, in seeking the dog, but in the silly thoughts
which drove him out and brought him home again,
and which, though unexpressed, made him somewhat

ridiculous, so that even Phillis and Daisy did not know quite how to deal with him, and consequently dealt instead with Alexander, kissing his nose and giving him biscuits. And then he fell to contrasting shrewd Miss Elizabeth with his kind aunt—wondered if his aunt had got quite well, and whether she would be badly disfigured. And then the doctor came in, and said : "Make your arrangements for next week, Burnet ; we are going to get rid of you."

CHAPTER XLVI

FRANK spent ten days in the South of France, and then, obliged to confess to himself that he was still weak as a rat, he prolonged his holiday, and determined to find some quiet spot in the Italian Lakes where he might spend another ten days, or more if he felt inclined. He intended stopping at Cadenabbia, and then changed his mind at the last moment, and pitched upon Baveno, for no particular reason, unless you could call it a reason that his father and mother had spent part of their honeymoon there. He came by steamer to Stresa, and, as they drew near to the land, he pictured his father and mother together, and saw a figure watching the boat which might have been Phillis— and lo ! it was.

He had time to turn hot and cold, and hot and cold again, before he could struggle through the gangway, lugging his yellow bag, and with a mocking bow approach.

"Why, Frank, what are *you* doing here ?"

"What are *you* doing here ?"

They asked each other questions ; answers seemed superfluous.

"You look very thin," said Phillis, "but you've got a little colour."

" That's the heat," said Frank. He wished he did not flush so at the least excitement. He always had, and always would, and since the smallpox he was worse than ever.

" I can't tell you how sorry we all were. You must have been very ill. Did you ever get the grapes from home ? I ordered them to be sent."

" Yes, rather," said Frank ; " they turned up the day before I left."

" Oh, then they weren't much use. Perhaps the nurses ate them. How did everyone treat you ?"

" Splendidly, royally—spoilt me horribly." It seemed years ago—years ago—years ago. Why, the last thing of any consequence that had really happened was his talk with Phillis on the terrace that late summer night. " Well, when are you going home ?"

" This spring, this May." (*She* was flushing now.) " I've turned my tenants out, and I'm in affluent circumstances ; anyhow, affluent or not, I can live in Marchington again. How long is it, Frank, since you were there ?"

(She went out of her way to call him Frank. . . . Out of her way ? What an ass he was ! She must call him something, of course.) " Oddly enough, I went down this winter—in January."

" Why odd ? Don't you go often ? I know *I* should. . . . How did you catch the smallpox ? I suppose you don't know ; and then you went and gave it to your poor aunt or cousin or somebody."

" That's near enough. Are you staying in Stresa ? I'm not."

" Nor am I. We are at Baveno."

" Where I'm going," said Frank. They both laughed. He wanted to say to her, " Phillis, you *do* look well," but he refrained. She *did* look well, and that was sufficient.

" What's your hotel ?" he said instead.

She told him. " The Bristol."

" Mine is the Beau Rivage," said Frank. He was sure there was some such name.

One thing was evident to Frank : that she liked him better now than she had ever liked him before. He could not *prove* it—no ; there was nothing in what she had said, nothing in what she had looked, but he could feel a friendliness—more than that, a sort of nearness, hard to define, as if every step she walked at his side she walked closer and closer ; and yet, of course, she *did* no such thing, and perhaps he had no right to feel it. Anyway, grant him the right to feel better ; and better he did feel—quite eager to go out at nine o'clock, and gaze up at the stars, stare over the shimmering waters, stroll a bit in this direction, then a bit in that, find out where The Bristol lay, and keep a proper distance.

But there seemed no sense next morning in keeping this distance, after all. He would go up and see what they were doing, and who *they* were. He found them planning an expedition. Phillis's aunt was in the hall ; she shook hands with Frank, and said :

" You'd better go, too, Mr. Burnet, and help them carry the lunch. "

" Help them to eat it," said Frank, and wished he did not always show up so ill before her.

Into the hall ran Daisy, under a thick white veil.

" Oh, Frank, I heard you'd come. Won't you climb Mottarone ? The others have gone on ; I ran back for this veil. You can't think how the sun burns you. There's only the German to follow, and I don't want to walk all alone with him. You will come, won't you ?"

Of course he would. They started out. After them possibly panted the German, whoever the German might be. What did Frank care ? In front he could see winding upwards four or five figures on the path.

" Who are they all ?" he asked.

Daisy informed him.   Except for Phillis, the names were unknown.   He half thought Phillis must be aware who was pressing along behind her.   She certainly did not slacken speed ; at each bend of the way she had bent another ; there was always an equal space between them.   But then they suddenly halted.

" They are going to rest," said Daisy ; " now we shall catch them up."

" Whew !" said Frank, and flung himself down. " Let's give this fellow a chance," he said, and he looked round for the German.

" You won't like him," said Daisy.

" Oh yes, I shall."

" And there's Phillis beckoning.   No, it's his wife."

" If the German's wife is to the German as Phillis is to the German's wife, you are very rude to Phillis."

" Oh, she's not half as fat.   She always starts ahead of him."

" She shouldn't," said Frank ; " and you *mustn't*.   I can't support him alone."

But he turned out quite a decent fellow.   Everything seemed good to-day.   So hot a sun, so fine an air, such green banks and snowy chasms !   " Isn't the sky blue ?" Daisy kept saying.   So it was ; Daisy was right ; let her say it as often as she chose.   " And doesn't the lake seem to swim ?"

" Yes," said Frank, though he thought it didn't ; he thought it seemed steady—miraculously steady ; but why should he mention that ?

Meanwhile the party toiled on in front.   Daisy despaired of catching them, and accused Frank of lagging.

" You wait till lunch ; we'll catch them then," said Frank.

" We could catch them now, if we chose," said Daisy, " if only you'd hurry."

" But I won't hurry ; I utterly refuse to hurry."

" There ! they have stopped.   I don't believe they

mean to go on until we come up. Look, they are waving."

Both the ladies waved this time.

" Oh, well," said Frank, " come along."

" What an age you've been !" said Phillis.

Everyone talked, and they climbed to the top.

CHAPTER XLVII

It was really very jolly. Frank was rather surprised at himself for not feeling stiff. It was just the sort of occasion when he was apt to feel stiff, but now he believed that even if Fred had been there he could have forgiven him. He seemed more sure of himself. And when they suggested going home, and Daisy got up, Frank got up, too, and went after her without any awkward hesitation. He fancied the German lady came next, and possibly Phillis after that. He heard a good deal of shouting, but did not look round—only waved his stick over his head, and faithfully followed Daisy.

Daisy was quite a pleasant companion—a little too talkative, perhaps, but natural, and open, and kind. The difficulties of the descent, besides—the circuit of boulders, the fording of rills—made breaks in a conversation which might otherwise be monotonous. She talked of Rome and Florence, and her horses and dogs, and her father, and now and then Phillis's name was thrown in with a certain careless discretion.

" I don't see any of them," she said. " Are you sure we are on the right path ?"

The right path ! Frank laughed. When there were hundreds of paths, and all of them wrong or right, as you chose to regard them. But this was ever the way of women.

He began to comfort Daisy. They were, at any

rate, going *down*, and below them must be Baveno. And yet he himself tried to judge of his bearings.

" Perhaps we have dropped a little too soon," he said ; " but it really doesn't matter."

" How do you know it doesn't matter ?   We might be lost.   You'd better shout."

" There's no need to shout."

" Yes, shout ; do shout."

" Well, what shall I shout ?"

" Shout ' Hallo '! "

He shouted " Hallo!"   Some birds flew up in a hurry.   The shout died away.

" What makes it so still ?"

" That's only the after-effects of my shout."

" What do you mean ?"

" Why, haven't you ever noticed that after a shout there's always a silence ?"

" No, I haven't.   I've noticed echoes.   I'm sure we are miles from everyone.   What are you listening for ?"

" Their answer, of course.   I'll have one more try. . . . Hallo ! hallo ! . . .   How we scare the birds ! . . .   This is a beautiful ravine !"   He fell into a reverie. . . . " Isn't it beautiful ?"

" Oh yes, very !" said Daisy.   " But hadn't we better get out of it ?"

" Forward !" said Frank, and on they went.   " Let me go first, and beat back the bushes.   Besides, I can pick the way."

" It looks to me," said Daisy, " as if we were going on and on into a sort of trap, and shall presently find we can't get out."

" Oh no !" said Frank.   But, indeed, it was true : the arms of the mountains seemed to be closing.   " I'll shout again. . . .   Hallo !"

No answer.

" They must be deaf," said Daisy, and added her little voice.   Three times, four times, she shouted, and the last shout broke with a sob.   " We must do

something," she said. " Try another path, Frank,
why don't you ?"

" All right, I will," said Frank mildly. Of course,
there was no other path, but he must somehow reassure
her.

" We can't *see* anything here," said Daisy.

" If the worst comes to the worst," said Frank,
" we must clamber up and get a view."

" Let's clamber now."

" It will be harder than you think. Come on a bit."

" You keep shouting, Frank—keep shouting."

He shouted at every half-dozen steps. Never a
single reply. Frank felt uncomfortable, partly because
he knew that Daisy was within an inch of tears—a
woman is easily upset over the matter of losing her
way—and partly because this morning's climb was
beginning to tell upon him, and he wished he had not
lent his brandy-flask to the German, or that the German
had given it back. . . . And, as he feared, *now* they
were stuck. Daisy could certainly not get on. There
was a gash in the ravine, and only by working along
a ledge could they turn this hulking piece of the
shoulder—a perilous ledge, too, in itself—and how
could he know that at the end it would lead them out
on the mountain-side ? " We'd better scramble up,"
he said. There was no need to mention the unpleasant
alternative. " *Do* go on shouting," said Daisy.
" Shout louder." He strained every vocal chord,
and whether it was the shout or this morning's climb,
he did not know, but the blood surged in his head like
fury. " I heard an answer," said Daisy. " Listen !
I did !" Frank heard nothing. His ears were full of
a swelling flood.

" Hallo ! hallo !" cried Daisy. " There, they've
answered again. They are ever so far above us."
She began to climb. Frank followed. The flood was
sinking now. He could see what he was doing. He
could direct her steps. He *must* direct her steps, for
she slipped back at every struggle forwards.

" Go on your hands and knees," he said. " Give me your stick. It doesn't help you." She gave it him without a word. She fought with her petticoats. Far above they heard the others shouting—shout after shout, shout after shout.

" *It's no use your shouting!*" cried Daisy ; " *we can't come any quicker.* . . . Oh, Frank, we'll never get up ! I wish you would take my woolly coat—I kneel on it—and my purse, it's empty ; and *do* be careful, because I really can't keep the stones from rolling."

" We are half-way up," said Frank. " Don't look back."

" It seems to get steeper and steeper. Perhaps we ought to turn."

Turn ? Impossible now ! Roll like the helpless stones giddily down ! Not to alarm her he said : " Go on. You're doing it famously."

Not much sense in that remark. He never knew skirts so tiresome, or woman so clearly the weaker vessel. But what a change at his words ! " You're doing it famously !" *Famously !* All at once she was possessed with power, and just as *he* was deprived. She was moving stoutly forward, upward ; cursed her petticoats royally ; suddenly gave a whoop of joy.

" There they are ! What fun ! Come along, Frank !"

He was coming as fast as he could—two sticks, a basket, and woolly coat, and his head going round like an insane windmill, staring and stark, legs and arms all abroad.

" You'll have to give me a shove," said Daisy. . . . He heard her say that, and he heard her ripple. He knew there were (but he could not hear them) other voices beyond. . . . " *Shove*," said Daisy. . . . He felt something hard (the heel of her boot) pushing against his hand. He was not conscious of pushing himself . . . he was dimly conscious of slipping . . . slipping . . . then of being stopped suddenly short in the back.

. . . " Hallo, Frank !" He opened his eyes. . . .
He was here after all, lodged on a withered bush, and
faces were peering down from the chasm's edge—
grinning faces they seemed.

" Hallo ! What's happened to *you ?*"

. . . Was that Daisy, full of surprise ?. . .

" I thought you were just behind me."

. . . No, he was dreaming—dreaming. . . .

" You have let fall the young lady's coat." (That
was the German, of course). . . . He was not dreaming
at all. He had been scrambling up a ravine with
Daisy, and Daisy had got to the top, and he was
supposed to be following—with two sticks (here they
are), one basket (all right), and the coat which hung
on the withered bush. He reached for the coat.

" Where's my purse ?" said Daisy. " I gave you
that as well. It's empty, but it's got some addresses."

" Have you hurt yourself, Frank ?" That was
Phillis. Her face was serious.

He made another effort. The stones shuffled under
his feet. He saw the German's hand held out, but
he grasped the rock instead, got one leg up, then half
his body, then the rest of him flat on the ground.
Then he sat up.

Daisy was asking what had happened.

" Now then !" said Phillis. . . . " Daisy, *you'd*
better *wear* your coat. . . . It's getting chilly. We
shall be late. Go on, and I'll follow with Frank. . . .
Frank, you should never have come. You're not
fit."

" I'm all right," said Frank. " I can't think why
I took her down there." This was malicious.

" Daisy never looks where she's going."

" Oh, *I* led the way."

They were walking together. How refreshing the
air on the mountain-side ! Phillis said nothing. They
walked in silence, zig-zag down, after the others. They
were now on the regular path cut in regular lengths,
and they swung along at a steady pace. Was she

trying to catch the others up ?   Or was she sometimes
trying to linger ?   He could not tell ; he only knew
they had nothing to say—or everything !

It was dark as they wound out on the road.   All
over the lake was a sullen darkness.   The lamps
burned sullenly on the shore.

Frank's hotel came first.   " Good-night," he said,
and he slipped inside.   He went straight up to his
room.   He did not feel ill exactly : he did not know
what he felt.   He certainly thought he should dine
as usual.   Still, he sat on and on in his chair.   There
was no light in his room, but he had no particular
wish for light—some sort of light came in from the
street below.   He was not sad (there was nothing much
to be sad about) nor dull (there was plenty of company)—merely quiet, quiet, quiet ; and when most
quiet of all, the door was quietly opened.

" Frank, are you here ?"

He stood up.

" Are you here ?   Yes, you are.   Well, you
ought . . ."

. . . Somebody spoke ; he heard his name. . . .   They
were calling him—time to get up !   His mother was
saying, " Frank, Frank, Frank !" . . .   But what an
odd dream !   Was he *dead ?*   He would stave *that*
off ! . . .   He was ill of the smallpox.   It was night
in the white-tiled room.   *That* was a candle . . . on
the floor ?   Himself on the floor ? . . . Phillis !
Phillis !   What is this ?

" You're coming round.   You fainted."

That was Phillis's voice.

" Shut your eyes.   You are in your room at the
Beau Rivage."

He shut his eyes . . . never mind . . . wait a bit. . . .
Had he sat in his chair ?   Was he sitting there when
Phillis came in ?   And had they walked down together
from Mottarone ?

" Phillis !"

" I'm here."

" *Why* are you here ?"

" I thought you ill."

" I wasn't."

" You fainted dead away."

He was silent. " You couldn't tell."

" Tell what ?"

" That I was going to faint."

He got no answer.

" Could you ?"

" Could I what ?"

" Could you tell I was going to faint ?"

" I thought you *ill*."

" Was that why you came ?"

Why did she not answer ? He asked her again. Why did she not answer now ?

" I can't bear to think——" Oh, she was crying ! Now she was sobbing. Somehow she sobbed upon his breast. " I can't bear to think . . ."

" *What* cannot you bear to think ? . . . Phillis, child ! dear child, dear woman ! *What* cannot you bear to think——"

" I cannot bear—I cannot bear," she sobbed unreasonably. He knelt beside her ; now supported her. . . . " Those weeks in London . . ."

" What weeks in London ? What do you mean ? Never mind the candle. I'll put it out." It was guttering. Now the room was dark.

" . . . All those weeks. I can't bear to think of them. Ill, with nobody to look after you."

" Three very competent nurses."

She tried to laugh.

" Phillis !" He changed his tone. " Phillis, tell me. Did you *care* ? Do you mean . . . you don't mean . . . oh, you can't mean *that*."

" What ?"

" That you cared all the time ?"

She nodded.

" You wrote such a funny little note. You spelt ' discriminate ' wrong."

" Did I ?" She was drying her eyes.

" I'm such a *pig !*" she said. " I've often been such a pig to you. You always are with the people you like the most."

" Always," said Frank loyally.

It was a collective sort of statement, but it included him, anyway. He leant against the chair, overcome by a sensation of intense fatigue, not altogether disagreeable. She felt the movement, and stood up. He stood too. What he did he did instinctively. He held out his arms, and they folded round her.

CHAPTER XLVIII

To live now for the first time ! To have had breath in your body for twenty-six years and never lived a single day until this day in March—*this* day, when he woke at five o'clock, and dressed, and went out and drank in the morning air, and felt all impatient and yet in no hurry ; for the thing *had* been—he *had* lived— and he cared not a straw at this moment for the past or the future. Having lived, you can't die. He who denies it has never lived, that is all ; has never walked at Baveno by the lake in the mood Frank walked in now—the mood infinitive—" to love, to walk, to live."

And he found Phillis, of course, all in due time. They found one another, and they wandered off for a morning stroll and got back late, and agreed that they would not let everyone know all at once. But still, they must plan some sort of excursion for that afternoon with the rest, and Frank half believed that by common consent they were left to themselves, and that nobody would have pitied him if he had been lost in another ravine with Phillis, who may have been looking a little confused. She looked charming, though, confused or unconfused (he liked both looks

the best), and he was rather more pleased than annoyed
that the afternoon party should see her confused,
see *him* confused, and take it for granted that the rest
of the world must keep out of the way. And he knew—
yes, he knew—that Daisy was bursting with kind
thoughts she longed to impart ; and even, perhaps,
the German's wife guessed more than she dared pretend.
But who cares for that ?   Let anyone guess that can
guess, and be glad or sorry, whichever he choose ;
did it trouble Frank's head as he lived those days—
one, two, three days—three lives in one ?

Aunt Elizabeth must be told.   Frank thought she
would be surprised, but, according to Phillis, she
appeared to have received the statement calmly.

" She always *has* liked you," said Phillis, as she
gave the result of her interview.

" Oh, I don't think so," said Frank.   " She used to
disapprove."

" Only of some of your ways, which would aggravate
anybody who didn't know you.   She thinks you are
one of the few gentlemen left in England, but that you
ought to have been a parson."

" I know.   She doesn't like my pictures.   We
shan't quarrel over that."

Not over that, nor over anything, as it proved
presently.   Frank, who expected some sharp attacks,
had prepared some mild defences—very mild and very
ill-prepared ; in fact, they would have been quite
useless had Miss Elizabeth challenged them.   But
she did not challenge them, and at the very first hand-
shake he threw them overboard, and heard her say :
" Well, Frank, it is a long time since I saw you."
And Frank remembered that night by the open
drawing-room window, and falling upon his knees.
And then he heard her asking questions about his
health, and the smallpox, and the hospital, and his
aunt (whom he hoped was well again), and how they
had both caught it (and Frank hadn't the slightest
idea, but they had taken tea together), and then about

his holiday, the South of France, and Italy, the scramble up the mountain, and Daisy's little adventure ; and so they talked and talked, and only just before he left did she say very kindly : " And now I suppose I must give my best congratulations to you two young people." And Phillis said, " Of course you must," and Frank said, " Oh, well, yes."

" She told me in private," said Phillis afterwards, " that no engagement had ever given her more satisfaction ; that we were so well suited."

" I think we are, don't you ?" said Frank. He would have liked an answer.

" I suppose so. I never troubled to think about it."

" Well, perhaps that is best," said Frank, and laughed. Phillis was always unconscious.

Not that Phillis was lacking in natural affection. Generous, warm-hearted, without meanness, without fear, she made a royal surrender. But a girl does not want to be for ever giving demonstrations of that which should require no proof. Having plainly told and plainly showed she loved him, could she do better than laugh, and smile, and talk, and walk, and eat, and drink, and be merry? If the sun shines, must it be asked *why, why, why ?*

Once he seized on her and stopped her, stopped her in her gaiety, *made* her conscious—she *should* be. " Do you know that you are the most attractive creature——" he began.

" I know that it is your business to think so," was what she said. " But, Frank, be sensible. I would ever so much rather you did not go on these long mountain excursions." (She had released herself.) " You came back yesterday so fagged and white, and Daisy never supposes anyone can be tired as long as she isn't tired herself."

And Frank went on about the mountain excursions, but he was not thinking about them. He was dimly thinking that Phillis was right, and that perhaps, after all, in the long-run, it was better that she should have eyes quick to detect when he looked white than ears always burning to know that she was " the most attractive creature." There was some sense in that. Meantime, though she delighted to care for him, she might be pleased to see him restored again to perfect health, fit for mountain excursions, and not only that, but for the affairs of life—fit for work like other men. And by a happy coincidence, what should come to him next morning but a letter from Raikes, which letter wanted to know why on earth he should be in Italy (rumour had said he was there), when everyone else was back in town getting their pictures suitably framed for the Royal Academy show. Raikes wrote a capital letter, and Frank read the first two sheets and put the other sheet in his pocket, and thought Raikes a capital fellow, and felt himself in capital form. And Phillis, when she saw him, remarked on his improved appearance, and said she was glad he had been persuaded to stay at home yesterday afternoon.

" I'm all right now," said Frank. " I shall have to be going back to work."

" Oh !" said Phillis. She made no attempt to hide her genuine disappointment.

" It is the busy time in town."

" What a bother ! Can't you wait till we return at the end of April ?"

" What ! Another six weeks' holiday !"

" Can't you work here ?"

" You won't let me paint you. I've asked. "

" Paint *me ?* Paint the lake, the mountains, the valleys. I thought you loved Nature, Frank."

" So I do—to talk about and walk about. Isn't she lovely this morning ? But I'd give the whole lake, Mottarone, and that Fisherman's Isle, and that boat with its queer little sail, for — for what ? Why, for the look on your face at this minute. . . . It's gone !"

" Of course it's gone ! and the lake and mountains remain. All that is artist's rubbish. *Me* you should love (not the look on my face)—*me* you should love better than mountains, or lakes, or Fisherman's Isle, because—because—because—— I don't know exactly why, but because I can *speak*, and you can't get on without somebody speaking, even if they don't say anything very particular. But this has nothing to do with your leaving us. Does your work matter so much? It didn't matter before."

"Oh, didn't it?" (But, by the way, perhaps she was right.) "I've half a notion I may send up for this year's Academy."

Phillis said: "Oh, do! How jolly!" But she had no time to say more, for here was Daisy with Aunt Elizabeth, and everybody talked.

It was when he was dressing for dinner that night that Frank chanced to come on this morning's letter. He had not yet read the last sheet, and he read it now. There was a good deal of information about mutual friends: So-and-so was "very fit," So-and-so "getting on like a house on fire"; Raikes himself had had a "stroke of luck"—had sold a twenty-five-guinea picture; So-and-so was producing "first-rate stuff"; So-and-so would "make a name."

. . . Yes, it was time to be back at work. *He* also was "very fit," had had *his* "stroke of luck"; but was he "getting on like a house on fire," "producing first-rate stuff," and would he "make a name"?

He answered Raikes' letter: told him he was coming home, that he had one or two things he hoped to show, that he was well again. He sealed and stamped the letter.

Of course, it was not exactly a true letter—that is to say, the facts were incorrect. He might or might not be going home. The doctor forbade his return to London before the middle of May. He had *not* one or two things he hoped to show, because he did not believe he had anything fit to show—the portrait, perhaps, and that was unfinished. And, as for being

well again, one gets into habits of saying " Well." . . .
He would order some more of the tonic.

He ordered the tonic that very night—first wrote
for it, then telephoned. He would get it to-morrow
now. He had heard by the last post from Dolly. The
envelope had a broad black edge. This meant somebody's death. . . . His aunt had died. His aunt !
How ? Never really recovered her strength ; ought
to have stayed where she was ; *would* come back
because of her servants ; reached London that very
cold week ; got a chill ; nobody knew how bad she
was, until she suddenly became much worse ; Helena
telegraphed for (attending some women's meetings in
Birmingham) ; both there when she died. She would
be buried in Elmer's End Cemetery.

Why should it seem so cruel ? He had sat there
with the note in his hand, as if a blow had been struck
from which he should never recover. His aunt was
over sixty, and some day one must die ; and considering
all the terrible deaths which may overtake a man,
whether they cut him off in his prime or not—violent
deaths, shameful deaths, painful, neglected, bitter
deaths—one might be considered lucky to die very
quietly in one's own home of nothing worse than a
chill. He could not, however, tell Phillis that night.
He had had half a mind to excuse himself from looking
in at The Bristol, but if he did he should only be ques-
tioned, and this headache and feeling of sickness was
not a sufficient reason to give. So he went, but he
did not stay long, and he said not a word to Phillis—not
a word, that is, about this—this particular matter
which filled his mind. How could he ? She looked
so healthy herself—health and strength in every
glance, in every movement, she betrayed. How could
he talk of death, sudden illness, a week of cold weather,
Helena sent for, then the end, and the burial in the
cemetery. How could he ? Well, after all, why
should he ? This was *his* aunt—no aunt to Phillis—
and possibly here, in little Baveno, there might be a

dozen persons at least whose aunts were just dead or
just dying. He must have more sense. It was the
old evil creeping back, never thoroughly worsted—the
magnifying of detail and incident out of all proportion
to outline of fact. His aunt had caught the smallpox.
Somebody must! She had never really recovered.
At her time of life that was not unnatural! And having
never really recovered, she died. That follows as
a matter of course! The very cold week, Helena
being at Birmingham, suddenly getting much worse—
these were all details, pieces of colour, such as people
without imagination borrow for occasional use, while
the people *with* imagination . . . Oh, God help them !—
the people *with* imagination! How could he drive
these images away ? . . . He saw her—*saw* her coming
back that very cold week, on the boat, then through
the gangway, white and chilled and blown about ;
saw the dull, black, cruel weather ; flew to Birmingham ;
saw Helena on a platform of ladies . . . ladies, ladies
everywhere . . . then a telegram comes in ; Helena gets
up, crosses the platform hurriedly ; . . . flew to London
again, saw his aunt upon her bed, lit the fire for her,
put at her feet a hot stone bottle . . . in comes the
doctor. "*Sans doute. How long is it since you were
vaccinated ?*"

. . . Oh, would he never sleep that night ? . . . Never,
never. . . . Why, he *had* slept. Here he was this
morning. Morning light peeped in at the window.
Hope again ; but he lay exhausted. It was as if he
had been beaten, beaten in battle. He knew that
sensation of old. It is something to know a sensation,
recognize an old friend. He had given up repining ;
he had given up expecting things to be different.
He should always expect these knock-down blows.
Meantime he was as weak as a rat . . . *that*, however,
must wait; only temporarily he would remark to himself
that he had better not go back to London. . . . Lying
in bed he would make his plans. . . .

Ought one, or ought one not, to avoid a knock-down

blow ? Was it wiser, since Fate set a mark upon you, to put your head out of Fate's way ? . . . An awful thought then followed. *Should he keep Phillis ?* Had he in that tempted Fate too much ? No, no ! *One* thing he would have if God lived above ! He should be happy in *that* to his bent ! Yes, whatever a man believes or disbelieves, so much he believes—that God's Hand *is* over him (God's kind hand ?), however far, however high ; and that though it permit the devil's worst, it will never permit just *this* or just *that.* Take Job for an illustration ! . . . Phillis should be spared to him. Then what else mattered ? Fame, wealth, ease, pleasure—let the devil have them ; they might *go* to the devil ! Let him have Phillis and hide his head. He thought of home in the Midlands—quiet Marchington village—but he did not think of the Manor. He was thinking of home, real home—the house where you are born : the drawing-room, dining-room, study, kitchen, the bedrooms on the floor above. . . . Still, he had chosen to be an artist ; he had studied, and he had worked ; and if one retires from a profession, one should retire, not escape. Phillis had every right to expect that he should take his part in the world, as a man amongst men — do, in fact, what others were doing, push his way where others pushed, and not sneak off at a critical moment with everyone saying, " What's happened to Frank ?" Whatever *did* happen, let it be known ; let people say, " He showed in this year's Academy (or " He was crowded out "), but he is giving up painting—taken on another job." It was said, of course, that a man should stick to his last ; but if it had never been *his*—if he found his own last afterwards—which should have been his all the time . . .

He got up and came down to breakfast. He believed he was going to be ill. You surely can't have the smallpox twice in one year ; but you can catch chills and die. Here was Phillis. Good ! . . . No, he wished she had not come. He was not fit for her this

morning. Why had he not stayed in bed ?—wretchedly
ill as he was—going to be wretchedly ill.

"Only just finished ? For shame ! Come out in
the garden. I've something to tell you."

What would this be ? Perhaps she had heard about
his aunt. But her tone was strong, and her eye
was clear, her step was steady—when was it not ?

"I'll give you a shilling if you can guess—no,
sixpence, it's so easy—no, a farthing."

"Guess what ? Say good-morning to me first."

She was almost too impatient.

"Well, what am I to guess ?"

"The engagement ! The engagement !"

"Oh, it's an engagement, is it ?"

"Yes ; I said so."

"Excuse me, you didn't. Well, I suppose—I
suppose—well, yes, it's Bob and Daisy."

"Oh, Frank, you dear ! you genius ! I thought you
were so stupid you'd never guess. Is he quite, *quite*
good enough ?"

There was the oddest shade of disappointment,
and over that such wondering admiration as she
watched his face. Frank laughed. "Quite, *quite*
good enough ? You must ask *her* that."

"Oh, Daisy thinks him perfect ; but, then, she
ought."

"And if she is satisfied, that's enough."

"Of course. Naturally, I can't understand anyone
being fond of anybody but you. Have you really
made up your mind to go ?"

"Certainly not. I have more or less made it up to
stay."

"Well, there seemed no earthly reason for going.
How glad I am !"

All at once he remembered his wretched night, and
the wretched feeling of illness. "No, I shall stay
another few weeks. By the way, can one get at a
doctor, supposing one wants to ?"

"There's a very good man in our hotel—a well-known London man. You looked rather poorly when I came in. Why don't you send for him ?"

" He's out here on a holiday. He won't want patients."

" Oh no ; he's here for his health !"

" That makes it worse."

" But I know he has doctored one or two people, and I believe they got better."

Frank laughed, though he had not felt much like laughing. " Well, I'll see," he said.

" Then you hadn't really *decided* to go ?" said Phillis. She seemed puzzled.

" Not really decided. The only thing I must do is to write to Raikes, and get him to see my pictures sent in when he sends in his own. He's had a stroke of luck — just sold a twenty - five guinea picture."

" Has he ? Well, tell him to send in your pictures. Why should *you* bother ?"

Why should Raikes ? But Raikes was a very good fellow, and Frank had no compunction when he wrote and explained just what he wanted. Not a difficult matter for explanation : he had only to name three or four pictures, and he named them, and where exactly they would be found.

CHAPTER XLIX

RAIKES, of course, must needs write back two sheets, and must needs fill one and a half with football " shop," and cramp all the news in the last few lines. The news was this : that he had had the deuce of a trouble to find the pictures Frank had mentioned, and when he had found them, he could not honestly say that he felt himself repaid. He had, however . . . At this point the doctor entered. Frank was reading his letter in bed, where he had lain all yesterday. " And you'll lie in bed to-day," said the doctor. " If we don't look after you, you'll be ill."

It was very good-natured of this man—a well-known London man—to come round from The Bristol. Frank thought about him and about his good-nature for quite a quarter of an hour after he left the room, instead of picking up his letter and reading to the end. There was nothing in the letter to make it interesting to Frank. He *did* pick it up again, however, and went on from the point where he had stopped when the doctor had rapped on the door. . . . Hallo ! What had Raikes been up to ? . . . " *Had found a jolly portrait*" . . . (Yes, but it was unfinished.) . . . "*poked behind a portfolio.*" . . . (Perhaps it would do as it was.) . . . " *Also behind the portfolio a sort of twilight effect in the city.*" (Oh yes ; that was done last year.) "*Also in the portfolio a rather good study of horses.*" (What could that be, by the way ?) " *Also a landscape all about nothing—open gate, glimpse of garden, field and harrow.*" (From below the church, of course ; the bit he had done as a boy. He had taken it out not so long ago, and had thought of getting it framed. The associations were powerful ; but he could bear them now—at any rate, alone, with nobody looking on.)

He wrote to Raikes that afternoon. As to the choice of pictures, Raikes' choice was probably best. Somehow he muddled his own affairs. Raikes it was who had told him the year before last that he sent up quite his worst work for show, and no wonder it was rejected. This time he would be wiser. He only wrote a card, and gave Raikes leave to please himself.

At the end of the week Raikes wrote again. He had taken another opinion, and a verdict had been passed. The portrait, the study of horses, and the little landscape all about nothing—those had the votes. The opinion, if he wished to know, was the opinion of Jackson, R.A., and he might think himself lucky.

He did think himself lucky. Fancy Jackson commending his pictures !—Jackson, who used almost to sneer ! This was something of a joke ! Just like Raikes to do a good-natured turn. . . . Of course, Jackson, R.A., was engaged to Raikes' half-sister, which gives the connecting-link. She had a title too ! . . . Jackson was rather a rising man. But he must say something about those horses. What horses could they be ? Had he ever painted a horse which anyone on the view would call a horse ? He had sometimes tried the Manor horses just to please Phillis. It might be that some of these sketches survived, but he usually tore them up. Or Raikes, in his rummaging about, might have lighted on another man's work. This was just possible. It looked rather stupid now to write and disclaim the horses, having not disclaimed them at first. Besides, it appeared there was only one which had gained Jackson's approbation. However, he would write. He would first glance through his other letter, which bore the London post-mark. By a most odd coincidence (no, the most natural thing in the world), this letter was from Jackson. The very kindest letter ! He wrote in the warmest way. It was short—all contained on one side of a sheet—but the tone was distinctly encouraging. He said that he had been very glad to accede to Mr. Raikes' request, and that some of the pictures had struck him as of unusual merit. There was promise and performance. Reading the letter through again for the fourth or fifth time, Frank rather regretted that Raikes' future step-brother-in-law had not been more explicit, had said in point of fact *which* of the pictures struck him most. But there was no doubt that the letter was genial and hopeful, and also that it must be speedily answered. Raikes must wait.

It was not an easy task to reply, to express oneself *just so*, to be discreet—gratified, yet not elate ; and Frank had torn up one attempt and begun to scratch another, when Phillis and Daisy came in. They wanted him to dine at The Bristol. Daisy was very pink and pretty.

" Of course I will," said Frank.

He thought at first that he would say nothing to them about his pictures. He would rather it should be a surprise. Besides, it was not as if the Royal Academy Hanging Committee had said their final word. But eventually he told them all about Raikes and Jackson, and the two letters which had arrived, because the conversation happened to go that way ; because Daisy had asked him whether or not he intended to send up his pictures for show, and it seemed foolish to keep the news back.

Daisy was over-joyed. " How fine ! Phillis, aren't you horribly proud of him ? Tell us what the pictures are."

" Oh, well, just ordinary pictures."

" Landscapes ?"

" I believe there's a landscape—two landscapes. There's a portrait."

" A portrait ? Anyone we know ?"

" Phillis knows him. That chap at your forge."

" Wattie ? Not really ! What fun ! I don't believe he would like it, though, to be hung in the Academy."

" Any animals ?" said Daisy.

" What is the boy but an animal ?"

" I mean real animals—nice animals—horses."

" Horses, cows, dogs, and cats ? Well, there might be a study of horses, but I doubt if it gets in."

" I was going to say," said Phillis, " that I did not know you considered yourself much of a hand at horses."

" Referring, I suppose, to my equestrian capabilities."

Phillis laughed.

" I suppose it isn't Choice or Necessity," said Daisy.

" Oh no! They must have been creatures of my imagination. But I really forget. I can't remember much about them."

" Phillis, aren't you horribly proud?" Daisy had said that once already.

Phillis was pleased, but cautious. " If an R.A. says they are good, they *must* be," she said. " An R.A. ought to know."

" I suppose nobody else but an R.A. is *allowed* to know," said old Miss Elizabeth.

" Oh, of course, if you *can* know, you *may* know," said Phillis. " I never *could*."

" And what relation is Mr. Jackson to Mr. Raikes, your friend?" asked Daisy.

" No relation at present. Jackson is to marry Raikes' half-sister, who has a title, by the way, Raikes' father having married somebody, I don't know who."

" And I suppose, if Mr. Jackson admires your pictures so much, and has anything to do with the Academy show——"

" My dear Daisy! We don't talk about such things."

" Why not? Well, I call that stupid. I don't see how he can say he admires them, and then exclude them from the show."

Everyone laughed, and Frank the loudest. He was beginning to feel a good deal better. Yes, he was feeling better, decidedly better—so much better as he walked back, that he sat down and wrote to Jackson and Raikes, and posted in the box before he went up to bed.

CHAPTER L

HE should have to return to London. There was nothing else to be done. Here was another note from Raikes—a postcard. "Why hadn't he written ? Was he coming back ?" (How absurd ! Frank had expressly told him he wasn't.) "Should he himself be responsible for the pictures ?" (Yes, of course ; who else ?) "And everyone wanted the horses, and nobody wanted the landscape. What was F. Burnet's own opinion ?" etc.

What was his opinion ? Why, he hadn't one ; only the whole affair threatened to fall in a muddle, and Raikes appeared a bit of an ass. The porter was in the hall. It might be just worth inquiring if last night's letters had gone. The porter looked at the clock and said yes, and then went and opened the box, and said yes again, and then explained that the box was invariably cleared at such and such and such an hour. Frank gave half his attention ; with the other half he was thinking that had the letters *not* gone, had he *not* written them late last night, he should have written quite other letters this morning. An explanation was wanted. He would bring it himself. He would go to-morrow. To Raikes he wired. Then he must bid good-bye to Phillis. Phillis said : " Well, never mind ; we shall all be home in a few weeks' time, and if you think you ought to go, I should hate to keep you. Why is there so much hurry ?"

" Why, Raikes is such a wild chap ; you never know what he is up to. I told him the pictures I wanted sent in, and he seems to be sending a lot of others."

" Well, but why doesn't he do what you tell him ?"

" I can't conceive, except that, of course, he thinks he knows best. He thinks himself a first-rate judge of a picture, because—oh, well, I don't know."

" Perhaps he *is* a good judge of a picture."

" Oh, well, perhaps he is."

" And some people are very bad at judging their own performances, just as some people never make mistakes except in their own affairs."

Frank had heard that before. . . .   Oh yes, at Surbiton, in the drawing-room . . . it was his aunt . . . that day when Helena told him he ought to paint the miseries of twentieth century existence. . . .   Ah, but we bring our troubles on ourselves. . . .   Meantime Phillis was still philosophizing—very rare for Phillis— and she was looking over the lake with the softest of dreamy looks.   He changed his position a little.

" And some people always make the worst of them- selves," Phillis was saying ; " and I've seen *you* do that, Frank, and you can't think how annoying it is for anybody who's fond of you."

" Tell me.   I'll improve.   I'm not above it."

She laughed, of course.   " You're very, very nice," she said, " though not at all with the kind of niceness you imagine."

" I imagine no niceness," said Frank abruptly. This was the plain and simple truth.   " I must go and pack."

It was a glorious day for the start.   He said good-bye to Phillis before breakfast.   He took her up the winding path which led to Mottarone.   They had to get under the trees, for the heat of the sun was already terrific.   He begged Phillis to stay indoors during the hottest hours.   Then he began to talk about the posts, and when they would write to one another ; and this he did to distract his thoughts, if he might, from the numbed feeling, the blank in his mind, the nightmare creeping over his soul.   He must not break down.   He never did ; he never dared.   Did he once break down, he should break down again, and again, and again.   He kissed her hurriedly. . . .   No, that was unkind. . . .   He kissed her a second, a third time, tenderly, tenderly. . . .   " The one woman for me," he kept saying.   " The one woman for me."   Oh, if he could have ventured to tell her of the yawning pit which seemed to widen. As he stood there, held her, looked far beyond her—up to the slopes of Mottarone, where, two weeks ago, they had zigzagged down—he seemed to know, to see it written, to hear it spoken in the air, that an enormous gulf did now, or would (it was all the same), separate them, silent and proud, as before.

It was a bitter morning—a bitter Sunday morning—when he arrived in London. Everyone looked pinched and chilled : the old starved porter most pinched of all as he struggled for a cab. Frank gave him a shilling, it was so cold. There was a fire in his room at No. 14—still No. 14. This was warming, and warm was the landlady's welcome ; and there was the smiling landlady's girl just starting for church. He said he was glad to get home—very glad. He hoped it had not been a great nuisance forwarding all his letters. Letters ? What, another pile ? He stood by the fire to open them, tore off the wrappers, ripped up the envelopes, flung this into the flames, stuffed that into his pocket, shoved the other behind the clock, and all the time giving ear to his landlady's conversation. Then, whilst she laid the table for lunch, he turned the key of the studio and walked in to have a look round. The landlady soon pursued him there. She hoped he found everything as he had left it, except for any damage which Mr. Raikes might have done. Frank asked if Mr. Raikes had called yesterday or the day before. He must, of course, have received the wire. No, Mr. Raikes had never called, not since he took the pictures away, which the landlady hoped was quite correct.

" Perfectly," said Frank ; and when she begged him not to remain in the cold, he said, " All right, I won't," and sat down and remained. However, when he was left alone, he got up and prowled about. He had the queerest sensation as of never having been away, as of waking up from a vivid dream ; and if so, he should have to reckon where the dream began

and ended, what was the false and what was true.
The smallpox had been true, for there, in the mirror,
he saw reflected the signs of it upon his cheek. . . .
And, by the way, the portrait *had* gone. So much
was certain. And the portfolios, which leant in their
accustomed corner accumulating the dust, these had
been disturbed, and one was pushed aside on the floor.

He impatiently jerked and unknotted the tapes.
The covers fell apart, and there was a flutter of sheets
between. He pulled out things here and there. Some
of them he could have vowed he had never before set
eyes upon. . . . Some, of course, came back—studies
of years ago, bits which he perfectly well recollected
in Paris, and bits, too, which he had borrowed to copy,
or kindly accepted, or good-naturedly bought from
fellow-students in London, or Paris, or Rome. How
should he know? What a flood of memories! . . .
A couple of sepia drawings taken in *Notre Dame*
brought to his mind a whole chain of events. He had
given two guineas apiece for them to a young Belgian
in distress. . . . These water-colours in tissue-paper,
tied with ribbon, he must also have been plagued to
buy. They were initialled in the corner ; but W., that
might stand for William, and S. might stand for
Smith. . . .

" Hullo !"

It was Raikes. Frank jumped to his feet.

" I heard you'd come. Got your wire? Oh yes !
How are you? You look fit."

" Oh, I'm all right again." Senseless phrases.

" What brought you back? You said you weren't
coming. I could have managed the show. What
sort of a time have you had ?"

" I thought I'd better . . . What sort of a
time? Oh, grand ! . . . I thought I'd better come,
because——"

" You needn't have bothered. Decent weather ?"

" Out there? Oh yes ! Fine ! It's brutally cold
in London."

" We've had a disgusting spring.   Everyone's down
with influenza."

" Are they ?"

" It simply ruined the University soccer match."

" Did it ? . . .   Well, look here, what have you been
up to, rifling my rooms and——"

" Oh, that's all square. I quite enjoyed the job ;
and I can tell you Jackson is most awfully pleased,
and he isn't any too easy to please. He says you've
come on no end."

" He never saw my work before that I'm aware of,"
said Frank—" never looked at it, that is."

" Well, he's seen it now, and you've got to thank
me for not showing up the appalling stuff you suggested."

" Will you stay to lunch ?" said Frank.

" I can't. I've got to get back. I came to tell
you to be round at my place sharp at three this
afternoon. Jackson is coming, and wants to meet
you."

" What does Jackson really say ? Your letters were
utterly vague."

" Oh, he has plenty to say. Don't swallow all he
says. He's an enthusiast, you know."

" I didn't know. Then he appears in rather a fresh
light. He used to be a bit of a bear."

" In old days, oh yes. He's promoted now to a
lion. That makes all the difference. He can afford
to be very polite, and he has a new protégé every
year."

" That's flattering," said Frank, and laughed, and
he shouted after Raikes, as he ran down the stairs,
a final promise that he would come.

He ate his solitary lunch, glad to be alone, for there
was a good deal to think about—not that he had any
very definite conclusive thoughts, but must keep
arguing up and down, *if* this and *if* that. Well,
this afternoon would settle the matter.

Raikes, of course, never explained anything. He

had never explained that at three o'clock his studio was to be filled with twenty or thirty striving artists, striving at this present moment not so much for fame as for elbow-room.

Frank was greeted on every hand. It seemed as if all his old friends were there.

"You've been abroad, haven't you?" . . . "*Ill!* You're looking all right!" . . . "Influenza? No, not *smallpox!*" . . .

Frank fought his way in and out. He was sick of answering questions—all about himself, too! Also provoked with Raikes, and wondered what he meant, for here were pictures, pictures, pictures. It was a regular show! . . . And, oh yes, *there* hung the portrait. . . . Well, it didn't look bad, and they had shoved it up in a first-rate light.

"Hullo, Burnet! You're coming out strong." That was an old Academy fellow.

"I don't exactly understand," began Frank; but he was jostled aside.

"Oh, here you are!" This was Raikes. "You'll find your things this end of the room. And I want to introduce you to Jackson."

"I say, Raikes, you never explained——"

"Explained what?"

"Why, this is a regular show!"

"Isn't it!"

Raikes was swept away. Frank pushed on. Here was the portrait, and here was the landscape, and there, by the side, on an easel apart . . . was *this* the study of horses? *This!* But he had never painted *this!* . . . So much was certain. Then who had? That was another matter. He *could* not have painted it—*he* could not.

. . . Somebody jogged his elbow. He hoped it was Raikes come back again, but it wasn't — somebody shoving through. What a horrid buzz and confusion! . . . Perhaps, after all, he was dreaming. Very likely, and he should find himself in the little bedroom over the lake. . . . Somebody else was shoving now.

" Hullo, Burnet ! how are you ? I like your things most awfully. Where have you been all this age ? Abroad, haven't you ?"

" Yes, abroad. I say, where's Raikes ?"

" He was here just now."

" I know ; so he was. He's all over the place."

" Here he is."

" Here I am," said Raikes. " Now then, my friend, what do you say ?"

" I say thanks very much ; only——"

" Only the portrait isn't finished, is it ? Just what I thought you'd remark. Still, Jackson likes it, and it isn't bad."

" Oh, it isn't *bad*, but——"

" But you wonder that I didn't prefer some of your own absurd suggestions ?"

" Yes ; but look here——"

Raikes did not look. He spun round and seized on another fellow. The other fellow spun round too. Frank dimly recognized his face. He was turning faint and giddy, and yet it was all so horribly plain. He must say to them both at once, then : " *One of those pictures is not mine.*"

" Hullo, Burnet !" (The fellow knew him.) " Glad to see you. You've got some jolly things this year. I like your strawberry roan."

" As a matter of fact," said Frank. The blood surged in his head. . . .

" Here's Jackson," whispered Raikes.

. . . What was happening ? . . . He was shaking Jackson's hand. . . . Jackson had grown considerably fatter. Perhaps he afforded more to eat. . . . And he talked very fast ; no, not fast, very slow ; only he talked persistently, so that you could not stop him, and fancied you could not even keep up. . . . He must wake himself out of the silly state. He must either *stop* Jackson, or *listen*—listen first, for there might be no need to stop him.   He might not be talking about the horses. . . .

"*Capital! Capital!*" . . . And yet not really enthusiastic.   You could not pretend to believe what he said, and therefore you could not disclaim his praises without making a still worse fool of yourself. . . .   "*Capital! Capital!*" . . . Say it again! Wait a bit, though ; he must keep his senses. Suppose Jackson asked him a question now ! . . . Oh, well, *now* he was talking about the portrait, nodding his head that way.

"You had a charming subject."

"Oh yes !" said Frank. It *was* the portrait.

"The merits in this are perhaps less obvious than the merits in the study of horses, but I incline to think I prefer *this*."

"Oh, thanks very much !" said Frank. "I am keener on this myself. As a matter of fact . . .   Oh, thanks very much. . . . Good-bye !" For Jackson was warmly pressing his hand, and already had moved some yards away.

Frank had a wild idea of pursuing him. He was seized with a sort of panic. This must be controlled. He began struggling round the room, and he would employ himself in recalling how shrivelled poor Jackson used to look seven or eight years ago, and how he so rarely opened his mouth, and how, without troubling to open his mouth, he could make you feel very uncomfortable . . . and how, in the heat of the hurry, he had never yet properly faced the question whether or not the study was his. The most sensible thing to do would be to have another look. He used in old days to try his hand at every sort of subject ; only in comparatively recent years had he arrived at the conclusion that he was better at faces than anything else. The delineation of character—that was his strongest point. He might know something of Nature, but he knew best of all the human soul : *one* soul, at any rate—*his own*—and one is quite enough to know. . . . .   Here he was again.   No crush round the easel this time.   Of course, at first sight he should have said he had never set eyes on those horses before ; but then, was he here to judge at first sight ?   It was a matter of some importance.   Everyone else except himself seemed so positive they were his ; but if he was not quite satisfied, he had better make certain of the fact by a proper unprejudiced investigation. . . . The letter B. !   Why, that was odd !   What a fuss he had made about nothing !   Yes, that was B. sure enough—plain B. staring him in the face. . . . And in the bottom right-hand corner, which was where he always put his initials,—his initial.   Any F. to be seen ? . . .   F. . . . F. . . . F. . . . .   No, unless that smudge was an F ; but then, he would sometimes put B. alone, and sometimes F., and sometimes F. and B. in a monogram.   Certainly in the days when he painted those horses, which must have been about the same time that he painted the landscape . . . when he was barely seventeen . . . certainly in those days he used to sign his name and initials in every sort of fashion, being fond in those days of his name and initials.

" Why have you never showed them before ?" Here was Raikes, turned up again.

" Oh, well, to tell you the truth, I'd forgotten them." Now quick, quick !   " To tell you the truth, I should even have doubted if they were mine."

" What do you mean ?"

" Well, I mean if it hadn't been for my initial. . . . There's my B.," said Frank, and he pointed it out.

" Did you paint them so long ago, then ?" said Raikes, of course without looking.

" Oh, well, yes, I suppose so.   Why, as long ago, I suppose, as before I left Winchester."

" Then, my boy, let me tell you you've made a big mistake.   You should have stuck to animals.   It's all very well for Jackson to praise that portrait, but the horses beat it by chalks. Those horses you could *ride !*"

" Oh, well, the portrait was never really finished."

" No, it isn't, is it ? Finishing wouldn't do no good. You changed your opinions half-way through. You've got two different fellows there."

" Whatever makes you think that ?"

" Why, the eyes and the mouth don't match ?"

" Why should they ? What do you mean ?"

" The eyes are tragic—tragic, sir, tragic !"

" Tragic ? Stuff ! No more than the mouth."

" That's my point : they *are*. The mouth is the mouth of a reasonably happy individual."

" The mouth, then, tells the truth. He was happy enough ; but he only gave me a couple of sittings. Jackson said nothing about the landscape."

" Won't do," said Raikes, and shook his head. " Jackson remarked that the foreground wanted work."

" Did he ? Oh, very likely. That, also, was done an age ago."

" It seems to me," said Raikes, " we none of us improve with years ;" and Raikes was off again.

Frank very soon went out. It was four as he walked away. He walked alone. At that moment he could not have endured company. He was in a very strange, uncertain mood, feeble, hesitating. He turned aimlessly up one street and down another, and then he was aware that he wanted an empty street where he would be undisturbed. Such a street he found—a respectable street, a street perhaps for lodgers, and this being Sunday, drawing towards five, the lodgers would be in or out—one thing or the other—not to and fro, and up and down, nor (as in the poorer streets) lounging about the doorsteps. To the far end of this street he walked. It had a definite end, came to a full stop, with the backs of other houses in a street running across at right angles to block the way. And now he was here, why had he come ? To stand staring

stupidly at the houses, to stand in a dream, able only
to dream, not to think ; too dull, too dead to think ! . . .
Ought he to think ? Why, yes, he ought. Had not
things happened this afternoon enough to set him
thinking ? He set himself to think, urged himself,
bade himself—what was the good ? He still stared
vacantly down the street, wondered who lived in these
sleeping houses, and whether on Monday the houses
would wake.

. . . One woke now unexpectedly. A young man
opened a door and came out. Bang went the door !
One, two, three, down the steps he trotted, turned up
his collar, and caught sight of Frank, took an unerring
line down the path, and swept the corner in full sail.

CHAPTER LI

FRANK went home. In the passage the girl greeted
him ; a lady was upstairs. Was it Phillis ? Oh, if
it was Phillis !—oh, if it was Phillis, he must go—go
somewhere ; they could not meet.

Who ran out to the top of the stairs ?

" I've been waiting, and waiting, and waiting." . . .
Why, Dolly ! Why, only Dolly !

" I couldn't think who on earth it was," said Frank.

" I heard you were coming to-day. You dear old
boy !"

" It's awfully good of you to look me up." Dolly
was all in black. Of course, she would be all in
black.

" I want you to give me tea," says Dolly, " and then
take me to church."

" I'll give you tea," said Frank, ringing the bell.

" *And* you'll take me to church."

" Will I ?"

" Oh, but, Frank, you must. If you won't, I can't
stop for tea. No, really. It gets so dark."

" What's all this about ?   What's tea got to do with church ? ...   Yes, please, bring the tea up. . . .   Explain, Dolly, explain."

" I've quite lost my nerve."

" Have you ?"

" I can't bear being out alone after dark, and I like going to church, and there've been so many horrible murders and mysteries.   I hardly dare look at the posters ; there is always some dreadful news."

" Oh, that's all right.   You think there are more murders and mysteries because you happen to notice them more.   That's an overstrung imagination ; we know all about that."

" I never thought I had any imagination.   I was always supposed to be without it at school, and when I went to the Extension Lectures on Keats ; but now, whenever I go down a street after dark, I turn hot and cold."

" Well, if you manage to turn hot to-night it's a wonder," said Frank ; and he smashed up the coal on the fire, and shovelled another shovelful on.

" But you *will* take me to church ?"

" Rather !   What church ?"

" I go to St. Philip's.   It's very high.   I hope you won't mind.   You're a dear thing to come.   Warner gets horribly bored, and I've a great notion of letting people go their own way.   If I choose to go, I shall go ; and if he chooses not to, he needn't ; but I was sure you would, as you always did."

Well, if Dolly wanted someone to see her home in the dark, why not go ?   It was just about what he was fit for, to pioneer people through the streets.   As they went along side by side Frank could have cried to some-one to come and menace this queer little woman, and give him the chance of showing fight.   But nobody seemed to wish to molest her.

" The murders and mysteries to-night, Dolly," he said, " must be at the other end of town."

Dolly laughed boldly.   " I don't care where they

are when I've got anyone with me. It seems so odd to have a companion. I go about so much alone."

" Do you ? Then you ought to get used to it."

" Oh, I think nothing of it now. I go pretty well everywhere alone, especially now since mother's death. Not that I saw half as much of mother as I should have liked ; still, you never do see the people you want to, and I felt I could always go round there. Why, I haven't seen *you* since—since—when ?"

" When ?"

They were under the shadow of the church, mixing now with the congregation gathering from the adjoining streets. Inside the pews were silently filling. . . . What a mad idea to be here in church for no particular purpose ! Was there anyone else out of all this number who had come with so little purpose—that is to say, with *avowedly* so little purpose ? For, of course, the whole thing was outside him now. At any rate, until he knew what, in the first place, he had done, and what, in the next place, he was going to do, he could hardly sing, and kneel, and pray. Kneel ? Yes, because everyone knelt ; but pray ? he had not a word to utter. With the Psalms it was different. It was, perhaps, a little odd that he should feel such a wholesome relief in the singing of God's most righteous judgments, His furies and indignations. It was like going through some dreadful storm, hailstones sputtering round his head ; he could stand that sort of thing. Whether he could stand the preacher was rather another question. Dolly sat down, put her gloves on the top of her Prayer-Book, and settled herself in the corner. So does everyone settle himself for a sermon. So used Frank of old ; so had he settled himself for years, most of the Sundays of his life, in every kind of humour, and yet, whatever the humour, there had always been but one way to fit your shoulders to the pew. For the first time now in his life he sat awkwardly. Should he shut his eyes and dream of the past, of Sundays in Marchington

Church ? Should he dream that it was his father preaching ? . . . It was not like one of his father's sermons ; his father had always something to say. Where he got it from, that was a puzzle, seeing that he rarely went out of Marchington village, and saw very little company, and preferred the old standard books in his library to the morning and evening news. *This* man studied his news. He was touching on many current topics. Frank saw the trend of it all, and knew he might just as well not listen, and yet as each fresh topic was mentioned he noted every one.

This was annoying, for none of these topics concerned Frank, nor, by the way, would they much concern Dolly, who suddenly sneezed and looked round for a draught ; but still, this was always so with preaching, and only the few here and there, like his father, have something to say.

Besides the present-day topics, there were naturally various references to God, and temptation, and sin, and other ingredients of religion. They did not materially signify ; they brought no weight or value with them, and might just as well have been omitted. God was strong, and man was weak ; but the preacher did not *know* any more about God's strength than he did about the present-day topics—ah, but Frank's father at Marchington knew !—and as to man's weakness—had the preacher ever been weak ? Had the preacher always been weak—born weak, lived weak, died weak ? If not, let him hold his tongue, his idiot, idiot tongue ; for what do the strong know of strength ?

" It wasn't too high for you, was it ?" said Dolly, as they crushed out through the porch.

" Oh no," said Frank. " It's raining. Let me put up your umbrella."

" It didn't bore you dreadfully ?"

" Bore me !"

" And you don't even want to say, ' Oh, let's get home, and have some supper ' ? That's the usual cry."

" Oh, well, I'm not particularly hungry. Here, I'll hold the umbrella ; you've got your skirts and things."

They splashed through the swimming streets.

" It must have rained like fun," said Frank.

" Didn't you hear it in church ?" said Dolly. " I did, all through the sermon. Why, you must have been asleep !"

" Oh no, I wasn't ; I was listening."

" Were you ? I tried to, but I don't think I have got a brain for any sort of consecutive argument."

" Consecutive argument ?" said Frank, wondering.

" I mean," said Dolly, " he's what you would call rather a deep thinker."

" Carried you out of your depth ?" said Frank. " Well, I confess I floundered about a bit myself."

" Rubbish ! *You* understood him. You're logical, only you're much too nice to say so."

" Oh no, I should say at once if I were logical."

" Frank !"

" What ?"

" Do you ever know what it is to be really wretched?"

" I fancy I did two months ago."

" Why ? When ? Oh, when you had smallpox. Yes, but I mean really wretched."

" Well, for real wretchedness try the smallpox."

" I shouldn't mind."

" So you said when you wrote to me. I didn't reply for fear of giving you the very thing which you wanted to have ; but I might have replied that you did not know what you were talking about."

" And you don't know what you are talking about when you say I've no cause for wretchedness."

" I said no such thing. I hope you have ; there is some chance, then, of a cure. If there's no cause there's no cure."

" I suppose there is always a cure."

" There is with the small-pox."

" That's what I mean. If I had the smallpox
there'd be a cause for wretchedness."

" Then, you *do* want a cause. You inferred that you
had one ; at least, you were vexed with me for inferring
you hadn't."

" Perhaps I have. I don't say everything."

" Sometimes it is better not."

" Ah, so people tell you when they don't wish to be
bothered with your affairs. You're not going to see
me back to the very doorstep ?"

" Yours is number twenty-four. Lights in the
dining-room window."

" That's Warner wanting his supper. Won't you
come in too ?"

" Not to-night."

" Warner is sure to say, ' Why didn't you ask him
in ?' "

" He'll ask for his supper first. Besides, you
have asked me in. . . . Take the umbrella. Good-
night."

" Good-night. . . ." She was on the step. " One
minute !" She came back again. " I'd something I
wanted to say. . . . Wait a bit, I forget. . . . How
silly I am ! It isn't anything I forget . . . it's only . . .
loneliness." She gave a sob, and caught hold of his
arm.

He released it, and took hers. " Loneliness ! Oh
no, you're tired."

" It isn't that . . . it isn't that . . . it's . . ."

" It probably *is* that," said Frank, " and you miss
your mother. As a matter of fact, so do I."

" It isn't that. . . ."

" Oh well, yes, I expect it is."

" I tell you it *isn't*. Don't keep on saying it *is*. Of
course, I *do* miss mother, but——"

" Of course you do. Still, you've got Helena
left."

" Helena !" She stopped sobbing. " Helena ! Oh,
Helena has the poor."

" That is absurd.   You are sisters."

" I wish I'd never told you."   She wiped her eyes.

" Told me !   Told me what ?   You've not told me anything that I know of."

" I—I said I was lonely."   She was screwing her pocket-handkerchief.

" So is everyone."

" My dear Frank "—she put the handkerchief into her pocket—" that is a very old consolation."

" Well, I suppose it doesn't console one much, but it's common-sense.   I shall be lonely walking home ; your respected husband is lonely now ; possibly Helena——"

" You needn't go on.   I'm not utterly stupid.   I'm not so utterly stupid as to suppose that I'm the only person in the world who—who . . . give me the umbrella.   I'm sorry I brought you out of your way."

" I'm afraid I've not been a particularly lively companion," said Frank ; he shut the umbrella with care. " That's all my fault."

" I think we are both out of temper," said Dolly. " I am much obliged to you, Frank. . . . No, thank you ; *I'll* ring the bell.   I can manage.   Good-night."

" Wait a bit, Dolly ; look here."   An odd feeling came over him of *power ;* he was fit to speak to anyone, fit to speak to thousands—a feeling closely akin to the old feeling of *reality ;* but now what he knew in the back of his mind he could bring to the front and utter. " Wait a bit, Dolly ; look here."   He opened the umbrella again.   Her hand was on the bell.   " It's all my fault for not giving you a straight answer to a straight question.   I will speak like the Bible.   ' *Do I ever feel wretched ?*' you ask.   Answer, ' *Yes.*'   Only listen : when I do I can generally trace the cause to myself."

" My dear Frank, anyone might think that you thought me an idiot."   Her hand dropped from the bell. " Naturally the cause is in yourself ; I mean *my*self ; that is, *our*selves. You don't suppose I should feel wretched if the cause was in somebody else, except by way of sympathy . . . though I don't believe much in sympathy ; it's very, very hollow."

Frank considered ; he was really considering. " *Say* something," said Dolly ; and he jumped.

" I don't know what to say," said Frank. " You put so many ideas in my head."

" Do I ?" said Dolly.

" Yes, but it all wants sorting. Go along. You will catch cold."

" Oh no, I won't ; besides, never mind : I dare say I shan't see you for an age, and I know it was stupid of me to take offence, when really it was I who was wrong."

" Stop !" said Frank. " There you go again ! An entirely new set of ideas ! Now I intend to lead you back to the point you started from."

" Where was that ?" said Dolly vaguely. It must seem a long way off.

" Wretchedness. You were wretched."

" Oh yes," she hesitated ; " I said so. I think perhaps I was exaggerating."

" Good-night," said Frank.

Dolly laughed. " You *are* so funny. Well, everyone exaggerates. But *you* said *you* were wretched."

" Excuse me ! You asked if I ever knew what it was to be really wretched, to which I meekly replied ' Yes,' adding subsequently that the cause—no, that was where you went astray ; I'll put it differently—adding subsequently that I generally found myself to blame."

" Oh yes, people are always ready enough to say that sort of thing of themselves. You wouldn't like it in your most miserable moments, if somebody came and said it for you."

" No, I shouldn't like it," said Frank, " but that wouldn't make it less true."

" But I don't believe it *is* true. Why "—Dolly brightened—" think of some of the dreadful things which happen to people—deaths, and diseases, and losses ; I knew a girl who was engaged to a man, and he died the day before they were married—I mean *were to have been* married. You can't blame her for that. I call it very dreadful."

" Very sad for her," said Frank—" very."

" And yet you say people are to blame for their troubles, and for the things they haven't got." That was an after-thought.

" I didn't say that," said Frank. It flashed through his mind that it did seem a strange dispensation which had made Helena the mother, who already " had the poor." " I didn't say that. I only said they were to blame—it's a cruel word—to blame for their *wretchedness*, which is another affair. The trouble is the cause, the wretchedness the effect ; but if you can see an inch—mind, even only one inch—*beyond*. . . . ' Beyond *what ?*' you were going to ask me."

" No, I wasn't. I don't know what you are talking about."

" But you *might* ask me ' Beyond what ?' and I should say I hadn't the slightest idea ; only if you *can* see an inch beyond, you have leaped over the wretchedness—a pit it is, a snare, a gulf—and you stand on unassailable ground." What a sermon ! What a sermon !

Dolly yawned. She held out her hand for the umbrella. " Well, I want my supper," she said. " There, I've rung the bell. Frank, you're an angel. Goodnight."

" Dolly, you're a human being. Good-night."

CHAPTER LII

HE woke next morning with joy, perhaps with a shout
of joy ; a shout seemed ringing in his ear.   Such a load
was off his mind !   He *had* painted those horses after
all . . . he had painted them in the study for his mother
years ago, and his father had stood by the table with a
paper in his hand, and said, " Frank is no longer a
child." . . . He had painted . . . wait . . . where was he ?
in bed ?   In his room ? . . .   He thought he was back
in the hospital ; there was the washhand-stand, only
they had papered the walls. . . .   Why, he was dreaming ; he had woken up now.   He was here in his room.
Dreaming—stop !   Was it all a dream ?   He buried
his face.   Let him dream again !   Let him never,
never awake.   Oh, if he could have waked in the study,
and found his father and mother there ! . . .   He must
get up ; he must move, keep moving ; he should go to
see Raikes to-day ; he should get those pictures out of
Raikes' hands ; he should find some good excuse.   He
should go round directly after breakfast (Raikes would
probably still be in bed), and say outright : " Look
here, I don't want those horses sent up."   Raikes
would say : " Why not ?"   Frank would say : " Well,
I don't believe they're mine."   Raikes would think him
crazy.   Or, of course, he might soften things down, and
give no reason, or Raikes might really not care.   What
are one man's works to another ?

Raikes was out.   When was he coming back ?
Next week.   Next *when ?*   Next week.   Where had
he gone ?   He had gone playing golf.   Did anyone
know what he had done with the pictures for Burlington
House ?

The landlady shook her head ; on second thoughts
her daughter might know.   Would she please ask her
daughter ?   When she came in she would.   When was
she coming in ?   To-night.   To-night ? . . .   Oh, well,

that was not so bad.   He called again at nine o'clock.
. . .   It struck him that after all the horses might not
be accepted.   Jackson liked the portrait best. . . .
Would the girl be there ?   Yes, she was.   Good !   She
had just arrived.   In she came with her hat and
feathers.

Did she know anything about Mr. Raikes' pictures
for the Show ?   What pictures ?   what show ? etc.
Oh yes, the young man had called, and taken them.
What young man ?   The young man from the shop ;
she didn't know his name ; she would run and ask if
her mother happened to know the young man's name.
Oh, never mind *his* name ; what was the name of the
shop ?   That she could not say.   Would she find out ?
She seemed doubtful ; besides, she did not see how she
could find out.   Frank was very patient.   He explained to her that, knowing something of the young
man, she might learn where the young man worked.
Well, perhaps she might next Sunday.   " I mean *now*,"
said Frank, and he left in despair.

He must trust entirely to himself and his own
ingenuity.   There were certain well-known shops in
that particular district where artists dealt.   He would
try one after another ; perhaps before the day was out
he should have traced his pictures.   He began with the
hope of visiting a dozen shops if necessary in the
morning, and a dozen in the afternoon ; but he heard
a church clock boom half-past one as he came away
from his fifth endeavour.   Everyone seemed so un-
conscionably slow.   But he himself was in better
spirits—without reason, perhaps ; still, one can't help
that.   Condemned men sleep before they are hanged,
which is a mystery.   Yet there was reason enough ; he
had at least something to do, something to expect,
and when the pictures *were* found, what a relief—oh,
what a relief to get them safely home !   An explanation would be easy ; the horses should light to-
morrow's fire, and never, never, never again should he
put brush to canvas. . . .   *When* the pictures were

found ! But then, he had not calculated that, as each step took him further afield into regions less well known, he should have to stop for inquiries, and possibly might toil along street after street without passing a single picture-dealer. . . .

He came back on the top of an omnibus. There was no room inside. A girl like Phillis jumped in just as he was about to take the last place. He slowly climbed the steps. He turned up his collar ; the wind whistled through him ; what had he done to-day ?

What had he done to-day ?

Nothing.

And supposing he *had* done anything, what would it have been ?

Nothing.

Supposing he had found his pictures, would he be any the better for that ?

No.

Why not ?

Because he should have to tell lies about them. Raikes would want to be satisfied, so would Jackson, and how can you hush up a story like that, or any sort of a story ? Was he sufficiently skilled in the art of deception to satisfy all the world, or, rather, at the outset to check any further suspicions ? . . . Moreover, had he the smallest *wish* to deceive ? Could he live with a truth untold ? . . . In a very short time those pictures would be passing before the Committee in Burlington House. He was confused in his own mind now as to what he really hoped. He felt as if he did not care whether they were accepted or not ; whether he went to see them hanging upon the walls ; whether someone came back from the dead to claim them. . . . Really, *that* would be best of all ! If only someone would claim the pictures, get up and make a fuss at the Show—a public fuss, so that everyone knew, and no explanation was required.

Then there would be no need to tell Phillis. He could slip off, and that would spare her much. The

engagement had never been announced; those who
were in the understanding would naturally hold their
tongues, and Phillis would suffer no disgrace. Phillis,
poor Phillis! . . . He must not say that; he was
dealing with facts, remember! Besides, love can easily
turn to hatred (*true* love cannot turn to anything else),
and it merely remained for all concerned—namely,
himself and Phillis—to readjust their lives. Phillis
would readjust hers, of course, ruling her fate with
proper control. He himself? What did that matter?
He might be fortunate and die; he should go where
there was a chance of dying, and in the next world all
is known: there was that piece of sure satisfaction.

He gave it up, the whole affair from beginning to
end! He should go mad at this rate, if he were not
half mad already! What purpose was served? Why
should the scenes of the past two weeks go round and
round in his head—the letters Raikes wrote, Jackson's
letter, the letters Frank wrote in return, the talk at
The Bristol Hotel, the uncertainty, the delay, the questions which had to be answered, the answers which led
to more questions, which led to more answers, which
led to more questions again? What was the good *now*
of imagining what might have happened *then* had
everything happened differently? Was there any
profit *now* in wishing that *then* he had said, " *What*
studies? I never painted a horse in my life"; had
said it, and stuck to it—truth first, manners afterwards?

Why had he *not* said it? It was interesting to try
to find out. There were perhaps three causes. First,
vanity; the belief that now at last somebody had been
found with sufficient sense to appraise his work, a
belief admitting not a shadow of doubt as to the value
of that somebody's opinion, or the value of the thing
appraised. Secondly, intoxication; he was off his
balance. For this he was not altogether to blame, but
much to blame for not noting the fact, and watching
carefully every impulse. He should have curbed himself at once, tightened the reins, as one steadies a weak-

kneed horse downhill. His recent engagement to
Phillis—climbing all at once to the heights of happiness, a whole kingdom of joy held under his hand—this
should have made him specially careful. . . . Ah, but
it *had* made him careful ; on those happy heights he
had trembled. . . . And this brought him to consider
the third cause and the last—timidity. What does
it *mean* ? Timidity—what *is* it ?

He clambered down the steps.

CHAPTER LIII

WHEN Raikes came to congratulate him on getting
both pictures hung (the news was written in his face),
Frank thought himself too dead to care, and yet at the
first words something quickened ; he was alive again.
His whole manner and appearance must have changed,
for Raikes looked at him, and said : " Well, *that's*
settled. Two of mine are in."

" Are they ? I'm most awfully glad." So he was
glad. Now let the storm burst overhead. It had
brewed long enough for him. But whence would sweep
the storm-clouds up ? Which way would blow the
current ? This was his only dread—that he might miss
his chance, speaking too late for fear lest he should
speak too soon. Too soon he had not spoken. All
those efforts to anticipate the storm had failed—dis-
honest honest efforts. The storm would break in
order, first the murmur, then the tumult then the
silence. From such storms there is, thank God, no
escape.

Phillis was now his only care. The storm would
whistle about her too. Yes, but the storm would not
matter to Phillis, consumed with a storm of her own.
She hated cowards and liars ; that was one consolation ;
and if she hated with such good cause, she would suffer
no pangs of love. The very fact that he had written

every third day to her since they parted—each word in her sight a deliberate lie—would crush down the scales (all in her favour), and she would hate him so much the more, so much the more righteously, gleefully, royally ; so sure of herself—the case so open, no excuse, no possible misconception—that she would trample the past underfoot, rising supreme to a future, a happy, reasonable future. This was best for Phillis.

No other course would do. Was it not thousandfold best that awhile she should suffer the sting of his shame and the pain of a separation than to suffer for ever the soreness of wrongs half righted, truths half told ? Was it not best that she should be free to hate him out-right (so easy for her) than be fettered by makeshift pardons ?

Ah, yes, in theory this was well. How would his theory serve him now—now that she was coming, now that no pen could be forced to form words which the lips could never be brought to utter ? But the lips must speak, and the lips must meet ; well, she would hate him hereafter so much the more.

Would she detect a difference ? Phillis ? Oh no ! That was not Phillis, wholesome Phillis ! Her first thought would be pleasure—a ready look, and a ready kiss, and ready conversation. And he need not have vexed himself as he stood there alone on the platform, out of the wind and the rain, for the boat was delayed, and they met after all in the squash at Burlington House.

PART X

WATTIE

Had I said that, had I done this,
So might I gain, so might I miss.

CHAPTER LIV

ONE day—it was early summer, in May—Wattie was spreading some sheets of newspaper down in the church for the plaster and paint, when his eye was caught by a name at the top of a column, and he found himself reading the paragraph through from beginning to end. . . . "The Royal Academy" hung again ! Bravo " The Royal Academy "! How he laughed over recollections of a couple of years ago ! . . . But here were six, eight, ten—no, fourteen lines, and all about Mr. Frank, his " tones " and his " values." . . . Wattie sighed, and he sighed and took up his palette. Mr. Frank hung . . . he should like to see that. Well, and why not ? Moreover, he had been wishing of late to learn what real masters and students of Art could do, who gave the whole of their time to their work.

He got to Burlington House at two o'clock in the afternoon. At first he wished he had never come. There were too many laughing ladies, and they pushed him into a corner, and, not being able to edge away or turn himself about, he could only avoid the ladies by staring through to the opposite wall. Here, strange to say, he was caught again. Faces looked back at him, women and men of startling reality. How could you tell the true from the false, the men and women in frames from the men and women walking about ? . . . And there, bravo ! the Royal Academy ! What fun to thread your way in and out and come nearer yourself

at each step ! . . .   Mr. Frank must have worked at
it since—since those long afternoons at The Bell
a couple of summers ago. It was not so much of a
likeness, but more of a clever study. " Tones " and
" values " the paper said, but fancy as well, and character—not Wattie's, perhaps, but character all the same.
Mr. Frank knew something of faces and characters,
having face and character of his own. The odd part
was the look in the eyes. They should not be so dark,
so deep ; and they should look *out*, not *in*. . . . If he
could get quite close . . . but here were the laughing
ladies again. One of them put up her spectacles and
said what she thought of the face. Everyone seemed
to be talking, and they jostled so, there was no escape.
And then they all talked about something else that
was lower down on the wall, and Wattie got cooler and
struggled to see, and an opening came, and he saw. . . .

Now this was a very remarkable thing. He should
never have dreamt it possible. Still, here it was, and
it looked all right, far better than he could have ever
imagined. Not that he himself would have hung his
own picture there, for this was a place for laughing
ladies and masters and students of Art ; but if somebody else thought it good enough . . . he supposed he
was just a bit flattered ! He remembered how much
that canvas had cost him—eighteen pence—and the
trouble he had to get over to Brinkley to buy it one
Saturday afternoon. . . .   And yet the old flaw mocked
him, and he was ashamed. Were they not free, yet
fettered ? wild, yet restrained ? Standing alone, un-
harnessed, unbridled, was it not clear to anyone's
senses that they had been curbed by a human hand,
and not only had been, but still were curbed ? Some
check upon them was evident now — some check,
some presence, vaguely felt, then more than felt—
visibly seen—for could he not trace the weight of her
body, trace it through every limb and sinew of each
of the beasts as they stood—wild beasts, tame beasts,
fretting the ground—while she asked an honest opinion,

or wanted an earthly reason why they should stand in the sun ?

" They are perfectly charming !" somebody said, and then they began all over again about the portrait above. The crowd was closing. Wattie pushed through ; he would not be pinned there any more ; and for the future Burlington House should be for the laughing ladies. His immediate plan, to get out of this room. . . . Yes, he would go in here, a room by comparison empty, with hundreds of little pictures dovetailed upon the walls. Empty ? No, one very old gentleman wandering round with a glass in his eye, and on the couch with her back towards him . . . Should he stay ? Should he go ? . . . She turned while he faltered, and all at once was a laughing lady coming towards him.

" How odd I should just be thinking about you !" This was what Miss Phillis said.

CHAPTER LV

SHE was waiting, expecting a number of friends. What was *he* doing ? Why had he come ?—Why should not he come if he wanted to ?—Had he come on purpose to see his portrait ? Wasn't it good ? Wasn't it like ? Or *wasn't* it good ? *Wasn't* it like ? A sudden change of inflection, a sudden anxiety, almost a tremor. Wattie must laugh at once, and assure her that inch by inch it was true to his face. Then she was satisfied.

" Tell me what *you* have been doing ?"

" Nothing."

" Nothing ?" Miss Phillis spoke in a dream. She was looking towards the door all the time. " Wattie, I've so much news !" She woke with a start, so happy and jolly. " In the first place, I'm coming home."

" To Marchington ?"

" Yes."

" You'll be glad ? "

" Glad ! I should think so. How I loathed
Italy ! How I *hate* London ! You know all the
money I lost ? Well, it's found. And then I've got
another piece of news. . . . Let us go and look at the
pictures."

Well, no need to tell her news ! He followed her
back to the stifling room. The crowd was thicker
than ever ; yet nobody brushed her as she passed.
" *Now* give me your honest opinion."

" You give me yours, miss."

She coloured and laughed. Miss Phillis, when she
looked at a picture, never knew what to say.

" Everyone tells me they are clever," she sheltered
herself, then sprang out : " I don't understand about
cleverness, but the portrait is just like you, and the
horses I simply love. They remind me of Choice and
Necessity. Poor Choice !"

" I think they were meant to, perhaps." Why, by
the way, poor Choice ?

" Oh no, they were not. Mr. Frank said not. He
said they were imaginary."

Very nice of Mr. Frank !

" I have never seen horses I liked so much."

" You have seen them before." She must have
forgotten.

" Just now—oh yes, before you came in."

" I mean before that."

" How could I, in Italy ?"

" Long before Italy."

" Oh no, I had never seen them. This is the first
year they have been shown."

" Is it ?" It was awkward to know what to say.
How they got there he could not imagine. Perhaps
she had sent them to town, or asked Mr. Frank to sell
them, only neither Miss Phillis nor Mr. Frank would
forget to hand him over the money. " I've never set
eyes on them since you had them."

" What are you talking about ?   *I'm* talking about the horses."

" So am I."

" *Since I had them ?*   *I* never had them.   What do you mean ?"

" Well, I'm sorry, miss, but you *did* have them. I lent them to you, and then you went away, and I didn't trouble, because, miss, to tell you the truth, I'd dozens at home every bit as good, dozens much better, perhaps.   I can see the mistakes."

He had no intention of pointing them out, but he stepped instinctively up to the picture, and put his hand first on one horse, then on the other, where the saddle should (or should not) have been.   Then he stepped back and saw her face. . . .   He was frightened. . . .   He had felt giddy himself just now. . . .   It was the atmosphere.

" It's hot," he said abruptly.   He thought she was going to faint.   " Let us get into the other room."

" Why ?" said Miss Phillis.   " How people push ! I cannot hear one word you're saying.   What is it about the picture ?   You lent it to me ?   *What* picture ?"

" This !"

Miss Phillis was puzzled.   She had forgotten.   It was only one circumstance in her life.   Was it to punish her or himself that he entered into an explanation ? " I lent it to you, and you told me that afternoon in the church that you had passed it on to a friend ; and you told me my horses couldn't compare with the horses in the rose-window."

She put one hand on the rail before her.   A sudden idea occurred to him.   " Let me look at your little book."   He thought he would slip it from her hand (she was too much dazed to read for herself), but she clenched the book with her fingers and, under her breath, flashed out at him all at once.

Without a word he took it from her.   It was open

there as he took it. He found the number and name. . . . Oh, it was *that!* . . . Never mind. . . . What a strange thing to happen ! . . . But there was the immediate present, the need of something to be done. The future would come, and pass.

. . . Where had she gone ? The empty room ? He must follow. He struggled through. He stood with the hundreds of tiny pictures winking at him from the walls. She was there on the same low leather couch. He sat down, too, which seemed odd. He heard himself distinctly say, " It is a mistake." She was going to speak, but he stopped her. " No, not an error ; still, a *mistake*. It needs explanation. No, not excuse ; I said *explanation*."

He did not see her ; he did not look. Where he looked he did not know. He saw nothing certainly ; so much he knew.

" Put it down."

She meant the little book. He put it upon the couch, where she might have it if she chose. Her voice was hard and cold. She would, of course, be unfair and unreasonable, wronging herself and Mr. Frank.

" What have you done ?"

" What have I done ?" said Wattie. " I looked in the book. Why not ? It was much the best thing to do. I see now what has happened."

" Do you, indeed ? I should be glad, then, if you will inform me."

" I only know what you know—that is, just as much as this book has told us. Why should I pretend that I don't know that ?"

" I said nothing about pretence. You said you could see what had happened."

" I can see quite enough. I have no more concern in the matter."

" Is that for you to decide ? Are *you* to be judge ?"

" Judge ! Judge of what ? This has nothing to do with me."

. . . Should he speak to her—plead with her ? Better not. No, imperceptibly he would draw out of the web, disentangle himself. Had he ever a place in it, besides ?

"It is useless to talk. You had better go." She picked up the little book and laid it upon her knee. How could he go, and leave her there ? . . . She stood. Very swiftly she rose. He heard a catch in her breath. . . . Friends came in at the door . . . Miss Daisy and Major.

"Oh, Phillis ! At last ! Here you are !" Miss Daisy seized hold of her hand. "We've been hunting for ever so long. How white you look ! You have just arrived ? The whole of the way from Paris ?"

"I was travelling all last night. How are you, Bob ?"

"First-rate," said Major. He seemed very jolly. "What's wrong with you ?"

"Nothing at all."

"You poor old thing !" said Miss Daisy. "If you had started with us last week you would have had a better crossing. We've come to see Frank's pictures ; we couldn't come before."

"We read of 'em in the *Times*." This was Major, and when he spoke Miss Daisy listened.

Wattie got round the couch ; but Miss Phillis turned upon him. "There is no need for *you* to go. You can stay." Her look commanded him. "Daisy, you remember Brett — Brett, who shoes horses and paints them ?"

Miss Daisy smiled uncertainly. She had forgotten, that was plain, and all about the empty purse ; but then, she was dreaming about Miss Phillis. "Where's Frank, by the way ?"

"Yes, where's Frank ?" said jolly Major.

"He is coming. I think he said three o'clock."

"You think," said Miss Daisy, and laughed.

"Frank's a young swell with his pictures," said

Major. "Who would ever have thought it possible ?"

"Anyone but yourself," said Miss Daisy. "You
know nothing of pictures. I'm sure Frank deserves
it."

"Well, come along and let's see."

"Come," said Miss Phillis, and Wattie came.

They were caught in the throng together. Miss
Phillis was thrust up against him, and yet they
seemed scarcely to touch. "I wish you to stop,"
that was all she said. She had no sort of right to
command.

Major was in front with Miss Daisy. He had one
hand on her arm. "Which way ?" he turned back to
inquire.

Miss Phillis nodded her head. She went on. Wattie
would follow. He supposed that she knew. There
was a block, and they came to a standstill, people
pushing to left and right. Miss Daisy suddenly in the
pause felt for Miss Phillis.

"I haven't seen Frank yet," she said, with such a
sweet look in her eyes.

CHAPTER LVI

"How do you do ?" said a voice from the rear. Wattie
was shoved aside. "What a squash !"

"Here he is !" cried Miss Daisy, pulling at Major.
Major looked round. "Hullo !"

"How nice !" said Miss Daisy. "We've all of
us met." There was nobody else in the room, of
course. ·

"Am I late ?" Mr. Frank consulted his watch.
He did this first, then turned to Miss Phillis. Wattie
heard what he said. There was no escape.

... "You're pale. ... What's the matter ? Had
any lunch ?"

" Yes, I've had lunch," said Miss Phillis.

" What possessed you to come to this show ?"

" I wanted to come. I'm glad I did."

" Did you travel straight through from Paris ?"

" Yes."

" I missed your train."

" It didn't matter."

" And you've got a racking headache."

" No."

" Naturally not. Well, we'll get out of this as soon as we can. . . . I knew you'd be tired. You're white as a sheet."

" I'm perfectly well."

" Good ! . . . I say, I'm glad it's fixed up about Daisy and Bob. . . . June it's to be, I hear. Bob is a very good fellow really."

" So I have always believed."

" And Daisy . . . well, Daisy is Daisy. . . . Dear girl, what's the matter ? You're not fit to be here. Why didn't you send a message ? I would much rather have met you in Eaton Square. . . . I wish people would *not* push. . . . It's no good ; you can't see anything. Look here, shall we go ?"

" I prefer to stay," said Miss Phillis, and she slipped ahead through a sudden channel, and murmured something . . . " Daisy and Bob . . ."

The channel closed. They were caught once more— Major against Mr. Frank.

" Bravo, Frank ! two bits of good fortune rolled into one. Nothing like going sick, and running abroad to be nursed up." He laughed, and being so free and jolly, dug Mr. Frank in the ribs.

Mr. Frank laughed too, but another laugh, for beyond their joy he and Major had nothing in common.

" Mum's the word," said Mr. Frank ; " it is not formally announced."

" Frank," said Miss Phillis suddenly, " don't you remember Brett ?" The tone of her voice was sharp.

" Brett who ? Brett what ?" said Mr. Frank.

He started a little, anxious to please, fearing a hole in his manners.

Miss Phillis was trying to draw Wattie forward. Mr. Frank saw Wattie, and kindled at once.

" Why, of course," he said. " Is this Brett ? I don't think I ever heard your name. . . . I thought you were called something else. Have you come up to see your portrait ?"

Major was mystified.

" He has come to see the pictures," Miss Phillis explained ; " he is an artist himself." This she explained to everyone. One or two ladies looked round. . . . *Who* was an artist himself ? . . .

" Do you exhibit ?" asked Major, surprised at his own intelligence.

" No," said Wattie.

" He does not exhibit—no," said Miss Phillis.

" Brett an artist ?" said Mr. Frank. " You were a blacksmith last. What did I tell you ? Not to paint pictures, not to smoke, not to have any ambitions."

Major was staring at Wattie. " Bless my soul !" he said. He had recalled, in all probability, Marchington village and Marchington forge, and " *Which of the two are you backing, my boy ?*"

" Look here "—Mr. Frank was speaking—" let us run and show Brett his remarkable likeness, and then cut away and get tea."

" Running and cutting," said Miss Daisy, with a great broad coat in front of her, and just at that minute the broad coat moved.

" Here we are !" said Mr. Frank, keeping a way for the ladies. " Behold the portrait and the original."

" Why, it was *you* brought my doggie back !" Miss Daisy turned with tears in her eyes. " It is very, very . . ." She could not say what. Funny Miss Daisy, with nothing to say. " You know, Frank," she burst out, " *it isn't all you.*"

Mr. Frank smiled a shrewd quick smile. " No, it isn't, is it ?" he said. " Well, have you stared enough ?"

" By Jove !" said Major ; he had not spoken. " By Jove !" They waited to hear, but he did not say anything else.

" Now then," said Mr. Frank, " I vote for a move."

" Oh !" cried Miss Daisy. " We must look at this. What dears !" She had gone quite close, then drew back. " Phillis ! Bob ! What are you doing ? I'm sure this is a beautiful picture ;—and these are your horses, Frank ?"

" They are only studies," said Mr. Frank.

" *Are* they yours ?" asked Miss Phillis. (What was she going to do ?)

" They are nothing to boast of," said Mr. Frank. " I can't think how they got in."

" I can't think either," said Miss Phillis. (Let her punish herself if she chose.)

" Phil darling, what do you mean ?" cried Miss Daisy. " Why, I'm not sure if I don't like them better than *that*." She was gazing again at the portrait. " I *do* like the portrait—I *do*. It reminds me of something I thought very pretty, and I *was* so unhappy about my dog. . . . Only there's one thing : the eyes aren't straight. I don't believe the eyes *are* straight. . . . Frank ! Where's Frank ? Do you call those eyes straight ?"

Mr. Frank looked into them darkly. " I know nothing about it," he said. " I thought they were. They were meant to be. You know, it was finished from memory."

. . . Wattie was back outside The Bell, with the room on the first floor deserted. . . .

" Well, they're *not*," said Miss Daisy ; " and now I have noticed it once I should notice it always. . . . But the horses are lovely. . . . Only, I'm sure, Frank, you meant them for Choice and Necessity ; poor old Choice !" (Why poor old Choice again ?)

Mr. Frank came forward a little. " Do you think so ? There's bound to be some similarity ; horses are more or less all alike."

" My dear Frank ! You paint them, and talk such nonsense !" Miss Daisy was quite annoyed. " Horses are no more alike than human beings. I can't bear to hear you speak so, and of Choice and Necessity, too— the sweetest and best——"

" You'll catch it now !" said Major. " But, by Jove, they are capital ! That roan, you know— capital ! . . . I'm with Daisy, in duty bound."

" You two would rave over anything that happened to go on four legs. When you've done !" said Mr. Frank. " Here's Phil with a racking headache."

" I've no headache at all," said Miss Phillis, " and I like to hear Daisy's opinion. . . . You don't care for the portrait ? Neither do I."

" Oh, I don't say that," cried Miss Daisy, " but the horses are dears."

" So they are ; dearer than human beings. . . . The eyes are like Frank's."

" Like Frank's !" said Miss Daisy. " How funny ! It's the eyes I object to."

" I never said——" began Miss Phillis.

" What did you never say ?" asked Major.

" I never said," persisted Miss Phillis, " that I did not object to the eyes. I *do*."

Major burst into a roar of laughter. He clapped Mr. Frank on the back. " I think we had better go," he said.

" I think so too," said Mr. Frank ; he laughed as well, though not so loud.

" Don't plague Phillis," said Miss Daisy; " she's utterly fagged and tired out. And do for goodness' sake let us admire what we choose. There is only one thing," she went on—" one thing so small that it hardly matters, and it's no good talking to Frank."

" Talk on," said Mr. Frank. " We are getting in everyone's way."

" I don't care," said Miss Daisy ; " everyone got in our way before. It's only a sudden idea. . . . Those horses are done from life ?"

"Well," said Mr. Frank, "perhaps more or less. What are you driving at?"

"What do you mean by 'perhaps more or less'?" Miss Phillis wanted to know.

"Never mind that," said Miss Daisy; she had got her sudden idea. "Just tell me this: were they hunters?"

"Choice and Necessity were." That was how Mr. Frank replied.

"Why don't you answer the question?" This was Miss Phillis again.

"It's only because," said Miss Daisy, "they look as if they are meant to be free, and yet as if someone was holding them in. . . . It looks even as if . . ." She went and put her hand over the picture.

"Oh, you mustn't do that," cried Major.

"*Now!*" cried Miss Daisy, quite heedless. "You would almost suspect I was hiding two figures."

"I dare say a figure would be an improvement," said Major. "You might have a man at their heads."

"That's not what I mean," said Miss Daisy. "It's here in the saddle . . . just here . . . they look as if they were carrying someone . . . and then it would fill up this space in the sky."

"Brilliant idea. Frank, is that right?"

"I don't know what you are talking about."

"Daisy wants . . ."

"No, I don't." Miss Daisy turned suddenly round with her shining eyes and her very flushed cheeks. "What do *you* think?" she said, for nobody else understood.

"I think like you do, miss."

"Very gallant," said Major, bursting out with a laugh.

"I know I'm right," said Miss Daisy, laughing too, for she did not mind. "But it all depends on the figure. *You* said a man, Bob."

"So I did. Well, what *was* the figure? Frank shall tell."

" I would tell if I knew," said Mr. Frank.

" Brett knows," said Miss Phillis.

Everyone laughed.

" If I do," said Wattie, " whatever it was, it is wiped out now."

" What does he say ?" asked Mr. Frank. " You are all very frivolous. Ladies and gentlemen, tea or I die."

CHAPTER LVII

WATTIE must now put his thoughts in order. On one point he was convinced : Mr. Frank had not the remotest idea who had painted the pictures. Mr. Frank would never make mischief. Suppose he had said to Mr. Frank—yes, even before Miss Phillis, Miss Daisy—suppose he had said, " Those figures are *mine*," Mr. Frank would have yielded his claim directly ; he would have told the truth, every word, as honester people so rarely did, too much absorbed in arranging his facts to care one jot for public opinion. But, then, it was quite impossible. How should *he* intervene ? Was not confession due to Miss Phillis ? Was not he, Wattie, nothing more than an unfortunate accident in the case ? It happened that this was *his* picture ; let him push that well to the front ; let him shelter himself behind the merely fortuitous chances, and so, under cover, escape. He had no business there. There?—no, nor anywhere within one hundred thousand miles ! Was he not always dumb—a beast ? Could he fathom such passion or such pride ? . . . He would flee the thousand miles away. Somewhere out there was his life. He saw that life, too, in a flash, stretching before him—sunny meadows—and he should be mad for joy. Why not ? Just because this had been in another age, in another world, should it spoil all worlds, all time, for him ? Let her spoil her own world, her own time, if she would ! And yet, if she wished to be reasonably happy, she had only one reasonable word to say. He was sure one word would be sufficient, or to what purpose had they committed their souls to each other? They *had* committed their souls. So much was easy to see. Like Miss Daisy and Major, they had come to an understanding, but recently, so it appeared; it was not yet "formally announced." "Mum's the word," said Mr. Frank. Mr. Frank had "gone sick," so said Major; had been "nursed abroad"; had been standing too much in the sun perhaps. All else was idle conjecture. They might or might not have met since Marchington days. One thing he was certain about, and that was Miss Phillis's happy face as he came on her in the empty room with her two bits of news to tell.

But could he stand by and do nothing—see her suffer, destroy herself? That was where pride would lead her, to utter self-destruction—pride, judgment, and obstinacy. . . . This brought *him* back to the canvas; he leapt the thousand miles. Once more he was intervening. He might speak, upbraid her folly, give her an honest opinion again. She would never forgive him, of course, and now you could not just turn up your collar; you were bound to feel chilly for good and all. . . . Ah, *there* he thought of himself. Well, if he put himself out of the question, would he find that he spoke to any real purpose? Had she not always loved Mr. Frank from the day when she cried for him under the tower? Was there anything else to be said?

He would refrain; he would hold his tongue; he would work; the work, at least, might go on.

He was working when Miss Phillis came. He heard the key in the door of the church, and then her footsteps approaching. Such an afternoon to come! There were hailstones rattling on the roof. She must have her reasons for braving the weather, these April storms in May.

She began at once. " Brett, I have something to say to you. I knew I should find you here. I suppose you have no objection to telling me what you are going to do ?"

" Nothing."

" You cannot do nothing."

" In that matter I can. It doesn't concern me. I've told you that before."

" This is absurd. You said yourself it required an explanation."

" That has nothing to do with me."

" Can I live with a lie ?"

Wattie was silent. Then he said : " I've my own life to consider."

What thoughts were passing he could not tell. There was some change of view.

" I don't think you do with your life what you might. You have genius, I suppose. You should move away from here—go up to London, and make some money."

Wattie held his peace.

" You might be quite a successful animal painter, and I fancy that sort of thing pays very well."

" Do you know any successful animal painters ?" The best thing was to quarrel.

" I can't say that I do. I am not interested in Art."

" And yet you are sure that it pays very well— animal painting, I mean ?"

" I said I believed it did. You could, of course, get any information you required from one of the big schools of Art. Meanwhile I must thank you for this work you have done at my request."

" It was my request," said Wattie.

" Oh yes, I remember now ; I gave you permission. It looks very nice. These horses are very much like your horses in the Academy."

" They are the same, only differently treated."

" The same, are they ? So I thought."

" These are the best," said Wattie. He would feign

a complete absorption in his work, an utter indifference to matters outside.

" Am I the first to see them ?"

Why did she want to know ? And she asked in a careless way which betrayed a good deal of eagerness.

" Almost the first," said Wattie.

" Who besides has seen them ?" She was vexed.

" Two children."

" Not old enough to understand."

" They would understand the picture — nothing else."

" How long will it take you to finish ?"

Wattie stared up at the wall. She might just as well look at it upside down. " What more would you like put into it ?"

"I ? Oh, I know nothing about it. It seems to me as if it were done." . . . (Done, yes !) " By the way, you have my key."

He was sure it was not " by the way." He turned the key out of his pocket.

" Thank you," Miss Phillis said ; " you can give me the key. I think, for the present, your picture must do."

Must do ! " The key is yours," said Wattie. " The painting is mine."

" Yours ? How yours ?"

" Well, I paid for it, paints, brushes, and everything."

" Of course. I know. I could not possibly let you be put to any expense. Besides, you must charge for the labour."

" I did it to please myself."

" I am glad it has given you pleasure. Still, on no account could I allow your work to go unpaid. You did it to please yourself perhaps, but you did it for me——"

" How for you ?" said Wattie.

She coloured. " At my request ; at least, I mean, by my permission."

" I could not have done it without. But, all things considered, since it was my idea, my time, my trouble, my money, the painting belongs to me."

" Not if I buy it from you."

" Of course, not if you buy it from me. I don't think I want to sell."

There she stood without a word.

" Brett," she said suddenly, " you are a fool ; you are a boor. Do you imagine that I cannot see through your intention ? You mean to wipe this picture out ; but are you so dull as not to perceive you can never wipe out the *fact ?*"

" I have no fact I want to wipe out ; nor shall I wipe out the picture. It meant a good deal of pains, and just for somebody's fancy, to satisfy somebody's pride, shall I give it all up ?"

" I hope not. I hoped you had more sense. There is one little thing you might do for me, Wattie—a small favour I have to ask."

He was on his guard at once. She who so hated *liars* was now deliberately playing him false.

" Will you ?" She waited for his answer. He would not help her tell these lies.

" Will you ? I'm afraid I was rude and ungrateful, and you have always been kind."

" Well, what is it ?"

" I want you to *finish* this picture. It was stupid of me to take the key. I can't think why I asked for it. Here it is." She had some cruel purpose.

" I don't want the key," said Wattie. " I've done with the key."

" But you cannot get in without the key, and I want you to finish the picture."

" The picture *is* finished," said Wattie. He could have laughed and cried to see the way she looked up at it.

" Had you really done all you meant to do ?"

Wattie said " Yes." He was putting together his box and his brushes, without any noise or fuss.

" Then I may as well keep the key. I shall be busy

all next week. After that you can be sure I shall
let you know what I mean to do. I perfectly well
understand your claim on your own handiwork, but,
of course, it is quite absurd to argue our rights. The
church is mine."

Wattie said nothing.

" In a sense it is mine—not, perhaps, a religious
sense." (Not a religious sense, no !) " Still, it *is*
mine ; but you do not suppose I had nobody else but
myself to consult when I gave you permission to paint
the walls. There were one or two people—at least, by
courtesy—who had right to some say in the matter."
(These were all after-thoughts. Wattie just nodded.)
It might raise a point of law," said Miss Phillis.
(Wattie just nodded again.) " Anyhow, wait till
next week is over. I shall be more at liberty then."

She swept away from him with a smile. What she
intended he did not know.

CHAPTER LVIII

It was the following Friday evening that Wattie
noticed a light at The Bell in the room on the first floor
over the parlour. He dreamt that night of Mr. Frank.
He was walking up and down in front of the forge,
reading the news, in his Norfolk coat and shiny slippers,
and Wattie made sure when he woke that he should
see Mr. Frank that day—not that he wanted to see
him, but he made sure that he should. He did not see
him, however. Either Mr. Frank went out very early,
or else he did not go out at all. Perhaps not at all,
since it rained all day. Nobody stirred at The Bell,
but the room on the first floor was occupied, for the
window was open, and one of the curtains was blowing
about. Wattie looked for the light again at dusk, but
this evening no light appeared. The rain was still
persistent—drip, drip, drip off the roof. What had

happened to Mr. Frank ? And then, as he wondered, came a spark, a glimmer, a steady glow, and a shadowy arm pulled the curtains across. He dreamt again of Mr. Frank. He wanted to dream of anything else ; and as he dreamt he strove with himself to curb his imagination, and then the waves rolled over him, and he was with Mr. Frank. . . . Marchington railway-station, crowded with boys and girls, and Master Frank in cricketing flannels struggling through to shake hands. . . . How Master Frank shot up ! and his long legs walked the whole length of the train to the van where the porters were sorting the luggage, and he hit a bright yellow bag a whack with his walking-stick. . . . " *Carry this up to The Bell.* . . ."

He could have sworn it was Mr. Frank's voice, and before ever he knew he had sprung out of bed and gone to the window, but he only looked over the bit of yard. Dark, very dark, and raining fast. . . . He got back to bed, and dreamt again. . . . This time they were sitting in church, and although there were people in every pew, there seemed nobody else but Master Frank. He was gazing up at the little rose-window, gnawing his lips, and then all at once he looked round with his chin lifted over his collar, and everyone stood . . . and Mr. Frank suddenly went to the door, very white, and then he came back and walked up the aisle, and Wattie had covered his face with his hands . . . and woke hot and cold, and buried his burning cheek in the pillow.

And then he thought he would think about riding in on a jolly day from Brinkley to Marchington, by every bend and curve of the road ; and he started away from the saddler's shop, and presently found himself slipping, and he pulled Choice (now a strawberry roan) up a side-alley, where, over the hedge, came horse upon horse and the sweet young ladies ; and a little brown cub ran into his arms, and he carried it to some iron gates which a couple of men were painting ; but when he tried to get in they told him they always closed early on Saturday afternoons ; and the man who told him sneezed and shivered, and it was Mr. Fred, in his riding-breeches, warming his hands at the fire, as if he would make up his mind to speak. And then Mr. Fred grew tall and dark, and threw his cigarette out of the window, and said : *" I remember certain days . . ."*

He woke, to find it morning, and the troublesome night was past. Raining still, but it cleared at noon with a watery gleam of sunshine, and Wattie decided that he would go out. There was nothing to keep him indoors. More rain, but the clouds were lifting. He could, anyway, shelter in the porch.

Exactly a week ago he had finished his task. "Task" was a cruel word for the work which had yielded him so much pleasure. He was thinking now as he walked up the path how strange it seemed to have nothing to do — nothing to do in those few short hours for which all the other hours were lived. It was never so in his life before. He could not remember a time when there had not been something to do, somewhere to go, to make his brain whirl on Friday night and set it dancing on Saturday ; and now he was suddenly without scheme, or plan, or purpose, or even a reason for going on. The plan which he thought had been filling his mind had exhausted it drop by drop ; his mind was not filled, but emptied ; and the final touch last week had drained, not brimmed, the goblet. Part of himself had died. But, then, you died in one part to live in another ; the blossom makes room for the bud ; and had it not been for the cheerless day and the lowering clouds, he should know even now what the buds would be, and what sort of spring would succeed.

Meantime there were other creatures in trouble. A couple of daws, crying piteously, flew over his head. Something must be amiss with them. Very likely their nest was destroyed, for they built in the tower, and the Marchington boys still climbed for the eggs as they did in Wattie's day.

" Those birds have been screeching round and round ever since I came up." That was Mr. Frank's voice. There he was in the porch. Wattie ducked in to get out of the rain.

" A wonderful wet week, sir," said Wattie.

" It has rained now for forty-eight hours on end," said Mr. Frank, " to my certain knowledge." He turned his collar up.

They stood and stared before them.

" They're flooded out at the Manor," said Mr. Frank presently.

Wattie both nodded and shook his head.

" The rain has got into the stables, and come through the roof into one of the bedrooms. It never ceased all night."

" And very close, sir," said Wattie.

" There may be thunder about," said Mr. Frank, and he turned his collar down.

The daws flew screaming back again.

" I should reckon they may have been flooded out too," said Wattie ; but Mr. Frank looked away through the porch.

" Here they come," he said. Who were coming ? That was the path from the Manor.

" They are coming to see the church," Mr. Frank suddenly explained.

" They'll never come through this weather."

" Oh, well, yes, they will. They are half-way here already. You know they are going to complete the church ?"

" Yes, I know," said Wattie. He tried to make out the figures crossing the field. They were all of them under umbrellas.

" It has been suggested," said Mr. Frank, " that I am to put the finishing touch."

" Oh !" said Wattie.

" It's a job, by the way, to interest *you*. Do you remember a roan and a pretty white mare ? They must often have been at your forge."

" The mare had four black feet ?" said Wattie.

" Four black feet ?   Very likely—yes, I think she had.   I never noticed."

" And the roan was a sort of a strawberry ?"

" That's the beast.   I can imagine him not very pleasant to shoe."

Wattie laughed to himself, for he thought all at once of the mate and Mr. Marshall, the groom.   " Well, he wasn't so wonderful pleasant at times."

" You won't see him down at your place again.   The poor brute strained himself over a fence, and they say he will have to be shot."

Oh, then, that rumour was true !   Wattie had heard of it in the village—how Miss Phillis had put Necessity to a big jump, when he wasn't fit, so everyone said ; and everyone said she should not have done it, and might have broken her neck besides.

" And it comes rather hard now the mare has died."

" Died !"   Blow upon blow.   " She was good to live for years and years.   When did she die ?"

" Oh, its some weeks now.   You remember her well ?   Yes, you're right : she had black feet."

Wattie said nothing ; a lump seemed to rise in his throat.

" I think that suggested the idea of painting the horses on the wall."

" That was suggested ages ago."

" Oh, well, yes ; I suggested it first myself in church." (It was Miss Phillis *suggested* it.)   " But I mean this new idea—that I should take those animal studies which you saw last week at Burlington House, and copy them on the Tower Wall."

" Are *you* to do *that?*"   Wattie's brain reeled. This was her cruel plan.

" I have been asked to do it."

" Only you're going to say you won't."

" Why should I say I won't ?   But I shall say I can't, which amounts to the same thing.   That's why they are coming here—everyone soaked to the skin,

I expect. We are to look at the wall. I remember
I thought it a good idea ; but we must seek out another
artist. You've forgotten the little rose-window ?"

" That artist is dead," said Wattie. " You're not
thinking of him ?" Oh, Choice and Necessity—one
going, one gone ! Miss Phillis's heart must be broken.
This was a big excuse. " Have you got the key ?"
he said all at once. " If you have, we'll go inside."

" They are bringing the key," said Mr. Frank. He
stood there calmly waiting. " What an array of umbrellas ! No, there is only one man who could paint
those horses, and nobody knows where he is."

Bang went the old lych-gate. Someone was running
up the path. Wattie moved to get out of the way,
but he had to slip round Mr. Frank, and Miss Daisy
ran into his arms.

CHAPTER LIX

" WHOEVER is that ?" she said. . . . " Oh, Frank,
there you are." She found Mr. Frank. " Phillis has
got the key. Isn't it awful ! It's rained for forty-
eight hours on end."

" Just what I was saying," remarked Mr. Frank.
" You are dreadfully wet. I hope your things won't
spoil. Mind the drippings from the roof." He drew
Miss Daisy into the porch.

" We've all got cloaks and umbrellas," Miss Daisy
said. " What an age Phillis takes ! Here she is !"

. . . Here she is ! Major, a little in front, Miss Daisy's
papa, Miss Phillis, and Mr. Fred. Miss Phillis went
straight to the door.

" Allow me," said Major. But Miss Phillis was
turning the key in the lock. She was pale. Wattie
made up his mind to follow.

" My dear," said Miss Daisy's papa, " I hope you
won't all catch cold."

" I can't think why we've come," said Major. He was steering Miss Daisy.

Mr. Fred only shivered and sneezed, and looked up at the roof, whence the water came pouring.

" Wipe your boots," said Miss Daisy to everyone. " And we'll leave our umbrellas outside."

Major was helping with the umbrellas.

Miss Phillis passed on.

" Well, where is the work of Art to go ?" said Miss Daisy's papa, and he slapped Mr. Frank on the back.

" The church is too dark," said Mr. Frank. " Wait a bit." And he suddenly turned and went back to Miss Daisy.

Wattie heard all, for he could not escape, partly by reason of Miss Daisy, partly by reason of Major, still stacking umbrellas, and partly by reason of Mr. Fred, who was gaping now at the Latin motto which ran along under the porch.

" Daisy, you are not nervous ?"

" Nervous ? What of ? No. Why ?"

" I want you to do something for me."

" I will do anything for you, Frank."

" I want you to take care of Phillis."

" What's the matter with Phillis ?"

" Nothing at present. Go to her now."

Miss Daisy was very good. She went at once to Miss Phillis.

Her papa was coming out in a hurry. " I say, you fellows, do you know what has happened ? Here's no end of a mess inside."

" What's up ?" said Major. He pushed in first and Wattie behind.

" A regular mess, and you can't see a thing. Hasn't anyone got a taper ?—a match, then ?" Miss Daisy's papa was fumbling.

Major had struck one first.

" Good Lord !" said Mr. Fred ; and he looked at the pavement, then at the roof, then at the tower wall. " What the dickens does this mean ?"

" Seems like a flood," said Major. " A pipe burst probably."

" Mind the ladies' skirts," said Miss Daisy's papa.

" Ladies, mind your skirts," said Major. " Wait a bit ; I'll strike another. . . . It's only plaster and wet. There's nothing wrong with the wall. Is that where Frank is to put his horses ? Frank, my boy, a very nice field !"

" If this is what we came to see," said Mr. Fred, " we may as well go home—at least, I mean, of course, if it *isn't* what we came to see." And he laughed.

" Where's Phillis ?" said Miss Daisy's papa.

" Phillis is here," said Miss Daisy. They were seated together side by side. Miss Phillis was hidden away.

" Another match," said Major. " Take a look round. No, this is the only damage. The damp has got in through the wall."

" It's a horrid swamp !" said Mr. Fred. " Hadn't we better send a message for somebody ? Here's somebody would go."

That meant Wattie.

" Look here," said Mr. Fred : " you go and tell somebody they're wanted up here pretty sharp. There's a pipe burst, or a hole in the roof, or something gone wrong somewhere." Mr. Fred was quite excited.

" Perhaps you understand pipes," said Major, striking another match.

" It's a leakage from the top," said Wattie. Anyone ought to be able to see where the water was coming in. " It's something got down the head of the pipe."

" Very likely," said Mr. Frank—" very likely a jackdaw's nest. I remember that once in my father's time. Wait a bit, please, before you go. I've something to say."

He stood by himself in the aisle. It struck Wattie as very odd, not to say laughable, that as Mr. Frank took his stand in the aisle the whole congregation sat down.

" I want you all to attend."

Major flung his last match on the ground, and stamped upon it heavily.

" Never mind lights. Besides, it's clearing. I've something I want to tell you. You know that study at the show ? It wasn't mine. I mean the horses."

" Eh, what ?" said Miss Daisy's papa. " Who's that talking ? Why, bless my soul, I thought it was somebody strange got in ! It's you, Frank, is it ?"

" Yes," said Mr. Frank. " Do you understand ?"

" Understand what ?" said Major, half in, half out of his pew. " Somebody lend me another light. I believe I've dropped a sovereign."

" Never mind the sovereign. I want you to listen, Major, as well ; I want you all to listen."

" Listen to what ?"

" To what I tell you."

" I don't see that," said Mr. Fred. " I'm going home." He got up to go.

" Oh dear !" cried Miss Daisy, standing too (Major looked round) : " Please everyone pay attention. Something is dreadfully wrong, and nobody cares. What *did* you say, Frank ? Do be plain."

Major sat down.

" I wish to be plain ; I thought I was," said Mr. Frank. " I tell you *I did not paint those horses. They were a fraud.*"

" My dear chap, you're mad !" said Major. " Far from being a fraud, they were truer than life."

" *I didn't paint them,*" said Mr. Frank—hammer and tongs !

" Well, then, who did ?"

" I don't know."

" Rats !" said Mr. Fred. " I'm going home."

" Do let him speak ! Do let him speak !" cried Miss Daisy again.

" He can speak if he likes," said Mr. Fred. " He said he'd got something to tell us."

" So I have. Sit down, Fred. Doesn't it seem

to you odd, by the way, to send in another man's work as your own ?"

"Odd! I should call it confounded impertinence. . . . I—I say, is that what you have been doing ?"

"Yes."

There was a silence in the church. Wattie flushed crimson. Possibly, though he could not see it, everyone else flushed crimson too.

Major spoke first in an odd, abrupt way.

"Is that true ?"

"Yes."

"Then it oughtn't to be."

Mr. Fred sniggered.

"Are you sure it's true ?"

"Yes."

There was another silence. Major sat forward, with his head hanging over the pew in front, and Wattie could hear him softly whistle. Then he said : "Humph ! Well . . . I should have kept *that* fact to myself."

Mr. Fred sniggered again. Sometimes Wattie longed in his heart to get Mr. Fred down alone at the forge.

"Yes," said Major, standing up, "I should have kept that fact to myself."

"I—I must confess I don't yet *quite* understand," said Miss Daisy's papa. Mr. Frank turned his face. "You sent up two pictures—very good pictures, so I've heard—to this year's Academy. Is that so ?"

"Yes," said Mr. Frank patiently. "One picture was mine—that's all right. I am speaking now of the study of horses."

"Very well, the study of horses. . . . But by some unfortunate accident——"

"It was no accident," said Mr. Frank. "I knew what I was doing."

Major and Mr. Fred went to the door. They stood side by side looking out.

"What did you do it for, Frank ?" asked Miss

Daisy's papa. "There must have been some provocation." A funny word to use.

"Anyone who wishes to hear the facts of the case can hear them at his pleasure," said Mr. Frank, looking all round. "Some of you won't be interested. It was by mistake, first of all, that the particular picture I mention was chosen out for the show."

"*Mistake* now you call it?" said Major, wheeling round. Wattie heard him say under his breath : "The fellow's a fool. What does he mean? He doesn't know what he means."

"I'll tell you what it is, Frank," said Mr. Fred : "you're making the deuce of a hash of things. You'd better come home."

"Your late successes," said Major, "have turned your head."

Mr. Fred thought that a first-rate joke.

"The choice of that particular study," Mr. Frank went on, "for exhibition was a mistake. It was the mistake of a friend ; but it was a mistake which I might have rectified any time during the last two months."

"You'd much better have left it another two months ; that's my opinion," said Major.

"I cannot agree with that," said Miss Daisy's papa. "I beg to differ. If Frank Burnet or anybody else has done a wrong to this man, or any other man, he owes it to that man or any other man to set it right."

"Who's injured now?" said Major. "I didn't know anyone was."

"As a matter of fact," said Mr. Frank—"as a matter of fact I don't believe anyone is injured. I cannot be sure, but I think it is more than probable that the artist who painted those horses has forgotten them long ago ; he may be forgotten himself—may be dead, for all I know. They were found in an old portfolio."

"Whose?"

"Mine."

" My dear chap," said Major, " *you* painted them. *Now* are you satisfied ? You painted them, and you forgot them, and you remembered them—I mean, you didn't, but somebody else did—and they were hung on the walls of the Academy, and the unprecedented success has turned your head, as I told you before."

" That is just how I have been trying to reason," said Mr. Frank, " but it doesn't fit in with the facts."

" Then the facts are out, that's all I can say."

" No, the facts are facts, and they are all known except for the artist's name, which I fear we shall never discover. If ever I learn it, you shall be told. Meanwhile I have communicated all particulars to the Academy authorities, and I am glad to say they seem thoroughly to appreciate the situation, which you, I think, don't."

" Not in the least, I assure you," said Major. " Never heard such a yarn in my life."

" Nor I," said Mr. Fred. " Don't understand it at all."

" For my part," said Miss Daisy's papa, " I fail to see what need there was for bringing the matter forward if nobody has been injured."

Mr. Frank was silent.

" Oh, but, papa !" began Miss Daisy, " people *are* injured."

" It is a most unpleasant affair, I'll allow, but, like Fred, I confess I don't understand."

Nobody spoke. Perhaps they all thought it unpleasant ; perhaps nobody understood.

" *I* understand," said Miss Phillis. At last she had risen. Risen ? Yes, and came out of her place and walked straight to Mr. Frank's side. " *I* understand, and, really, now that the truth is known, or the greater part of it, anyway, and Frank and I shall take every step to let the rest be discovered and known— everything known that can be known—really, the understanding of it only concerns our two selves."

Here she took Mr. Frank's hand ; here she bent her

head and kissed it. Major opened his mouth to speak, but had the sense to shut it again. Mr. Fred, good riddance, slunk out through the door.

"And we've none of us any business to think the story odd," said Miss Daisy emphatically.

"It *is* odd," said Mr. Frank, looking at her with a curious smile.

"Well, Frank," said Miss Daisy's papa, "I think——" There he stopped.

"It isn't easy to know what to think," said Mr. Frank, after giving him time. "And one of the things I most regret is putting you all in such awkward positions. But that will come better presently."

"I'll tell you one thing I think," said Miss Daisy's papa, "and that is, that you've grown the very image of your father."

"Anyway," said Mr. Frank, "I know something my father knew."

Wattie was puzzled to guess what he meant. He guessed it had something to do with Miss Phillis, but Mr. Frank never once looked at Miss Phillis, and only kept hold of her hand.

"And it seems to me," said Miss Daisy's papa, "that where you ought to be is up *there*."

"In my new pulpit when it arrives," said Mr. Frank. "But something will have to be done to that wall. I don't understand even now how there comes to be such a lot of plaster."

"About the wall, dearest Frank, I have much to tell you." Miss Phillis took his other hand and kissed it in just the same way.

"Come along, Daisy," said her papa. "It's stopped raining, and Bob has gone."

It was Wattie's chance to make good his escape—round by the tower, over the graves, through the hedge, and across the meadow. He had determined to go straight home, but passing the forge, as the sun came out, he lingered a minute to speak to Gracie, the foreman's daughter.

I have finished my story. Strange that somebody tells me it is not sufficiently plain that Frank has since become Vicar of Marchington. I should have said there was no doubt ; born to preach, I always thought. You will remember, too, that Phillis preferred the Vicarage. Tom, she says, may live at the Manor. Tom probably will ; he likes things jolly. He is called Tom because Phillis saw no earthly reason why they should all be Seymours and Hedleys ; but the second boy is Frank. There are two girls as well, and I have heard of other children. At five years old they learn to ride. The house is much the same as ever. If you go there on a winter's night, you see the big lamp in the hall, and a broad stream follows you down the path. Mrs. Burnet generally runs up to look at the children after dinner. Tom is asleep—sleeps like a rock, breathes through his mouth, the boy ! Frank awake ; wants to know if, when he dies, he will get to heaven. His mother gives him a drink of water, smooths out his pillow, and kisses his head. Two at a time upstairs comes her husband. There is really no need for him to come, but he stops and talks for a bit. He says the boy suffers from indigestion.

THE END

AFTERWORD

Dorothy Vernon White (1877-1967) published five books between the ages of thirty and thirty-five, the first three under her maiden name of Dorothy Vernon Horace Smith, which read now like the beginning of a dazzling career. *Frank Burnet* (1909), her second, is a great novel, rich in psychological and moral insight, powerful as drama, and masterfully written. And then she stopped. She spent the rest of her life, as she had spent much of it since her early twenties, teaching religion (Episcopal Christianity) to young people, in Bible class and Sunday school. Why did she stop? It is a mystery, and the few available clues point in different directions.

One clue is something she told me in 1950 – I met her then while doing research for a book on William Hale White ('Mark Rutherford'), the more famous novelist who became her husband. *Frank Burnet* brought her a grand total of five pounds. This is not surprising. In its art her fiction was too far from the solid social realism of her most successful fellow Edwardians, Bennett, Galsworthy, Wells, to please the larger novel-reading public. And though that art is akin to Forster's and to Woolf's in its concern with the inner life, their more 'advanced' readers – devotees of feeling, of the superior sensibility, of art – could only have been dismayed by her ideas, which were decidedly not advanced. So she may well have stopped because her work utterly failed to win a response.

But there are clues to suggest something else, that she gave up writing because her real vocation was precisely the one she chose. Her husband, though he admired her fiction, predicted that her life-work would be a kind which had 'more a personal influence, and religious', a comment which she noted in the manuscript of *The Groombridge Diary*, but omitted (from page 113) in the published version. And in 1950 she wrote me herself, 'In all humility I say . . . you cannot really penetrate either of us [the other was Mark Rutherford] without entering by way of our religion.' In fact, each of her novels – the other two are *Miss Mona* (1907) and *Isabel* (1911) – poses the religious view of things against that of the 'world', although in the third religion makes its effect by its absence; and it is startling to realize that *Frank Burnet* is the story of an abandonment of art very much like her own. To all this, however, it must be added that if she did deliberately choose that teaching vocation, she had her own idea of its subject matter. 'We are entirely at one,' this Anglican Sunday-school teacher wrote after a discussion of creeds with Hale White – and this of a man who had so completely rejected institutional beliefs that he had forbidden *his* children to attend Sunday school. They could be at one because her faith confirmed, as much as it inspired, her natural response to life. And what this was like is suggested by a note he set down in 1910 (in the unpublished '1910' manuscript) to explain their strange coming together. His love, he said, 'included reverence for genius more remarkable than any I have ever known in woman. It is genius not for this or that, but for living, genius which shows itself in all the events of common existence . . . ' Her religion, like his, was religion as wisdom.

She grew up, one of eight children of a police magistrate for Westminster, in an orthodox Anglican family, and it may be that she never needed to rebel because she was never an 'intellectual'. Until her meeting with Hale White in 1907, cricket and her teaching meant more to her than books. (An essay of 1906, 'The Lady Cricketers', vividly conveys the thrills of the game for a group of women players.) It was within, not outside or against her religion that her intellectual life developed. In early years this led to difficulties. A note of hers in an unpublished collection of her letters and talk made by her husband between 1907 and 1913 (the 'Dorothy Book') speaks of 'the sense of guilt and the dread of damnation' she suffered from at thirteen. But later on it worked the other way. In her account of her Bible class, *Twelve Years With My Boys* (1912), she says she began teaching at twenty-two because 'I had passed through a dark cloud that summer, but God had been with me in the cloud, and I had come out of it with a desire for service.' As it happens, she came out of it, more or less, for good. In her 'battle with timid melancholy . . . hope and . . . courage conquered.' And explaining why she was liked by her boys, she tells us frankly, 'I cannot help knowing that there was a great deal of brightness in me, an immediate expansion of body, mind, and spirit when touched by another human being, an instinct to love without criticism . . . a great deal of life and fun.' It is this brightness of temperament, underlying and determining her religion, that made the thirty-year-old author of *Miss Mona* seem to the gloomy seventy-five-year-old Mark Rutherford a 'miraculous' answer to his life's deepest need and led to the surprisingly passionate relationship recorded in *The Groombridge Diary* (1924), by which she is best remembered.

But before Hale White there was someone else who impressed himself deeply on her imagination and who is worth mentioning here because he became the basis for characters in her fiction that embody her most cherished values. This was her brother, a promising biologist killed in action in World War I. In a privately printed collection of his letters (*Geoffrey Watkins Smith*, Oxford, 1917), which also contains testimonials from army associates to his remarkable selflessness and bravery, she describes him as 'absolutely healthy and happy by temperament', free of the ambition to be 'anything he was not justified in being', and possessed of a 'sweetness of temper' which was 'no credit to him, if you like' because it was 'a gift straight from Heaven'. Not only did he take the difficulties of life 'without unnecessary fuss'; he didn't even let others draw him into 'fuss', for he 'did not . . . strive to live everyone's life as well as his own.' But though she concludes that he was no 'saint' because a saint must have 'a self to subdue' – a conquest involving 'sorrow', 'faults and besetting sins', 'darkness' – there is reason to believe she was in that essay, written immediately after his death, repressing her memory of a self he did subdue. The man who was to die so bravely speaks in a letter written at twenty–four of the 'ghastly funk of the water' that prevented him until recently from learning to swim. But more striking is what he revealed in an autobiographical fragment Mrs White showed me in 1950 about his traumatically brutal experience at public school. The experience confirmed him, he says, in his besetting faults, which were 'coldness', 'self-centredness', and physical cowardice. The essential traits of the happy brother she remembered we will see again in her second novel in Wattie. (They are also in Miss Mona's star pupil John Smith.) Those of the troubled brother she (briefly) forgot we will see in Frank Burnet.

It was the religious teaching begun in 1899 which enabled her, as it were, to see her brother, as well as a great deal more. *Twelve Years With My Boys* shows her acquiring precisely the psychological and moral realism at the heart of that second novel, a kind that may well have startled her fellow Anglicans. Among the 'evils' she fought in her boys, for instance, was 'cant', and her method was to try 'never to utter a religious sentiment I did not feel' and 'never to accept . . . unfelt sentiments from the boy himself'. This required 'very often . . . a long holiday from all religious phraseology', and sometimes 'even . . . a direct attack upon religion, the stripping off of some religious mask', for words like 'Repentance' and 'Love of God and our neighbour' can become 'the merest gabble'. Still more shocking: 'A good boy is better than a bad boy,' she says. 'There is no doubt in my mind about that. On the other hand, a good boy is not better than a bad boy; that may also be true.' In judging people, as well as in teaching religion, we must beware of the conventional pieties. We must go beyond what 'people say, or do, or think' to what is 'much harder to discern', the 'springs and the channel' these come from. Impatient with religion as parroted dogma, she quotes with delight a recently discovered maxim: 'Religion is caught, rather than taught. It is the religious teacher, not the religious lesson that helps the pupil to believe.'

What it is she believes we find in a pamphlet of four *Discourses* privately printed in Beckenham in 1902, which anticipate not only the theme of *Frank Burnet*, but even the relation to its theme of the novel's chief characters and events.

In the first, 'Character', we are told that God looks not at 'the petty sin' or 'the petty deed of virtue' but deeper, and asks, 'Why art thou cramped and small and withered – a creature of no sense, *doing ill and doing well*, and *art* nothing?' – in other words, that there may be a difference between what we do and what we are. The next, 'Completeness', reminds us that in Christ's injunction 'Be ye perfect' the word 'perfect' comes from the Greek *teleios*, which means 'complete', and that it is 'lobsideness' He is asking us to avoid. For 'we let our strongest virtues grow rank; they rampage.' So 'we must walk with open eyes. We must not blindly follow even virtue.' (Is this a Sunday-school teacher or is it André Gide?) In 'The Father-hood of God' she suggests that the sense of God as a 'trusted Parent', far from lulling us with fantasy, is identical with the confidence in ourselves and our world that sets us free to do our work as it should be done, and that the life of the 'true son of God' is 'a life of energy', not the 'feverish restless energy' of the fearful, but 'the energy of one who can say calmly, I serve, I wait, I know,' that is (surely), I serve what for me is highest, I wait without impatience for results, I know what for me is best and what is not. Even the last discourse, on the belief in 'Life Everlasting', shows this same grasp of religion as insight into our experience on earth, for her emphasis here is on the source of that belief in the hunger for 'a better life, a better country' which is the 'Divine spark' in us all. Like Browning ('A man's reach should exceed his grasp/Or what's a heaven for?'), what she seizes on in the promise of an utter best in heaven is its encouragement to believe in those glimpses of a better on earth that do in fact give life its meaning and purpose. In fact, the God of her *Discourses*, though a living Father to her, is also a name for reality, which must always stretch infinitely beyond the small circle of light shed by our temporarily useful theories, and her faith in Him is also that trust in the world and ourselves we must all attain if we are to make the most of our lives.

It is not surprising then that this faithful Anglican was recognized at once by the churchless Hale White as profoundly congenial. 'Although you have bound yourself to a community,' he wrote her in a comment on *Frank Burnet*, 'you are essentially revolutionary or, properly, anarchical . . . [Your "ethical theory"] is anarchy in the true sense of the word, as opposed to control or subjugation.' And later: 'O! my dear, do you know why I love you? It is because you can dispense with duty; it is because you can trust an impulse to do everything for you; it is because you are unexpected and spontaneous.'

All of the foregoing in her life and thought came together like so many tributaries in the deep and urgent – and also sparkling – river of *Frank Burnet*. And though her first novel, an account of a Bible-class teacher and two of her pupils, was a promising and delightful beginning, its simple, fable-like story hardly prepares us for the quality of her second. In *Frank Burnet*, everything – characters, their world, her language and her art – shows an amazing advance into full mastery.

More than once Frank encounters as a flash of light the rebuke of Christ to His disciples which was to have been the text of his father's last sermon: 'Ye know not what manner of spirit ye are of.' This assertion of a reality concealed by what is visible hints at the novel's theme, which we will come to in a moment. But it happens to suggest its art as well. In its method and its style the novel presents us with a vivid surface only darkly shadowing forth what is hidden beneath. It is a story of an education by life that comes to us from the point of view of two characters in alternating sections bearing their names, Frank himself, descendant of a line of ministers who rejects the family vocation for that of artist, and Wattie, the blacksmith's apprentice seven years his junior, who also develops a talent for painting and who, from his forge, observes and guesses at the lives of his 'betters'. What we are told of Frank's story is what these two can see, feel, and understand, and one element of the novel's mastery is its strict faithfulness to this dramatic method. There is no dead wood of exposition, everything is presented as felt experience which requires us to stay alert to details, to the way things are said (or thought), to what is left unsaid. But the mastery is also in the style. It is a style remarkable both in the freshness and intensity with which it registers the qualities of experience and in its economy;

character and meaning are conveyed in strokes so few, swift and accurate that each rereading shows us things we missed before.

But if there is more in every scene than meets the eye, there is also that lively 'surface', where we encounter characters, a society, flashes of insight into the tangle of life that are interesting at once and in themselves. The three principal characters, for instance, have a most lifelike way of resisting and contradicting our judgments. Frank, whose childhood fear of death persists in his fear of heights, water, horses – a disgrace he can't bear to admit to, becoming, as the young Phillis asserts with sobs of anguished disappointment, a 'liar' as well as a 'coward' – and who turns to art out of a demeaning itch for personal distinction, is somehow right, though wrong. Phillis, the fearless, truth-telling horsewoman he loves and regards, reasonably enough, as a 'starry' creature far above him, is somehow wrong, though right. And Wattie, 'healthy in body and soul,' as Frank enviously observes, and for Phillis – and the reader – a guide to moral sanity, remains silent when the other two are facing their terrible crisis because he has his 'own life to consider'. This is not quite selfishness; it belongs to his sanity that he knows it is fruitless to try to live anyone's life but one's own. And yet, in the face of Phillis's danger and need he is not happy to feel himself 'dumb – a beast'.

But although these three are always in the centre, the novel gives the impression of a broad canvas and a sharply observed society because of the many other characters who, however briefly seen, spring at once into life, their talk charged with personal flavour and hinted thought and feeling. There are the Vicar and his wife, delicately at odds and yet delicately united in contending with their 'superior' son. Among those who work out in the world there are first Wattie's mates at the forge, and later Frank's colleagues Raikes and Jackson, the sort of artists who have both the talent and the vocation, as distinct from the kind who have only the talent. As for the leisure classes, in addition to Phillis's horsey guests, there are the two aunts, Phillis's bitingly intelligent old Aunt Elizabeth, coolly pricking the thin bubble of Frank's conceit and then wryly encouraging what he becomes in his despair; and Frank's own 'dull' aunt, with whom, as life darkens around him, he takes comfort in talking about 'things that matter, the truth once in a way'. And in the latter's two daughters are rapidly sketched the sexual and political attitudes of Edwardian sophistication.

Then we keep getting the sense that life in its complexity is being illuminated, although, again, we must listen closely to hear how much is meant by apparently modest, off-hand remarks. A good deal of this comes quite legitimately from Wattie, as living evidence of that inner 'health' from which Phillis twice seeks support. Consider his response, for instance, after she has publicly shamed Frank (again she has been stung into insult by her own pain) for pretending to have jumped his horse over a hedge like herself and her guests, and has come to Wattie, uneasy, for his 'honest opinion' of her outburst. 'Well, miss,' he says first, 'you're not *obliged* to jump.' Next, of the deeper disgrace of the lie – and after a small hesitation – 'Well, miss, do you know I don't blame him.' And finally, as she keeps after him about what happened during the breakfast chatter, 'What I can't see, miss . . . is why, when you jump, you talk about it.' As her intensity has made clear how much more than the jumping of horses is involved, his resistance too has deeper implications. In fact, these modest replies are the modesty of wisdom before the mysteries of human nature – of the soul, if we may use the old word. He has rejected the demand that every rider be brave when one, for reasons others can't know, is not. Where he can't know, he has refused to 'blame'. And since he is unlikely to be rebuking Phillis for mere bragging, his final remark is a hint, like Miss Smith's in her *Discourses*, that people make too much of actions, that there is more to us than what we do.

Some of the understanding we are challenged to come up with, like this of the large meaning in small remarks, is the kind that flashes on Frank when Phillis persuades him to visit his father's grave and he suddenly grasps that sermon text cut into the stone. He used to think the words 'merely scriptural' or 'Biblical' something you had to put meaning into. 'But the meaning was in them already. *Nobody knows our manner of spirit.*' The meaning that is in such things already is, of course, the universal, the secular meaning of religious formulations. So, when his aunt forces on him his father's notes for that sermon and we read that Christ's rebuke to His disciples is 'hardly rebuke at all . . . Comfort rather . . . *You* do not know; God knows . . . Blessed security', we should be ready – should we not? – to follow him here too in finding such meaning. Very well: why 'blessed security'? Surely because if what we are issues from the infinite reality which is beyond our knowing or tinkering, we can stop worrying, we can entrust ourselves to that reality and *live.* Thus he sees the next moment, with a surge of relief, that he has no right 'to dwell upon the past (his own futility) or look into the future (Is life worth living?).' His concern is 'the immediate present. A day's work, a day's wage, a day's sunshine, a day's storm.' And though his work is still painting, he is aware soon after that he no longer confused life with a '"career" . . . It was something more intricate than that – a web to take all your time weaving. Not that *you* wove it. It got itself wove, whilst *you* continued to live – as indeed, you are bound to live, without question.'

This sketch of the pleasures on the novel's surface has also, necessarily, hinted at something deeper. In fact, *Frank Burnet* is a work of highly conscious art in the service of a profound vision, all its parts related to a central development, all the threats and promises of the beginning fulfilled in the confrontation and revelation at the end.

We catch an obvious hint of a unifying intention in Phillis's symbolically named horses, the fierce strawberry roan Necessity Frank shrinks from and the ladylike white Choice he prefers – though they remain utterly alive as horses and far from obvious in what they signify. A more delicate kind of suggestion arises from the repetition of certain phrases, which, as in Woolf – or in Mann, with his *leitmotifs* – begin by being meant literally and then, as they recur in varying contexts, expand in their meaning. Phillis's abrupt remark (overheard by Wattie) when she sees Frank's discomfort at the forge, 'There's no earthly reason why we need stand in the sun,' seems quite innocent at first. When it is repeated in the 'Frank' section which comes next, we learn that the heat which bothered him was internal. Later, for Wattie that remark about the sun, and also Phillis's demand for 'an honest opinion', enter into his paintings of her two horses as if 'spoken' by their posture, and as if the horses have become an expression of what fascinates him in her. And as the years pass both remarks keep coming back into his mind, in fragments or disguised, whispering of connections and correspondences. Most important, finally, is the recurrence of certain kinds of experience, and especially the experience of fear. So, when Frank understands near the end that 'timidity' is a reason for his climactic error and asks himself, 'What does it *mean*? Timidity – what *is* it?' the question is left unanswered because it is answered by the whole novel.

The novel's subject is planted in our first glimpses of little Frank learning about death from the memorial plaques in his father's church and asking his mother doubtfully if God is 'kind'. It is a story about the fear of life which results from the fear of death, and to which Dorothy Smith's religion-as-wisdom is the answer. And it is about three ways of relating to that religion – of living it, of being in the right – a good way, a better, and a best.

Both Phillis and Wattie are in the right – to quote the author's words about her brother – 'as a gift straight from Heaven'. They are absolutely honest and brave by nature, and they have no need for self-assertion. (Thus for Wattie his painting is not a career, a means to distinguish himself, but a rapt response to what he loves, and when he has caught this fully in his painting of Phillis's horses, and of her too as an invisible presence among them, he is ready to move on to other things.) That Frank could be made worthy of such human excellence – of Phillis – by a career success he can only think during the brief period of his euphoria. At heart he knows well that his triumphs as an artist are nothing beside the beauty of what she is.

But, as we have seen, Phillis and Wattie can differ. Phillis is a 'blessed unconscious creature' (as Frank calls her in pure admiration) and to be unconsciously right is not enough amid those mysteries of the soul. Our virtues may 'rampage', we may follow them 'blindly'. So the anguished recoil of hers results in that burst of cruelty to Frank for which she must go to Wattie for reassurance. Of course, she could not really have learned from what he said. It would diminish the beauty of her natural rightness if she could.

Wattie is her superior because he is not unconscious; he sees and hears and understands – and he can respect the mysteries he cannot plumb. But there comes a time when he too is found wanting, when he must acknowledge to himself, as we have noted, that he is 'dumb – a beast' where others are in trouble; he cannot say the saving word. For this power, the power to say what will touch and help, one must have one's own trouble, one's own 'sorrow', 'faults and besetting sins', a 'self to subdue'. One cannot have it if one is right by nature.

Frank Burnet is clearly not among those fortunate beings who are right by nature. Even as an artist he seems haunted by a question working not calmly, for the work's sake, but – like those in the *Discourses* unable to believe in the 'Fatherhood of God' – with 'feverish restless energy', for success. But, as Hale White observed, 'Nothing but the whole book will give you a notion of Frank,' for his is a story of how one grows. 'I can grow,' he exults when, like the author's brother, he conquers his 'funk of the water' and dives into a pond. Not that his growth is always a matter for exultation. A spirit he knows not of must emerge from within a self that resists, that goes wrong, that feels sorrow and despair. This is why each section of the novel has for its epigraph a verse from Browning's 'The Last Ride Together', in which the last ride granted to a horseman by a woman he has lost becomes a metaphor for the clinging to nearly hopeless hope required by life at its darkest. So, it is the pain (almost 'physical') of Phillis's public insult – and the recognition that she is right – which scourges Frank to ride and jump Necessity and leads him afterward to wonder 'whether Phillis was justified or not; whether lies were lies and terrors terrors, to be meek a vice or a virtue; whether one ought to bluster and brag, and to get back as good as you got, and see to it that when you were hurt, somebody else suffered too.' But this is nothing less than a questioning of the ways of the world, the questioning of Christ. And it is a measure of the quality and meaning of this novel that he has been led to such questioning, not by a church or a book, but by the realities of his life. 'She says,' Hale White noted in the "Dorothy Book", she has not taken her Christ from a book, not even from the N.T.'

What Frank grows into the reader discovers. All that need be said in conclusion is that the best in him owes its existence to what was worst. As he observes himself one day after a fashionable minister's sermon about 'how God is strong and man weak', '. . . had the preacher ever been weak? . . . If not let him hold his . . . idiot tongue: for what do the strong know of strength?'

Irvin Stock, Massachusetts 1984